LITTLE PEOPLE

T0386744

FOR DAVID

LITTLE PEOPLE

A NOVEL

JANE SULLIVAN

ALLEN&UNWIN

First published in Australia in 2011 by Scribe Publications

First published in Great Britain in 2012 by Allen & Unwin

Copyright © Jane Sullivan 2011

The moral right of Jane Sullivan to be identified as the author of this work has been asserted by her in accordance with the Copyright, Designs and Patents Act of 1988.

All rights reserved. No part of this book may be reproduced or transmitted in any form or by any means, electronic or mechanical, including photocopying, recording or by any information storage and retrieval system, without prior permission in writing from the publisher.

Every effort has been made to trace or contact all copyright holders. The publishers will be pleased to make good any omissions or rectify any mistakes brought to their attention at the earliest opportunity.

Allen & Unwin
c/o Atlantic Books
Ormond House
26–27 Boswell Street
London WC1N 3JZ
Phone: 020 7269 1610
Fax: 020 7430 0916
Email: UK@allenandunwin.com
Web: www.atlantic-books.co.uk

A CIP catalogue record for this book is available from the British Library.

ISBN 978 1 74237 885 5

Printed in Great Britain by the MPG Books Group Ltd

10 9 8 7 6 5 4 3 2 1

A woman of considerable physical courage mounted a horse, rode side by side with her soldier-husband, and witnessed the drilling of the troops for battle. The exciting music and scene together inspired her with a deep thirst to behold a war and a conquest. This event transpired a few months before the birth of her child — his name, Napoleon.

During the period immediately preceding the birth of Dante, his young mother saw a startling vision. She beheld a populated globe rise gradually out of the sea and float mid-heavens. Upon a high and grand mountain stood a man with brilliant countenance, whom she knew to be her son.

A woman gave birth to a child covered with hair, and having the claws of a bear. This was attributed to her beholding the images and pictures of bears hung up in the palace of the Ursini family, to which she belonged.

— Dr Foote's Home Cyclopedia of Popular Medical, Social and Sexual Science, 1858

DRAMATIS PERSONAE

THE LILLIPUTIANS

General Tom Thumb (Charles Stratton), the one and only Man in Miniature

Lavinia Stratton, his wife: the Queen of Beauty

Minnie Warren, Lavinia's sister: a pretty, plucky lady

Commodore George Washington Nutt, a sharp fellow
with a deal of drollery

THE MERELY SMALL

Rodnia Nutt, the Commodore's brother: coachman and horse wrangler

THE FULL-SIZED

Mary Ann, an unfortunate young woman

Sylvester Bleeker, manager of the Lilliputian troupe: destined to save the day

Hannah Bleeker, his wife: sharp with her needle

Franz Richardson, a pianist and aspiring virtuoso

Ned Davis, an agent: a provocative fellow

THE OUTSIDERS

Matilda, a tattletale child

Her terrible papa

Dr Frederick Musgrave, a collector of marvels

Alfred, Duke of Edinburgh, a Prince of the Realm

SAGACIOUS BEASTS

Erasmus, an Australian bird

Mazeppa, a Wild Horse of Tartary

Innkeepers, lackeys, cabbies, ladies bountiful, poor ruffians,
sporting gents, the great Australian public

CHAPTER 1

One day, she will ask me the inevitable question. There is much to tell, and I am not certain how to tell it. At least I know where to begin.

I will remind her that I was young, and had always been told that wanting was nothing but covetousness, a sin before God. I had no idea how dangerous the world could be.

· · · · · · · ·

It began with a game a gentleman taught me.

'Matilda tells me you have been wicked, Mary Ann.'

'No, sir.'

The first time, I tried to explain. Matilda's papa seemed calm, faintly amused. 'I think you deserve a forfeit,' he said when I paused in my awkward story. Gravely he closed the study door, took my hand in his, raised it to his lips. What kind of forfeit was that?

'That will be all, Mary Ann.'

Later he took to summoning me to his study when no one was about. He would close the curtains, light the lamp, sit on the edge of his desk and talk about a calf that had died at birth, or the time one of his dogs had a thorn in its paw, or the green fields of Norfolk. Now that he lived in the locality of Emu Flat, Victoria, he missed that green: it was very restful. I had not seen him so pensive. He was handsome in a bullish way.

I spent most of my time with Matilda, my pupil, and her family of sulky dolls. *You don't belong here*, they said. *You have frog hands. We shall tell Papa.*

The maids and the cook kept to different parts of the house. I had occasional words with Matilda's mama, who liked to wander around the vegetable garden with a sweet smile and a covered basket. I never saw inside the basket. Matilda's papa was a distant rider on his dusty estate, pausing at a gate or whistling to his retrievers, except when he called me to his study. Before he dismissed me, he would take a forfeit. 'That is for vexing Matilda,' he would say. And then he began to add: 'And for bewitching me.'

In time, his hand-kissing extended itself. He was always gentle, respectful, but his words hissed like steam in a kettle. I was driving him out of his mind. Did I not know the torments a man could suffer? I should take pity on him.

What I felt for him was many things, but pity was not among them. He was uncommonly tall, robust, the king of his domain. When he sat on the edge of his desk with his hands over his eyes, I came to him and took his hands away from his face. That made him smile, and I understood then what form my pity should take. I collected his smiles, took them to my attic bedroom and stored them in a red lacquered box he had used for his cigars. It was my most precious possession.

One day, I passed the drawing room and heard Matilda's papa and mama talking in low tones. Her voice was cold, his almost unrecognisable. 'Please, Emily. Please.'

An hour later I was summoned to his study and I waited for him to take me in his arms and guide me to the chaise longue under the window with the closed curtains. But he paced the carpet, would not meet my eye, talked about how dissatisfied he was with my teaching. 'You may have a month's wages and I will give you a good reference.'

I forgot myself. 'I have done nothing wrong,' I cried.

'Take your money, go. If you say a word to anyone I will tell them what a madwoman you are. You will be placed in an asylum for the insane and never released.'

I left Emu Flat and came back to Melbourne alone. My menses, always punctual, had not come. I prayed, but the words stuck. I paid for a tiny miserable room in the attic of a hotel by the river and took the rest of my money down an alleyway to a small dark house I'd heard about in whispers. Inside, hanging from a hook in the ceiling, was a cage with a silent canary in it. An old woman was shaving soap into a bucket of steaming water. She looked me up and down, took my money in her glistening hand.

She gave me a blanket and told me to take off my clothes and lie down in my chemise. I kept on my boots and stockings. My bed was a low bench draped with a much-darned sheet; the scratchy blanket smelled of lye. The woman lifted it up over my knees and prodded at my still-flat belly, my thighs, around and inside my private place, and I held my breath until black spots swarmed in front of my eyes. She straightened up. 'Only just fallen, have yer? That's good. Most of 'em come in late.' Then she left the room.

Surely there must be more.

Shadows passed on the ceiling. I tried to relax each tense limb in turn, tried not to imagine what might be done with a bucket of soapy water. A door opened into the adjoining room, voices murmured, old and young, both female. Another young woman must be lying there, under a scratchy blanket. Business was brisk. An odd fancy came to me: we were in the pages of a picture book, and the young woman next door was myself, on another page, recovering a few hours later. The canary in the cage shuffled back and forth on its perch. It had pecked out all its breast feathers. Every pore in its skin gaped at me.

All at once a scream from the next room seemed to rip open the wall. I did not even sit up. I rolled off the bench, pulled my dress over my head, threw my shawl over it, ran out the door into stinging rain. More screams and sobs followed me; I ran as they sliced me open. I did not stop running until, back in my little garret, I flung myself face down on the bed, damp dress gaping where I had not buttoned it. No tears; all I had was wheeze.

Why had I run? Stupid terror, but a spirit whispered to me something else: You refused to lie down and be tractable. A second spirit whispered: You're just finding an excuse for your cowardice. This second spirit was practical: You've paid, you can go back. But I knew I would not return.

When darkness came, I changed into my nightgown and brushed my hair like a good girl, but in the mirror was a witch face. I could not sleep because the spirits argued, and the whispers crescendoed to a roaring. So I rose from my bed, holding the red cigar box, crept onto the moonlit lawn. This was what madwomen did. They let down their hair and stumbled about in their nightgowns.

The roaring was in the Yarra Yarra. At the end of the lawn was the river, a black racing tide splintered with fragments of moon. I had not thought a river could run so strong. *Come*, it roared at me. Was that what I was looking for? Where was the best place? Here, at the edge of the water, a few steps in? Or from the bridge, where my weight would carry me deep? Either way would be quick. I opened my lacquered box, inhaled the scent of tobacco, turned it upside down, shook out all the smiles and hurled it into the water. The wind whipped my hair. *Come*, roared the river. Then a new thought anchored me, a firm little voice.

You are not mad enough for this. Go back to bed. You will have to carry your burden as best you may.

I turned upriver towards the bridge. On the parapet, at its highest point, I saw a white shape like a bundle of clothing. As I watched, the shape expanded into a star with five stumpy points. The little star clutched and held itself round the middle, jerked and flailed as it faced down to the water. A child. Sick, or frightened, or trying to pass water? But why did it tremble so? Then the child toppled and fell towards the water in precisely the arc I had contemplated for myself.

There was too much noise to hear the splash. The shape disappeared, then bobbed up again. The river was sweeping it in my direction. It would pass very close to the bank. I ran to the water's edge and slid down, gasping as an icy grip closed around my ankles, my knees. I floundered, nearly fell, but righted myself, waist-high in the flow. The child was within arm's reach, swirling in an eddy; still nothing but a bundle, ballooning with air. I pulled it into my arms, but I might as well have grabbed a sack of cannon balls. The fabric, now dark with mud, stretched over the child's dangling head like a caul, hiding its face.

All at once it convulsed. Limbs snaked around my neck, my waist, gripped with astonishing strength. It would drown us both. I staggered backwards into a fountain of bubbles, the child starfished across my chest and belly, and then a black hum as the Yarra Yarra closed over me.

I rolled onto my knees, scraped my shin on a submerged rock. Kneeling on the rock's sloping surface, chin above the flood, I held on with both hands and pulled one foot, then two, from the mud. I scrambled up the bank, leaden child dangling beneath my breasts, its legs crossed over my back. I swayed on all fours, reached to prise its arms from my neck. It fell beneath me, slopped like a bag of dough. Did it breathe? Where was its face? Was it even human? Or something that deserved to drown? I straddled it, tried to find its chest through layers of waterlogged fabric, to push water from its lungs, to hear it squeal or snarl. The creature clung, clawed, had me by the ears, pulled my head down. We wrestled in silence. My hand reached its skin.

Lanterns, shouts, splashing, harsh barks. I sprawled on my belly. The claws had gone. I was nothing but stink and blood and icy mud, throat raw, shin athrob, every inch of me shivering. Yellow lights bobbed over my head as I vomited up the Yarra Yarra through my hair, emptying all my cavities, becoming as clear as jelly. A dog ran up and down the riverbank, barking.

CHAPTER 2

When I woke from my stupor, with daylight in my eyes, a strange woman was sitting by my bed, holding my wrist and measuring my pulse.

'How do you feel?' she asked.

'Have I been unwell?'

'You have coughed up half the river. I took the liberty of washing off a deal of mud. I also gave you a sleeping draught.' I groaned, tried to sit up. 'Lie still.' Under a twist of greying sandy hair were freckles, shrewd grey eyes and a sucked-in mouth. The voice had the nasal twang of an accent I did not recognise, and the elbow on the arm that pulled up the bedclothes had a sharp point.

'The river ... what happened?'

'You don't remember?'

'Not much.' A faint roaring. A dog barking.

'You're a heroine, dear.' Her twang emphasised the r's. That voice: it was the one you use to children so they will not be puffed up with praise.

'I don't understand, Mrs ...'

'Mrs Bleeker. Sit up. Drink.' She handed me a glass of warm milk. 'My husband is Sylvester Bleeker, the General's tour manager.' She spoke as if I should know who the General was.

I sipped the milk. My locket lay on the table by the bed; but the table was marble, not plywood, and the sleeves around my wrists were not my sleeves.

The strange spiky woman watched me frown. 'I moved you into a more comfortable room. Rest assured, there will be no expense.'

'You are very kind, but I really am fine.'

She gave me a long look. I thought that the wrinkles at the corners of her eyes might mean kindness or calculation. I pulled the nightgown up around my neck. When she reached out with both hands, I began to shrink back, thinking she would touch, dispassionate as a doctor, my swollen breasts and tender nipples. Instead, she took both my hands in hers, drew them into the light, pressed them as a phrenologist measures a head.

'We must notify your family, Miss ...'

One word swam into my head, and then another. 'Mrs ... Carroll.'

'We must notify Mr Carroll, then.' She let my hands go.

I waited, and more words swam in. 'Mr Carroll passed away.'

'I am sorry.'

I ran my gaze along the mantelpiece, the clock, the Toby jug. 'He was of the clergy, he had red cheeks ...'

Mrs Bleeker raised an eyebrow.

'But very sober in his habits,' I went on hastily.

'You were both English? Your voice is refined.'

'We came from England to better ourselves. But then he was

8

taken with the pleurisy. It was very sudden. Now I have no one, no family. I cannot pay you, I have spent the last of my money.'

Now she would leave. But all she did was pat my right hand. Then she held the fingers apart, examined the webbing that stretched between them to the lower knuckle. She picked up my left hand, spread the fingers again; I fought the urge to snatch back my hand.

'I was born so,' I said. 'I cannot wear gloves, or rings.'

'You will want a position. Have you been in employment?'

'I was a governess: I taught reading, writing, drawing, pianoforte. It is true, I am in need of a position. I was told there were many opportunities for governesses in Australia. I have a good reference. Do you know of anyone who —'

'Can you sew a fine seam?'

'Pretty fine.' A strange question to ask a governess. She squeezed my left hand, took the empty milk glass and left the room.

* * * * * * *

When I woke again I was alone, but on the chair beside the bed was a large bundle of black fabric, and on the coverlet just below my chin was a white glove and a bobbin of white cotton pierced with a needle. I sat up, turned the glove over and over: silk, smelling faintly of lilacs, about the size to fit a five-year-old with slender hands, three of the finger ends and thumb frayed and gaping. I sewed up the finger and thumb ends with small, tight stitches and embroidered two rows of fancy stitch along the hem before a memory rose, with a wave of nausea, of white fabric ballooning on dark water.

Mrs Bleeker returned with chicken broth, bread and more milk. She waited behind the door until I had used the chamber pot under the bed, then put down the tray and fetched a jug, soap and a bowl of water. While I washed, she picked up the glove, turned it inside out, stretched it, thrust her little finger inside. 'Not half bad,' she murmured, then looked at the hem and sniffed. 'What counts is strength. All the clothes must endure hard use. Yanked on and off, tugged at by ragamuffins —'

'Mrs Bleeker, do you have a position for me?' I paused, tried to slow down my eagerness. 'Does your child require a governess?'

'Child? What child?' Her voice was sharp. 'There is no child. Eat your broth.'

I sat meekly at the marble table.

She lifted the mass of fabric from the chair by the bed. 'I wore this when I played the mother of one of Bluebeard's wives,' she said in a softer tone. 'Excuse me for saying this, but my cries over my dead daughter were heart-rending, everyone said so.' The black gown had stripes of alternating matte and shiny silk. 'This would fit you well.'

The broth smelled delicious. I was suddenly starving.

I spent another day and night in the room, eating meals at the marble table, sitting by the window in the soft woollen nightgown, mending seven pairs of little gloves of silk and kid, repairing a rip in a tiny muff of black fur that sat like a kitten in my lap. The window faced away from the road and river; a calm rain fell on rows of carrot tops. From time to time, Mrs Bleeker swept in and out with trays and garments. Once she stayed a little longer, picking up the locket and dangling it from her fingers. I felt a brisk rummaging through my heart.

'Do you have a job for me? I sew, I sketch, I do anything. Surely there is a job for me?'

Mrs Bleeker took the tray and left. I held myself back from running along the corridor after her like a puppy.

• • • • • • • •

I woke early, covered in sweat. I wrapped myself in the coverlet and waited in the chair for dawn. My breasts tingled, I felt slightly sick. Rain pattered on the window. This was what it was like, to be in limbo. I forbade myself to think of my burden, the past, or the future, and I would not try on the black dress. But I did pick it up when daylight came, and in the pocket I found a piece of folded paper. I opened it and the print shouted at me.

Sylvester Bleeker, manager
Positively Twenty-Nine Days Only
at the Polytechnic Hall, Melbourne
Four of the Smallest Human Beings of mature age in the World
Perfect Ladies and Gentlemen in Miniature
The original and only GENERAL TOM THUMB and his WIFE
(Mr and Mrs Chas. Stratton), COMMODORE NUTT and MISS
MINNIE WARREN in their BEAUTIFUL PERFORMANCES
consisting of SONGS, DUETS, COMIC ACTS, BURLESQUES
and LAUGHABLE ECCENTRICITIES.
Ned Davis, agent March 1870

I put down the paper, grabbed the nightgown I was wearing in my fists and pulled the folds up over my head. I felt with my hands how the cloth flattened and distorted my nose and mouth, turned my eyes into ghostly hollows. Was this how a simple garment, soaked in water and mud, turned into a caul? Was this how a man became a monster?

Footsteps at the doorway. I whirled, pulled the gown from my head. Mrs Bleeker stood with her arms full of white linen. She put down her bundle, and frowned and sniffed over the latest glove I had repaired.

'You have ladies,' I said. 'Mrs Charles Stratton and Miss Minnie Warren. I would be a very good ladies' maid.'

'It is not a position for a governess, or a clergyman's widow.'

'But I can mend their clothes, dress them, run errands. I can help you too. I can be your assistant. Please, Mrs Bleeker.'

She hesitated. 'I will have to ask my husband.'

When she came back, she had an offer.

'Twenty-two pounds. That's for nine months, the length of our tour of Australia. Board and all expenses paid, including travel. You will be assistant wardrobe mistress and ladies' maid to Mrs Stratton and Miss Warren when required.'

I thought of the meagre governess's wage, held my breath.

'There will be much hard work and constant travel,' Mrs Bleeker went on. 'We will not always stay in such pleasant hotels. The people who come to see us can be rude and vulgar. But then, Mrs Carroll — what is your Christian name?' I told her. 'Mary Ann, you know more of Australians than we Americans.'

The twang. Of course. Our friends from the New World.

'I am most grateful, Mrs Bleeker.'

'This is all conditional, mind. If the post is agreeable to you,

I shall arrange for the sisters, Mrs Stratton and Miss Warren, to interview you. It will be up to them. And the General. And my husband.' She tweaked the curtain at the window. 'The rain has stopped.' She picked up the dress from the bed and held it against me. 'Black becomes you. I have brought clean underclothes. Will you not try it on?'

She retreated behind the door and waited while I took off the nightgown and put on the camisole, pantaloons, corset, petticoat and hoop. Then she helped me into the dress, showed me the looking glass: pale face and feet, dark tangled hair, black and silver stripes rippling like the moon on water.

'This gown is too fine for me,' I said.

'Nonsense. It's stage finery.'

In the mirror, over my striped shoulder, Mrs Bleeker stared at me. I saw myself with the same gaze: startled-deer eyes, face still childishly round, but for the jut of my chin. Her gaze travelled down, up, hovered just below my waist.

'I had almost forgot.' She took my left hand and slipped a gold ring onto my third finger. It stopped at the joint, just above the web of skin, but it stayed in place. 'There. You can wear a ring after all. Only painted gold, I fear. We have many such props. Perhaps it will serve as a reminder of poor Mr Carroll.'

I could not help myself. I took Mrs Bleeker's thimble-callused hand in mine, pulled it to my heart and began to cry.

'Oh, there, there,' she said, looking around furtively as if someone would appear and blame her for the tears.

• • • • • • •

Of course I was curious about the little people. I had never seen any kind of little person, but I had touched one, as we struggled by the Yarra Yarra, and nausea rose when my fingers recalled the fishy wet skin.

I thought of Mr Quilp the dwarf in Mr Dickens's book, with his hook nose and villain's smile. I fell asleep while sewing a glove and I entered a hall where the Perfect Ladies and Gentlemen in Miniature stood on a high platform, their eyes level with mine, to judge me. They were not perfect. They were hunchbacked, and their limbs were stumps ending in claws. Their ruddy Toby-jug faces were wizened and crushed and they wore smocks fit for madmen and women. They pointed at me and screeched like bats, *You must be tractable*, and threw out strings baited with hooks that caught in my clothes and drew me towards them. They would tie me down like Gulliver. I woke, the glove crushed in my hand.

Then Mrs Bleeker came to tell me it was time to meet the ladies, and I wanted to hide behind the curtains, but I scolded myself for such childish fears.

In the sisters' boudoir, bright dresses, shawls and underwear lay strewn over the beds and furniture amid an overpowering scent of lilacs. At the heart of scent and colour, the furled bud, was Mrs Lavinia Stratton, her eyes fixed on mine.

Imagine a society beauty, and all the things people say about her. Tiny waist, lustrous black hair, exquisitely modelled neck and shoulders, velvet skin, finely shaped eyebrows and black eyelashes. Imagine hair loose, slim form wrapped in a Japanese robe of rose and white silk, dainty feet in matching rose slippers. Now imagine she is just a fraction less perfect: cheeks a little too round and babylike. Now imagine she sips from the magic bottle labelled *Eat Me*, and she shrinks down, still in perfect proportion, until she is no taller than my hip. And this shrinking concentrates her beauty, as cordial sweetens the strawberry.

Beside her was Miss Minnie Warren, a bonny fairy in a green silk wrap and green slippers, a little smaller, a little chubbier, hopping from one foot to the other. If she were not so close to her incomparable sister, and her own cheeks were not unfashionably ruddy, many would declare her a beauty in her own right. Lavinia, hands folded, could pass for a figurine; but Minnie was a blur of movement. Everything from her hair to her fingers was flyaway.

My eyes filled with tears; whether from wonder or the scent of lilacs, I could not tell. I could scarcely believe that one such creature existed on this earth, let alone two.

'Kneel,' Lavinia said to me, her voice imperious, musical. Did she demand a queen's homage? But she was pointing to a pincushion on the floor in front of her, and I saw the hem of her robe was half pinned, the edge ragged. Behind me, Mrs Bleeker cleared her throat. I kneeled and continued pinning.

'Look at me,' Lavinia said. She was fanning her hair out over her shoulders. Her eyes were a startling violet. 'What do you see?'

'A beautiful lady,' said I.

'Not a beautiful *little* lady?'

I hesitated. Was the question a trap?

Lavinia smiled. 'Always remember when you look at me that you are in the presence of a wonder of the world.'

'Two wonders of the world,' said Minnie, her voice high and a little sharp. Both spoke with Mrs Bleeker's twangy accent.

'I am the Queen of Beauty,' Lavinia continued. 'I sing like an angel. I am all that the most fastidious fancy could desire in a woman. Everyone says so.' She shrugged the robe down a little, giving me a glimpse of powdered skin, then pulled it tight. 'And I am highly intelligent, but nobody says that. At all times, my talents must be presented to best advantage.'

'And my talents too,' said Minnie. 'Don't forget my talents.'

'As if we could,' said Lavinia drily, shooting her a look. Then she turned back to me. 'We are very much indebted to you, Mary Ann.'

I nodded, bent to her hem. Mrs Bleeker stood silently behind me, but her eyes were needles in my back.

'You are a clergyman's daughter,' Lavinia went on. 'And a clergyman's widow. You look very young. What are you, seventeen?'

'Twenty. I am newly widowed.' I felt about to sneeze. I wanted to tell Lavinia a story of my blameless life, but the lilacs swelled my tongue.

'Such is fortune for us poor women.' Lavinia put one hand to her chin, tapped her rosebud lips with her forefinger. Her rings flashed. 'You have worked with children. You sewed up my gloves. You braved the Yarra Yarra. You must have a cool head in a crisis. It is all crisis with us, is it not, Minnie?'

Minnie chuckled.

'And yet,' Lavinia continued, 'I am not convinced we need a ladies' maid on this tour. We have managed very well so far without one.'

A sneeze rose into my head, but I fought it back. 'I believe I am not the panicky type,' I said firmly. 'I am very diligent and hard-

16

working, and I use my head. I'm sure I can rise to any challenge you might set me.'

'You are not backward in coming forward,' said Lavinia. Was that a rebuke? 'Very well, you shall have your challenge. Mrs B, what is the time?'

'Twenty past three.'

'So. Here is your task. You must dress me in my Worth lavender grosgrain gown and put up my hair, and then you must dress my sister in her primrose gown and put up her hair too. Just a simple knot. Mrs B, you can give her hairpins but you must not help her.'

That was easy enough.

'And it must all be done by half past.'

Ten minutes? I might as well leave now, I thought, and beg in Melbourne's alleyways. But it must be possible: no harder than dressing Matilda's dolls. I turned to the bed and flipped through the rainbow of silks, satins and velvets until I glimpsed lavender, pulled out the gown and rushed to Lavinia. She stood with her arms held out, let me pull off her Japanese robe. I felt the faint trembling of her effort to keep herself calm, still, as if she stood balanced on a tiny point. Beneath, she was in her crinolette and underthings. She stepped into the dress and I coaxed her arms into the openings, smoothed and pulled the dress tight. Confusing braids and fringes, tiny hooks and exquisitely covered buttons set my fingers afumble, but somehow I got her fastened in, wound her hair into a hasty knot and pinned it in place. She patted it as if reassuring an unruly pet.

Mrs Bleeker consulted the clock on the mantelpiece. 'Twenty-three past.'

Good, that left more than half my time to attend to Minnie. But when I drew out the primrose gown, she laughed, flung off her wrapper and twisted away from me like a child playing chasey. I could not get her to step into it: I had to throw the silk over her head and then grab each flailing arm in turn and push it into the sleeves, wanting to smack her but not daring to hurt her or rip the delicate fabric.

'Minnie dear,' Lavinia cried in reproach, but she was laughing too. It was a much simpler dress than Lavinia's, but Minnie kept wriggling out of my grasp, and when I tried to do up the buttons, she did can-can kicks under her frothing skirts. I despaired over her curls, pinned up the long locks and left the rest to dance Princess Eugenie–style around her cherubic face. We stood panting, eyeing each other.

'Thirty-one past,' said Mrs Bleeker.

'That's not fair,' I cried. 'You saw —' Mrs Bleeker frowned and clicked her tongue at me.

'I saw,' said Lavinia. 'But if we were backstage, we would miss our cue.'

I glared at Minnie, who widened her angelic eyes.

'However,' Lavinia went on, 'in view of my sister's skittishness —'

'I am not skittish! It's my natural spirits!'

'— in view of my sister's spirits, I will allow that you were very quick, Mary Ann ... Minnie dear, you absolutely must let that hem down. I have told you time and time again. When you walk along the runway, all the gentlemen will see your ankles and Lord knows what.'

'Oh, bosh. It's exactly the length that Paris is wearing this season,' said Minnie.

'Nonsense. Think how fast you will look.'

'Better fast than frumpy, Vin dear.' Hands on hips like a tiny washerwoman, Minnie looked as if she were about to stick out her tongue at her sister.

Lavinia's tone grew stern. 'Altogether too much spirit. Have you had your medicine today?'

'She will take it with her tea,' said Mrs Bleeker. The parlourmaid had arrived with a trolley, and the sisters fell on it, jostling each other as they reached on tiptoe to the top tier of the cake tray. A scent of honey competed with the lilacs. Was I hired or not? I looked towards Mrs Bleeker, who gave a slight shrug.

'Are you ladies decent?' The cry came from the doorway, in a high tenor twang.

'Come in, Charlie,' said Lavinia.

Mr Charles Stratton, known as General Tom Thumb, strode into the boudoir, spurs clinking. A fine-looking fellow with strong eyebrows and full cheeks, his portliness suited him. He was dressed as Napoleon and moved with a stiff-legged strut as if surveying his empire. He had an erect carriage, a sparse gingery beard, a brave cockade in his hat and high boots buffed without mercy. He gave Lavinia a smacking kiss on the cheek, smiled at Minnie and Mrs Bleeker, took a slice of cake from its stand, broke off a piece and tossed it into his mouth. A hair's breadth taller than Lavinia, he seemed to fill the room.

'First-rate plum cake. You ladies have the best teas.'

His voice, high for a man, was deep compared to the ladies'

chirrups. Littleness concentrated his wife's beauty; for him, littleness concentrated his masculinity, and this seemed to me even more marvellous. All three little people had the plump, fresh look of sparrows who might beg for crumbs, then hop under your nose and devour your whole dinner.

'Is everything all right, Charlie?' said Lavinia, gazing at him fondly.

'Right as rain. How lovely you look, my dear. And you too, Minnie. And …' He smiled at me. 'Who might you be, missy? Come for my autograph?'

'This is Mary Ann, General,' said Mrs Bleeker. 'She is a clergyman's widow, we are considering hiring her to help out.'

Charlie — for so I would come to think of him, though I always called him General — looked me up and down, and I straightened like a soldier on parade. He stuck his thumbs into the armholes of his white waistcoat and thrust out his chest and stomach until the buttons were in danger of popping open. He drew his head back to catch my eye, his top chin sharp, his lower chin more rounded, and it seemed as if he were looking down at me. As he stared, I began to feel that my fancy of cheeky sparrows was all wrong. Charlie and the ladies were the right size, and Mrs Bleeker and I were clumsy giantesses.

I hid my huge hands behind my back as he began to frown.

'Has Mr B approved this? Do we need any more help?'

'She is the one, Charlie.' Lavinia nudged his arm.

'What's that, Vin?'

'The one who rescued you, when you lost your footing on the bridge and fell into the Yarra Yarra.'

20

Charlie's gaze dropped. He gently brushed Lavinia's hand from his arm, and a flush crept across his cheeks. My head roared again with a cascade, a slithery monster, and I averted my eyes as we stood like bashful children.

He will never let the troupe hire me, I thought, if I make him remember.

I felt his eyes on me once more and returned his gaze. His face was still flushed, but now it glowed with hope and an anxious little smile.

'How is your health, Mary Ann?'

'Very well, thank you.' My reply was automatic, but I was sure my puzzlement showed.

'Are you sure? Just lately? Ever feel a little peaky?'

Surely he could not know of my burden. I opened my mouth to insist I was well. He watched me, still smiling, gave me a little nod, his right eye twitched in something that was nearly a wink, and I realised what I should say.

'I have felt a little indisposed lately. But it is nothing. I am more than capable of any amount of work.'

'Well said,' he cried, sweeping off his hat. 'General Tom Thumb at your service, young woman. The General is totally in your debt. You saved him from oblivion in a spiteful river at the ends of the earth, and we will reward you handsomely.' He took my hand in a firm paw, a little sticky with plum cake, and pumped it up and down.

'How do you do, sir. I am glad to see you so well,' I said.

He gave off a comfortable man scent of brandy and cigars.

'What a warm hand,' he said. 'I have a feeling you will bring us

21

good fortune. Let us drink a toast. Mrs B, do we have brandy?'

'We have tea, General.'

'That will do. Let us charge our glasses — I mean, cups.'

The three little people held out china cups, and Mrs Bleeker poured from the teapot.

Charlie raised his cup high, held my gaze. 'Let us drink to youth and hope, to a new dawn. Not — as some in this troupe would have us believe — a false dawn.' For a moment, his voice deepened. Lavinia and Mrs Bleeker exchanged a swift glance. *Four of the Smallest Human Beings of mature age in the World*, the pamphlet had said. Where was the fourth, and why wasn't he here?

The cups rose, clinked together, and I felt an almost pleasurable dizziness as I stood in a circle of smiles. 'To the future,' said Charlie. I had no idea why he wanted me to act a little peaky, but I would have no trouble doing it.

Mrs Bleeker drew me back from the circle. 'Well done,' she whispered. 'Now all you have to do is impress my husband.'

SIDESHOW

Mrs Charles Stratton,
née Miss Lavinia Warren,
aka Mrs Tom Thumb

Mr and Mrs Tom Thumb

ACT ONE

The girl looks all of a puzzle. We have that effect sometimes on those who have never seen us before. Or perhaps she is wondering why she had to kneel to me. It was not just so she could pin my dress, or so I could look her in the eye. This is what one does before a queen, and I think I have been a queen for most of my life, long before Mr Barnum manufactured me so. It was necessary for a young person such as myself to have dignity and command. Otherwise I would be nothing but a doll, to be dandled and discarded. Look at the Queen of England: not tiny, to be sure, but certainly a plain little dumpling, as my husband irreverently calls her. Even her crown is little. But Lord, such dignity. Such command.

My reign began on a sled in Middleborough, Massachusetts, during the winter I turned six. Father said I looked like a Chinese emperor. I sat wrapped in woollen shawls, wearing a red stocking hat, while my schoolmates pulled me. When I yelled directions, they swerved whichever way I wanted. We played that game every winter for five years. Sometimes the little brothers and sisters rode on the sled, but they whined and fell off and got left behind in the snow. They did not have the knack of command. Minnie was always too young to go with us (there are eight years between us sisters), and though she cried and begged it was just as well: she would have tossed and rolled and sent us all skidding to perdition.

Dignity came later and was harder won. I thought I would be the queen of Colonel Wood's floating theatre until I saw Miss Hardy's button boots. I was sixteen then and quite the heir presumptive. But those boots gaped at me in all their enormity on the threshold of the stateroom we were to share on the steamboat. There was a bulge in the leather of each boot where the big toe poked up. Who could fill those shoes?

Miss Hardy was more nurse than queen to me. She came from Wilton, Maine. She was double-chinned, gentle and affectionate, smelled of gardenias and measured eight feet tall. Once I had overcome my awe, I would climb into her lap for a sleep, or to have my frequent headaches soothed as the steamboat throbbed its way down the Mississippi.

Colonel Wood was my cousin, had a well-trimmed goatee, wore white suits without a speck of soot on them and always carried a pair of white gloves; and because of all these things my parents trusted him when he asked me to travel for a season on his showboat. Every day, wearing one of the three matching ensembles in royal blue that Colonel Wood had made us pay for out of our wages, Miss Hardy and I took a promenade on the floating theatre stage. The customers greeted us with gasps and cheers and cracks about the long and the short of it. I assumed Miss Hardy caused all the commotion, until some visitors approached me, stooped down and peered most impudently at my face and my bosom.

'Why do they stare so?' I asked Miss Hardy afterwards.

'Don't mind them. They just want to be sure.'

'Sure? Of what?'

'That Colonel Wood isn't humbugging them with a little child.'

'How do you do,' I said, curtseying to the next gentleman who came close to inspect me. 'I am Lavinia Warren and I am sixteen years old.'

'Of the Plymouth Warrens? Who came to Massachusetts in 1650? Three brothers. One was lame and had a humpback, one had very large ears, one had six fingers on one hand. I am descended from Stephen, who had six fingers.'

I watched him in silence.

The gentleman cleared his throat. 'Has any member of your family six fingers on one hand or six toes on one foot?'

I drew myself very straight, looked up into his watery eyes. 'I am descended from William, Earl of Warren, who married the daughter of William the Conqueror. We came to America on the *Mayflower*. General Joseph Warren laid down his life for his country at the battle of Bunker Hill. I am sorry to disappoint you, sir, but no one in my family ever had six fingers on one hand, or six toes on one foot, or a limp, or a humpback, or very large ears.'

The gentleman looked hard at my hands and feet, then back at my grave face. Could he tell I was chaffing him?

'Or a deficient brain,' I added.

'Well done, dear,' whispered Miss Hardy. 'You tell 'em.'

· · · · · · · ·

26

Then the war began, and we had to leave the South, where it was not safe to stay, in case we were caught up the creek behind enemy lines.

'You are never going away again,' my mother told me when I returned home. 'The world is not safe for you.'

'It seems no less safe for me than for any other soul,' I replied.

For a while I went back to my old school to teach, but standing on a chair to rap knuckles with a ruler did not seem work I was cut out for. So I resumed my old round of cooking, sewing and housekeeping. I would not give myself airs, pretend I was too good for such tasks. And yet they vexed me, and Minnie vexed me more.

She was nine then, my little raggedy shadow, grown almost up to my shoulder. She followed me everywhere, as she had always done, asking me again and again to tell her stories of Miss Hardy and the gentlemen who inspected us. I am sure I was very patient. I told her that if she wished to meet the public, she must fix her deportment and learn tidier ways. She took to pulling the pins out of my hair and using them to fasten impertinent and badly spelled labels to my back. *Steme Bote Quene*, *Hoyty Toyty Miss* and the like. I ask you.

I felt I had to get away. I could choose between another river tour with Colonel Wood, in a safer part of the country, or an offer from a Mr Barnum to appear at his American Museum, on the corner of Broadway and Ann Street, New York, to be followed by a tour of Europe. I was inclined to take the Colonel's offer, but then Mr Barnum invited my parents and myself to his home in Bridgeport, Connecticut. Let me pass on the opulent appointments of his magnificent house and say only that I found him a tall dark fellow with a florid complexion who gazed at me as if lovestruck.

'Miss Warren,' he boomed. 'You are a miracle. A Queen of Beauty.'

Well. Such soft soap. I told him I was sorry, but I was already engaged. Then my mother said I was not exactly engaged at present, which made me frown, and I assured Mr Barnum that Colonel Wood was making my worldwide reputation.

Mr Barnum found that very funny. 'On a paddleboat up a creek? Miss Warren, you deserve better than a bunch of Southern riff-raff. You deserve kings and queens and emperors at your feet. I can give you the entire Americas, Britain, Europe, Asia … Australia, if you wish it.'

I told him there was no need to get barbarous. He made to say more, but I hushed him and told him I would not wear royal blue, it did nothing for my complexion. He positively danced around me, told me I would wear any colour, style or fabric I desired, no expense spared, gowns from Madame Demorest of Broadway and jewellery from Messrs Ball and Black. He offered me his hand, which swallowed my own. My mother was clinging to my father's arm, both smiling. I felt light, ready to float away, except for the red hand anchoring me.

· · · · · · · ·

On Sundays, when the American Museum was closed and the crowds had gone home, the Great Skeletal Chamber became a nursery and playground. I was surprised that the resident children of the museum were not frightened by the thunder lizards and their still greater shadows flickering on the wall. But they had seen the miracles so many times.

One evening, soon after my arrival in New York, I stood and watched as Madame Josephine Clofullia tried to get the children to sit cross-legged on the floor and look at their Bibles. Her luxuriant beard did not help her to impose discipline. Hendrik the albino boy ran up and down the hall, chuffing and whistling, his phantom train echoing round the arched ceiling. Malcolm the fat boy, pocket knife in hand, was trying to chisel a thunder lizard's toe bone out of its socket. The five Indian children, wrapped in threadbare blankets, crouched on the floor in a sullen knot.

'Oh, Miss Warren,' said Madame Clofullia, in her breathy Swiss accent, 'I have such a nice story for the boys and girls, the story of Jacob and Esau, but they will not be told.'

I wondered if I should offer to take over. It would not take me long to get the children's noses into their Bibles, but I did not wish to usurp Madame Clofullia's duties. And I had spent all morning trying on my new gowns and jewels, and all afternoon playing hostess in the museum, in peach silk with amethysts at my throat and wrists, standing on a pedestal table, smiling and shaking hands and murmuring greetings and laughing. The room had been as full of gaping heads as my mother's preserving jars were full of pickled onions. I supposed I had been a success. My feet ached, my stays pinched, my face was a dead mask of smiles.

Malcolm looked up from his chiselling, and a grin split his moon face. 'Here he is!'

Hendrik stopped in mid-whistle; the Indians shrugged off their blankets. They all ran towards the figure entering the chamber, who I first thought was another child. Then General Tom Thumb gave a big masculine laugh and emptied his pockets, showering them with bonbons. The children pounced, then fell back, sucking their treasures.

'Mercy,' he cried. 'You have cleaned me right out of treats.' Then he greeted us, the ladies, and asked how we found the children.

'Obstreperous,' said Madame Clofullia.

At once he suggested she go and rest; he would supervise them until their bedtime. 'Perhaps, Miss Warren, you would care to keep me company?'

I had no reason to refuse. He made no attempt to organise the children, just stood back and let them play. Malcolm chalked squares and numbers on the floor, then hopped slowly down his row of squares, wheezing and chanting. Hendrik followed him. At the end of the row, Malcolm jumped, turned, jumped again, thighs a jelly-wobble, and looked to the General for approval. I too looked. For some reason my frank gaze was difficult to summon: I could only manage sidelong glances. Everything about the General spoke manliness. When I had seen him before, from a distance, holding court, he cut such a fine figure I suspected he might be one of Mr Barnum's automatons. At closer quarters he was broad of shoulder and chest; hair in glossy waves; faint scent of cologne and cigars; hint of portliness about his chin and below his waistcoat; moustache my mother would hate.

He felt my glance and turned. 'How did your levee go today, Miss Warren?'

I told him it went well, although it was very crowded and hot, and I asked him how he dealt with all those people.

'I don't find it hard — I've been meeting the public all my life. That is my profession, meeting the public. It comes to me like breathing. It will come to you the same way soon.'

I tried to imagine a world packed with pickle-jar heads.

'It is a noble and profitable profession,' said the General, his hands behind his back. I was about to say that nobility was more important than profit, but then my hand went up to my collarbone and encountered the amethysts, and I stayed silent and confused, feeling his gaze, wondering where my queenliness had gone.

'What do you think of these children, Miss Warren?'

'They are most singular,' I said. 'Like everyone in this museum.'

'Some are more singular than others,' said the General, smiling into my eyes. 'I like to come here and watch the children. They don't watch you back. Not much.'

I looked down hurriedly. He turned back to the hopscotch game, his smile growing wistful, and his left knee began to bend, his left foot slowly rising behind him, until he stood on one foot with the unconscious grace of a heron.

I have often wondered since if that was the moment I fell in love with him.

· · · · · · · ·

The proposal came at Iranistan, Mr Barnum's grand house at Bridgeport, the town where the General also lived. For months he had made frequent visits to his sister in New York and always dropped by at the museum to see me and talk to me. I grew very impatient for his visits. Then when I visited Mr Barnum for a weekend, the General took me for a ride in his carriage around Bridgeport, stopping at his mother's house and showing me his apartment fitted out with fine furniture designed for his size. His mother, who wore too many diamonds on her fleshy neck, grinned at me with broken teeth and told the General that his girl was a damn fine filly. I smiled and pretended not to hear. We drove on. He pointed out several of his properties and when I remarked that it seemed he and Mr Barnum owned all Bridgeport between them, he swelled and smiled.

After dinner that evening, Mr Barnum and all his guests excused themselves one by one, leaving me alone with the General, huddled by the fire in the cavernous drawing room, playing backgammon. The General did not seem to care for the game. He stood up and took to the fire with the poker. Then he took a piece of paper from his pocket and unfolded it into a sheet as big as a newspaper. It trembled a little in his hands. He sat down, handed it to me and asked me if I knew what it was.

'It is an insurance policy,' I said.

He leaned forward, hands on knees, explaining the policy to me, pointing out clauses and signatures. His house was mortgaged and insured, he got the interest, and the man who had given him the mortgage had to pay the taxes. That was the way he did all his business. I tried not to smile. He drew his chair a little closer, cleared his throat and asked about my forthcoming tour of Europe. Would I not be lonely? Would I not like him to accompany me so he could explain all the strange customs and peoples?

'You told me you had plenty of money and were tired of travelling,' said I.

'I should like it first-rate if I were to go too.'

'Perhaps Mr Barnum will fix it, if you ask him.'

He put his arm along the back of my chair. 'Don't you think it would be pleasanter if we went as man and wife?'

I had expected it, and yet I felt a thrill of surprise. It was like a play. A familiar, wonderful play. He called me *dear*, asked me to call him *Charlie*, kissed me on the cheek and asked me to say *yes*.

I remember I was so happy, and yet so afraid the whole scene was some dark plot of Mr Barnum's. But that kiss had such fervour. My cheek glowed.

'Well, perhaps I might love you enough. But I can never say yes without my mother's consent.'

'Then may I visit your mother and ask, pet?'

I sat for a moment as if in deep thought. He kissed my ear and I felt the kiss as something between a tickle and an explosion. 'You had better shave your moustache first.'

· · · · · · · ·

When she knew of our engagement, Mother said we must have a little talk. I thought it would be about property, or Charlie's supposed haughtiness, or that moustache.

We sat in the old family parlour in Middleborough under august pictures of the Warren ancestors. Mother reached out and took my hand.

'Marry by all means. But you must not have children.'

I was too stunned to reply. Mother said that after seven children, she knew what she was talking about. 'Giving birth would kill you. It cannot be contemplated.'

Rallying, I said that Charlie and I would surely have children like ourselves, and what was wrong with that?

'You cannot be sure. Look at me. Don't risk it, Lavinia. Do

whatever you must to avoid it. There is a curse on us Warrens. It
follows us down the generations, it looks for a chance to strike.'

I laughed and assured Mother I was not in the slightest danger,
and I did not believe in curses. But I began to dream of formless,
heaving things. Mother's words had planted a cold blue embryo
in my womb. On the eve of my marriage, I had a little talk with
Charlie, and we came to our arrangement.

• • • • • • • •

These nights, we lie under the covers and listen to the river and the
strange Australian birds and Charlie rubs my hands. He says he will
give me everything I want. There must be a way. The miracles of
science can achieve so much. I pat his hand, say it is not necessary,
ignore the faint ache in my belly.

I try not to think about babies, even when they sit in my lap. I
imagine they are clockwork creatures you might wind up in Mr
Barnum's museum. It's easier that way.

CHAPTER 3

I could not see the little people when their tiny walnut-shaped coach drew up that evening outside the Polytechnic Hall. When they alighted, I was on the other side of the road with Mrs Bleeker, and carriages and drays choked the thoroughfare. All Melbourne wanted to catch a glimpse.

I did see the driver, sitting high on the box seat, raising his whip at the young ruffians teasing his pair of miniature ponies.

'Mr Rodnia Nutt, the Commodore's elder brother,' said Mrs Bleeker. 'He always drives the Commodore's coach.'

He was a small man, but not extraordinarily small. He was in sky-blue plush, with a cloud of white wig and a handsome face of thunder. I could not stop staring. How tall would he be if he stood next to me?

'Come on,' said Mrs Bleeker. She led the way across the road, weaving through the traffic, and down an alley to a side door.

'My husband will be backstage. Get him anything he needs.'

'How shall I know him?'

Unexpectedly, she giggled. 'Look up.'

Look up, I thought, suddenly alone but for two stagehands hammering a defenceless plank. Lamps sputtered and hissed around my feet. Swirls of smoke made me cough as I threaded my way through a maze of dark corridors and came out into a large space. Before me hung a huge red curtain. A streak of a man, six foot five at least, stood with his back to me, peering through the slit between the folds.

'Mr Bleeker?' He turned, frowning. 'I am Mary Ann, sir. Mrs Bleeker sent me to see if you need anything.'

'Hannah sent you?' Sylvester Bleeker stared down at me with watery eyes. He had a narrow drooping face, sparse hair and beard, and his frown was not anger but bewilderment. Then he snaked out a skinny arm, laid a hand on my shoulder and drew me to the curtainfolds. 'Look.'

Beyond the curtain was a large, handsome hall with friezes in the Grecian style. Hundreds of people sprawled on seats, backs of seats, stood at the rear and in the aisle. Still more were filing in. Chatter, waving fans and handkerchiefs, baccy spit, gusts of cologne, orange peel, sweat, farts, all heading straight for me.

Quickly I closed the curtains. 'Oh Lord, we are onstage.'

'So we are. Onstage in Melbourne, the Chicago of the Orient. Population, one hundred and seventy thousand. All here tonight, by the look of it. What shall we do?'

He was asking me? I licked my lips. 'Put on a show, sir?'

Mr Bleeker laughed without mirth. 'How, with the theatre about to burst? Always one thing or the other. House miserably small or stuffed to the gills. And who's the miracle worker around here, hey?'

As he rubbed his chest with his great hand, little Napoleon approached him and tugged at his coat-tails like an importunate child. 'Mr B. Let me see the order of scenes.' The manager took a sheaf of dog-eared papers from his pocket. Charlie scanned them, then thrust them back towards Mr Bleeker, his voice squeaky with outrage.

'What's this? General precedes Commodore?'

'This is the same order of scenes as Japan.'

'But I need hardly remind you, the General is the star act and the Commodore the warm-up.' Charlie grabbed the papers back, squinted at them. 'Will not do. And what's this? The Commodore's drum solo? *Again?*' One plump be-ringed hand slapped the page.

'It's very popular.'

'It is very horrid. Bang bang bang until our heads explode.'

Mr Bleeker got down on his knees to study the papers. Charlie saw me. His face was blank for a moment, then broke into a huge grin, and I smiled back.

But he was stern again, back to his papers. 'Not on. Not on.'

'Mr B, come quick. We can't hold 'em off.' The cry came from a lean dark fellow in a bowler hat, crossing the stage towards us. Mr Bleeker waved him away. 'Not now, Ned.'

'The coppers say they'll close down the show if we don't stop folks coming in.'

Mr Bleeker stood, made to lay his hand on Ned's shoulder, then paused as if the touch might be unpleasant. 'Forgive me, General … Mary Ann, come.'

I trotted in his wake, dodging sets and trunks and a long pole where the ladies' little gowns hung, brushing me as I passed with the smells of lilac and mothball. Somewhere a piano jangled up and down the scales. How my bladder grumbled. Where was the nearest privy? How could I keep up with these whirlwind people? Calls came from all sides.

'Mr B, I can't fix …'

'Mr B, this isn't …'

He strode on, leaning forward as if into a gale. Already I was out of breath.

Then a little man, a truly little man, in a navy uniform and jaunty cap ducked under Mr Bleeker's arm, and finally he paused.

'I hear you're changing the order of scenes, Mr B,' said this fourth little person in a high singsong voice.

While the other three all had something round and cherub-like in their faces, Commodore George Nutt was the only one who appeared really young. A little shorter and slimmer than Charlie, he seemed not much more than a boy, the kind who would charm you with his antics while he stole your purse. His merriment pushed up his face, slitted his eyes. His apple cheeks and snub nose glowed with health and rouge.

'I hope the show still closes with the star act. All the world loves the Commodore. And the Commodore loves all the world — especially the young ladies.' He winked at me, whistled, tilted his hat, nudged Mr Bleeker's kneecap.

'Commodore, please. I'm not changing anything. Ned, get me outside.'

At last, by way of a door in a hidden side alley, we reached the open air and the front of the Polytechnic Hall, where a mass of men, women and children shouted and surged, battering on the closed doors with their fists. An umbrella poked Mr Bleeker's side. He towered above the throng, rubbing his chest, like a bather with his head above choppy water. I flattened myself against a wall, my head full of sharks and drowning, while the man called Ned waited companionably beside me.

He lifted his bowler to me in slow ceremony, revealing a pate black as liquorice and glossy with pomade, as if it had seeped out of his brain. He thrust his head towards me and shouted above the din. 'Ned Davis, agent and treasurer and Mister Fixit of the General's tour. Pleased to make your acquaintance, ma'am. You want anything fixed, you come to me.' Then he lounged back to watch the entertainment. I would have clung to his greasy-sleeved arm, but something was wrong with his smile: his teeth were too yellow, and one canine stuck out from its neighbours in a most predatory fashion. Besides, his pomade smell stirred my nausea.

Mr Bleeker pulled himself higher, filled out his chest. 'Ladies and Gentlemen,' he bellowed, winning a silence. 'Ladies and Gentlemen, I am Sylvester Bleeker, the manager of the show. The House Is Full. There are No More Tickets. Come back tomorrow. Come back for the best show yet. The Man in Miniature and his Diminutive Queen and the Incomparable Commodore and the Charming Miss Warren will perform for your delight …'

'I've come for tonight,' growled the man who had poked Mr Bleeker with his umbrella. He stood very close to me, and his drooping eyelids and blubber lips made me feel still more queasy.

'You Have Waited Years for these Magnificent Lilliputians to Visit,' shouted Mr Bleeker. 'One More Night.' He thrust his face into umbrella man's, pressed something into his hand. The man opened his hand, stared at a piece of cardboard. 'Come back tomorrow, sir,' Mr Bleeker whispered, 'and you may take the Queen of Beauty's tiny hand in yours.'

The umbrella man spread his fleshy lips in a grin. He tucked the card into his breast pocket.

Mr Bleeker fumbled in his own pocket, drew out a crumpled handkerchief, a bunch of keys and a cloth bag. He undid the bag's fastening and pulled out handfuls of little cards. 'Here, Ned. Here, Mary Ann. Handouts. Free, tonight only.'

The top card in my pile showed Lavinia smiling, silk-clad, the perfect fairy. I imagined the blubbery lips kissing the card. I fought down the urge to retch.

'Free *cartes de visite*!' shouted Ned, holding handfuls above his head. 'Unrepeatable offer! Pick 'em up now, get 'em signed at tomorrow's show!'

The men surged towards him. Would he fall beneath their trampling feet? But his hands rose higher and his cuffs slipped down from his scrawny wrists, scarred with white slashes. Mr Bleeker was waving his hands at me. Women and children pressed against me, my bladder ached and stung, and as fast as I doled out the cards, more hands clutched at my arms, dress, hair. They would drag me down, stamp on me, pull off strips of my flesh. With a shriek I threw the cards into the air, and as they fell and people scrabbled for them, I turned and rushed back into the theatre. Privy. Quick, before my bladder exploded. Inside the theatre, the audience was chanting.

Fee-fi -fo-Thumb!
I smell the blood of a LITTLE one!

It didn't rhyme. Nothing in this place made sense. All hunger and savagery. Mrs Bleeker bustled past, arms full of satin.

'Where is the privy, Mrs B?'

'Down the alley, out back. Get him his tea, for God's sake. And his tablets. Kettle on the hob. Blue teacup, mind.'

I ran out to the alley, hiked up my skirts and crouched on the privy seat, holding my breath against the stink. Oh, relief, what a stream of it, and blessed solitude. What a fool to fear a circle of grabbing hands. Yet I waited trembling for some other person to burst in and snap at me to do something, for God's sake.

My nausea faded as I reached fresh air. In the room with a fireplace, I found the kettle, and as I came out, carrying the cup and the bottle that had stood next to it, Charlie pushed past me, pale as a mushroom under his cocked hat, and led the way to the wings. He stuck his thumbs in his waistcoat armholes, thrust his two chins and his chest out at Mr Bleeker.

'Mr B, I must insist. Change the order of scenes or I won't go on.'

Mr Bleeker rubbed and patted his own chest like a thin gorilla. 'Course you will. It's you they want, man. Listen.'

Fee-fi -fo-Thumb!

Charlie folded his arms, did a Napoleonic glower.

Mr Bleeker sighed. 'I'll change the order of scenes. From tomorrow.'

'So the Commodore will precede the General?'

'Of course.'

'And no drum solo?'

'A shorter drum solo.' Charlie reddened. 'Melbourne folks love

41

a good show,' Mr Bleeker said quickly. 'Last week at the opera, someone threw a gold nugget onto the stage.'

Charlie's face cleared. 'They will appreciate us more than some fat Lucia.'

'Jove, they will.'

'We'll give them a twenty-four-carat show, eh, Mr B?'

'You bet, Generalissimo. Now where's …'

'Your tea, sir.' I held out cup, saucer and bottle of Dr Foote's Magnetic Anti-Bilious Tablets. Mr Bleeker grabbed the cup, inhaled the fragrant Foochow steam, and I understood then that time would stop while he drank his tea. 'Good work, Mary Ann.' He sipped, took a tablet, began to speak. Charlie was smiling at me.

I felt the nausea rise: would I have time to dash away before I had to heave?

'You see, Mary Ann, we're all tools. I'm Mr Barnum's tool. You are my wife's tool. Mr Barnum says there is no tool you should be so particular about as living tools.'

I was about to disgrace myself. They would all recoil in horror, the show would stop, the audience would flee the theatre and everyone would shun the madwoman.

'If you get a good tool, keep him. He learns something new every day.'

Something was rising in my throat. Slowly the stage began to revolve.

'A good tool is worth more to you this year than last. He's the last man to part with. If his habits are good and he continues faithful …'

Behind me, a young man I had never seen before strode out

to the piano in the wings, flipped out his tails with a flourish, sat down and began to play. The audience cheered, then gradually fell silent, and I began to feel a little calmer. The young man crouched low, leaned back, flung his cascade of dark red hair from his eyes with a toss of his head, a lion afire with the chords from his fingers. His eyes were closed. Who was he? I wanted to see his eyes open. I reached for Mr Bleeker's cup and saucer, but the manager had gone. I was alone at the edge of the stage as the jaunty overture stomped and swirled, and the audience clapped along. As I stepped away from the lights, and the curtains swept open, another wave overtook me. The floorboards rose, slammed into the side of my face, and my last sight was Napoleon's boots.

Mr Charles Sherwood Stratton,
alias General Tom Thumb

General Tom Thumb

ACT ONE

My name is Charlie Stratton, and I am what the General used to be.
The General is thirty-two years and three months old; he's pulling
himself together, he's going onstage to astound the Antipodeans
with his Napoleon. I'm four years old and I'm not going anywhere.
I have been four for a long time. You can't see me, can you? I'm
hiding. I'm good at hiding. I'm like the boy in the picture puzzle.
The boy in the fork of the tree, the boy-shaped space the branches
make. It's kind of lonely up here, but it's the best place for me. As
long as I keep still, you can't see me.

What happened was the General came. He strutted in and he
sat down, plonk, with his chest out and belly up and legs spread.
He filled up all the space where I used to be. I had to climb up into
the puzzle tree. I don't mind, not really. The General is great and
good. You know that old story, the one where the king of the gods
had a splitting headache, it hurt so bad his head split open, just like
a plum?

• • • • • • • •

Out sprang the goddess of wisdom, fully grown, with all her armour on. That's how the General was born. He sprang out of Mr Barnum's head. I guess it didn't hurt Mr Barnum too bad — the General was much smaller than the goddess, and he didn't have a helmet and spears and such.

But he was fully grown. He smoked cigars and drank wine and walked with a swagger and a stick with a lion's-head handle and a man-about-town way of wearing his hat and saying howdy-do to the ladies. His waistcoat held a manly chest and a thumping great heart and his breeches held I don't know what, but it was something mighty important. He knew everything and he was afraid of nothing. Did he know about me, then? I cannot tell.

Of course he had to learn first what to know and what not to fear. But he was a mighty fast learner.

'Show me how small you are,' said Mr Barnum.

The General stood in the study by the fire. It blazed hot all down his right side. Mr Barnum kneeled before him, as he might with a favourite dog.

'Come. Show me.'

The first time Mr Barnum said it, the General crouched down.

'No, no.' Mr Barnum frowned. 'You must do the opposite. If you want everyone to notice how small you are, you must try to appear big.'

The General held his breath and spread out his arms. Would he float off the floor like a balloon?

Mr Barnum smiled. 'Watch me.' He drew himself up and walked all round the room with straight legs. It made the General think of a rooster. He had to tip back his head to watch. He gurgled with laughter. 'Now you try.'

He did the walk, but it was harder than it looked.

Mr Barnum watched him. 'Stretch taller. Raise your chin towards the ceiling. Pull back your shoulders. Oh, you are a big man, a big man. A general reviewing your troops. No, that's too solemn. Strut, boy, strut.'

'Cock a doodle doo,' crowed the General.

'That's the boy. You're cock of the walk. Look me in the eye. You are equal to anyone you meet. Puff out your chest. Strut, strut.'

The General did his best. Legs of tables and chairs bumped into him. The hungry tongues of the fire licked towards him.

Mr Barnum took down the looking glass from the mantelpiece and placed it flat on the rug. 'Stand on that. See how you look.'

He stood on the shiny surface and looked down. He saw great thick tree-trunk legs, a big belly, small shoulders, a tiny head.

'What do you see?'

'A mighty fellow, Mr Barnum.'

Mr Barnum laughed and laughed. 'A mighty fellow indeed … No, don't stop.'

Strut, strut, until long after the fire died.

The wine and the cigars were harder. Both tasted worse than the most horrid medicine. They made the General so sick he could hardly strut and twirl his cane. Mr Barnum put out a spittoon so he could empty his stomach if he needed to. He would kneel down and pat the General's back as he heaved.

'I am truly sorry, Charlie. But you must learn to smoke and drink before you can be a man.'

'But I'm not a man, Mr Barnum. My ma says I am four years old.'

Mr Barnum's merry face quite lost its ruddy glow. He stood back and looked at the General the way his father would look at a plank of wood he planned to turn into a table.

'Eleven, Charlie. You're eleven. It's being such a little fellow that makes you feel a child.'

He put the cigar back in the General's mouth. One puff, and then he coughed and coughed.

Mr Barnum laughed. 'Don't look so doleful. You want to grow up, don't you? All boys want to grow up.'

· · · · · · · ·

I still fancied then that the General and I were pretty close. Other times, I fancied that if he ever met me in the street, the General would smile and pat me on the head and slip me a coin and walk away, twirling his stick with the lion head. He always had a soft spot for children, the General did.

I was a good boy, mostly. I sat very quiet and still in my boy-shaped space in the puzzle tree while the General did his stuff. I came out sometimes when he was asleep. I'd creep around his fancy bedroom and sit in the red velvet chairs that were specially made for him and were just the right size for me too. I felt like Goldilocks before the three bears came home. He had a dressing table with a stool and a mirror, all his size, and two silver-backed brushes. I'd sit and look at the boy in the nightgown in the mirror and pretend to brush my hair. But the bedroom didn't have any toys, and in the end I'd get bored and go and hide again.

I never came out when the General was performing. I knew I'd only get into trouble. Well, I did peep out once. I was so excited, I couldn't help it. The General and Mr Barnum were visiting the Queen of England. She was all in black, a bit of a dumpling. She looked like someone who was kind pretending to be fierce. The General was doing his show, and it was a good house — all the royals loved him. What the General saw was a long picture gallery, and the royals and their attendants, and Mr Barnum secretly mouthing his lines at him in case he forgot. What I saw was a poodle. I don't know why it was, I'd seen lots of dogs before, but when I saw that poodle, I remembered how much I'd always wanted a dog. I wanted so bad for that poodle to come over and lick my hand, and jump up and fetch my stick when I threw it. I wasn't thinking of anything but that poodle, and so I stepped out of my boy-shaped space, just for a moment. And it saw me. You know what, it didn't like me. It froze, and then it growled and barked and came at me. It was only a little toy dog to the royals and to Mr Barnum, but it was as big as a bear to me. I turned to run, right out of that great room and down the marble steps of the palace and out into the streets of London and find somewhere I could hide again.

It was the General who saved me. He stood firm and raised his stick like a sword and he had a fencing match with the poodle. Parry, feint, lunge. Mr Barnum had taught him some nifty swordplay. The royals were in fits, they laughed so much. The little dumpling Queen had tears in her eyes. In the end the dog had enough and retreated, and the General bowed and there was great applause while a flunkey grabbed the dog by its collar and dragged it out of sight. I hope he didn't hurt it.

The only creature who ever saw me was that dog, and it didn't like me. Everyone came to see the General, and everyone loved him. Kings and queens, princes and princesses, dukes and earls and counts and marquises shook his hand and patted him on the back and kissed his cheek or even his cherub lips. Hundreds, thousands more jostled to get near him, cheered and hollered for him. They wrote songs and plays, polkas and quadrilles in his honour. They painted his portrait, they made models of him from clay and dough and spun sugar. It never went to his head. He was a man, he had money, could do anything he liked. He married the sweetest, the most bewitching little beauty in the world. She called him Charlie, and I liked that, I must say. He travelled everywhere and he thought it would go on forever. When you have always been fully grown, you never think you will grow old.

Now he looks in the dressing-table mirror when he thinks nobody else is around. He's forgotten I can see him. He looks and he looks and he fluffs up his hair, or combs his whiskers, or tries buttoning and unbuttoning his waistcoat, but the picture doesn't change. I don't know what he sees, but it isn't a mighty fellow anymore.

He tries to stay away from that other little fellow, Commodore George Nutt, but sometimes he just can't avoid him. He watches him sideways, watches the mob and the way they cheer and clap for him, the way they once cheered and clapped for the one and only General Tom Thumb. He'd like to land a fist or two on that snub nose. But he doesn't go in for fisticuffs. And anyway, George might hit back, hard. He's awfully young.

The General tries to remember his mother and father. But all he knows are the Strattons, who are very amusing. They considered themselves so hoity-toity, and he always Thundering, and she always Damning, and both forever asking poor Mr Barnum for more money. Mr Stratton is dead now. He was a carpenter who thought he knew about things other than wood. He had red eyes and a grumbling way of talking and rubbed his mouth with the back of his hand and picked his teeth with his fingernail. And he drank like a fish. Mrs Stratton's still around, though the General doesn't see her much. She has boobies that bulge so from her low-cut gowns, she might as well yank them out and push them in your face. She flashes diamonds in her ears and on her wrists and rolling about on those boobies, more diamonds than the General ever saw on even the Queen of England. All paid for from his shows, of course. Her voice is loud and cracked and she has a whooping laugh that can end in a shriek like these Australian cockatoos. He'd laugh when Mr Barnum made fun of the Strattons behind their backs, but sometimes he just wished the ground would open up and they'd fall into the centre of the earth, particularly when everyone was in a grand restaurant in Paris and Mrs Stratton ordered duck by flapping her arms and quacking. Don't be too hard on the General. He wasn't unfilial. They weren't his parents, remember. He was Mr Barnum's brainchild.

I don't recall much of the time before the General sprang fully armed out of Mr Barnum's head. I was only four, remember. Still am, though I've learned a thing or two. I think my ma used to sing me songs. She never sounded like a cockatoo to me. She had a soft, wistful singing voice and a blue apron warm from the fire.

Sometimes I want to comfort the General. I want to come out

and tell him it's all right. You can be unhappy and afraid. You can howl and rage in a tantrum because it's not fair, this getting old and fat and tired — nothing is fair anymore. You can suck your thumb and cry for your ma. I do that, sometimes. It doesn't do me any harm. But then I'm stuck in my boy-shaped space in the puzzle tree, and he's a man. He can do what he likes. He does things, in his head and for real, that I don't understand at all. Especially the things he does with ladies. So why should he understand me? And what's to understand, anyway? He is a General, great and good, and I am only a very little boy who hides.

Now there's going to be a baby. A tiny, tiny baby. The smallest baby in the world. I don't know much about it, not even where it's going to come from, but the General knows. He's all perked up again. He can't wait. This time, everything will be right. A proper childhood. No wine, no cigars, no strutting. Everyone in the whole wide world will love this little boy, forever and ever, and no one will love him more than the General himself.

I can't wait either. I'm going to have a little baby brother. Oh, I know Tommy isn't really my brother, but that's how I think of him. I'll come out for him, and he'll see me and know me straight away. We'll build mud forts and shoot each other with sticks, we'll catch minnows, we'll sail paper boats, we'll shout and run along the beach trailing seaweed. We'll have a dog with curly hair that follows us everywhere. And if by any chance anyone doesn't love us, we'll just go away and hide. I'll teach him everything I know, and I'll never have to sit in this puzzle tree again.

CHAPTER 4

'The time has come to put our cards on the table,' said Mrs Bleeker, as she swung the tip of her folded umbrella at an impudent patch of grass in the road. Something heavy and painful rose in my chest.

We were walking back to Craig's Hotel from the Ballarat orphanage, a carriage ride from the town. The little people were making charity appearances during their three weeks in Ballarat; they had met the orphans and had begun a short show, when Mrs Bleeker took my arm and quietly suggested the walk.

Still walking, she turned and stared at me gravely. 'The General has asked me to talk to you about the infant.'

I thought of the row of the youngest orphans, in clean smocks, wet hair plastered to their skulls or yanked into tight braids. 'Which one?' I said. 'The bold boy who shouted?'

'Don't be obtuse, Mary Ann.'

I could not mistake the direct gaze. 'How did you know?' The heavy thing in my chest sent tentacles up into my throat.

'I did not come down with the last shower of rain. Your queasiness. And may I remind you that you fainted backstage in

Melbourne. Yet you seem a strong, healthy girl. How far along are you now?'

I stared at the path, my face burning. I knew how long, give or take a few days, but was there any point in admitting it? Best get it over with. I hid my trembling hands in the folds of my skirt. 'When we get back I will look at once for a cheap passage to Melbourne.'

'Whatever are you talking about?'

'I will forgo my wages. I have scarcely earned them yet. You have all been very kind but I cannot impose on you any longer.'

Mrs Bleeker scowled. Would she hit me with her umbrella? 'You are not going anywhere, you foolish girl. The General wants you precisely the way you are. Precisely.'

'I don't understand.'

'You must have noticed how much the General loves little ones.' Her voice took on a persuasive tone. 'Did you see his moist eyes at the orphanage? If there is one thing the General regrets, it is that he never had a childhood. He began with Mr Barnum when he was four years old; he had to learn to drink wine and smoke cigars. It has left him with a very soft spot for children, but he and Mrs Stratton have never been blessed.' Mrs Bleeker sighed. 'Lord knows, a hard fate ...' Her voice quavered, her mouth took on a drooping shape. Then she screwed her lips into a brisk line. 'He will adopt the infant. A dream come true for him. And for you too.'

'For me?' This could not be right. There was never any chance of my dreams coming true.

But Mrs Bleeker spoke slowly, as if to a child. 'The infant will grow up in his new house in Middleborough, Massachusetts. Do not let the General's comicalities deceive you. He is very wealthy, wise and generous. No more perfect childhood could be imagined.'

The thing in my chest had lifted a little. 'I still don't understand. The General could have his pick of any child in that orphanage. Why me?'

Mrs Bleeker looked up at the eucalypts, which shivered in a rising breeze. 'Call it his gratitude towards his rescuer.'

I wrapped my shawl tighter around my shoulders. 'I never wished for gratitude. So ... must I hand over the infant?'

Her eyes widened. 'Lord, we are not barbarians. And they are so much attached to you. They wish you to come back to America with them at the end of the tour.'

The New World? The land of Indians and grizzly bears? Images from a child's picture book whirled before me, but Mrs Bleeker bundled her umbrella under her arm and ticked off points on her fingers and I did my best to concentrate. 'The dollar equivalent of thirty-five pounds a year, plus board and travel expenses. This is a raise on your salary as assistant wardrobe mistress, and exceptional pay for a nursemaid. When a little time has gone by, you can choose.'

The trees were slowly spinning. I hoped I was not going to faint again. This was far more astounding than Indians and grizzlies, and of all the words to issue from Mrs Bleeker's pinched mouth, the most extraordinary was *choose*.

'If you wish to remain in their employ, they will find you duties where you can be close to the infant and perhaps continue your care. If you wish to leave, the General will provide references and a very handsome settlement. You will have your pick of positions. And who knows, perhaps your pick ...' She clapped a hand over her mouth. 'Oh, my dear, what am I saying? I know how devoted you are to the memory of poor Mr Carroll.'

We continued to walk in silence, Mrs Bleeker swinging her umbrella at the dust, while I tried to think. All that came into my mind were pictures: the bench and the thin darned sheet in the mean house by the Yarra Yarra; and then Charlie and Lavinia bending over a tiny cradle with nothing to be seen inside but a soft curve of blankets. Behind me a small door opened and light flooded into the room. I turned my back on the little couple and the cradle, walked towards the New World.

Mrs Bleeker's voice cut into my pictures. 'Well? What do you say?'

'I don't know what to say. Never, in my wildest dreams …'

'You can trust the General's word. He is an upright gentleman. And his anticipation of this happy event will take away his bad humours and his eccentricities. You cannot believe how much he longs for an heir.'

'And Mrs Stratton? Does she long too?'

Mrs Bleeker's voice softened. 'She is a woman.'

I am a woman too, but not a rich, married woman who can have whatever she longs for. I forced down the unexpected stab that leaped from beneath my heart and remembered what my father had said: *The Lord giveth, the Lord taketh away.*

'Feeling queasy again?' said Mrs Bleeker. 'I have medicine in my basket.'

'No need.' I attempted a brisker walk, tried to think of the cradle, but all that came was a picture of a parcel in my lap, bright with curls of silver ribbon. What was inside the parcel? Nothing. That was the gift. The Lord was taking away the burden I had thought immoveable. I would bend down to go through that little door into that bright New World, with a clear conscience, since the infant would grow up in the most loving home that could be imagined. Then I would straighten my back and look up, and coming towards me ... My heart gave a great thump and I was light, ready to float above the trees.

'Are you sure you are well, Mary Ann? I had expected you to be glad.'

'Oh, I am much, much more than just glad. The dear, kind, generous ...' I blushed at the thought of the momentary stab from beneath my heart. Now I wanted to kiss the hand of the radiant Queen of Beauty.

'Hold my umbrella.' Mrs Bleeker bent to the basket on her arm, pulled out a square of pink cotton, wiped her brow and fanned herself. 'Of course,' she murmured, 'there is one condition.'

'There is?'

'The General must first consider the infant suitable.'

Healthy? Without blemish? 'That only God can decide,' I said.

'Quite. But the General already seems certain he will find the infant suitable. He has great faith in you.'

'I must make sure I do not disappoint him.'

She nodded, folded the cotton, pushed it back into her basket. 'I nearly forgot. Some things for you.' She drew out a small brown bottle and a pair of black kid gloves, rubbed shiny at the fingertips. 'This is Dr Foote's Magnetic Elixir, a boon for all kinds of female complaints, including queasiness. Take a sip whenever you need it. And the gloves should fit you. I have unpicked the stitches along the seams between the fingers, below the knuckles.'

I thanked her, put the bottle into my pocket and pulled on the gloves. They covered the thimble callouses and the burns from the iron and a spilled kettle. If I kept my fingers together, I had ladies' hands.

'These are the first gloves I have ever been able to wear,' I said. She gave me a small smile and I returned it. 'What will happen next?' I asked.

'We continue the tour. You continue your duties, health permitting, until your confinement. But don't go bothering the General and Mrs Stratton about it. Any questions, come to me.' She held out her hand as if to shake on a deal or to clasp in friendship. Just in time, I realised what the gesture meant and handed back the umbrella.

I watched her beaky profile as we walked on. My gloves were snug, and the sun was breaking through the cloud ahead of us, lighting up the wire on the fencepost at the top of the next hill. The outlying tents of the mining settlement came into view, white and festive.

'I do not deserve such fortune,' I said. 'But I will take it.'

Mrs Bleeker allowed herself a larger smile. 'If I thought you were the sort of girl who cared for such things, I would tell you about the made-to-measure gloves you can buy in New York.'

• • • • • • • •

So the deal was done. Now I look back on that day and am astonished at myself. Why was I so humble and obliging? Why did I not stamp my foot, demand to know precisely what would become of me and my child? Why did I not insist on contracts and lawyers, hold out for the best possible arrangement? But I was so grateful to be housed and fed and given purpose and future. Above all, to be spared disgrace and destitution. And I had so little power — or so I thought.

I was lighthearted, nervous, full of questions back at Craig's Hotel, as I sorted out costumes and props with Mrs Bleeker, but she seemed too distracted to reply.

Later, I came across Charlie studying himself in the big looking glass, adjusting his cravat, and I ventured to thank him for his astounding generosity. He never took his eyes off his own face, and we both watched him blush almost purple.

'Do not speak of it,' he murmured, waving me away, and his voice made me think this was no modest disclaimer. This was a command.

'I am honoured,' I said to Lavinia as I pinned up her hair, 'to be chosen ... you are so kind ...'

'Not at all,' she said, 'but really, this will not do, I must teach you how to plait in a chignon'. Then she produced a silk bag containing a nest of coiled hair identical to her own, and I was soon lost in her instructions for twisting ropes around high-backed combs and padding knots as her hair grew more and more voluminous.

Was the subject of adoption considered too indelicate, or was everyone just too busy? Certainly I myself had almost no time to think about it. While the troupe performed at the Mechanics' Institute in the evening, I sprayed seltzer water onto Minnie's tonsils, helped the ladies change their costumes, mended a coat, swept up the dung dropped by one of the miniature ponies as it wandered unheeded about the rooms, put out a fire when a lamp fell over, hunted down a fine new blue cup and saucer for Mr Bleeker and poured his tea. I heard a drumbeat, shrill singing, roars of laughter and applause, and the tantalising tinkle and crash of the piano; but all I saw was people running on and off the stage.

I did sneak another look at that tall pianist with the red hair. His name was Franz Richardson, I had discovered. This time he played with his eyes open, squinting at the sheet music, fumbling and pausing as he turned the pages. It was not incompetence, I divined: it was a kind of magnificent rage at being forced to play such inane jauntiness. He made me so curious. I wanted to get closer to him, but Mrs Bleeker called me away to fasten yet another row of buttons.

· · · · · · · ·

Sometimes I wondered if the relentless demands made of me would become too much to bear given I was already so constantly indisposed. But in truth, I was glad to be busy. I believed that hard work would be my salvation, and the Lord was taking away my burden.

It was hard work I had turned to when I thought I could save my mother and father. I do believe I came close to succeeding. But in the end, no one could have saved them.

What should I say about my parents? That they were virtuous, and kind to me. I remember my mother lifting me to the white towers of horse-chestnut blooms in the rectory garden. Laughing, chasing me round the sundial. My father did not run or laugh or lift me up; he was a grey pillar of a man, but sometimes he would smile and lay his hand on my head in such a gentle way. Together they went out, baskets over their arms, to give to the poor. But that was why they fell sick.

It happened so fast. One night I lay in bed listening to the bells — they tolled all the time in London the year I turned eleven. The doctor, Cook, Molly the maid and Mrs Utley the housekeeper had all gone. The door opened slowly. Mother stood by my bed, her arms folded around her stomach. Her hair, usually coiled tight, hung in damp wisps around her neck.

'I want you to see to Father. Now.'

This was a house where I did what I was told. If I wanted to play outside among the fallen horse-chestnut leaves instead of sewing my sampler, Mother would say I'd get dirty. Father would say that wanting was the sin of covetousness. I should do what God wanted. So I took the candle to my parents' bedroom, and when I opened the forbidden door, the sweet odour almost choked me. The room was crisscrossed with lines, and on them hung sheets and towels soaked in perfumed water. Candles glowed hazily through the white veils. I pushed through the maze of wet cloth to the bed, where a darker smell rose. Father lay on his back, grey chest hair bristling from the neck of his nightshirt, muttering.

'Father?'

He watched the ceiling with a preoccupied frown, as if he had detected sin or peeling plasterwork. When I put my hand over his, it felt like the snails in the garden after rain. I took down a hanging towel, wiped his brow. I pushed up the sleeve of his nightshirt and wiped his arm and he moaned.

'Thou art become cruel to me.'

'No, Father.'

'I cry unto thee, and thou dost not hear me.'

He was not talking to me. He was talking to the Lord. I unbuttoned his nightshirt and rubbed the towel over his chest. I had never seen so much of his skin, was surprised at how soft it was. Father had seemed made of marble.

When the candles had burned down and Father had fallen into an uneasy sleep, I crept back to my bedroom. Mother lay across the bed, also asleep, with a sour smell under her cheek, and I realised she had vomited. Should I clean the coverlet? But that would mean waking Mother, so I curled up on the floor and waited for dawn.

I was so sure I could save them.

In the next two days, I whisked from one bed to the other, fetched water, poured it between flaking lips, washed snail skin, cleaned off vomit and watery faeces, washed and wrung bedclothes and towels, shovelled coal into the kitchen stove, heated water on the hob, hung the wet sheets in front of the stove. When they were half dry, I wrapped some around Father and Mother and hung the rest in the bedrooms, soaked in eau de Cologne. I stood at the sink in the scullery, scrubbing my hands with soapy water until they stung. Father muttered. *The Lord giveth, the Lord taketh away.* Mother never said a coherent word. Gradually the foul odours stopped rising, and the snail skin dried out. Surely by now they must be getting better.

I don't remember exactly when Mrs Utley came back. I do recall watching, dull and light-headed, as she turned away from me and heaved with sobs and hard-won breaths.

· · · · · · · ·

I was thinking of my parents one evening as I sat alone in a pool of candlelight in the parlour of the Craig's Hotel suite, long after the Ballarat urchins who patrolled the street in the hope of glimpsing the little people had given up and left. I squinted at a rip in Charlie's tiny shirt in my lap. The collar had a faint sweetness: eau de Cologne. I held it to my face and shivered, Father's voice scratched in my ears. *The Lord giveth, the Lord taketh away.*

I took deep breaths as I continued my stitching. I would work hard, and this time all would be well, for nothing could be so bad again. I smiled to myself, and my needle twinkled as it healed the wound in Charlie's sleeve.

A clink of glasses and the clearing of a male throat came from the balcony overlooking Lydiard Street. So not everyone was in bed after all. It was a calm and unseasonably warm night, and the window was wide open, though a large davenport blocked my view — and, I realised, hid me from whoever had moved onto the balcony. Should I declare myself?

Instead, I blew out the candle. A match flared, and I heard a glug of port from a decanter, a trickle of tea, and murmurs: one drawling, the other high. Sylvester Bleeker and Charlie, having a gentlemen's confab.

They were talking about a proposed meeting with a certain Ballarat doctor. 'Quite the collector,' said Mr Bleeker. 'His fame has spread.'

'I don't think I'll come with you. I have never cared for the genus collector,' said Charlie. 'If he sees me, he might whip out a giant butterfly net.' Mr Bleeker laughed. A pause; then Charlie spoke quietly. I could not catch the words.

Mr Bleeker spoke louder: 'Nonsense, General. Tonight's show was full of all your wonderful vim and vigour.'

Again, Charlie's reply was inaudible, and I prepared to leave; but as I was packing my sewing basket, Charlie's voice rose: 'Lavinia tells me our Mary Ann is still indisposed.'

I froze.

'I'm sorry to hear it. She's already such a favourite with the ladies …' Mr Bleeker's voice dropped away.

Father used to say: *Listeners never hear any good of themselves*. And yet I strained to hear.

Charlie's reply was clearer: 'She is only a little indisposed. It is a good sign, what we should expect at this stage. Tell me, what do you think of my plan?'

I leaned forward. Surely there was only one plan Charlie could be talking about.

'You sure it's a good idea?' said Mr Bleeker. 'We don't need an infant for business these days.'

'This is not for business. This is for quite another purpose.' The chair creaked again, the glow of a cigar lit the room. Charlie's voice, lower but also closer: 'May I speak in confidence? Man to man?'

'Of course, my dear fellow.'

My breasts were tingling, they gave off a high-pitched vibration. No, it was a mosquito whining around my nose. I did not wave it away, sat utterly still.

'What do you know of the Coming Man, Mr B? What do you know of the Moment of Generation?'

'As much as any non-medical man, I guess.'

'There is more to that moment than most men would guess.' A pause, a shift in the cigar glow, then one hissed word: 'Electricity.'

Had I misheard?

'Beg pardon, General?'

Louder: 'Electricity is the catalyst. I am speaking of something other than the vulgar method of congress …'

'Ah.' Mr Bleeker sounded uneasy.

'All that is needed,' Charlie continued, 'is close proximity between a healthy mature male and female. There is no need even for touch. The male must be an individual of uncommon magnetism. There must also be an extraordinary excitement, and a great deal of water. And — *alakazam!* — a new life is formed.'

A spluttering, as if Mr Bleeker's tea had misdirected itself. What had I learned at school about electricity? Something about using a comb to make one's hair stand on end. Whatever did this have to do with the adoption?

'I will explain,' Charlie said. 'Every human being can generate electrical charges. Forgive my frankness, Mr B, but I must speak of male and female generative organs. They produce acidic solutions and alkaline liquids, and together, in water, they make quite a soda.' More spluttering from Mr Bleeker. 'Cicero, Napoleon, the great men of history — they are all uncommonly magnetic, electric. By an effort of mind, they can sometimes retain their electricity, and at other times discharge it through their spermatozoa, with the power of a cannon ball.'

He sounded very excited. A muffled exclamation from Mr Bleeker.

'Involuntary discharge is also possible, under the influence of a great shock to the nervous system,' Charlie went on.

'I don't know what you're talking about, General.' What a relief that I was not the only one. 'I've never heard of such a thing. Are you telling me you jumped into the Yarra Yarra on purpose?'

Charlie laughed. 'No, but accidents can have fortunate consequences.' His voice dropped, and I crept to the davenport, peered over the top. For a moment, I saw nothing but a faint glow from the stars, and then a match flared: Charlie was relighting his cigar. His face, florid by daylight, was transformed into a Chinese lantern. His voice rose again: 'It is a rare occurrence with great men of destiny. As to where we might find such a man, that is not for me to say. But we have our woman, Mr B. Our Mary Ann is a treasure, Vin says. We will take good care of her. She saved my life, after all. She is an excellent —' His head turned towards the street and a breath of wind carried away his next word. *Vestal? Vessel?*

'So,' said Mr Bleeker, 'this, ah, Coming Man won't be like the others? I don't want to go through all that again.'

'Dismiss them from your mind, Mr B. What is it the Good Book says? They are not worthy to touch the hem of his garment.'

Mr Bleeker grunted, waved an arm as if to swat a mosquito. They talked on of other matters as I crept to the door.

Our woman? Our Mary Ann? I had heard good of myself, and it was more puzzling and disturbing than a complaint. Outside the door, I put down my basket. My stitching on the tiny shirt looked clumsy and fragile. I clasped my hands over my navel. Who exactly was this General I had wrested from the river? What was it that he was so convinced had happened in the water?

· · · · · · · ·

There was little sleep for me that night. My head was buzzing with the mysterious conversation I had overheard but, no matter how I turned it back and forth, I could make no more sense of it.

Very early the next morning, before most people were awake, I was sitting out in the hotel courtyard cleaning the ladies' boots when a *tock, tock* of hooves made me lift my head. Three men were leading horses across the yard towards the stables; the third man was much shorter than the others, his left leg had a slight limp, and his horse, a stolid bay with a white blaze, towered over him.

It was Rodnia Nutt, the Commodore's elder brother, without his coachman's wig and blue plush. He was whistling a tune. As the first two men and their horses disappeared into the stables, Rodnia came abreast of me. Without any warning, his horse suddenly reared up on its hind legs with a furious neigh and began to plunge down on him, as if to shatter his head with its hooves. I jumped up, letting the boots, brush and polish fall from my bench, and made to grab at the horse's bridle, but it was too high above me, so I lunged at Rodnia, knocking off his hat, pushing him out of the way of the falling hooves. As we both rolled onto the gravel, he gave a long hissing whistle. Had I knocked the wind from him? Slowly we got to our feet, brushing ourselves down. The bay stood silent, docile. Where was its fury? Something, probably blood, was trickling down my leg from my knee. Rodnia picked up my shawl, handed it to me, and I wrapped it around myself as if it were a cloak of invisibility.

'You all right, ma'am? The bab's not hurt?' said Rodnia anxiously.

For a moment I was baffled. Then a hot wave, something between shame and relief, swept me, and I staggered back to the bench where I had been sitting and almost fell onto it. Rodnia jammed his hat back over his mop of brown curls, hitched the horse to the bench leg and sat beside me.

'God's teeth, you're hurt. I'll fetch Mrs B —'

'No, I am fine, just a little shaken.'

He stared at me, and I was not sure whether I should feel threatened or comforted. His brows had ferocity, but his brown eyes and gruff voice were gentle, like a wild animal that chose to be tamed. In his livery as the little people's coachman, driving the walnut coach round and round Melbourne and Ballarat every day to drum up business for the shows, he had seemed a puffed-up piece of sky. Sometimes Charlie and George and the ladies would sit inside the coach, waving like kings and queens, but Rodnia would sit stiff on his perch, ignoring cheers and jeers alike. Now, in his stained leather vest and dung-encrusted boots, he seemed unaccountably larger. And yet he stood no taller than my armpit.

The two men who had led horses into the stable came out the door and stared curiously towards us. Rodnia stared back, gave a quick jerk of his head, and the men touched their caps, walked away.

'You look all in,' he said. 'They should treat you better, you being the goose and all.'

'What did you say?'

'No offence.' He smiled. 'I meant you're the goose that lays the golden egg, 'tis your good fortune. The General was longing for a son and heir, and then along you came to rescue him. The bab'll have a fine home.'

So he knew. All the troupe must know. Did they also know of Charlie's strange talk of electrical discharges? Was I the only one left in the dark? I rested against the rough wall behind the bench. The ladies' little boots lay in the dust in front of me, but I made no attempt to pick them up.

'Don't you worry, ma'am.' He was calm, a little amused. 'They'll hang on to you like billy-o, keep you in clover. Ain't that so, Zep?' The horse snickered. 'Let me introduce you. Missus Carroll, Master Zep, the Wild Horse of Tartary — though he don't look too wild at the moment.' The horse nudged his shoulder and he scratched its nose. 'Me and Zep've been pals for a long time. He used to belong to a Hungarian with tremendous moustachios. Zoltan juggled balls and swords on horseback.'

'A circus horse?'

'And very well trained. It was my job to seize Zoltan butt-naked — well, in a body costume — bind him to Zep here, give him a whack on the rump — Zep, not the Hungarian — and send him galloping round the ring. The girls shrieked, they loved it so.'

I stared at Rodnia's sturdy build and stubbled jaw. A damp warmth came off him, sweeter than the horse smell.

'Old Zep's a wise beast. Watch.' He let out a whistle, and the horse reared on its hind legs; he whistled again, and it dropped and stood still.

'Oh, I see … So you were not in danger after all. Mr Nutt, I feel very foolish.'

'Rodnia, please. And you're far from foolish, ma'am. What you did was very brave. You're a dandy rescuer.'

I shook my head, smiling. The hotel door opened, and Ned Davis emerged in his shirtsleeves, blinking and scratching his groin, his unpomaded black hair flopping loose over his forehead. He gave us a hard stare, keeping his head turned towards us as he walked by.

'I must go,' I said. 'The ladies will be waking soon.'

'Come see me when you have a mo,' said Rodnia. 'I'll be about. I'll teach you how to make Zep wild.'

Mr Rodnia Nutt

P.T. Barnum and Commodore Nutt

ACT ONE

She's a brave girl, this one. The way she jumped at Zep, could have been trampled for all she knew. And smart. Doesn't know much yet, but she'll cotton on. How she puts me in mind of … but no, that's all over now. Yet it monkeys around in my head, that other brave, smart girl, and her downfall.

They say the long train on her gown tangled around her feet. What do I know. I'm good with horses, but not so good with women. Maybe that's because of this notion of mine that I was made to love my little brother.

He was an uncommon large baby, weighed ten pound. At last, said Ma and Pa, a big strong boy to work the farm. Not like me, bonny Rodnia, named after my father, a sturdy lad with a bumpy brow and curls like a young billy goat, but not tall, not even at four years of age.

To love means to protect. I stood on tippytoe to peer into the crib at the baby's curling fingers and vowed that I would take care of George Washington Morrison Nutt, even if George grew to tower above me.

I grew slowly and made it to forty-nine inches. George stopped at twenty-nine inches, though he grew a bit more later in life. So I did the towering. When George wanted to see the world, he sat piggyback on my shoulders and together we were as tall as a big boy. Then he felt free to shout all kinds of rudeness at his boy enemies. We raced around the town of Manchester, New Hampshire, me scowling and George crossing his eyes and poking out his tongue. We were so like an Indian totem pole that some folks started and crossed themselves in the Roman way when we rampaged past.

We weren't much use around the farm, so Ma and Pa fixed for us to join Mr Lillie's Travelling Circus and Show of Wonders. My brother at fifteen was the wonder — Tiny George, the Smallest Man in God's Creation — and I at nineteen was *Hey, You*, to work for my keep at whatever came up. I had some notion to save up all my money and run away from the circus, but I had no idea where to run, and in any case I couldn't abandon George. Whenever I thought of my little brother, the muscles in my arms went tight, and I breathed hard and locked my hands together and pulled, one arm against the other. I had taken on all the bullies at the Manchester school and I would take on any blackguard, were he as big as an ox.

George's ambition was huge. He wanted to be the biggest little man in New Hampshire, in America, in the world, bigger even than General Tom Thumb. But Mr Lillie would have none of it. He wore a ring on every finger and he turned purple when provoked. He turned purple a lot around George. 'I must have tone,' he said. 'Your antics, George, they will shut us down. No profanity, no trousers down, no farting. Stay in your booth and walk up and down and doff your hat to the ladies.'

'Aw, Mr Lillie, can't I go in the ring? Can't I wear a red nose and big shoes? I will be a sensation.'

Mr Lillie's jowls darkened. 'Roddie, can't you keep this rascal under control? George, you don't understand. You are not a sensation. You are a wonder.'

I did my best with George, I lectured him and cuffed him about a bit when he misbehaved, but he knew full well I'd never hurt him bad and he took no heed of me.

Meanwhile, I sought my own trick and thought it might come from study. So I studied Miss Emmeline and her brother Mr Ludovic at practice, to and fro on the trapeze above my head, to and fro. Their strength was not just in their arms or arched backs or their streaks of red hair. It was in their ankles, insteps and toes. And in Miss Emmeline's smile.

I don't know what it was about Miss Emmeline. You could say it was her queenliness or her grace or her beauty, and you'd be right, but that wasn't it. It was maybe something in her eye when she looked down or looked away, when she thought nobody was watching her. I'd seen that look with a horse that's been trained too hard, too cruel, but its spirit is still there, deep down. And then she'd look up and see me watching and she'd put on her smile. A dazzling smile, even if it didn't quite reach her eyes.

With the brightest of her smiles, Miss Emmeline got me to take charge of their trapeze apparatus. Every night after the show, for the next day's performance, I took a lamp into the circus tent and took down all the rods and poles, ropes and ladders. I held each load-bearing part and connection close to the lamp and tested it by hand for fault or weakness. Then I put the apparatus up again, spread and pegged the safety net, checked it for holes. I climbed ten, twenty, thirty foot, nimble and hard-handed as a sailor in the rigging, worked my way arm over arm along the horizontal poles. But I would never take to the trapeze. That was Miss Emmeline's place.

Another task I had was to clean out the Sapient Bear's cage, and there I could practise my speechifying. *I can offer strong arms and a true heart. One day I will inherit a half-share of a farm. I want you to be free. I want to save you from hard training, from a dangerous trade. I want to save you from* … The bear yawned, showed its yellow teeth. I caught a blast of mucky banana.

Sometimes Miss Emmeline would listen to my wisdom about struts and ropes and weights as she did her callisthenics on the grass. At least, I fancied she listened. I would hold samples of poles and leather straps in my hand and tell what load and stress they might carry while she stretched and swung. Sometimes she gave me a breathless, 'Yes, 'twill do,' over her shoulder, and twang, my chest swelled.

Alone in the circus tent, I practised my own trick. Over and over again I jumped across a short gap from one rope ladder to the next. Sometimes I leaped to a single rope. I braced myself for the landing. I gripped hard to stop the slide that might scorch my palms. I flung out one fist, hard as iron, twirled lazily on a rope and smiled at the upturned faces, the drum roll, the clapping hands, Miss Emmeline reaching out her white arms. Then I looked down and saw a spider stretch of netting, a circle of sawdust, tiers of blank seats.

At the end of each day I collapsed onto the straw pallet I shared with George and fell into a void of sleep. But one night, George kept me awake to whisper to me his new plan.

'It's all worked out.' He was trembling with excitement. 'Only keep mum, so Mr Lillie can't stop us. I'll mount the trapeze with Mr Ludovic and he'll fling me to Miss Emmeline to catch. To and fro, to and fro. My costume will be red and green silk. I'll tumble and fly like thistledown, like a hummingbird. Think of it, Roddie — Tiny George, airborne! How they will gasp and cheer!'

'Are you crazy?' I said. 'You're no acrobat. One slip …'

'No slips. Maybe my trousers will fall down though.' He was jumping on our pallet.

I grabbed him, forced him down, hissed in his ear. 'Forget it. I forbid it.'

He looked at me, panting, all sly. His hair bristled with straw. 'Roddie, I love you, Lord knows. But you ain't Pa.'

I realised I'd get no more sense out of him. I couldn't go to Mr Lillie; I was no snitch. Nor could I go to Emmeline's brother Ludovic, who always looked at me as if I were a scraping from the Sapient Bear's cage. But I made up my mind to talk to Miss Emmeline while she did her callisthenics.

She listened, stretching her leg above her head so I grew faint to see. 'Tiny George will be safe with us, never fear.'

'But he is not a sack of potatoes you can toss about. He'll wriggle and twist out of your grasp. He'll fall.'

'I don't think so. But if he does, he'll land in the safety net.'

I shook my head. I could not see it. George was never one to land in safety.

Miss Emmeline smiled and stretched her other leg. 'It does you credit though, how you care for your brother.'

'No more than you care for yours, I'm sure.'

She frowned, put her leg down. 'I have no brother.'

'But I thought … Mr Ludovic …'

'Then you thought wrong.'

Her voice, and the dark roses in her cheeks, made me cold. I picked up a leather strap and pulled it tight between my fists. When she spoke again, she sounded brisk, practical.

'If we don't do this, I will have to offer Ludo something else. He is very insistent. It is not enough to entertain, he says. We must astound.'

I swear, I was so near to saying something foolish about how she astounded me already. But then Mr Ludovic slid by, as he always did sooner or later, with his panther's ease and his soft call — 'Come, Em' — and clicked his tongue twice. She stopped in mid-stretch, folded
herself up like a tent and followed him.

I watched their shadows behind the canvas. No brother?

It was time to take down and put up the trapeze apparatus. I trudged slowly to the circus tent. High up, feeling my way along the poles, I wondered for the first time what it would be like to fall, to have the ground rush towards you. Would there be time for terror, for pain? Or would it all be the ecstasy of speed, of letting go? My eyes blurred, I reeled, dizzy. I waited for the fit to pass, then I turned, leaped from the ladder towards the guy rope.

Dozens, scores of times I'd done it, launched into nothing, slammed into the rope, knotted my fist tight around the heft of it, my body jerking back from the fall. Nothing different about this time. Yet I sailed past the rope, several inches wide, my outstretched hands clawing at empty air.

Much later, I heard a thin whispery voice. 'Lift up your heads, O ye gates; and lift them up, ye everlasting doors; and the King of glory shall come in.'

I am told the pious Living Skeleton found me lying still as a statue, but not in a statue's pose. I was half on, half off the safety net, my left leg thrown wide, my head under the front row of seats.

When they pulled me out, my head was full of nothing but swamp reek. They carried me to my pallet and sent for a doctor. I kept my mouth agape. I was choking on the stench of rotted grass under the bleacher seats. I gulped for air, for words.

'Calm yourself,' said George, attacking my arm with anxious little pats.

A mountain of pain was growing in my left leg.

Sometime later, George peered at me over the foothills of my mountain. 'We are tough Nutts. It takes a lot to crack us.'

I didn't answer. Cymbals crashed. I rose through the cooling air to the trapeze, where Emmeline waited for me. We were both naked as babes. Side by side we swung on the same trapeze, to and fro, to and fro. Emmeline reached out and grasped the bar. She swung onto the platform as my swing moved back. Everything moved slow as molasses. She turned towards me, her arms high, one hand holding the second trapeze. She was tiny, so far away. And took off. Now my trapeze swung towards hers. We rushed slow, slow, towards each other. Blood pounded in my veins. Trumpets blared. Slow, slow. I saw her smiling face, with her dark nipples and dark triangle beneath like a second face. I knew that when the trapezes met, our bodies would melt together. Closer. I reckoned my nose would reach and touch her between the eyes of her second face. Sweat sprayed off her hair, sparkled in the lights. Closer. A drum roll. My nose was there, between the eyes. Nothing but mushy apples and bananas, and rotting grass, and a pimply hairy snout and rough tongue. No Emmeline, just the Sapient Bear gripping the trapeze with his paws, hard as iron, and Mr Ludovic laughing, and light flashing in my eyes, and George buzzing round, just his head with wings, a pestering cherub, saying, *Please get better, Roddie*, and my leg on fire again.

When the doctor took me off the laudanum, he said there was a difficult break in the femur, it might take some time to heal. He had put a splint on my leg, said it was a miracle I had not hit my head, I must have fallen into the safety net and then bounced or slid half off it. I had escaped with one broken bone and a mass of bruises.

In time, the pain faded, and I learned to swing my body around on crutches, with George running round my feet and threatening to trip me up.

'You still here, you pest?' I said. 'Not tumbled from the trapeze yet?'

'Oh, that.' He sighed. 'Roddie, I changed my mind. Seen you lying there, day after day … I'm figuring, I ain't about to put you through what I felt then. No, sir.'

Something swelled in my chest.

Then George grinned. 'But you still ain't my pa.'

I swung a crutch at his shins and he shrieked as he scampered away.

Mr Lillie grumbled about mouths to feed and insisted I take up all my duties again. George threatened to walk out on the circus unless Mr Lillie waited until I could walk without support. They shouted at each other until I dropped my crutches and hobbled towards them and said I was ready for work.

My leg still ached in wet weather, and I could not help limping. But I could do most of my tasks. So I went into the circus tent to the rods and poles and ropes of the trapeze. Something cold seeped down my veins into my fingers and toes. I could not lift my feet even by one step onto the rope ladder. I sat down, still as a statue. A sour taste rose. The ring spun round. A rotten-grass smell clogged my head.

Miss Emmeline stood and listened as I hung my head and told her I could no longer take down or put up her trapeze for her. I wondered if she might despise me for a coward. But she nodded gravely. She seemed quieter and smiled less, though everyone said she was performing better than ever. In her arms she cradled spanking new pink boxes.

'New costumes?' I said.

Those dark roses again in her cheeks. 'We are announcing it today. We are engaged. We will have our wedding on the trapeze.'

Something fell down, down inside me, and kept falling, and there was no ecstasy or peace in letting go. I put on a smile, said a glad word or two. I wanted to tell her that I did not blame her for marrying Mr Ludovic, that the circus was outside the rules, a special place for special people who belonged together. Or again I could tell her that she should run away from the circus, and especially from Mr Ludovic. But I looked and said nothing. Her hair was drawn back under her bonnet, her arms were in wide sleeves, her thighs hidden in her skirts. Her miraculous strong ankles were all buttoned up in boots. The secret second face I had seen in my dream was no more than something for dirty boys to guess at.

I told myself she was no different after all from the New Hampshire misses who strolled the showgrounds on the arms of their beaux, mouths hanging open at the wonders.

· · · · · · · ·

The wedding took place as planned. The circus was packed; we all looked upwards. The couple stood on high trapezes, facing each other across the ring, he in black, she in white satin with a veil and a long train. A priest shouted the service from the floor. Then the band struck up the wedding march, and the happy newlyweds began to swing towards each other. Perhaps he would put the ring on her finger as the trapezes met. She stood high and worked her arms and knees, and her veil and train flew out in a silver arc behind her.

It was so fast, no one even had time to scream. At the top of her longest swing, she sprang out and up, silver thrown into space. Her arms were out as if to meet a lover, but she had already passed Mr Ludovic, still clinging to his trapeze. I saw where she would fall, way beyond the safety net, and I ran forward with my arms up and out, but there was no time. I could not meet her, could no more stop her than I could stop a horse bolting.

· · · · · · · ·

That was a few years ago. Now I drive two miniature ponies round and round the streets of Ballarat, and George sits behind me in state, in his walnut-shaped coach, wrinkled like a golden brain, and the crowds cheer for Commodore Nutt. Sometimes as I drive, and the people shout, and George sits safe in his shell, thoughts go round and round with me too. I had to take George from her and Ludo, had to, had to, could not let him be the one to fall …

The thing is, I'm good with horses. And if I'm quick, I can stop a horse bolting.

I don't remember what I felt when I fell. I hope she felt the ecstasy, the letting go.

CHAPTER 5

When in doubt, I always asked Mrs Bleeker. So I enquired whether she knew anything about what happened when electricity and generative organs were combined with a great deal of water. She sniffed and said it sounded dangerous to her, but she left all that sort of thing to the men of science, it was hardly a suitable subject for the female mind, and when I had finished the ironing would I come help her on the sewing machine? So I could only hope all would become clear in time.

Even with that mystery unsolved, I was beginning to feel I had the measure of these people. I had no idea how short that measure fell. In particular, I realise now, I did not have Charlie's measure.

He came storming into the suite in Craig's Hotel in his shirtsleeves and waistcoat as I sat feeding green velvet under the sewing-machine needle.

'I will not stand for it,' he shouted.

Mrs Bleeker's foot rose from the treadle, Lavinia paused over her sheet music, and Sylvester Bleeker groaned as he saw the sheaf of papers waving in Charlie's hand.

'Who gave you those?'

'A very good friend. And I am glad he did, for if he had not, I would never have discovered what these Australian so-called critics are saying about me.'

Lavinia raised her copy of *The Cottage by the Sea* and resumed her trilling, while Mrs Bleeker returned to her seam, and I fed her the velvet. But the singing and whirring could not drown out Charlie.

'Listen to this.' He held out one paper at arm's length. '*The life and soul of it all was Commodore Nutt, who possesses a large fund of humour, and can sing a comic song in a capital style. His Captain Jinks of the Horse Marines was exceedingly clever and had to be encored.* Can you believe such stuff?'

'There was an encore last night.'

Charlie pulled out another slip of paper. '*Commodore Nutt is a host in himself and displays a very tolerable amount of histrionic ability, with an inexhaustible fund of varied humour, which has the effect of keeping the audience in a state of agreeable surprise, and relieving the otherwise monotonous nature of the entertainment.* Were you aware our entertainment was monotonous, Mr Bleeker?'

'Man's a jackass. You shouldn't read critics. You've told me that yourself.'

Charlie shuffled through his pile. 'Listen … *Commodore Nutt is fast becoming a universal favourite. He possesses all the facial expression of a practised comedian and the number of characters he assumes is proof of the versatility of his genius.* Do you hear that? A jumped-up farmer's son who cackled under canvas for the rustics of New Hampshire at five cents an hour until Mr Barnum plucked him out. Genius. Hah.'

Mrs Bleeker's needle swerved away from her seam. She fumbled for her pocket scissors. Lavinia sang on, while Mr Bleeker held up his hands.

'Come, General. These same critics have also praised the whole show very highly. Every time they single you out for special mention.'

'Special mention. Hah.' Charlie held up his last sheaf of paper in clenched fists. 'To speak plainly, the General has become something of a "bloated aristocrat" and except when disposing of his pictures seems to carry a "retired from business" air with him.'

The paper dropped. Charlie put one hand to his head, and Lavinia stopped in mid-trill, moved to her husband's side, put a hand on his arm.

'The rubbish they use to fill these rags,' said Mr Bleeker.

'I cannot tell you how much this pains me, old friend. *Bloated* … the General can endure cheap abuse. *Aristocrat* … that I suppose is a backhanded tribute to the General's dignity. But *retired from business* … to a man who works night and day to delight his public … that is the unkindest cut of all.' He moved his hand from his head to his chest, and pressed as if his heart were about to spring out from his waistcoat.

'Scum,' Mr Bleeker said. 'But this here's a free country with a free press. What would you have me do, cowhide the skunk?'

'Just make the Commodore less … prominent.'

Mr Bleeker was silent.

'I will leave it to you,' said Charlie. 'Now the General has to work at this business he is supposed to have retired from … Mary Ann? Looking glass.'

I jumped up, hastened to the bedroom and picked up Charlie's gilt-framed looking glass. It was almost my height and heavy. I bore it carefully back into the centre of the room and held it up for him to see his reflection, as I had done many times.

Charlie turned first to Mr Bleeker. 'I mustn't keep you from business.'

'No, indeed. Must have a word with Ned Davis.'

The manager left the room, and Lavinia made to follow.

'Stay a while, my love,' said Charlie. 'And Mrs B and Mary Ann, if you please. Mary Ann, put the looking glass flat on the floor. Glass side up. That's it. Now. Observe. Especially you, Mary Ann. It is as Dr Foote says. When any great national hero draws the attention of a gravid woman, especially if he is constantly before her eyes, the prominent mental and physical characteristics of this conspicuous individual are impressed on the plastic little creature nestling beneath the beating heart.'

What on earth was he talking about? But I had no chance to ask. Breathing deeply, he began to strip, handing each item to me as he went along. Coat, waistcoat. Surely he must stop soon, surely … Cravat, shirt. I kept my eyes downcast and my hands out, resisting a painful urge to cover him. Boots, socks, trousers. Dear God.

'Charlie, what are you up to?' said his wife. I sneaked a look. He was enclosed in nothing but a tight garment like an acrobat's costume, the colour of cooked salmon flesh, that covered him from neck to wrists to ankles and glittered over the swell of his breast and paunch. I kept my eyes averted from his crotch. As we women stood transfixed, he stepped onto the mirror like a brave skater treading the ice. He glided slowly from one pose to another, pausing, staring constantly at the mirror beneath his feet. Muscles flexed, legs bent, arms swung, fat trembled. I wanted to laugh, then to vomit, but kept my face frozen. All I could think of was a raw sausage dancing on a skillet.

Charlie was whispering. 'Stretch tall. Raise chin. Pull back. Cock of the walk. Glide. Strut.' Had the reviews driven him mad? He stood with his legs apart, leaning forward, left knee bent, held out his left arm straight ahead, while his right arm bent and his elbow moved back, level with his ear. A sharp tearing sound: the sausage had split its skin, gaping at the seam, from the back of his neck to his buttocks. He paused. Then with a whiff of sweat and moth balls, he continued to stretch.

'Mrs B,' whispered Lavinia, as if she feared to wake a sleepwalker. 'Fetch a blanket.'

Mrs Bleeker ran into the next room and returned with a blanket from the couple's bed. Charlie stood as quiet as a steaming horse while she threw it over his shoulders and pulled off the sausage skin.

'I feel a little tired, Vin,' he said composedly. 'I will go and lie down.' He turned to me, gave me his full beam smile. 'You should take care of your health, my dear. Plenty of rest, that's the ticket.'

I swallowed my nausea. 'I am fine, sir.'

'Oh, Charlie.' Lavinia's voice held infinite sorrow. She put her arm round her husband and escorted him to bed, the blanket trailing in his wake.

I propped Charlie's mirror against the wall. In the glass, I saw the rumpled dresses and sheet music strewn across the sofa, two little dressmaker's dummies, the sewing machine with its spill of velvet, Mrs Bleeker dangling the shredded remains of the horrible shiny undergarment from her fingers.

Lavinia put her head round the door to the bedroom. 'He is resting. The poor wee man. Oh, I'd like to get my hands on whoever showed those notices to him.'

Mrs Bleeker held out her handful of fabric. 'Should I mend this?'

'Better throw it on the fire. I will talk to him.'

When Lavinia had returned to her husband's bedside, Mrs Bleeker crouched by the fire. The star of the show and the prospective father of my infant had just gone insane and all I could do was sit and sew.

'What is going on, Mrs B?'

She was quiet, running the wrecked body stocking back and forth through her fingers.

'You should have seen him as Cupid,' she said finally. 'I made him such gorgeous wings, they fitted at the back, here ...' She pointed out the spot. 'He carried a little quiver. A classic manly build in miniature. So slim and light of foot and so agile, and the ladies shrieked when he tossed his curls and pointed his arrow at them.'

'When was that?'

'Long ago, in London.' She stared into the flames. 'They called it his Pantheon. Samson carrying away the gates of Gaza. The Fighting Gladiator. The Slave whetting his knife. Ajax. Discobolus. Cincinnatus. Cain swinging his club. And everyone's favourite, the infant Hercules strangling the snakes. I made him gutta-percha pythons. They flocked to the Egyptian Hall. We made five hundred pound a day.'

So Charlie was not mad, merely nostalgic. 'He was doing those poses again? But why the mirror on the floor?'

'That's how Mr Barnum used to teach him when he was a tiny boy. Then he'd make him strut. Chin up, shoulders back, chest puffed out. Round and round on the mirror for hours on end.'

'He still has that walk,' I said. 'But why is he doing those poses now?'

'The notices. And the Commodore, of course.'

'The Commodore is a very funny fellow. But he is smaller than the General.'

Mrs Bleeker looked up sharply. 'Don't you ever remind the General of that.'

'But the General is the one and only Tom Thumb.'

'Is he? When they were first on show together, everyone thought that Commodore Nutt was Tom Thumb. They looked at the General and thought he was some older, fatter little person Mr Barnum had dug up.' She held up the withered skin, flames glowing through the rips and ladders. 'Did you know he and the Commodore were rivals for Miss Lavinia's hand?' I shook my head. 'It's a famous story — Mr Barnum has seen to that. When the General began paying court, the Commodore was jealous. He began to talk about bowie knives, about his pistol, Widowmaker. They had a scuffle one day, and the Commodore threw the General on his back.'

'Was he hurt?'

'No, no. And of course the General won in the end. He proposed at Mr Barnum's house, and she accepted. Mr Barnum said the Commodore was strutting about like a turkey bantam, all red in the face.' I laughed, and Mrs Bleeker frowned at me. 'Don't forget bantams have spurs.'

She stood up, cast the salmon garment into the fire. A sudden sizzling and a foul smell as she stirred the blackening heap with a poker.

'Mrs Bleeker, forgive me asking, but … do you think the General is ready for fatherhood?'

She stared at me. 'Lord, what a question. He could not be readier. Don't you understand the simplest thing? He will give the little one the childhood he never had.'

I wanted to tell her how, in that salmon costume, he had looked like a bloated baby; but she looked almost about to strike me.

Then she spoke more calmly. 'He will work as hard at fatherhood as with anything else he does. He will be the perfect papa. It is just … a difficult time. It will pass. As long as he and the Commodore continue to keep their distance.'

I thought of the times I had seen the little people lined up. Charlie was always at one end of the row, George at the other, with the ladies in between. Their brief appearances on stage together were done in silence. They rarely shared a carriage. When not performing or meeting the public, Charlie visited the ladies, or sat drinking port with Mr Bleeker, or skulked alone in his room. George drank brandy or tickled the balls on the green with Ned Davis; they would commandeer the billiards room in any hotel and close the door on their gusts of laughter.

I could remember only one exchange between the two little men. They had attended a performance by Mr Robert Heller the Prestidigitator when they shared the bill with him at the Theatre

Royal in Melbourne, and afterwards Charlie was in raptures. 'Such a capital trick, seven shots fired point-blank at Mr Heller and not a mark on him! And then he smiles and shows seven bullets between his teeth! Should we not incorporate something of the kind into our show?'

He had looked at Mr Bleeker. But it was George who had replied. 'By all means, if you'll let me prestidigit a bullet or two between your teeth.' He opened his jacket and grasped the handle of his pistol Widowmaker, tucked into its holster, and grinned into Charlie's face.

'Still armed, Commodore?' said Charlie. 'What are you afraid of? Fierce kangaroos?'

'Shame on you, Commodore,' said Lavinia. 'Put that horrid thing away. We will have no more talk of guns.'

And George had obeyed. 'For you, Mrs Stratton, anything.'

I drew my chair back from the guttering flames and spread the dress I was sewing across my stomach.

'So are the General and the Commodore enemies?' I asked.

'There are no enemies in my husband's troupe,' Mrs Bleeker said sternly. Then she sighed. 'They rub each other up the wrong way. They produce the wrong electricity.'

I made a few more stitches. Maybe I should not be in a hurry to leave the Strattons' employ when they got to America. But that might mean no freedom, no prospects. I thought of Mrs Bleeker's swiftly curtailed promise. *You can have your pick of …* Sometimes it seemed I could never have my pick of anything. It had been that way since I was a child. I could only reach out to touch beautiful things that drifted by, like the russet leaves that had blown around the sundial in the rectory garden before winter set in. But I would reach out once more.

'Mrs Bleeker, I have noticed how frustrated Mr Richardson gets when he is playing the piano and he has to lean over to turn the page. I read music, I could do that for him.'

'That is a capital idea.' Mrs Bleeker turned to me with a broad smile. 'You may help Mr Richardson whenever you are free from other duties.'

'Is he the kind of man who would welcome my help? I mean … what kind of man is he?'

She looked at me in surprise. 'Well … he is a rescuer, like you.'

'Mr Richardson?' A little needle ran through me when I repeated the name.

'He rescued Mrs Stratton from an alligator in a swamp.'

'Good heavens.' I imagined Franz Richardson standing chest-deep in evil water, holding Lavinia over his shoulder with one hand and beating off a gape-jawed monster with the other. I leaned forward to ask Mrs Bleeker more.

'Hannah, what's that horrible stink?' Sylvester Bleeker asked his wife as he burst through the door. 'Why are these dresses strewn about? Why is this sheet music all higgledy-piggledy?'

'We are in the middle of a few tasks, Silly dear.'

'Hannah, how many times must I tell you? Please don't call me by … that name.' Tossing the dresses onto the floor, Mr Bleeker flung himself down on the sofa and began to massage his chest.

'You haven't taken your anti-bilious tablets, have you?'

'Tablets be blowed,' said Mr Bleeker. 'What am I to do? That insolent Ned Davis more or less admitted it. He gave those notices to the General. I expressly forbade it. How dare he?'

'You should send Ned packing, Sil — I mean, Sylvester. He loves nothing better than to snoop and stir up trouble.'

'Sack a devilish good agent? I'll never find another. No, but I won't take him to see Dr Musgrave on Friday, that's for sure. The fellow is bound to wrangle all sorts of deals behind my back. I'll just have to make a memorandum myself.'

'No you won't, Silly. Why not take Mary Ann? She has a good hand.'

Mr Bleeker stared at me. 'You can take notes? Fine, you're booked. Now I must go sort out the gathering storm clouds. Unless there's a miracle, we'll have mutiny. And who's the miracle worker round here?'

I turned to Mrs Bleeker as he left. 'Dr Musgrave? Is Mr Bleeker not well?'

She laughed. 'He is not that kind of doctor. He is more … oh, I would say a legend hereabouts. My husband is keen to do business with him. He lives at Athena Hall, by the lake. It is said the whole building is made of solid gold, and Dr Musgrave and his servants wear tinted spectacles to reduce the glare. How lucky you will be to see it.'

'He must be very rich.'

'As Midas! He is English, like you. He made his fortune among the speculators of the Beehive — that's the hotel where the business of the goldfields is done. He bought cheap and he sold dear. He bought up property and businesses in both Ballarat and Sydney. But at the height of his success, he vanished into almost total seclusion inside the mansion he built for himself. These days, he rarely goes out. But you know what?' She paused, raised a finger. 'Plenty goes in. Queerly shaped parcels, crates packed in straw and ice.'

'Whatever can they be?'

Mrs Bleeker sat back, enjoying her story. 'Nobody knows. But there are rumours. A fisherman out at dawn on Lake Wendouree said he saw Dr Musgrave with a white bird on his shoulder like a pirate, a big net over his other shoulder, walking on the water. Some say he preserves his own mother's hacked-off hand in a hatbox under his desk. Others say he keeps a beautiful woman in a trance inside a glass coffin, with hair coiling down to her feet, and nails almost as long, and no one knows if she is alive or dead.' She beckoned me closer, lowered her voice to a whisper. 'Some have it that he's a Bluebeard, with a secret room of walled-up wives. That he collects corpses, takes them apart and sews heads, limbs and torsos together, and studies the black arts to bring them to life.'

'Mrs Bleeker, you are making fun of me!'

'Well,' she said gravely, 'I'm only telling you what they say. You will see for yourself on Friday, when you go with my husband and Mr Richardson. Make sure you have at least two sharp pencils.'

'And a sharp needle, in case I have to sew up a corpse,' I said, and she laughed. It was all very exciting. Friday was two days away. I was sure I could face the most horrid Bluebeard with Franz Richardson at my side.

• • • • • • • •

Later that afternoon, I saw the devilish good agent, Ned, and George going down the staircase and turning into the billiard room. What did they do in there? And was it true that Ned liked to stir up trouble? The moment my chores were done, I made my way alone, down the stairs to the heavy oak door, which was slightly ajar. Carefully I pushed the door further open and peered into a fug of cigar smoke. The curtains were drawn, and the only lights were a lamp on a card table and a green-shaded one above the billiard table. In waistcoat and shirtsleeves, for once without his bowler, Ned sat at the card table, poring over sheets of paper, his pomaded hair sleek as pitch.

'Thirty-eight pound one shilling for that afternoon show,' he said. 'We would've done better, but for that fucking rain.'

'I thought Australia was supposed to be hot and dry,' said George. Under the lamp, his head rose like a green sun over the billiard table. He stood on a chair and a pile of cushions, his head and arms just above table level, squinting down his cue. He fired, and the balls sped obediently into their lairs.

'Hey, hey! Did you see that, boyo?'

'Another winner.' Ned picked up a piece of paper. 'We did better in the evening. Eighty-three pound five shilling and sixpence. That's a shitload of dollars in Yankee lingo.'

I wondered whether to go. All my spying could produce was dreadful language about pounds, shillings and pence.

'Fuck this.' Ned pushed back his chair, tugged a flask from his pocket. He took a long swig, then held out the bottle to George, who scrambled down and took an even longer swig. 'Now you can show me the glass again,' said Ned.

'Ain't you sick of the glass yet?'

'Never get sick of the glass.'

George shrugged, gave the flask back to Ned, and climbed

onto the billiard table, where his head reached to just below the green shade. He stood for a moment, gradually swelling, while his cherub's face acquired an extra chin. Then, with much huffing and puffing, he placed a large flat imaginary object on the table and with jerky movements, stepped onto the surface. He imitated an archer, a discus thrower, a warrior, a Napoleon, tottering and wheezing and grimacing as if his arthritic legs would hardly let him move, staring every now and then at the baize between his legs. The stares became longer and longer and more and more fascinated, and Ned was in fits of sniggers.

'It's Up Himself to a T, Commodore, you're a genius.'

'And now for my *pièce de résistance*,' said George in a pompous tone. 'My homage to the master.' He bent slowly down, like a hypnotised chicken, until his nose touched the baize and his backside stuck up in the air. A long pause, and then a huge bubbling explosion thundered out of his rear, leaving Ned helpless with laughter.

George straightened, bowed. 'The wonder of the world,' he declaimed. 'The one and only fart in miniature.'

His audience applauded and waved away the stink.

An involuntary gasp — astonishment, horror, laughter — escaped from me. George did not seem to hear, but Ned turned, stared and grimaced. That canine tooth that stuck out too far from its fellows flashed at me. He got to his feet and came towards me, right out into the hall; it was too late to run away, and for a moment I felt he would strike me. But he lunged forward, put his face close to mine. I fought the urge to step back, endured the whiff of brandy and pomade, a hint of onion.

'Well, if it ain't the busy little beaver.'

'I beg your pardon?'

'A tribute to your hard work. But you're in the wrong place, ma'am. Gents only.'

'I didn't know …' I changed tack, tried to sound defiant. 'You can't keep people out. There isn't a rule.'

'We don't need a rule.' I made to look over his shoulder, but he closed the door behind him, stood closer, covering me with his breath. 'Ever thought of making yourself a mint?'

'What do you mean?'

'You know. The golden egg.' He looked up and down the corridor, turned back to me, spoke fast and low. 'I have connections, I can fix it up. There are those as will pay very handsome.'

I had no idea why, but he reminded me then of the old woman in the house with the canary who had held out her soapy hand for my money. But wasn't he offering me money?

'Mr Davis, I don't know what you mean, but I don't want a mint.'

He stared at me, then grinned. 'Just remember, then.'

'Remember what?'

He opened the door behind him. 'Any hotel, it's the same. Billiard room, gents only. You remember that, you won't have no trouble.'

Then he was gone, and the door slammed in my face.

· · · · · · · ·

The next night, I discovered that George's performance in the billiard room had not been a private entertainment. It was a rehearsal.

At the start of the show, we were unusually dispersed. Mr Bleeker was in bed with an attack of dyspepsia, Mrs Bleeker was at his side, Rodnia Nutt was outside with the horses, the ladies were changing costumes somewhere backstage and I had no idea where Ned Davis was. I was sitting beside Franz at the piano in the orchestra pit. He had swiftly accepted my offer to turn the pages for him, and now he smiled a greeting at me, but we had not had a moment to talk. I remembered the first time I had seen him, with his eyes closed, at the piano; now I saw his irises were the green of a ripening apple, and his eyelashes were astonishingly long, like a woman's, and yet everything about him was decidedly manly. I reminded myself I must concentrate on reading the music.

The piano seat trembled as he played Charlie's entrance music, then all fell silent, as Charlie, thumbs hooked into his waistcoat, began his stump orator's speech, his most successful sketch: everyone loved the tiny pompous politician.

'Make no mistake,' he declaimed, 'a mighty wind of change shall shake this nation.'

At that moment, everyone began to shuffle and giggle, and Charlie swelled as if he would burst. But I could see, as he could not, the cause of the audience's amusement: George in his green Dandy Pat costume, looking oddly bulky, had come onstage and was prowling around behind Charlie. His bodhran was tucked under his arm, and his forefinger was pressed to his lips. Very softly he began to patter the drum, as if he brought his own rain. Slowly Charlie turned, started, gestured at George to leave the stage. George came closer, his drum beat louder.

'What is he doing?' I whispered to Franz.

'They must have changed the act.'

Charlie shook his fist under George's nose, and George turned to the audience and gave them a look that made everyone shriek in glee.

'Ain't ye had enough of polly parrot politicians?' he shouted in his stage Irish brogue. 'Wouldn't ye rather have a song?' They shouted their assent, and he began to caper and sing, '*I'm Dandy Pat from the Emerald Isle ...*'

'Why do they never tell me anything?' hissed Franz, lifting up his hands. Quickly I shuffled the piles of music, brought out the Dandy Pat theme tune, pushed it in front of Franz's nose, and he swiped at the ivories as if they were alligator teeth.

Now a discordant voice joined the drumming, singing and piano-thumping.

'Stop, Mr Richardson,' I cried. 'The General is doing his speech again, from the top.' Why was everything going wrong? Why didn't someone call a halt? Then I remembered there was no one around to stop anything.

The audience tittered uncertainly. George finished his Dandy Pat song but no one applauded because they were listening to Charlie, so he tucked his bodhran under his arm and shouted: 'Ar, enough of this twaddle, let me show you me little shillelagh.' This was said so roguishly the audience collapsed in laughter, drowning Charlie, who paused. George frowned and wagged his finger, and when the laughter finally died down, Charlie resumed his speech.

George was quiet, but he was not still. Behind Charlie, in full view of the audience, pausing only to put his finger to his lips, he was peeling off his Dandy Pat costume. Underneath he wore long woolly combinations, dyed pink, and a pillow under the vest to give him a paunch. Slowly he swung his arms and legs, striking his ridiculous poses, and my stomach lurched with every swing.

Franz sat still, hands balled into fists. 'This is unprofessional,' he whispered.

This is sabotage, I wanted to reply. The audience was laughing, and Charlie took it as a tribute to his own oratory. But it would take only one sound to make him turn round, and then he would know. One sound. George bent over. His woolly backside faced the audience. It rose as his head descended, his nose almost touching the stage boards.

'Excuse me, Mr Richardson,' I whispered. It was time for me to get busy again, and not a moment to lose.

I rushed to the door at the side of the stage that led to the wings, ran through. As I had suspected, no one was there. Quick, quick, what next? Several ropes dangled from the darkness above. Was this the right one? I grabbed it and pulled hard, hand over hand, praying it would not lower any scenery on the little men's heads. But as I had hoped, the curtains began to sweep across the stage. I could no longer see Franz, but heard the triumphant hammer of his end-of-scene chords. Obediently, yet a little puzzled by the abrupt ending, the audience clapped.

Charlie stormed into the wings. 'What poltroon pulled the curtain? Where is Mr B? I cannot believe this shambles.'

Was he furious with me?

Then a figure detached itself from the darkness beside the stage. 'I think you'll find Mr B in his bed,' said Ned.

Applause, mixed with hoots and whistles, interrupted him.

Onstage, George had scrambled back into his Dandy Pat costume and was taking his curtain call, sweeping off his cap in a flurry of bows. Ned gestured towards the stage: 'I believe you're wanted, General.'

Franz's piano plunked its way to a crescendo of Irishness. George turned, extended his hand to call Charlie back on. For a moment the stump orator paused; then, as Franz's piano switched to *Walking down Broadway*, he stalked back onstage to stand by George, hold his hand, bow, all the time as if a broomstick had been shoved up his bottom. Standing beside me, throwing me needling glances, Ned applauded like a madman. Finally, Charlie walked offstage, staring straight ahead. George ran out behind him in a crouching spider run and vanished behind a pile of props as the lights came up for a brief interval.

I rounded on Ned. 'That was cruel. And don't you dare deny that you put him up to it.'

'Well, well. Churchy la fem.'

'What does that mean?'

'When the fair sex are expecting a happy event, they get strange fancies. So, churchy la fem.'

'I think you must mean *cherchez la femme*, Mr Davis,' I said icily. 'And I am not prey to fancies. I knew exactly what was coming. If I had not pulled the curtain —'

'Aha,' said Ned. 'What's Mr B going to say about you interrupting the show?'

'Interrupt? Me? You did more than interrupt. You —'

'Yes, Missus Beaver?' The agent thrust his face at mine, bared his long yellow teeth in what might pass for a friendly grin, and I stared at the rogue canine, a little turned out in its socket, almost overlapping his lower lip. My nausea rose again.

'Are you insinuating something, Mr Davis?' said Franz. He had come silently through the side door, stood close, towering over the agent, who seemed to shrink a little.

'Just my Frenchy talk,' he said.

'Then don't bother Mrs Carroll with your Frenchy nonsense. I need her to help me perform.'

'Might I say, Mr Richardson, what a stupendous show you're giving tonight?'

What a wheedle had entered his voice.

'Perhaps next time the act is changed,' Franz said, 'someone will deign to inform the pianist.'

'You know how it is,' said Ned. 'When the cat's away ...' He winked at no one in particular and strolled off into the darkness, and my nausea faded as he went. I turned to Franz, expecting him to exclaim at the blackguard's insolence, but he was already striding back into the theatre and down to the orchestra pit. I hurried to join him, and by the time I sat down beside him, he was playing the run-up to *Cottage by the Sea* as the curtains opened again, and the Queen of Beauty and her sister swept into the lights.

Someone should give the agent his comeuppance, I thought. Watching Franz's shoulders squaring and straining against his dark coat as he leaned forward, the tawny hair grazing his collar, I thought again how like a lion he was; how Ned would run if he roared.

But what on earth had George been up to?

SIDESHOW

Commodore George Washington Morrison Nutt

Commodore Nutt in dunce's cap

ACT ONE

Ho ho, nearly got him that time, fat old fart. Maybe I'll get into trouble with Mr B, but it's worth it. Another salvo in my long-term campaign. It's all down to artistry, isn't it? I have it by the bushel-load and he doesn't have an ounce of it in all that puffed-up little body. Simple. So it's only a matter of time. But Lord knows, I get impatient.

Take the chair routine. We've been doing it for years. He comes onstage as Napoleon, tries to climb onto a chair, it's too big for him. So then I come on as a servant with a folding camp stool. I set it down for him and it's just the right height. He gives me a distant nod and begins to lower himself over the stool. At the same time, I creep up close behind him. Grab stool, whisk it away, Napoleon's bum falls onto the floor to a crashing discord from Franz's piano. Up he jumps, bewildered, but I've retreated behind the wardrobe and stand winking to the audience with a finger to my lips. Napoleon inspects the rogue stool from every angle, sets it up again, begins to lower his bottom. Out I jump: grab, whisk, crash. Several times, we do it. Everybody hollers to Napoleon to look out, but he hears them too late.

Oldest trick in the book, I reckon. But they laugh every time, harder and harder, until tears cascade down their faces. Why, I ask you? No thanks to Napoleon. He does it just the same way every time. Anybody can do that affronted-dignity stuff, legs in the air like a dead canary on its back. Me, I call the changes. Every audience is different, so why shouldn't every performance be different? I always remove the chair at exactly the same moment. But sometimes, I lift it high; sometimes, I knock it sideways; sometimes, very slowly and gently, I pull it back, so it looks as if for once his bum will land on the right place — and then whisk, crash, shrieks and bravos guaranteed.

I may be young still, but it's taken me a long time to get this right. I know I had a life before, on Ma and Pa's farm, and I had good times with Roddie, but it was like I was a little runt calf, no good for beef or milk, and didn't exist as a man until I was a performer. Started at fifteen in Mr Lillie's travelling circus as Tiny George, the Smallest Man in God's Creation. I've heard so often how Old Fatso got a head start, learning his trade as a young boy, strutting up and down for Mr Barnum on a gilded-frame looking glass on the floor by the marble fireplace. Well I didn't have fire or looking glass, just a broken hand mirror I'd found under the bleachers in the Big Top, and I didn't waste time strutting; any fool can strut. No, I stared into that mirror and practised my comical faces. Eyebrow up, cheek out, tongue sideways, nose scrunched, upper lip curled, lower lip thrust. Thirty-two faces I do, each one quite different, but when I'm firing they flow into one another, a nimble dance of the features. And the audience, God love them, they know the Commodore is silently telling them more than the most eloquent

107

of orators, and every one of those grimaces kills them dead. And that's before I've even moved or opened my mouth or beaten my drum. Don't get me started on that.

But if the audience gets it, why don't the people who run the shows? Old Turkey-jowls — beg pardon, I should say Mr Lillie — was hopeless. Always wobbling and gobbling on about propriety and not offending ladies and gents or ministers of religion. He killed me dead, and I don't mean the laughing kind. Take that great act I had worked out with my big brother Roddie and me. It went like this: all the punters paid to come into my booth to see Tiny George, and what they saw was Roddie, sitting still on my chair. And so they began to murmur, then grumble, then shout.

Tiny George, my eye, this fellow ain't tiny, he's just short. Where's the boss, we've been had, we want our money back!

And just when the booth was steaming up with their fury I came running in from the back, pulling up my pants and looping on my braces.

'What's up, can't a fellow answer a call of nature without starting a riot? Gee but I'm running hot, musta been those fancy chilli beans for luncheon,' and down the pants went again and six or so comical faces and a sudden hush and Roddie with his hands over his eyes and everyone wondering, is Tiny George actually going to poop right in front of us on his little bit of red carpet? And then an explosion and I ran round the booth with real smoke coming out of my bottom (don't ask, trade secret), and Roddie chasing me with a bucket of water, and the punters howling, not with rage but with joy. And next day the queue to my booth stretched all the way across to the next potato field.

But after two days Mr Lillie stopped us, said he wouldn't permit such vulgarity, it would get us closed down. Up your fundament, Turkey-jowls. If you could see me now. Who cares about touring New Hampshire when you can tour the world?

I remember when Mr Barnum rescued me from Mr Lillie despite all his gobbling, dubbed me Commodore, gave me a nut-shaped coach and hired me to perform at the American Museum for thirty thousand dollars, so they said (it was actually twelve dollars a week plus perks to begin with, but he wanted to make me sound priceless), and I thought at last I was going places. How nervous I was all the same, how keen to meet his star protégé, the great General Tom Thumb, performer for the Queen of England, the rage of London society. The excitable French nation had thronged to behold this darling of Nature's handiwork. And how New York roared for him! Oh, he was suave, and brighter than his polished buttons. They didn't threaten to pop off his swelling weskit in those days. And I thought he was kind to me, and delighted to meet a little man like himself. I kept mum about one thing, though: I was just a shade shorter than he was, and that perked me up no end, for I was still the Smallest Man in God's Creation.

But my awe at the General was nothing compared to my prostration on first beholding Miss Lavinia Warren. Oh, that I were a poet, to praise her alabaster complexion, raven hair, musical voice, rosy lips, divine form … In short she was beauty unsurpassed, made for none but me, and with her first smile at me I felt my heart leap up and land in a sweet net of chains that I understood at once would never loosen. But dare I speak my love? One tiny gesture of encouragement would embolden me. And after weeks of growing pale in her presence, and trying nevertheless to act the comic rascal that everyone thought I was, finally it came. She gave me a diamond and emerald ring. It was a present from Mr Barnum that did not quite fit her, she made plain for propriety's sake; he had said he would give her another instead. But I knew what she meant — or thought I did.

In the next few days I hid away with my old cracked mirror and practised my thirty-third face, the hardest I had ever attempted. Sincere, serious, ardent but respectful, and all the harder because it had to express in perfectly winning balance my real turmoil of feelings. Of course I practised words too, but it was the face and the gestures I had to get right. There would be a chance, soon. Several of the company were invited to Iranistan, Mr Barnum's house in Bridgeport, Connecticut, for a weekend, and I would come down on the evening train after my show at the American Museum, arriving at eleven o'clock. Over the weekend, I felt sure I'd figure out some way to meet with Miss Warren alone. All we needed were a few minutes. Bliss was within my grasp, and I could scarcely stop myself cartwheeling upon my little stage at the evening levee. Even so, there was some extra spark in me. I had never heard my audience roar so.

As my carriage came up the driveway to Iranistan, my whole body quivered at the sight of the brightly lit cluster of Oriental minarets and pleasure domes, modelled as I had heard on the Brighton Pavilion in England. Here was a palace fit for a princess, and I dared to cast myself in the role of the wooing prince. I've never felt so wound up, not even in those moments before I first met President Lincoln. I bounded out and rang the doorbell, expecting a servant to let me in, for despite those glowing lights I thought the company would have retired for the night. But it was my angel herself who opened the door, all pink from sitting by the fire, and just behind her in the hallway, even more flushed, stood Charlie. No one else, it seemed, was up. These two had been sitting in the drawing room all by themselves. I looked from one to another. Lavinia's violet eyes were wide and glistening — were those tears? Of despair? Happiness? — while Charlie shuffled and fidgeted and studied the golden tiles beneath his feet. I could hardly draw breath. All those pleasure domes and minarets above my head were thrumming and pressing down on me with some barely suppressed secret.

What could I do? I went to bed and slept not a wink. I think I knew even then what had happened. Lavinia was civil to me all weekend, but it was as though an invisible veil had descended between us. A few days later, Mr Barnum called me into his office and told me of her engagement to Charlie. What incensed me most was that Mr Barnum made a game of it, called it a prank of Lavinia's, when it was clear that all were quite serious. He even suggested I should court Lavinia's sister Minnie, but how could I ever look at another woman? And even if I could, Minnie might be pretty enough in her scatterdemalion way, but she was one of those minxes who could always uncover a man's heart, who would know whether it was hers or another's, whereas Lavinia, I believe now, never had any idea of the golden chains that bind my heart over and over. The end of those chains was in her little hand, is still there, and with one tug ... But of course she has never tugged.

I congratulated the happy couple. I had to find my thirty-fourth face, the rejoicing man, and that was devilish hard. The greatest ordeal was their wedding. I agreed to be best man, out of some instinct, perhaps, to watch over my darling; but the only way I could get through it was with the help of my best man at that time, the fivestar brandy bottle. The bottle also helped me sleep, perform, sleep, perform, sleep. That was my life then. I prided myself on my thirty-fifth face: the sober man. But I couldn't disguise the reek of brandy on my person.

Around this time, Mr Barnum and Mr Bleeker together began to devise a touring show that would star all four little people. Apart from some brief levees, it was the first time I had appeared with Charlie on stage, and I saw at once that he was not a natural performer. He had to learn every line, every gesture. Spontaneity and the felicitous ad lib were quite beyond him. Of course his stiff, pompous bearing was funny in itself, and the audience indulged him, but he hadn't the faintest notion of how to take up what he had and build on it. I thought about teaching him the rudiments of the comic art, but was sure he would never take instruction from such an upstart as myself. And then I had a better idea. I would work on my own act, my own personae, my Dandy Pat and my Captain Jinks and my Commodore, and polish them until they shone brighter than my angel's diamonds. I would study every means to win my audience, from grizzled miners to lords and ladies, from jaded critics to cheeky children. I would sweep all before me with the dazzling force of my comicalities. And what would happen to Charlie? Left stranded on stage, flapping and gasping, a milky puffer fish. All, all would adore me — including the one whom I adore above all.

It was not something to be done quickly, and besides I had to be wary, for Mr Barnum and Mr Bleeker did not wish their star to be upstaged, and Charlie himself would be furious if he ever got wind of it. But it's amazing what you can do by stealth. An encore here, a drum roll there, a wink, a nudge, a complicity with my followers that I play second fiddle to the greatest fool in show business. I build on it, little by little. And I have an accomplice.

No, not Rodnia, who for so long was my straight man and my protector, hoisting me up on his boulder-shoulders, defending me from the bullies and Lillies of this world. Ever since I was a mite, he's looked out for me, taking on ruffians twice his size, getting knocked over and coming right back at them until they just can't take his persistence and hobble off. Roddie has been a good brother to me, no doubt about that, but sooner or later, a fellow requires more than brute strength, a fellow has to move on from family. No, my ally is Ned Davis, a rogue if ever there was one, a man who practises only one face, but a fine one. He knows the art of appearing respectful and insolent at the same time. He knows what it is not to be appreciated for his skills, for Mr Barnum has never promoted him beyond agent. How he worships Mr Barnum, and yet he says it's as if the man just whisks by him and can't see him. There's nothing like being invisible to stoke a fellow's fires of cunning and vengeance. Sometimes Ned talks of the Gauls and their guerilla raids on the Romans, and I haven't the foggiest how an uneducated fellow like Ned knows of such things; at first I thought he meant the Gauls were a tribe of apes, but he is a great picker-up of info, and he bids me think of myself as a guerilla, all stealth and patience. He is my touchstone, my judge of the parodic art, and he encourages me to make more and more daring challenges, and rattle Old Fatso's complacency, until I am at last the conquering hero, the prince who enters the golden-domed palace and claims his rightful prize.

And it was Ned who told me what Mr Up Himself did with that young woman in the mud by the Yarra Yarra, and that means I have the measure of a man's weakness, which is what every conquering hero needs.

So I bide my time. What I must never do now is think of Old Fatso Up Himself and his good lady wife in private, for then I take out my trusty pistol Widowmaker from under my pillow and hold it in one hand and the cracked mirror in the other and I point Widowmaker at the mirror and I see the thirty-sixth face, a face I have seen nowhere but in my worst dreams.

CHAPTER 6

The calf had a sweet mild face and another, sadder face. I wanted to reach out and pat it, but I was not sure which of its two curly foreheads to pat. In any case, a glass wall stood between my hand and the creature, which seemed the most natural and humble of beasts. In the glass was a faint reflection of my face, and behind me was a tall presence crowned with russet hair. Was Franz Richardson looking at the calf, or at me? I bent my head to the notebook Mr Bleeker had given me, copying the label. *Polycephalous calf, born Bendigo, 1857.*

'A fine example of the taxidermist's art, is it not?' said Dr Musgrave.

'Jove, yes,' said Franz, much louder than my own murmur — 'Poor creature' — and Mr Bleeker's grunt as he pushed his dripping umbrella into the hollow elephant's foot by the door. We three visitors to Athena Hall stood in a hallway furnished in the style of a country gentleman's residence — lion and deer heads, tiger-skin rug — but also full of glass cases crammed with curiosities. I was in awe of anyone who could fit so many strange things behind glass.

My head was awhirl with so many things, but one feeling at least was relief. Nobody had even mentioned my act of closing the curtains at the previous night's performance. After complaints from Charlie, Mr Bleeker had issued a decree that no one was to depart from the script, or the running order, or work up any business, or even take an extra curtain call, without his permission. And first thing this morning Franz had sought me out, thanked me for helping him, hoped I would help again when my duties permitted, and asked me to tell him if Mr Davis bothered me any further. His voice was warm and melodious, and if Mrs Bleeker had not fetched me away I would have sat down beside him on the piano stool there and then.

And now here we were again, side by side — if only I could keep up with his swift steps.

'Look,' he cried, stopping beside a cabinet. A lizard reared on its hind legs, a ruff extending stiffly from its neck.

Chlamydosaurus kingii, I wrote. Mr Bleeker had asked me to record the name of any item that took my fancy. But everything took my fancy. All I could take in was a jumble of gaping mouths, tusks and teeth, pink gums; jars of liquid the colour of Yarra Yarra water, with blurred shapes floating inside; bones as long as Mr Bleeker's leg, or as short as my little finger. Now I had a good idea what had been inside those queerly shaped parcels that were seen going into Athena Hall.

Mr Bleeker was smiling at Franz like a father, and I felt the warmth of his pride. How alike the two tall men were, though Franz was more upright and muscular and incomparably more handsome. Our host stood looking up at them, hands behind his back. Like his lizard, he had a ruff. It was made of white hair, and it stood out broad and stiff from his head and chin, but his eyebrows and eyes were nocturnally black.

My only disappointment was that one story Mrs Bleeker had told me was clearly not true. Athena Hall was not made of solid gold. In fact the only gold I could see was a large signet ring on Dr Musgrave's right index finger. Why would anyone circulate such stories? Perhaps because he had retired so suddenly: folk do love a mystery.

I looked around for Franz. He was ahead, with Mr Bleeker and Dr Musgrave as they strode through room after room, past glass case after glass case. I ducked under a huge grey bird and trotted behind them.

'You have come across our *Ornithorhynchus*?' said Dr Musgrave, pausing, and as Mr Bleeker chuckled, he added, 'There is much argument as to whether she whelps like a cat or lays eggs like a duck.' Mr Bleeker muttered something about knowing a fake when he saw one, but Dr Musgrave was already ahead, out of earshot, and Franz paused only to press his face to the glass and mouth a solemn *Quack*. He turned, winked at me and I hid my face in my book. *Ornitho* ... But then I had to scamper again, towards a large case and a tiny skeleton, and Dr Musgrave was saying, '*Homo sapiens*, probably male, in his prime, found in the Kalahari region of Africa,' and Mr Bleeker was stooping and gazing into the eye sockets with the most melancholy look on his face.

'Nicely articulated, just forty inches tall. The same height as the General?'

'Exactly,' said Mr Bleeker, looking even more gloomy.

Dr Musgrave clapped him on the shoulder, and he winced a

little. 'Come, sir. We shall have a fine exchange of wonders in my study.'

I trotted behind again, writing *Homo sapiens*. I was an intruder in a gentlemen's club where my betters were circling each other with their ruffs extended.

But once in the study, the gentlemen seemed more at ease. No glass cases here, only tall cabinets full of drawers and a vast curtain of burgundy velvet that covered an entire wall at the far end of the room.

Dr Musgrave beckoned to me and led me to a corner table with a leather ledger on top, bigger than Father's gigantic church Bible. 'Take a seat, young lady. Here is a complete record of my collection, in alphabetical order. You may look up any item here, and anything you cannot find, please ask me.' As I began to turn the pages, densely covered with tiny handwriting, a servant wheeled in a trolley and withdrew. Mr Bleeker sprawled on a Chesterfield, his legs stretched across a Turkey carpet, with a pot of Foochow at his elbow. Franz perched on the edge of his armchair, beside a whisky decanter. Dr Musgrave offered round fruit cake, then sat behind his desk and presided with twinkling benevolence.

The stories Mrs Bleeker had passed on about the good doctor's Bluebeard secrets seemed more and more ridiculous. I smiled at the humbug. Still, I could not help staring at the hatbox below the desk where Dr Musgrave sat. The collector followed my gaze.

'Aha, you are mesmerised by the famous hatbox where I keep my mother's hand.' I wished I could disappear. 'A far older and much more interesting hand, from a tomb in the Valley of the Kings. But the good folk of Ballarat prefer to think of me as Sweeney Todd.

And I suppose you have heard the story about these fellows.' He pointed to the two human skulls that sat as paperweights on either end of his desk. 'Cornish and United. The first two traders I met at the Beehive. They took me for a raw new chum and tried to swindle me. So I had my revenge.' He stared at me and screwed his face into a startling mask of rage, and for a moment my stomach lurched so violently I was afraid I might vomit. Then Franz burst out laughing, and I smiled, ashamed of my queasy moment.

Mr Bleeker lifted his face from his teacup and explained he was seeking a Wild Man. He was a manager with a double mission: to conduct the General and his troupe around the world and return a profit; and to find a Wild Man for Mr Barnum's museum, preferably with a Wild Woman and Wild Children.

'I thought Mr Barnum was already supplied with Wild Men,' said Dr Musgrave. 'You have the What-is-it, do you not?'

'Ah, Johnson. Wears his animal skins for a dollar a day. Lately his savage gabble has been stuffed with rude Anglo-Saxon words.'

'And Indians?'

'Those shiftless brutes. Laze around and refuse to perform their war dances.'

'And an albino family?'

'The Lucasies? Pa's bad-tempered. Beats his wife and child.'

'So.' Dr Musgrave put one finger to his chin. 'You seek a Wild Man who is peaceable, industrious and kind to the weak.'

Franz gave his joyous laugh, so hearty and open.

Mr Bleeker looked grim. 'I'd hoped to find a good native family in the Antipodes. But I've seen nothing but miserable specimens.'

Dr Musgrave leaned back, steepled his fingers and began to

talk about Australia. A prodigiously large continent, most of it unknown. About an inland sea and a vast fertile region of lakes and plains, hidden far in the interior. About how he was associated with expeditions planned to explore this mysterious wilderness. His voice was deep and rumbling and, sitting before his huge record book, I began to tremble with his earth-shaking visions. He hoped to find new plants, new animals, and new people. A new race of men. A brace of specimens on their way to New York. An exclusive contract, for Mr Barnum's museum. His red lips moved in his white whiskers like an anemone seeking prey. Franz's eyes were glowing green.

Mr Bleeker had his eyes shaded with his hand, as if from too bright a light. 'You don't know of such a race, do you?' he interrupted. 'It's speculation.'

'Speculation has its fruits.' Dr Musgrave lifted a hand towards the lofty walls with their landscape paintings, the leather and gilt and mahogany. He swivelled in his chair and pointed through the velvet-draped window to the parkland and pastures sloping down through veils of rain to the lake. His hand dropped onto the skull on his desk. 'And speculation brings us new scientific insights. Now we know the human brain is not fixed for all time.' He patted the skull affectionately. 'No, sirs, humanity is a work in progress. Who knows the attributes of the Coming Man? A superbeing, for sure: but will he be fair or dark, smooth or hairy, large or small?'

My breathing quickened at the familiar phrase. I could not help myself.

'If you please, sir,' I asked, 'what is the Coming Man?'

Mr Bleeker frowned at me, but Dr Musgrave smiled. 'Ah, your

charming little secretary is a seeker of knowledge! Well, my dear, it is not an exact, scientific phrase. Shall we say it is an anticipation of mankind's brave new future.'

'Does it have anything to do with electricity?'

'Electricity is quite the thing these days, isn't it?' Dr Musgrave chuckled, and I had the sensation he was patting me on the head. 'But this is a very learned subject for a young woman. Perhaps you should read Lamarck, he has much to say on the development of species.'

I bowed my head, hot with humiliation. Mr Bleeker rubbed his chest. 'Let's get back to business,' he said. 'Mr Barnum's always interested in new wonders. How much ...'

All at once, I heard a child's voice. 'Bye-bye,' it said. We all looked round for the hidden little one. Dr Musgrave chuckled, walked to the window, took a velvet cloth off a domed object I had assumed was a clock. When he opened the cage door, a large white cockatoo sidled onto his arm and edged its way to his shoulder. Dr Musgrave returned to his chair, scratching the creature's poll with fingers as white as its feathers. Its eyes rolled up in ecstasy. 'Erasmus is a contented bird, is he not? As I am a contented man, or should be, for I have everything I could wish for. But I am a collector. A collector's passion is never satisfied.' He took a little bag from his top pocket and let the bird peck inside. 'I will never forget the day on the Sussex downs when I caught *Apatura iris*, my first Purple Emperor. I was twelve. I swished my net, pinched my prey firmly at the base of the wings, plunged it into the killer bottle. I can still smell it.' He raised his right thumb and forefinger to his nose, sniffed delicately. 'Lemon.'

How could he be so affectionate with one creature, I thought, and so deadly with another? Was that how men of science were?

Franz rose from his seat and strolled round the room, whisky glass in hand, examining the pictures and cabinets. I opened my notebook. *Wild man*, I wrote. *A new race of men. How much …* Franz was progressing slowly towards the curtain at the end of the room.

Dr Musgrave was telling Mr Bleeker that he had had another letter from someone in his troupe, a Mr Davis, who had offered his services to purchase collector's items anywhere in Australia where the tour was visiting. Mr Bleeker explained in a tight voice that Ned Davis was the agent of the troupe and there was a limit to his authority; if the doctor wished to do business, he must send his mail only to himself, the manager, he would provide an itinerary. Suddenly Dr Musgrave turned to Franz with a voice of command.

'Mr Richardson, don't open that curtain.'

Franz's hand, about to reach for the burgundy folds, drew back as if he had touched something red-hot.

'It conceals my most precious specimens,' the collector continued in a softer tone. 'I cover them to protect them from light, and also because, to the unscientific eye, some can appear … well, they are not for the eyes of the fair sex.' He smiled and nodded to me, and I folded my hands over my notebook. Then he turned back to Franz. 'You look like a young man of understanding. What do you know of passion?'

I felt a furious blush rising, covered my cheeks with the notebook.

Franz gave an innocent smile. 'I have a passion for music, sir. I play piano.'

'My dear mother played the piano,' said Dr Musgrave, his eyes twinkling again. They began to speak of sonatas and concertos and bagatelles. Franz perched on the edge of Dr Musgrave's desk, stroking Erasmus's crown of feathers while the collector fed the bird fragments of cake. Now Mr Bleeker prowled around the room, avoiding the curtain. My pencil flew over the page. Dr Musgrave had travelled to Europe, had been to concerts. Franz gasped when he revealed he had met Mr Liszt himself, had watched him play his *Dante* symphony with Saint-Saëns on two pianos at Gustave Doré's house in Paris ... How did you spell *Saint-Saëns*?

Then a hand reached across my page. 'Mary Ann,' said Mr Bleeker quietly, 'you don't need to write this down.' He raised his voice. 'Excuse me, doctor, we don't wish to detain you. Let's get back to the Wild Man. I can speak for Mr Barnum.'

'Of course. What a pinnacle of his profession he is, your employer. But let us understand our position. While I esteem him immensely, I am not of the same mind. He is primarily a collector of living curiosities, while I am a collector of the dead.'

'Well and good for science,' said Mr Bleeker, 'but nothing beats living curiosities. You should see the crowds for our wonderful performers.'

'Yet no performer lasts forever,' said Dr Musgrave. 'When he has gone to meet his maker, what remains of him but a few *cartes de visite*? But in a collection such as mine, marvels are preserved. Skeletons, full forms in formaldehyde, the creations of the taxidermist. I have been dabbling in the art of embalming. I like the sensation of driving the fluid inch by inch through the arteries, the veins, the lacy network of capillaries. The rubber bulb sucks and gasps as if the little creature were learning to breathe.' He paused, gazed at our stony faces; I gulped to keep down my bile. He sighed. 'I must sound macabre.'

'No, sir: scientific,' said Franz. 'First-rate science too, that lizard's a corker. I thought he was going to run up my arm.'

Dr Musgrave stroked the cockatoo's poll, stared at Franz. 'Gentlemen, I freeze time.' His words rumbled round the room, then faded until all I heard was the bird's clicking beak.

Then Mr Bleeker snorted. 'You're not telling me I should have my dear friend the General stuffed.'

The gentlemen laughed, Dr Musgrave loudest of all. 'No, no. And I am a specialist these days. I collect the young. They are most poignant. Would you care to see?' He stood and walked to a side cabinet, the cockatoo teetering on his shoulder, opened a drawer. The gentlemen peered inside, then Franz made way for me. The drawer was full of small skulls. They looked human, but too narrow, with low foreheads and elongated crowns. I wrote *Homo sapiens, New Britain, New Guinea.*

'The mothers bind their babies' heads with bark-cloth bandages, much as the Chinese bind their ladies' feet,' said Dr Musgrave. 'The infant skulls are soft. They take their new shape very quickly.'

Franz whistled. 'Say. How did you get 'em?'

Dr Musgrave reached into the drawer, held one skull up to the window as if it were a rare wine. 'This child was about eight months old. See how the light shines through?' On his shoulder, the cockatoo rocked back and forth. 'Bye-bye, bye-bye.'

Mr Bleeker gave it a furious glare, then stooped further towards the skulls in the drawer. I wrote Bark-cloth bandages.

'I think Mr Barnum deserves a wild Australian family,' said Dr Musgrave earnestly. 'I will do my best to procure one for you.'

A pause. Franz filled the gap. 'You are very kind, sir.'

'Not at all, Mr Richardson. I am a man in the grip of a passion' — he sighed — 'and I recognise a fellow sufferer. All I ask is that you bear my passion in mind. I crave the rare, the exquisite, the wonderful.' He had his hand on his heart. 'Above all, the young.'

I scribbled and scribbled, my eyes on the skulls. Fifteen of them, like eggs about to hatch.

Mr Bleeker straightened up. 'Come, Franz. Come, Mary Ann. My goodness, time flies. We'll be wanted at the theatre. Good day to you, doctor. Thank you for your time.' He strode at top speed out of the study, back through the rooms, ignoring the grins and snarls of the creatures in the glass cases, his coat-tails flying. Franz and I exchanged quick bewildered glances, then rushed to follow. Behind us came a demented screeching.

'Mr B!' called Franz. 'Wait! What is the matter? Is it your dyspepsia?'

We caught up with him on the doorstep, where he stood muttering in the rain, waving his arm to call the carriage he had hired for the journey. The horse splashed down the drive and we climbed in, Franz taking his employer's arm and holding the umbrella over his head as if he were an invalid.

All the time, in the rain, in the carriage, they argued. Mr Bleeker said he wouldn't trade with such a scoundrel for all the tea in China, and Franz insisted that the doctor was a capital fellow with a fine collection, and Mr Bleeker said it was nothing but pickled punks, and Franz said at least pickled punks did not have to pretend, to caper and gabble while people stared, and Mr Bleeker said that wasn't pretence, that was art, didn't he understand anything he'd been taught? At that, Franz took off his wet hat and pushed the brim around in his fingers. His hair was dry above where the brim had sat and wet below. I wanted to comb it all out and dry it in the sun.

'Shall I write you out a list of the doctor's marvels?' I asked Mr Bleeker. He held out his hand for the notebook, and I passed it over. He leafed through the pages, sighed, snapped it shut.

'Thank you, Mary Ann. You have a good hand. You've been diligent. Perhaps there were too many marvels. And by the by, you should leave the questions to us.'

I began my apologies, but Franz cut in. 'Perhaps she needed more precise instructions. And I am glad she asked questions: that shows initiative. I am curious myself. Tell me, Mrs Carroll, why did you ask about the Coming Man?'

A green spark leaped in his eyes as he leaned forward to me. Mr Bleeker frowned, rubbed his chest. I groped for words. 'I scarcely know, the phrase just took me.'

'It was a damned fine question for a man of science,' Franz said. 'That's the doctor to a T, isn't it? All those marvels, but he doesn't make a cent from them. And they are beyond hurting, are they not?' He turned to Mr Bleeker, who had his eyes fixed out the window, then back to me. 'Mrs Carroll, what do *you* think of his collection?'

'It is wonderful, quite extraordinary.' I spoke quickly, hardly thinking what I was saying. 'Of course I have not seen Mr Barnum's museum, but I have seen nothing like it.' Now both men leaned forward eagerly, staring at me, the representative of popular taste, and I felt pressed to say more. 'I wonder how he got all those poor creatures together?'

Mr Bleeker slapped his knee. 'Jove, she's hit the nail on the head. Thank you, young woman. As for you, dear Franz, you've still got a lot to learn about the wonder business. Think. Dr Musgrave opened a drawer. Showed us the heads of babes and little children. You asked the question yourself. How did he get them?'

Franz made as if to speak, then shook his head in bafflement, clapped his hat back on and stared out the window while Mr Bleeker brooded in his corner. We travelled back to Ballarat in rain and silence, and I thought of the great wall of burgundy and the skulls packed neatly in their nest. To my great surprise, I began to feel colder and colder.

CHAPTER 7

It was two days later when I slipped out the back gate of Craig's Hotel with a satin waistcoat of Charlie's in my basket, on my way to the haberdashery to buy new buttons. I had not exactly forgotten Dr Musgrave, but his mansion seemed like nothing but a fantastic dream, and there were much more solid prospects. I was wondering when I might share the piano stool again, and I almost felt like skipping through the puddles.

On the other side of the narrow street, two men were standing, watching me. Admirers of the little people, no doubt. These followers hung around the hotel at all hours, hoping to catch a glimpse of their heroes. But these two looked most particularly at me; one turned to the other, who nodded. Down-on-their-luck miners, to guess from their shabby red shirts, unkempt beards and trousers held up with string. Ballarat was full of them. Those who had enough money for grog shouted rude greetings at me, and a few came close enough in the crowded streets to brush their bodies against me. Yesterday one had grabbed at my breast, and Mrs Bleeker had bashed his arm with her umbrella until he ran away.

LITTLE PEOPLE

How I had wished that Franz was with us, to fend off the alligators.

These men did not shout or lurch towards me; they just stared. Should I duck back inside the gate? No, impudent strangers should not frighten me. Holding tight to my basket, I turned left and walked towards Lydiard Street, towards the shops and crowds. I heard footfalls and felt in my trembling muscles that they were following me. I walked faster, began to run, splashing through the puddles. The corner of Lydiard Street was a few yards away: I caught the shout of a distant spruiker, the rattle and clack of a carriage.

A hand grabbed my left arm, yanked me back. I screamed, swung my basket, kicked at invisible shins. Surely someone would hear and come running? Something seized my right arm, and a hand, stinking of tobacco, clamped round my mouth. I dug my teeth into the thumb. A yell, an oath.

'Bitch, you are scarce worth my hire.'

'Keep down yer noise,' said another voice. 'Let's go.'

With me pinioned between them, they frogmarched me back the way we had come. I began to shout and struggle, but something sharp pressed against my side.

'Try that again, Missus Carroll, and I'll cut you.'

Hearing my own name hissed at me was more frightening than feeling the tip of a knife. A boy carrying a sack over his shoulder ducked out of a doorway, and I turned to him in silent appeal, *help me, help me*, until the knife pricked the skin over my right hip. In a rush of panic I started forward until their arms dragged me back.

We walked on, not too brisk, two miners and their doxy taking the air. A force rose in my throat, choking me, suffocating me. I concentrated on my breathing — in, out, in, out — and kept up with their strides. Several twists down the network of alleys behind the hotel stood a covered hay wain with a horse in harness. Still holding my arm, the man with the knife let down the back of the wain and the other man stripped off the tarpaulin. He pushed a rag between my chattering teeth and tied the ends tightly behind my head, then took out a coil of rope and looped it round my wrists behind my back. I was nothing but jelly: at any moment the knife would slip between my ribs. Dear God, let it be quick, not too much pain. But they lifted me up and pushed me onto the floor of the wagon; and for a moment, too short, I felt nothing but wild relief. Then one of them held my head down, my face to the boards. Such a hand would not hesitate to press me to smothering. The boards trembled with the thump of hay bales piled around me. A sweet grassy tang, a whiff of horse dung, a shipboard smell of tar, a tobacco taste from my gag made me convulse in sneezes.

Rattling. Darker. The pressure on my head lifted, but I could not move, the bales were too close. More rattles and thumps, muffled; and then the wain lurched into movement. I lay sneezing and shivering, bracing myself against the heaves of the wagon. Now I could turn my head. Walls of hay in a dim green light. I rocked my body until the hay around me gave me space to sit up, and my head bumped canvas.

The worst thing was the slow speed of the wain. I wanted to make the horse fly, to get the ordeal over with, but what if they did more than ravish me? It was not money they wanted — they had ignored my basket and purse. Suppose they were keeping me alive only to put me through worse pain? And at the end, cut my throat?

My heart thundered in my ears and my breath came in gasps, but I forced myself to breathe in, out, in, out, deep and slow. *Think, think.* The rope that dug into my wrists was old, a little frayed: fronds tickled my palms. As I stared at the wain floor, the green light revealed a row of nails. One was not quite hammered in, it stuck out. I wriggled round until I had my back to it; my fingers felt for the metal, slipped the rope over, yanked. It was like trying to pull out a huge, tough thread from a canvas fabric, backwards, blindfolded. The rope kept slipping off the nail, my hands were slippery with sweat, but I looped the fronds back on, and slowly the tight twinings came apart. At last the rope gave far enough for me to slip one hand out, and soon I had the other hand free. I sat rubbing my wrists, then pushed at the heavy hay bales. They moved back a little, but the green light and the canvas over my head made me feel sunk in a sea where I could not break the surface. I began to gasp again through my gag. I pressed and punched at the canvas, slashed at it with my nails, but it would not give, and I sat back, heaving, wanting to claw my throat open. *You won't drown. Breathe through your nose. Think.*

Then it came to me. The men had had no time to lash down their load: they must have hooked the taut canvas over the back of the wain; all I needed to do was loosen it. I fought through the bales and felt along the upright board at the back end of the wain, tugged at the canvas folded over the board like a tightly made bed. A sudden slackening in my roof and a small triangle of day peeped at me, a pink light, an after-image from the green. I hauled hard: the canvas flapped back and I tore off my gag and drew in huge gusts of air in the dazzling pink light.

I wanted to shout for help, but there was no one to hear. We were rolling along between bare hills with an occasional copse of native trees. Behind me on the horizon was a haze of smoke and a glimpse of the huddle of brown buildings and shacks that was Ballarat, and still further away the pale flash of the tents around the mullock heaps. Ahead were the bales: I kneeled up and peered over them, saw the hats of the men, sitting at the front of the wain, nodding drowsily. At any moment, one would hear the flap of canvas, turn and discover me. I rolled to the edge of the wain, pulled myself up onto the low wooden parapet and stared at the muddy road passing slowly beneath me. As the wain lumbered over a rutty stretch of highway, I let myself drop, praying the ruts would distract the men and the mud would disguise and soften my impact. It still jarred. I landed on my feet, swayed, kept my balance, but the shock rushed up through my soles. I did not dare look behind me, but made my way quickly and silently to hunker down beside the road, behind a bush that did not offer much cover. I waited for the wain to stop, for the men to dismount, cursing, and haul me back into captivity; but the rumbling of their passage grew fainter, until all I heard was the *skark, skark* of cockatoos roosting in a nearby tree. The roosting tree flew up and danced around me, foul tastes filled my throat, my insides rose in revolt and splashed on the grass.

My burden. All the time the men had me, I had never given it a thought. Now I had vomited again, it was almost reassuring. As was its way, the nausea faded as suddenly as it came. I wiped my clammy face with my sleeve, my throat burning for clean water, and thought of the man who had growled as he held me. I had never had a proper look at either of them; all I knew was they were strangers. The man's words snarled in my head. *Bitch, you are scarce worth my hire.* Hire? Someone had hired him? And the way they had consulted each other, the nods, the naming of me: I was a bitch and I was also Missus Carroll. It was not that any young woman would do; someone must have described me most particularly to them.

Groaning, I staggered to my feet, still dizzy and weak, and all my left side ached, but I knew I must walk back to Ballarat while there was still light enough to see my way; and, because the men might still discover their loss and turn back, I would have to get off the road and cut across the hills. I imagined myself falling sobbing into Mrs Bleeker's arms. But what story should I tell? Someone in the troupe must have told these men about me, might even have hired them to abduct me. How else would these strangers have known of me?

I searched in my pocket for Mrs Bleeker's bottle of elixir, miraculously unbroken, and took a long swig. Then I brushed the worst of the mud from my clothes while the feather crests of the birds rose and the roosting tree shook with their screeches. It was all too hard to fathom. Maybe I was going back into the arms of an enemy. But there was nowhere else to go.

My legs worked well enough but, as I walked, my hands quivered and clenched, and my chest throbbed. At first I thought it fear. Then suddenly I knew what it was. *How dare they. Somehow, I will defeat them.* The storm in me all the more ferocious because it was not just for myself.

CHAPTER 8

I staggered back to the hotel, exhausted, bruised and muddy. Mrs Bleeker took one look at me and turned white under her freckles. I told her I had nothing worse than cuts and bruises.

'But what has befallen you?'

'Ruffians robbed me. The basket, the waistcoat, the money have gone —'

'Never mind that. Did they harm you? I will cowhide them with Rodnia's whip.'

'I am perfectly well.' But as I spoke, my head grew dizzy, and I swayed. Mrs Bleeker made me lie down while she fetched a tub and hot water, got me in and out of a bath, dressed me in a nightgown, fed me hot soup, talked to the hotel clerk and told me a doctor would come. And I succumbed gladly, though her rough hands scraped my skin.

Of course she wanted to know all. I told her briefly about the wain ride and my escape.

'White slavers,' she said through gritted teeth. 'It happens all the time in these rough mining towns with so few women. They abduct young females and use them for their evil ways.'

That too had been my first thought, but I remembered those names they called me. *Bitch, Missus Carroll.*

'They looked for me. They knew my name. And they said they were hired. Who could have hired them? Why?'

She shuddered. 'Best you don't know. You have had a miraculous escape, that's all. I blame myself for letting you out of my sight.'

'But someone must have told them about me — someone working in the Ballarat theatre, perhaps, or even in the troupe —'

'Poor child, your experience has robbed you of your senses. There is only one reason men would act so.'

'Will you tell the police?'

She sighed. 'I would like nothing better than to bring those rogues to justice. But my husband takes the view that nothing should be allowed to interfere with our itinerary, and here we are about to head off for Tasmania. Moreover, I do not think we should mention this dreadful episode to anyone. It would only upset them. Especially Mrs Stratton.'

'But —'

'Hush, dear.' She pulled the sheets around my shoulders, stroked my forehead. 'You must try to rest.'

I pushed the sheets off, closed my fists. 'I was special to them. I was not just any young girl. What is so special about me? What?'

She shook her head, smiled, put her fingers to her lips. At that moment, the doctor made his appearance, and I prepared myself for his probing and pummelling. But soon he pronounced all well: 'You will have a bonny one, missus. Sleep now.' And I was alone in the dark.

An enormous lethargy was creeping over me, yet I fought to stay awake. Someone in the troupe had stage-managed the ruffians and the wagon ride, I was more and more sure of it; but who kept this secret, and what was their purpose? Surely not Charlie and his wife, or Mrs Bleeker; all their interests lay in keeping me close and cared for. I had dared to construct a future that glowed and flickered in and out of focus like a magic lantern show. In moments of focus, I saw myself, containing the swelling under my ribs that I was beginning to think of as Belly. I sat with Belly, upright and dignified, against shadowy but solid drapes and furniture. Somewhere in the room, beyond the magic lantern's focus, was the little door that led to the New World.

Who was it, then, who threatened this future? Could it be Ned Davis? Was there that much malice in him?

Sooner or later, the one with the secret would act again. Then either I would know, or it would be too late. And with that uneasy thought, I drifted into sleep.

• • • • • • • •

When I woke, the dread was heavier in me. I could not recall my dream. I only knew it had been about my brother Robert. He was my eldest brother and he belonged to a much earlier time in my life. Now I see him as more than a bogeyman, I even feel sorry for him: when he was a child, he too must have felt abandoned and betrayed, and he never stopped looking for someone to blame. But when I was young, he was worse at some moments than the cholera. And yet he was my rescuer.

I did not meet him until I was eleven. For years I knew him

only as Bobby, a portrait of a serious young man with curly hair. There was a little version of him inside the silver locket Mother had given me, and a larger version on the mantelpiece next to the other strangers, Marian and Beatrice and James and Edward and Margaret and Hubert. They had all gone away to spread the Lord's word, Mother had told me.

When Bobby came from Nottingham, after Mother and Father were taken by the cholera, he was not Bobby anymore, but Mr Robert Teasdale, Esquire, owner of a fine cotton mill. Most of his curly hair had disappeared. He had Molly spread white powder on the bedroom floors and the stairs, had all the sheets and towels and clothes burned one by one in the stove. Molly and Mrs Utley fed them into the flames with wooden tongs. Then he had the beds and mattresses and shoes taken away in a handcart. While the rectory still stank of charcoal and tar and that strange white powder, Mr Robert had Molly sweep and scrub the floors and stairs and the front steps and path. He turned out the drawers and cupboards, brought in men to pack up the clock and the mahogany table, got Mrs Utley to pack silver and china from the dining-room cabinet. Now the rectory smelled of soap and sawdust.

One morning I saw Mr Robert come out of Father's study carrying something in his hands. I followed him to the parlour. He placed it on the mantelpiece, next to the pictures of Bobby and the other brothers and sisters. I stared at the new picture, a watercolour portrait of a strange lady with a wishy-washy smile and old-fashioned ringlets.

'Who's that?'

'Mrs Teasdale.' His voice was unusually soft.

'Your wife?'

Mr Robert gave me a sharp look. 'It is a portrait of Mother.'

'*That* isn't Mother.'

My voice must have been loud with scorn. Mr Robert frowned. 'Mary Ann, you are ill-behaved. Go to your room.'

'You're not my master. I won't go.'

Mr Robert looked as if he would strike me. Then to my surprise, he swept out of the room.

Mrs Utley explained that Mr Robert's mother, the lady in the portrait, was the first Mrs Teasdale. She had married Father when he was first ordained and had given birth to four boys and three girls. Some years later, she took ill and died, and Father had been so grieved by her death he forbade anyone to speak of her. Very shortly afterwards, he had taken Mother as his second wife.

'So is that why Mr Robert doesn't like me? Because I'm not his sister?'

'Don't be silly. You are his half-sister, he loves you.'

'Where are the others? Marian and Beatrice and James and Edward and Margaret and Hubert?'

Mrs Utley's breath wheezed. She raised her palms as if pushing against the air. 'Go to Mr Robert, apologise to him. He is your guardian and he knows what is best for you.'

When I found Mr Robert in the study, sitting at Father's desk, I wanted to knock him from the chair, but I remembered what Mrs Utley had said, gave him a deep curtsey, said I was sorry I had been so wicked, but I had not understood about the two Mrs Teasdales.

'If you do not understand, you should ask politely. One does not like to see impertinent little girls.' His voice had the grate of small waves on the shingle at the Thames's edge.

'Yes. I did wrong. Please forgive me.'

'So, Mary Ann.' He pushed back Father's chair, his hands behind his head. 'What is to become of you?' I understood he did not expect an answer, but my eyes moved to Father's globe of the earth, and I imagined it thrumming under my fingers.

'I want to see the world.'

'Wanting is the sin of covetousness.'

Mr Robert talked on, and I do not remember all his words. His voice was quiet and reasonable, but it grated. He said I should go to a good boarding school in London, a place of discipline. If I did not learn my lessons, if he heard of any more outbursts, he would take me away to a place where they would beat all the pride out of me.

• • • • • • • •

When I was seventeen and about to leave school, I received a summons to the headmistress's study, and there he was, shorter than I remembered, with more stomach and even less hair.

The headmistress excused herself, said she would leave us together, a brother and sister should have time to talk. As the door closed, I wondered for a moment who this brother and sister could be. Mr Robert stared at me, and I met his gaze steadily; we had not looked upon each other for six years. His head shone like a pink apple. He was the first to break eye contact; he walked around me and I could feel his eyes on me from the side, from behind. When he had completed his circuit and faced me again, he was chewing a thumbnail, a little red in the face.

'I expected a young lady. But I did not expect …'

'Are you displeased with me, Mr Robert?'

'Quite the contrary.'

'I have turned out well, have I not?'

'You have turned out splendidly.' He cleared his throat. 'At least, that is what your teachers say. You are a paragon, it appears.'

'I have enjoyed my lessons.' I looked down modestly. 'I like the other girls, and the teachers have been kind.'

Mr Robert rubbed his hands together, sat down in the headmistress's chair, just as he had sat in Father's chair all those years before. How like Humpty Dumpty he looked. 'And what is to become of you now?'

I was dizzy with the sense that this scene had played before. I looked round for Father's globe of the earth, to send it spinning beneath my fingers; but there were only bookshelves, an inkwell on the desk, and the headmistress's academic gown, a black pelt hanging on the back of the door.

'I want … I mean, I thought I might teach.'

'Excellent idea.' He put his elbows on the desk. 'Sara and Elizabeth are of an age to benefit from some rigorous instruction. Adam and John are a little wild, but boys will be boys. They need to sit down every morning and attend to their books.'

'Oh, Mr Robert, I did not mean …' I knew of his children from the letters he had written me from Nottingham each Christmas. Every now and then a letter announced a new birth. I would sit reading the letter by the stove in the school basement, wrapped in a shawl, eating my Christmas orange. The other girls had all gone home by then, only a caretaker and a couple of maids remained, and the classrooms were barren expanses of floorboards that creaked with shock at the passing of my feet. He always wrote that Mrs Teasdale was indisposed but there were strong hopes of improvement. Then he wrote how the cotton trade was doing and how his house alterations were going, and hoped that his sister was in good health and remembering their father in her prayers. I would write back promptly with best wishes and many questions, and then would wait eleven months for his next letter.

'Bed and board in our house,' Mr Robert continued. 'You may eat in the nursery with the children. Mutton and gruel and tea, a wholesome diet. Mrs Teasdale must on no account be disturbed. We have a bright little bedroom under the eaves; one can stand upright by the door.'

'Mr Robert, I have always appreciated your generosity.'

'And so you should. I have spent a pretty sum on you these last six years. One day off a month, shall we say.'

'Mr Robert —'

'Well, I must be quiet, I shall offer you the moon if I go on so, but it is not often I come across such an accomplished young lady.' That grating laugh again. He got to his feet and resumed his circling.

I took a deep breath, opened my mouth, and he lifted one finger. It was the same way Father had lifted his index finger before he spoke his words of wisdom.

'There is just one thing. Are you tractable?'

'Tractable?' A picture came to me of horses straining in harness.

'I think your education would make you familiar with that word. Tractable, biddable, docile, compliant, governable. A governess should be governable.' He snickered at his little joke.

'I don't know what you mean.'

'The last time I saw you, you were not tractable at all. You shouted wicked words at me.'

'I was a child and you were taking everything away. How was I to know I could trust you?'

'Not trust your own brother?' He stopped his pacing in front of me and stared close into my eyes — I smelled Worcestershire sauce on his breath. The dark bristles on his chin seemed strange against the smooth surface of his head.

'You are not my brother.' He stepped back. 'I have a brother. He is young and handsome and he has beautiful curly hair, he looks after me, and he doesn't worry about whether I am tractable.'

'I've had enough of this nonsense.' Mr Robert hit the desk with his fist. 'You monstrous ungrateful girl. You want this, you want that, you are all greed and capriciousness.'

'There is nothing wrong with wanting,' I protested.

'Don't you understand? You are in no position to want anything.'

I glared at him, fingering the silver locket around my neck, half expecting Mr Robert to reach out and pull it away, but he sat down in the headmistress's chair again. He slumped over the desk, his hand over his eyes. Father had sat in just that pose one night, after a visit to the unfortunate; Mother stood and stroked his shoulder while muttering spilled from his beard. *They don't deserve the Lord, they pawn our gifts for gin. Reek of it, the children too, God damn the whole tribe of them.*

'Perhaps you think I was badly brought up,' I said in a softer voice. 'But you must not think badly of Father. I saw how Mother loved him and supported him, even when he could not support himself, when he said bad things …'

'You take me for a fool. You insult the memory of our father, who never said or did a bad thing in his life. Who was left alone to die.'

'He did not die alone.' I could feel the blood draining from my face. 'I was with him.'

He shut his eyes, put his hands over his ears. I waited for him to listen, I still had so much to say. He began to mutter, with his eyes still shut. 'Is this what a fine new education does for a girl?' He opened his eyes, lowered his hands from his ears, stood and made for the door. As he brushed past me, I put my hand on his arm to stay him and he shook it off as if I were a street beggar. Then he turned, raised his index finger again. 'I have done all I could for you because you are my father's daughter, but there is too much of your mother in you after all.'

'I don't want your job anyway.'

'Want, want! Go out on your own into the hard world then, Miss Insolence, and see how you like it.' For a moment he paused, his hand on the door. He would not look at me. 'I should have thrown you out of the rectory with the boots and shoes.'

From the headmistress's window, I watched him stride down the pavement, his tall hat covering his baldness, abristle with rectitude. I clutched my hands together to stop them trembling. As Mr Robert receded, thinned, became one dark streak among many under the watery London sky, I felt in my veins the thrumming of Father's globe.

Not long afterwards, with glowing references from the school,

I obtained an interview with the Female Middle-Class Emigration Society, whose good ladies arranged my passage and lent me money to travel to Melbourne, Victoria, and seek a post as governess. Which led me eventually to Matilda, and her papa.

But it was not Matilda and her papa who invaded my head and my dreams at that time, when our tour truly reached the end of the earth, a town called Oatlands in Tasmania, and music drew me into the coach house.

CHAPTER 9

The music that lured me was a simple étude I had played with my pupils, but here the notes flowed in a way I had never mastered. At the centre of the empty floor squatted the piano, and Franz Richardson possessed it while chaff swirled around his knees. Mr Bleeker had arranged to have a piano brought over on a cart from Oatlands' largest public house for the day's performance. Later in the day, the troupe would improvise a stage, for there was no theatre in this town, a scattering of sandstone houses and barns dropped onto the green Tasmanian plain.

As I stood in the doorway, he looked up and smiled at me, and with a jolt I felt very well, for the first time in weeks, and full of energy. Perhaps it was the elixir Mrs Bleeker had given me; or perhaps it was crossing Bass Strait on the steamer *Tamar*, a journey that had reduced the ladies to bundles of misery. I had loosened their stays, raised their heads and given them water, held them as they heaved into tin buckets. Then I had wiped their faces and sat and fanned them with their own fans. It was as if my sickness had passed into them and out the portholes, to be lost in the strait.

Oblivious to the chaff storm, Franz seemed too large for his instrument, like a full-grown man trying to ride one of Rodnia's miniature ponies. He narrowed his eyes, peered at the notes. Was he too vain to wear spectacles? He had much to be vain about. Abruptly he broke off playing, patted the seat beside him on the long stool. 'It is most good of you to come, Mrs Carroll. I must learn a new piece, and you can turn the pages for me.'

That melodious voice again, only the faintest American accent. Should I sit down alone with this man? But it was part of my duties. So I sat, arranging my shawl over Belly. I always wore my shawl in those days, even when the weather was warm.

Franz embarked on a jaunty tune and I watched again the russet hair, the pale skin, the green-apple eyes. The chaff rose and settled on my skirt.

'The good folk of Oatlands have been pouring their ale on the strings,' he said, relapsing into disjointed chords. 'I never thought when I left the conservatory that I would be sitting in a stable at the ends of the earth playing *Walking down Broadway*.' He gave a short laugh, lifted his hands. 'Good piano hands, d'you see? Broad, with long fingers. Thumb loose in the socket. A good spread.' His right hand sprawled across the keys. 'Here, you try.'

Hesitantly I picked out a few bars of a piece from *The Well-tempered Clavier*.

'Bravo, Mrs Carroll. Nature has not blessed you with a good spread, yet you manage very well.' He placed his cool professional hands over mine: I told my racing heart he was being a good teacher. His trim white nails extended over several more keys than I could reach. 'Mr Liszt is the great master of the spread. There have never been such hands; he has taken plaster casts of them. His secret is that he has almost no webbed material between the fingers.' He picked up my hand, splayed my fingers. 'You are not so lucky. Your hand is a veritable mermaid's.'

'They called me Froggy at school.' I made myself laugh. 'I don't think you can have seen a mermaid, Mr Richardson.'

'I have seen the Feejee mermaid in Mr Barnum's museum. Her hands are nothing like as pretty as yours.'

I frowned, withdrew my hand, then worried that by taking it away I had made the fleeting touch important.

'Don't think me impertinent,' he said, 'I merely admire fine hands when I see them. But what happened to your wrists?' He was looking at the red marks where my captors' rope had dug into the flesh.

I mumbled something about tight cuffs.

He smiled. 'It is such a pleasure to have you with us, Mrs Carroll. It is most beneficial for the troupe — and for the General and his lady, of course. And I enjoy your assistance' — he gave me a swift glance — 'and your company.'

And I enjoy yours, I wanted to say, but could think of no ladylike way to say it. 'It is beyond beneficial for me to be with the troupe, I assure you.'

'I was sorry to hear of your bereavement, and I fear there is no way we poor entertainers can lighten that load. But we can help you pass the time.'

Why did he address me as if I were a bored lady? Was this mockery?

'If we are to share a seat,' he went on, 'you might call me Franz.'

'Franz,' I said softly. 'A beautiful name. Is it German?'

'Oh, I am entirely Yankee, I assure you. My parents gave me a rather dull name. I changed it in honour of my hero and my dreams. You know, once I dreamed of a solo career.'

'Like Mr Heller the Prestidigitator at the Theatre Royal?'

'Ah, Mr Heller. Did you know he played the piano for Mr Liszt when he was twelve years old?'

'He is a wonderful pianist.'

Franz shrugged. 'Yet see what he has come to. A mountebank with a box of tricks and bullets in his teeth, playing funny medleys and a thumping *Anvil Chorus* so the hoi polloi can join in with their boots on the floor.'

'The General was very taken with him. He loved the shooting trick.'

'I want something better than that,' said Franz. 'Recitals on stage before the crowned heads of Europe. World tours. People pursuing me in the street. Women sobbing at my feet.'

Was he mocking himself now? 'You are not so far out,' I said. 'You are on a world tour, people shout in the street and crowd to the shows.'

'But not to see me. To hear the crashing chord when a little man falls on his behind.' He brushed the chaff off the keys with his sleeve, closed the piano lid. 'You would not believe it, but I was the outstanding student of my year. Everyone predicted a glowing future for me. And then I was wronged. I do not believe any man was ever so wronged.'

'Wronged?'

'I do not speak of it, I let it lie deep.' He slumped on the piano lid, his face in his hands. 'What does the world care? So I am cheery and obliging, but it glows still, a coal in my heart, it will not be damped down.' Now his voice was dark and thick, choked with feeling. I almost reached out to take his hands from his face. Then he rubbed his eyes and looked up at the rafters. 'I fell back on teaching young ladies the piano, and together we would mangle *Autumn Leaves* or *Lightly Tripping*. I am sure you know all about that.'

I grimaced. 'I never want to hear another scale again.'

He laughed. 'Yes, and I never want to see another young miss fidget and twirl on the piano stool and smear toffee on the keys.'

'Oh yes. I had such a student, Matilda. She was a minx. Whenever I reprimanded her, she said she would tell her papa, and he would be displeased with me.'

'And was he, the terrible papa?'

I frowned and folded my hands. I must be more careful: he made me feel I could tell him anything.

Franz cleared his throat. 'And you taught other subjects? Poetry? The English poets, I suppose. Keats? Tennyson?'

'Very little poetry. I know only Cowper and Gray. And a Shakespeare sonnet or two … But pray continue your story.'

'Ah, the young misses … Of course I hoped even then to do better. I had a patron, a wealthy widow. I called her Madame. I handled some business for her, I escorted her to operas and recitals and afterwards she would peer at me through her jewelled lorgnettes and say, "You can do better, Mr Richardson, we must arrange your debut."' I laughed at his imperious quaver. 'And I would shake my head,' he continued. 'Secretly thrilled, poor praise-starved beast that I was, at her flattery.'

'So did she arrange your debut?'

'Yes, a small recital at her house before New York's most eminent critics. And then — you will scarcely credit this — I was wronged. Again.'

'But this is a dreadful tale,' I cried out. 'Who wronged you, and what did they do to you?'

Franz frowned, closed his eyes. 'It is painful still.'

'I'm sorry.'

'Don't be. You are kindness itself to listen to my tale of woe. Let me tell you the outcome. There was no recital. Madame dropped me, my students' parents dropped me. It was only thanks to the kindness of Mr Bleeker that I found employment with the General's troupe.'

'So it has been hard for you.'

He shrugged. 'I have seen the world, I have spent years braving danger and hardship, playing music that makes *Lightly Tripping* seem like a work of genius, upon primitive instruments, for people whom the world regards as oddities. But they are honourable people, and I have not abandoned hope … What about you, Mrs Carroll? Have you been wronged?'

Mrs Bleeker's words about Franz came back to me. *He rescued Mrs Stratton from an alligator in a swamp.* I imagined Franz hurling stones at a row of yellow teeth. Surely he would be a better rescuer than Robert ever was.

'I don't know if I have been wronged,' I said. 'That is for others to judge. But you have made me think of the time my brother came and took things away.'

And so I told the story to Franz, to the point where Robert sent me away to school. I tried to be fair, explaining how generous he had been, how he had paid to send me to an excellent school for young ladies in London. But I could not resist adding that I had to stay at school during the holidays: 'I was too loud.'

'That is monstrous. Why, you are the quietest, sweetest-natured little lady. Were he not your brother, I would call him a —'

'Hush, Franz.'

'Please forgive me, I should not have said that. And when you left school?'

'Mr Robert offered me a post as governess. But it did not … come about.'

'Poor little mermaid. How was it there was no one to save you?' He had chaff on his shoulders, in his hair. 'But of course someone did save you: the estimable Mr Carroll.'

'Yes.' I could think of nothing more to say but lies. There was a long silence.

'Let me play you some real music,' said Franz. He lifted the piano lid, closed his eyes, his fingers rippled. The notes floated, cascaded, and a softness rose from deep in me, way below Belly, until it prickled behind my eyes. At last Franz broke off, his hands suspended, and a fading chord hung around us. 'That was a little Liszt, Mrs Carroll.'

'You might call me Mary Ann. Everyone else does.'

'*Liebestraum*, Mary Ann. Love's dream.' He rested his splayed hands on his thighs, and I thought of the hands of Matilda's papa, warming themselves pink at the drawing-room fire. Then I looked away, across the floor, as if the notes would still be drifting with the chaff.

'It is important to have dreams,' Franz said. 'But our lives need more solid foundations. I am glad you will be well provided for — though I daresay signing all those documents was very tedious.'

'Documents?' I stared at him. 'I have signed nothing. Why, should I have?'

'What, nothing?' Now he seemed surprised. 'But in Mr Barnum's employ, it is usual ... I must have misunderstood. No matter. What you have is a gentleman's agreement, then.' He smiled. 'And you can't get much more gentlemanly than the General.'

'Yes, of course. But I confess, you've worried me a little.' I tried to laugh at my foolish worries. 'Should I ask for documents, I know so little of these things ...'

'I am quite sure that will not be necessary. As long as you are content with their plans. Tell me, what will happen to you and ...' His eyes ran over the folds of my shawl, and I tingled as if he were touching me. I told him what Mrs Bleeker had explained, and my options: to stay with Charlie, his wife and their child; or to go out on my own, with a generous settlement and my pick of prospects.

'And what will you choose?'

'Once the infant is well established, I will take the settlement and go out on my own. They won't need me, and I shall be free.'

Damn my red cheeks. What a thing to say to an unattached young man, he must think me a brassy widow prospecting for her next husband.

'Ah, freedom. Independence,' said Franz. 'I hoped for those things too once. And I do have prospects. Perhaps, one day ...' He glanced sideways at me, and my heart began to race again. Then his eyes dropped. 'But you know, most of the time, I just tickle the keys. That's what they want.'

∙ ∙ ∙ ∙ ∙ ∙ ∙ ∙

Cock crow, grey light, and I lay on a pile of grain sacks, stiff and sore and itchy. No one in Oatlands could provide us with an inn or beds. I had gone to my makeshift pallet with my head full of *Liebestraum*, but the music had soon faded, and I had lain awake, feeling again the lurches of the wain, smelling the hay, turning the questions over.

Now I made a memorandum in my head. Item One: Ned was a troublemaker. He might have hired ruffians to get me out of the way because I had spied on his games with George, stopped his sabotage of Charlie's speech.

Item Two: More likely something to do with Belly.

Item Three: Would George try to spite Charlie by stealing away the mother of his child?

Item Four: If Lavinia had a baby to care for, she might retire, and the tours would end. Was Mr Bleeker so devoted to raising money for Mr Barnum that he would see the child as a threat to the show?

Item Five: What if I had underestimated Minnie's skittishness? What if she was so set in rebellion against her sister that she could rob her of an infant?

Item Six: Could I rule out anyone? What of Franz Richardson, or Rodnia Nutt? I could not summon up even the shadow of a motive, but who knew what really went on in a man's head?

Item Seven: Back to Ned. He had told me I could make a mint.

So could he, if he kidnapped me and sold me to those that would *pay very handsome*. But why was Belly so valuable?

Item Eight: Perhaps there was no adoption plan. Perhaps Mrs Bleeker had spoken only to comfort me, before they tried to dispose of me. Perhaps they would try again.

It seemed so unlikely. And yet I had dreamed of unseen hands peeling me open from ribs to groin and yanking out a raw, bleeding lump. I shivered, groaned.

Enough brooding. I rose, fetched water for the ladies.

We spent the morning packing to move to the next town, Green Ponds, a place with no piano. Franz had persuaded Mr Bleeker to buy the Oatlands piano and take it with us, and it was his task to supervise the loading onto a baggage coach. When I passed the knot of men, I saw a flash of auburn hair and heard the creak of ropes and much swearing.

The troupe ate a luncheon of cold boiled beef and potatoes around a battered deal table brought out onto the gravel. Beyond the few buildings stretched vast oat fields and endless ranked clouds. Franz was still battling with his piano and did not join us. Charlie was morose and silent, and retired early. The usual bunch of children watched us with grave fascination. George pretended not to notice, but every now and then he flung bits of bread in their direction, and they competed with the pigeons to get it.

Mr Bleeker read out the names of our Tasmanian destinations: Green Ponds, Brighton, Richmond, Hobart Town, New Norfolk, Hamilton, Bothwell, Longford, Deloraine, Launceston.

'Full of chaff, the lot of 'em,' muttered Ned. He was cradling an animal skin in his lap as if it were a pet. He would not let it out of his sight. Before Mr Bleeker had arrived at the table, he had told George it was a rare hide from a Tasmanian tiger and he planned to send it to a collector in Ballarat. 'I'll make a mint, the doctor is mad for such odd critters.'

George had sniffed at it, scratched the hair. 'Smells rare, boyo, but how d'you know those stripes aren't painted on?'

'Musgrave'll know it's the real thing,' said Ned. 'We send letters back and forth — he's keen as mustard.'

So Ned had done deals behind Mr Bleeker's back after all, even though he hadn't gone on our visit to Athena Hall. Had he made a secret visit himself? What else might he be saving for the doctor?

Mr Bleeker was saying something about a tight schedule. 'Mustn't get behind. Have to catch the steamer back to the mainland on the 27th. Must be in Adelaide by August 8th. May have to cross the desert to get there in time.'

'We can manage a desert crossing,' said Lavinia calmly.

I looked up at the pale sun, felt the cool breeze, and then I heard hoofbeats from beyond the yard. Rodnia was exercising Zep, cantering up and down the flat. I had scarcely seen him since the day in Ballarat when I had thought to rescue him from his horse. Now he rode high on the bay's back with his legs tucked up, like a jockey, but with more strength and bulk, and it seemed he and Zep were both part of some great beast of silky tan. As they wheeled, he caught my eye, and raised one hand.

When we were about to depart, Rodnia approached me and beckoned me to join him on the box seat of one of the baggage carriages. If I could not ride with Franz, I decided, Rodnia would make a pleasant companion.

As the convoy lumbered out onto the road, the folk of Oatlands cheered and waved their hats. Dogs yapped and darted under the wheels. Rodnia clicked his tongue. The little walnut barouche was strapped into place on the platform behind him, and he sat on a sack of straw that made him as tall as me in my seat. He had cleaned his boots.

'Nero and Sultan,' he said, indicating the two brawny beasts in the shafts. 'Not like Zep. No brains. Prodigious pull.'

'I am sorry I didn't come and let you teach me how to make Zep wild, Mr Nutt,' I said. 'I never had a moment.'

'They work you too hard.'

True enough, I thought, but it would do no good to complain of it. 'Didn't you say Zep came from a circus?'

'Yep, and so did we. Mr Lillie's travelling circus and show of wonders. My brother was fifteen then. Tiny George Washington Nutt, the Smallest Man in God's Creation. Along with Zoltan the Hungarian Equestrian, Sigmund the Living Skeleton and a Sapient Bear that never got a name.'

'And you?'

'I didn't have a name neither.'

We rode between hedgerows, but Rodnia was back in New Hampshire, under flapping canvas. His gruff voice grew softer as he looked out over Nero and Sultan's bobbing heads.

'Mr Lillie, he was always bellyaching about my brother. Said Tiny George was rude to the punters. Said one gent wanted his money back because George had done a thing before his wife he'd blush to name. George said all he'd done was slip off his coat and weskit and shirt to show them the hairs on his chest because she sneered he was a half-grown boy. "Why, Mr Lillie," he cried, "what would you have me show them?" So I told Mr Lillie I'd learn my brother manners. I asked George, what's all this bull about hairs on your chest? You know what he showed me? A sticky chest wig. He'd got fur off the Sapient Bear and stuck it on with gum.'

'Your brother is a very funny fellow,' I said. 'But what did *you* do?'

'Ran errands. Fed and groomed the horses. Bound the Hungarian to Zep. Propped up, pulled down canvas and poles. Scoured saucepans. Lured the Sapient Bear into its horsebox. Scrubbed mushy apples and poo out of its cage. I was good at everything, except stopping George.'

Rodnia began to tell me of an idea George had had for a new act. His purpose was to make me laugh at George's antics, but I was laughing at Rodnia's way of telling the story. He sat up straight, his tone solemn, and then such voices sidled out of him: George's squeaky tenor, the slurring drunk and the rude boys in the audience, Mr Lillie's growls when he found out about the act and stopped it.

'So it was only a matter of time,' Rodnia said. 'The word went out, and Mr Bleeker found us. There was a lawyer powwow for months, but I always knew we'd end up with Mr Barnum. The thirty-thousand dollar Nutt, they called George. That was what Mr Barnum paid for him, with me thrown in.'

The horses had ambled almost to a standstill. Rodnia sat up, flapped the reins, and they picked up pace. 'I heard you rescued the show one night,' he said. 'Pulled the curtain before my brother had a chance to disgrace the General. That was well done.'

'But I don't suppose I pleased the Commodore.'

Rodnia laughed. 'He'll get over it, and you'll be the last person he'll blame. My brother is not a bad man, ma'am. Just bold and mischievous. And a mite prone to bad influence.' He frowned and fell silent.

I did not need to ask him where the bad influence came from. 'Do you mind me asking what happened to your leg?' I said.

'Fell from the trapeze.'

'Were you an acrobat?'

'Not me. I put up the apparatus and tested it for Miss Emmeline. She was the trapeze artiste, a dandy one.' His cheeks were a little red.

· · · · · · · ·

'I had this trick. I'd jump from one hanging rope to another and catch it. Just my own private thing, nobody ever saw it. But that day … My mind wandered off, and I missed.'

'You should have performed in the circus.'

'I'm not made to perform. I'm not made for a lot of things.'

I could not bear the wistful note in his voice. 'You're a funny fellow too, Mr Nutt, in your quiet way. Why don't you perform with your brother?'

'I take it very kindly you say that, ma'am. But that's not my job — I'm the big brother. D'you have brothers or sisters?'

'Seven of them. But I only knew one.'

We fell silent, and Rodnia lit his clay pipe, cupping it against a side wind. The convoy had spaced out, and we were in a dense stand of eucalypts. Branches crowded over our heads.

'Which one did you know?' said Rodnia.

I explained to him how I had met Mr Robert. Strange, that only a day before I had told the same story to Franz Richardson, but this time it came out differently. I looked at Rodnia's attentive face, told him of the days I had spent caring for Mother and Father when they had the cholera, and as I spoke I became proud of my childish industry.

'God in heaven,' he murmured.

'It was not so bad. I didn't have time to think. I thought I would beat the cholera with soap and eau de Cologne.'

Rodnia smiled. 'There you are. Rescuing again.'

'But I didn't rescue them.'

'Men aren't always as tough as we think,' said Rodnia, watching me closely behind his pipe. 'And women are sometimes tougher than we think.'

'But I was telling you of my brother ...' The trees were thinning out: we were entering oat fields again. I told Rodnia of my second argument with Mr Robert, in the headmistress's study, the day I left school and he left me. It took a long time to tell. At last I fell silent, my throat hoarse and my hands trembling as I waited for Rodnia to speak. Why had I poured out such long stories of Robert to Franz and Rodnia? Why had I not spoken to Mrs Bleeker instead? And why was Rodnia so silent? Did he think me an ungrateful hoyden?

Rodnia frowned, opened his mouth, then stuck his pipe between his teeth and puffed like a steam engine. Behind us came the thud of hooves, the rattle of wheels.

I looked over my shoulder. The other baggage carriage was gaining on us. Ned sat on the box, Tasmanian tiger skin at his side, giddying up his animals, and behind him loomed a pile of trunks and a canvas-shrouded piano shape. The road was wider here and as Ned attempted to pass, Rodnia dropped back and waved him on. As the carriages rode abreast, I looked past Ned's bowler and saw Franz perched beside him on the box seat, his coat collar turned up round his ears, a cigarette in his gloved left hand. He would not leave his beloved piano. He balanced a leather satchel topped by a notepad on his lap and was busy scribbling. He looked up briefly, then stared with utter astonishment at me. I smiled, waved, and Ned smirked, touched two fingers to his hat brim. I tried to shout a greeting, but the horses and wheels made too much noise. Franz glowered at me, then at Rodnia, then back at me. The way his eyes flickered suddenly reminded me that Rodnia was a man who came up to my armpit.

· · · · · · · ·

At Green Ponds, Rodnia drove his carriage into the stableyard of the little inn where we would stay the night. Not even a dog was about. We were the first of the convoy to arrive: Ned's carriage must have gone to the theatre to unload the piano and stage props. Nero and Sultan stood, damp flanks heaving, as Rodnia jumped down — always agile, despite his limp. He rolled up his sleeves: there was a line across the strong forearms where the tan stopped and a mysterious paler skin began. He reached out a hand to me. 'Careful. Remember you're the goose.'

I took his warm hand, stepped down, rested against the carriage wheel, watched a flash of cockatoos overhead, heard a great screeching, and then the scrapes and thumps of Rodnia as he climbed onto the canvas-shrouded baggage.

'Why won't the General and his lady talk to me about the baby?' I said.

'They're mad for smaller and smaller men,' Rodnia muttered, loosening the ropes. 'Think it's like breeding ponies.' His words seemed more like a private meditation than an answer to my question. 'Smaller and smaller. At the birth, the midwife must wear opera glasses. His first cradle is a tumbler. They must use a magnet to find him in the bedclothes, an ear trumpet to hear him cry.'

'I beg your pardon, Mr Nutt?'

'Rodnia, please … That's how my brother was when he was born. Or so they said. A bab who could up and crush mosquitoes in his fists like Hercules crushed the snakes.'

Something in his nonsense made me think of the way Father had tested me on Scripture, and I could recall the page of the Bible, the thin paper and velvet bookmark, and almost, but not quite, the words.

'What are you saying, Rodnia? Is it about the adoption?'

He had climbed up on the luggage pile, his back to me, bare arms level with the top of my head. Muscles rose like waves under his skin. I reached out and tapped him on the shoulder. He turned his head slowly towards me.

'Tell me, please,' I said. 'What exactly do they want from me?'

'A little bab.'

He held on to the ropes with one hand and reached towards me with the other, as if about to do a circus trick. The sinews stretched on his bare arm, the low sun haloed the gold-brown hairs. I thought he would seize me, crush me to his leather vest in a wrestler's or

161

a lover's embrace, and I shook with something I had not felt when Franz had put his manicured hands over mine at the piano.

Rodnia's hand hovered and stopped an inch from my hair. 'What exactly d'you want from them?' he said.

'Freedom. Independence. A chance to have whatever I want.'

'You'll get that.' His voice was gruff, dismissive. He dropped his hand, and I felt suddenly ashamed of the way I had tapped his shoulder.

'I must go and get things ready for the ladies.'

Rodnia nodded, turned back to the ropes. A flap of canvas came loose and the horses snorted. 'Hey there, Nero, Sultan, I'll be with you in a mo.' He spoke softly. 'We want you tractable, don't we? But it don't do you good to be too tractable. Wears you down, takes away your spirit.'

When he had told his circus stories, I had admired his will to do anything in the world for his little brother. Now I thought that if Tiny George asked him, Rodnia would hire ruffians to kidnap a young woman, bundle her up on a wain and take her God knows where.

I began to walk away, and he shouted after me: 'No one says a word against you, ma'am. And if they did, I wouldn't let them.'

CHAPTER 10

A passing bird might have seen us thus: a great desert of sand and scrubby hillocks, a mail-coach track. Two carriages with hired drivers, drawn by four horses; three full-sized men; one smallish man; two little men; and a gliding jellyfish of many colours, consisting of four overlapping parasols draped with lightweight shawls, petticoats and skirts, loosely sewn together and dangling almost to the ground.

But I saw nothing of this, for within our moving tent all was dim. We had ended our Tasmanian tour and had taken the steamer back to Melbourne, and now we were en route to Adelaide — the hard way. Mrs Bleeker and I held aloft the parasol handles, one in each hand, and peered ahead between flapping veils at the track, while Lavinia and Minnie walked between us. We had constructed our makeshift harem to hide the ladies from the glaring eye overhead. On our third day of crossing the desert, the troupe planned to travel thirty miles to Coolootoo station. The ladies could have ridden on the coaches, but had volunteered to walk some of the way to save the horses. Sometimes we paused to pass around the water bottle and shake the sand out of our boots and stockings, and from time to time we regrouped so that I had the support of the sisters' hands under my elbows. Sometimes, when their arms brushed against Belly, I felt a ripple.

Mr Hutchings, the proprietor of the mail coach, had come twenty miles to Melbourne to advise Mr Bleeker not to try to cross the desert between the settlements of western Victoria and South Australia. 'You cannot travel more than twelve or fifteen miles in a day,' he had told us all. 'Your horses will be up to their middles in sand. You will have to carry provisions and feed for them and pass the night in your coaches. It will be blistering by day and freezing by night.'

Mr Bleeker had explained again that the troupe needed coaches and horses in South Australia. He would send the two miniature ponies and the walnut barouche by sea, but for the rest to travel the same way would be expensive and would delay our visit by a week. All our schedule would be thrown out, and that would cost us more.

Mr Hutchings had stared at us from red-rimmed eyes. 'There's nothing out there. Just bark sheds every twenty miles, where we keep the relays.'

'All we need is pluck,' Mr Bleeker had replied, and a cheer went up.

Pluck we had in plenty. Especially Lavinia, with her determined merriment. 'Isn't this like washday?' she cried, catching at the edge of a sheet of lace that brushed her nose.

'It's stifling in here,' said Minnie. 'And you all walk so slowly.'

'We mustn't overtire Mary Ann,' said Lavinia.

'I am fine,' I said, ignoring the pain in my back, arms and feet, my throbbing head, my dry mouth and throat, the sweat collecting in every crease of my body. What was the desert to me? I was safe in the ladies' cocoon.

'You must keep your strength up,' said Lavinia.

This was as close as she had ever come to talking of the pregnancy and, despite Mrs Bleeker's presence, I grew bold.

'Mrs Stratton, what will it be like for me in the New World?'

'That is not a question you should ask Mrs Stratton,' said Mrs Bleeker.

'No, that is quite all right,' said Lavinia. 'Mary Ann, you cannot imagine the delights that await you.' Her voice slowed. 'In Bridgeport, Connecticut, you will see Iranistan. It is Mr Barnum's ethereal dream. Pillared and trellised, rimmed by satyrs, surmounted by Turkish towers, minarets, a grand central dome. Lit by its own private gas works, every room with a bath and hot and cold running water.'

'It is a house?'

'And what a house! But wait until you see his museum. What is your fancy? Giants, grizzly bears, dioramas of the Creation and the Deluge, industrious fleas? You will refresh yourself with oysters, ice cream and champagne. You will stroll in the roof garden, listen to the brass band. You will marvel at the fountain with its hundred jets. And at night, everything is as bright as day. You will lean from the balcony and see fireworks. And up, past your head, will rise a huge illuminated balloon.'

My ears buzzed. I had grown huge and round, I glowed, I floated, rising over ranks of chimney pots. Then two ruffians in beards and red shirts tugged at a string tied to my ankle, and I began to descend.

'I miss the museum,' said Minnie wistfully. 'Not the grizzly bears or the fleas. All New York society comes there, Mary Ann.'

'You mean all the young men come there,' said Lavinia.

'What of it, Vin? They know how to charm a girl. Not like these rude Australian rustics. All gape and guffaw.'

'What do you expect, with your skirts so outrageously short?'

Minnie groaned, pushed out of the tent, forged ahead. Her arms swung, her bonnet ribbons whipped back in a sudden wind.

'She must go her own way,' murmured Mrs Bleeker.

Lavinia sighed. 'If we were surrounded by fire, she would go into its heart.'

'She would go into other hearts than that,' muttered Mrs Bleeker. Lavinia frowned at her, and she tightened her lips.

Gradually Minnie faltered. We overtook her and she retreated beneath our shade, red-faced and panting. Flies spotted the back of her dress.

'Now you have tired yourself,' said Lavinia. 'You should take your medicine more often, Min.'

'Everything burns,' Minnie said in wonder. 'Even the wind.'

'Ladies, be thankful,' said Mrs Bleeker. 'This is the Antipodean winter.'

We were not thankful. We had passed two nights on the coaches, huddled together in blankets, our breath frosting, longing for the sun we had hidden from during the day. Now, we walked in silence, battling with hot wind that threatened to turn our parasols inside out.

Then the wind died, and I ventured again: 'Mrs Stratton, we were talking of my future in the New World ...'

Mrs Bleeker gave me a nudge, but Lavinia began to talk. 'A great bay window with tapestry seats.' Her voice was low, crooning. 'Mahogany panelling. A suite of armchairs upholstered in red velvet. Everything made to scale. In the window recess, the miniature piano presented by Queen Victoria. By the fireplace, the Chinese firescreens presented by Mrs Lincoln.'

We were walking past a skeleton, a cow spreadeagled in despair. I closed my eyes and imagined the cool rooms of the doll's house the Strattons planned to build in Middleborough, Massachusetts. 'Upstairs, five bedrooms. The small brass bed with the crowned canopy, and the carved mahogany bed presented by Mr Barnum. And the darlingest nursery. Peach-blossom wallpaper. A crib draped in apple green.' I tried to conjure up the baby in its apple nest, but all I could see was a hump of green coverlet.

'One door in the nursery will be wallpapered,' Lavinia continued. 'A peach will be the door handle. *Trompe l'oeil*. It will open onto your room, Mary Ann.'

'Will it be big enough? Will I fit?'

'Of course you will, silly.' Lavinia patted my elbow.

'You can't have peaches and blossom on the tree at the same time,' said Minnie.

The lace sheet in front of my eyes fluttered clear, to reveal a manly figure striding ahead of us, jacketless, swinging red-striped arms. I called out: 'Franz.' He stopped, turned, and I beckoned to him. A darkness blocked the way outside our hide. Then the light shifted, and green eyes peered through a lace sheet. At once I was confused: why had I summoned him?

'How are you, ladies?' He was looking at me. 'The General is concerned for you.'

'We are all very well, thank you,' said Lavinia. Minnie tilted up her chin. 'Fighting fit. We have faced grizzly bears, remember. A bit of sand is nothing.'

I extended one of my parasols, and Franz ducked gratefully into its shade, brushing my shoulder. Lord, how tall and broad he was. The tent was suddenly full of his Crimean shirt of red-and-white-striped cotton and its vigorous man smell.

'Are you very weary?' Again, he turned to me. 'Do you have enough water? Would you prefer to ride on one of the coaches?'

'We don't need a ride,' said I. 'But thank you — thank the General — for asking.'

'You do indeed look well,' he said, keeping his eyes on me. 'And your tent is a wonderful device. Very fresh and cool. Very inviting. What a pity I must rejoin the menfolk.' He smiled at me, nodded to Lavinia and Minnie and Mrs Bleeker, jammed his hat over his brow. We women huddled together and slowly Franz backed out of the tent.

As he left, the lacy fringe in front of my eyes, all tattered and clogged with sand, slipped away, the parasols collapsed, and the desert light struck me. *The veil of the temple has been rent*, Father would say. Franz had rent the veil. Fragments of ladies' fripperies danced around my shoulders, coiled in the sand or were whipped away by the wind into a scrub-dotted nothing. Franz was a way off at the carriages, shouting at the men; the sisters were tottering in circles; Mrs Bleeker was running after a taffeta shawl that floated just out of her reach. The horizon shimmered and boiled. With a slow thrill, I recalled that I had been the one who had beckoned to him, extended the parasol, invited him in. I plucked a slip of organza from my shoulder, turned my face to the relentless sun. Did it get so hot in the New World? The door was waiting, beyond the velvet armchairs and the miniature piano and the Chinese firescreens, and one day I would open it and step out, slim-waisted, in a new white dress, and there would be no veils, and already I could almost see who was out there waiting for me.

Then Mrs Bleeker was shouting at me and pointing at the strewn finery, and I ran to pick up the pieces. Lavinia and Mrs Bleeker chased them too, backwards and forwards in the sand. Only Minnie, usually such a blur of movement, stood stock still. Was she sunstruck? Then I noticed she was staring at me, and I felt a strange whirring in my ears. The whirring of Mrs Bleeker's inexorable sewing machine.

We repaired the tent and moved on. The sand followed us as we approached Adelaide. At first I thought we would escape it. We saw gum trees, flocks of white birds, geese rising from a lagoon, shade and a little green for the eyes. At Woods Well we stayed at a small adobe house on a plateau overlooking the bay, and a Scotswoman gave us kangaroo steak and hot scones. As we left the house a huge red kangaroo passed nearby, clearing fifteen feet with every bound. We skirted the shores of Lake Meningia. Then we took a ferry across the Murray river to the miserable village of Wellington, where we were to spend a night, and the sand caught us. It piled up to the windows at the front of our inn, and at the back it brushed the roof.

All this time, as we moved about, I had been between the sisters, Lavinia and Minnie valiantly supporting each elbow. Now Lavinia and Charlie went out for a stroll as the sun was setting, and Minnie retired to the parlour. In the darkest room, Mr Bleeker sat on the floor, wrapped in a blanket, his spine pressed against the wall. His wife sat in a pool of lamplight over her sewing machine. I lay on the floor with my back to them, my hair unpinned and unplaited, propped up with cushions and covered with blankets. I had been trying to help Mrs Bleeker but could not keep my eyes open, and had been ordered to rest. Exhausted as I was, I could not sleep. My face and feet glowed, an ache laced my ribs, I felt the weight of the sand piled to the windowsill outside like a giant hourglass.

Mr Bleeker was breathing heavily, muttering. 'Pickaxe? Fork? Tea strainer? Needle? Bludgeon?'

The sewing machine stopped its chatter. 'Silly dear, you have had too much sun on that bald spot of yours.'

I waited for him to chastise her once again for using the hated nickname. But he just sighed and said: 'If only I could talk to Mr Barnum. He'd tell me which tool to be.'

'You're not a tool. You're a very fine manager. You have accomplished the journey you were told it was madness to undertake. Everyone is well and in high spirits. We have eaten fat pork and pumpkin for dinner. The horses have all survived. By tomorrow we should be in Adelaide. And you have saved the company six hundred pounds. Let us leave poor Mary Ann in peace and find a place to bed down.'

The light shifted. I opened my eyes to shadows trembling on the whitewashed wall. Mr Bleeker in his blanket cast a shade like a giant bug in a cocoon, and I thought of that other cocoon which had borne myself and the ladies across the desert.

SIDESHOW

Miss Minnie Warren

Lavinia and Minnie Warren

ACT ONE

Sand, grit, all through my white silk gown and underthings, and sweat and flyspecks and squashed-bug marks, and my shawl tattered beyond repair, and not even a pitcher of water to wash myself. She used all the water, then went out with her man for a promenade, while I skulk and scratch in the parlour. No chance to change, of course. I have closetfuls of gowns back home; they burst out from the doors. I could wear a different ensemble every day for a month, a princess wouldn't have such a wardrobe.

But how come inside every gown I'm still a little farm girl?

There's nothing wrong with me, you know. Even the doctor didn't actually say there was anything wrong with me. When I was little, I mean really little, he came to see me, even though I wasn't sick. Mother said not to be afraid, it was the same man who had come to see Lavinia, years before. He said to lie down, there's a good girl. He blocked out the light when he stood over me, but he had a soft voice and clean hands and a smell of peppermint. He peered at my arms and legs and tapped them with a mysterious hammer. He murmured to Mother and she put her face in one hand, peering out through her fingers. I laughed. I thought she was playing peekaboo. I didn't realise until many years later that she had not wanted me to see her tears.

I used to follow Lavinia round the house, into the farmyard, back into the house with my muddy footprints. She ran, but I always caught her up. She hid, but I always found her. I don't think she was really cross about it. I asked her if I would be little like her, when I grew up.

'Would you like that?' she said.

I could think of nothing better, but I pretended to consider. I said I wanted to reach the cookie jar all by myself.

'Then you'd get roly poly from too many cookies. Anyway, if you can't reach, you can share the steps that Father made for me.'

Mother stood behind us in the kitchen, one hand holding a wooden spoon, the other hand over her mouth.

'Being little isn't so bad,' said Lavinia. 'You just have to act big.'

But I never thought being little was bad, not then.

Sometimes Lavinia would tell me we should not feel alone, for there were plenty of people like ourselves in the world. She had made a study of it in the schoolbooks. A Russian emperor had kept a whole court of dwarves and had built a palace of ice for them. It was said that somewhere in the deserts of Africa there was a race of miniature Hottentots.

'Then we will both have husbands,' I said with delight, 'and we can choose whether to live in ice or desert.'

She laughed. 'Minnie, only you would think of marrying a Hottentot.'

* * * * * * *

Father carved all our heights and dates into the wall by the barn door. George, James, Sylvanus and Benjamin had notches all climbing a steady hill to six feet. Caroline Delia had a gentler hill to five feet. Lavinia's hill began to flatten off into a plateau on October 31, 1845, when she turned four. By the time she was ten, the plateau at its highest point was twenty-four inches. My plateau was slightly lower. For years, Father piled bales of hay in front of the plateaus. But after Mr Barnum had taken up both of us, Father took the hay away and joined up the notches with a flourish of his finest whitewashing brush.

· · · · · · · ·

At the age of fourteen, on February 10, 1863, I made my debut in society in the most dazzling way possible. And yet I was not the centre of attention: I was still following my sister, down the aisle of Grace Church, New York, on her wedding day. Two thousand of the city's grandest folk, summoned by invitation only, filled the church to bursting. It had taken hours for their carriages to queue up and drop them off. When we four little people walked in, the worshippers craned their necks and aahed and oohed, and there was so much jostling and shoving you would never think you were somewhere holy.

As I walked beside Commodore George Nutt, my fellow little person and best man, I rested my right arm on his left arm. Just for a moment, I felt faint. Then he placed his right hand on mine and gave me a little wan smile, the kind of smile a man gives from his sickbed, and I wondered if he felt faint too.

We came to a stop at the altar, and I stood breathing in the scent from my bouquet of pink rosebuds and another sweet, mysterious smell that made me feel sick — or was it just my nerves? The clergyman stood over us and blocked out the light. His voice swooped and dived and thundered. Everything was echo.

Lavinia stood in front of me, a cherub wrapped in a starry white cloud. I'd helped her dress and I knew exactly what was in that cloud. White satin, embroidered with arabesques of beads and pearls. A crown of orange blossom, holding her lace veil in place. White kid gloves, white satin slippers with rosettes of lace and pearls. A point-lace handkerchief. The General's gift: a necklace with pendants, brooches, a star brooch, earrings, star hairpins for her veil. In all, two hundred and fifty-six diamonds.

I was trying so hard to see through that cloud, to the girl who had trudged just ahead of me through the muck of the cow yard, chewing grass stems until her tongue was green, her hair twisted up into daisy chains. Even then, she knew how to wear a crown. My daisies always fell into the cowpats.

Then I looked at the groom, so handsome in his black dress suit and blue vest and white gloves. He had a slight frown and his lips were pressed together tight. I didn't know him yet but I would call him Charlie, my brother, and I was determined to think well of someone so clearly in love with my sister. Everyone was in love with her, of course. But I knew where the happy couple's thoughts were. Not with the ceremony, not with the reception, not with the meeting with two thousand of New York's finest, not with cutting the cake topped by the Angel of Fame. No, their thoughts were with that moment at last when they would be alone together, when the Act of Love would take place.

For all my questioning, I had never succeeded in finding out what the Act of Love was, but I knew it was something very wonderful, not at all like the cock covering the hen or the bull mounting the cow or all the other shenanigans we'd seen constantly on the farm. Under my crinoline, I squeezed my thighs together. I had done this ever since I was a child. First, it was comforting, and then, it was invigorating. So invigorating, I wanted to do it all the time, and could not understand why Mother slapped me. I looked down at my puffed tulle and pink rosebuds and thought of the moment when I had first put on this bridesmaid's disguise, the time alone in front of the looking glass, trying to push my tiny breasts up and together. But all I had seen was a roly poly doll.

'Let us pray,' said the Reverend Taylor. I bowed my head. Lord, let my sister be happy. Let her have many children. Let her marriage be long and prosperous and filled with the Act of Love. Let her perform and travel, and when I am just a little older, let me perform and travel with her. I'm not greedy, am I, Lord? Let me have just one diamond. Let my hair be less wild. Let me have a bosom and a waist and shapely ankles and no pimples. Let the people admire me. Let me marry. Let me know my own Act of Love.

The teasing I had had, already. How well I looked with the Commodore. How it would not be long before another Fairy Wedding. And we did look well together: he was not quite as handsome as Charlie, but he had farmboy cheeks and a manly bearing and curly hair that floated when he ran. I had thought he liked me, but something was wrong with him. He was always a funny fellow, but he had been morose and silent these past few weeks. And there was that moment just before, as we walked down the aisle, that wan sickbed smile.

The prayers were over, the Reverend Taylor was asking the couple the questions that would bind them for life. Their replies were steady and calm. I looked over, beyond General Tom Thumb and my sister, to where George stood stiff in his pink vest. He took the ring from his pocket, fumbled with it for a moment, then placed it on a velvet cushion and passed it to Charlie. He watched to a chorus of *oohs* and *aahs* as Charlie removed Lavinia's glove and placed the ring on her finger.

Then I watched George's gaze travel slowly from Lavinia's hand, over the diamond bracelets, up the satin arm, across her décolletage, over her necklace with pendants, up to her face, just as Charlie lifted her veil and kissed her. How my thighs tingled. And I felt for a moment as if I could see with George's eyes, hear with George's ears: the rustles and sighs of the congregation, Lavinia's catch of breath. I smelled again the orange blossom and roses and that underlying odour that made me faint and sick. Like an icy breeze, the knowledge of what that odour was, where it came from.

George held himself as if his whole body was in a cast. I longed to go take his hand, but I knew he'd never feel my touch. And then suddenly I didn't want to touch him. Maybe I would catch the contagion.

That man is not for me, I thought. Maybe there is no man for me, not anywhere in the world. No Russian dwarf, no Hottentot. And then, a stab of feeling that left me breathless. How dare she? I squeezed my hands tight so that the thorns in my bouquet jabbed at me and I wished I had my old school memorandum book and pencil and a pin; I would write it down and slap it onto her oh-so-straight back so that, when she turned and walked down the aisle with her brand new husband, everyone would see what she was.

• • • • • • • •

But she won't keep me down any longer, not now. Even though I'm so tired, I kick up my heels, like I want to gallop around the dunes. I've brushed out most of the sand, but my white silk still clings, drags. Always littler, always younger, and my gorgeous dresses always just a bit longer than I'd like.

CHAPTER 11

I was walking through the rooms of Matilda's doll's house, past the tapestried windowseats, the chairs upholstered in crimson velvet, looking for the door that led outside. It was not on the ground floor. On the first floor the rooms were smaller. The room at the end of the corridor was tiny: I had to bend my head to enter. It held a white bed, hard as a coffin, and a white jug of water on a stand, and was covered from floor to ceiling with white-blossomed wallpaper. A baby's wails tore at me; they came from behind a further door, camouflaged by the wallpaper. The handle was shaped and coloured like a peach, but when I took it in both hands, it collapsed into a rotting mess. The door was shrinking, smaller and smaller, flies buzzed, the cries turned into screeches. I beat helplessly on the walls with my sodden hands, smeared brown pulp onto the white flowers. 'You don't belong here,' said Matilda's voice behind me. 'You are too big. I shall tell Papa.'

I opened my eyes to humped cushions. The room was empty and dark, a rising wind moaned. I got up and crept to the window, pushed apart the thin gingham curtains. The wind had swept away the piled-up sand. Under the half-moon, the horse trough was as white as bone.

A rustling came from the door behind me, and I whirled, fearing rats. A tall figure stood in the doorway, watching me.

'What do you want?' My voice caught with alarm.

'Mary Ann?' Franz's voice. He took a step into the room, as if I had summoned him. His shirt front gleamed, and moonlight caught his cowlick of hair, bleached of its russet. The air around him rustled — he was electric. 'I could not sleep. I was walking and I saw you against the moon … Your hair like an aura … You will think me foolish. Or intrusive.'

'No, I was still in a dream.' We stared at each other, a good three feet between us, impossible to move forward or back. I put a hand to my loosened hair, grown lush and abundant. Blood rushed around my body, pooling in the warmest places. My face still glowed; I hoped it did not look swollen. He cleared his throat but said nothing: his assurance and his compliments had slipped away with the daylight.

I grew bold. 'Why are you rustling, Franz?'

'Mmmm?' He crossed his arms over his chest and crackled. 'Oh, this is just my scribbling, I am always jotting down something.' He pulled a sheaf of paper from under his jacket and, at the same moment, the moon went behind a cloud, darkening the room.

'I have seen you writing.' My curiosity flared. 'Letters? Or are you a diarist?'

'I am trying my hand at poetry. I have been meaning to show you.' His fingers moved towards his pocket, paused. 'But perhaps you are more interested in horses than literature.'

'What do you mean?'

'You spend time with the little groom.'

I bristled as I caught the faint contempt in his voice. 'You mean Rodnia Nutt? On the way to Green Ponds? We were simply sharing a ride, as you were. I have no particular interest in horses, but I have a great interest in literature.'

'You are sure?'

'Of course. Especially in something you have written.'

'I would hardly call it literature,' said Franz. But he reached into his pockets, drew out more folded papers, held them up and squinted.

'Can I help?' I said eagerly. 'There is a candle somewhere …' I reached out, but suddenly he seemed to retract the papers back into his body, glaring at me as if he might hiss and claw. I stepped back, held on to the windowsill.

'Forgive me. My little weakness, I hate anyone looking at my unfinished work.' How passionate he was that everything should be perfect. 'Here, I have it.' He leaned forward from the waist and stretched out his hand, as if there were a line on the floor he could not cross. I stepped forward, and he handed me a tightly folded wad of paper. His eyes met mine, and some steely sheen was in them. Had he meant to give me this paper all along? Then he looked down at the floor. 'Read it when you have time. Or not. As you will.'

Before I could thank him, the doorway was empty. I looked for the candle, but it had gone. The moon had deserted me. I curled up in my nest of blankets, put the folded paper under a cushion nearest my cheek and lay open-eyed for an eternity, until the sun rose and we were off for Adelaide.

• • • • • • •

Mrs Bleeker's lips clenched over clothes pegs. While I held fabric against the snapping breeze, she spat out her pegs, rammed them into the sheets and shirts and petticoats and drawers on the line stretched across the courtyard at the back of our Adelaide hotel.

'Miss Minnie's plastron.' She pinned up a strip of lace. 'Always some hole that is bigger than it ought to be.'

The basket was empty. I picked it up, hurried into the empty washhouse, pulled a crumpled piece of paper from my bodice and began to read with one hand, while with the other I used the tongs to haul sodden garments from the copper and then pushed them through the wringer.

Who would be
A mermaid fair,
Singing alone,
Combing her hair
Under the sea,
In a golden curl
With a comb of pearl ...

A shout. 'Where is that washing?'

Curse the washing. It rose up around me, wall after wall of flapping sheets, keeping me from my dreams. All this work, would it really save me? But what choice did I have?

'Coming.' I pushed the paper back into my bodice, ran out with my filled basket. We resumed our pegging. *A golden curl.* I pushed a dark strand behind my ear. It was not my aura of hair. And yet.

'Keep up, Mary Ann. You are in such a daydream today. You are not indisposed again?'

'Not at all, I was just thinking …'

'About what?'

I handed her two more strips of lace. 'About … Miss Minnie.'

'Ah.' Mrs Bleeker smoothed down a sheet.

'In the desert, Mrs Stratton said she would go into the heart of the fire, and you said she would go into other hearts than that. What did you mean?'

'Mrs Stratton thinks Miss Minnie is a wilful child. But she is twenty-one years old. In some ways, she is more woman than her sister. It's a great pity she did not marry the Commodore, but it can't be helped. We must watch her.'

'Is it not children who need watching?'

Mrs Bleeker tweaked a shirt from my hands. 'Get me more linen, girl.'

Why was she so brusque with me? Why did so many of my questions go unanswered? Sometimes I wanted to remind her I was a clergyman's daughter and not a scullery maid. But in the wash-house, I would have another chance to look at the poem. So I ran back and drew out the paper. By now I knew every loop and slash of Franz's hand.

I would be a mermaid fair;
I would sing to myself the whole of the day;
With a comb of pearl I would comb my hair;
And still as I comb'd I would sing and say,
'Who is it loves me? who loves not me?'

185

The wringer handle jammed. Oh, it was a spiteful, horrid thing. I tugged at the sheet, spattering warm water onto Franz's poem, tried to read on. Something about a starry sea-bud crown: *I should look like a fountain of gold.* So strange, so thrilling. With a groan the wringer handle swung. I bundled the shrivelled linen into the basket, gave one last glance at the blotched paper. Please, poem, do not blur.

'For heaven's sake …' Mrs Bleeker was beside me, turning the handle with a far more practised hand. Dark circles bloomed under her arms. The basket quickly filled. 'Lord, it's Ceylon in here … What is that paper?'

'An old list I found in a pocket.' Quickly I tucked it out of sight. Would Mrs Bleeker command me to hand it over? But she was heaving up the basket. Outside, we set to pinning again, Mrs Bleeker muttering around the pegs.

'Why do we need to watch Miss Minnie?' I persisted.

'Men are collectors. They go to such lengths …' She swept a hand down the line, towards the ladies' tiny undergarments.

'They steal clothes?'

'Not just clothes.' Mrs Bleeker took the last peg from her mouth, held it up like a cigar. 'There are handsome, charming gentlemen who are not what they seem. Do you know what I mean?' I busied myself untangling the wadded linen. 'You are a clergyman's daughter, a clergyman's widow. And yet through no fault of your own you are acquainted with evil. Those dreadful men who abducted you in Ballarat … Can you imagine a further degree of evil? But perhaps this is too painful for you …'

'Mrs B, I can hear you talk of anything.'

'In New York, there is an evil house. Evil men go there. The females who work there are … unfortunates.'

She talked on in a half-whisper. It was not the afflictions of the Leopard Girl, Lucia the Limbless, Madame Fifi the Human Lobster, Ida the Tattooed Lady (Tortured by Tartars) and Amelia the Four-Legged Wonder that made them unfortunate. It was the fact they were slaves, made to work at a hideous trade. The busiest of them was the beautiful Amelia, who had not only four legs — always clad in the finest stockings — but two you-know-whats. Often two gents at a time would purchase her services.

'You do not mean …'

'Hush,' she whispered, glancing around, peering up at closed windows. 'Yes, I *do* mean.' The wind blew a sheet against her; she pushed it back. 'Some women can be lured. They are restless, they yearn, they are misled, they fall.' My hands froze around a petticoat. Could Mrs Bleeker have any inkling of my own history? 'And not just poor wretches. Respectable women. Ladies. Once they fall, there is no going back, they are lost forever. So you see, a young woman must always be watched. Especially a young lady, and especially a singular young lady.'

I relaxed, pulled the petticoat into shape: I was not a lady. As Mrs Bleeker talked, my mind entered water.

Till that great sea-snake under the sea
From his coiled sleeps in the central deeps
Would slowly trail himself sevenfold
Round the hall where I sate, and look in at the gate
With his large calm eyes for the love of me.

'Kidnappings.' The word cut like a whip into my dream. 'I beg your pardon, Mrs B?'

'Lord, are you deaf today? I was saying, it is not just enticement. It is abduction by force. Plotters lurk, plan, seize. We in the business are constantly on guard. They take anyone they can, even little children.'

'Do you think … I mean no disrespect, but could it be …'

Mrs Bleeker clicked her fingers towards the basket, and I handed over one of Charlie's shirts. 'What? Don't shilly shally.'

'Could someone inside our troupe hatch such a plot? I think that was why I was taken at Ballarat. In fact, I am sure of it.'

She dropped the shirt, stared at me. 'Whatever has come over you? No one in the troupe would do such a thing. What a wicked idea.'

'Not even Ned Davis? You said yourself, he is a troublemaker, we should get rid of him.'

'Mary Ann, you must understand one thing. Everyone in this troupe, yourself included, has been selected with the utmost care by either Mr Barnum himself, or my husband, or the General. There may be … foibles, but everyone with us is trustworthy, and the best in the business.' She picked up the shirt and pinned it to the line.

'But suppose —'

'Enough.' The word was a ferocious bark. 'Don't let me think we made a mistake with you. Because we can let you go.'

I thought of her letting me go, myself ballooning and drifting away over Adelaide like a lost sheet, and the courtyard began to spin. 'I am sorry …'

She sniffed loudly. I turned back to the basket and its last garment; I picked it up, held it between my face and her sharp glance, pressed the rough Crimean cotton to my face. The man smell had been washed out, but the shirt was still warm, the red and white stripes crushed into a thousand welcoming wrinkles. I clung to it, squeezing and kneading, praying for my vertigo to fade, until Mrs Bleeker gently prised it from my hands, shook it out and pegged it on the line.

'Well, you are new to us still, so I make allowances.' Her voice had softened. 'It's us against the wicked world. And the hardest thing is to keep us weak women from the abyss.'

The abyss did not concern me, I thought. But I was heartily tired of being a weak woman.

CHAPTER 12

The world was rain. Standing on the back steps of the Royal Hotel, I faced into blackness, but pinpoints of light flickered all around me. The roaring was constant, but not loud enough to drown the intermittent cries, howls, bleats and bellows. Carrying my tray of empty mugs, I stepped down and, almost immediately, I was drenched. As I shuffled down the slope from the main hotel building to the kitchen and bakery outhouses, icy water claimed my skirts, rose to my knees. Even when I reached the warmth of the kitchen, where pots hissed and spat and Mrs Guild the landlady and the cook and their helpers chopped and peeled and washed, water still swirled around our ankles. Mrs Guild, lank hair drooping loose from its combs, wiped her nose on her sleeve, took my tray without a word and gave me another. Like the first, it was loaded with mugs, this time full of cabbage soup. For once, I found a use for Belly: I could prop up the tray and take some of the weight from my arms.

I made my way back up the hill towards the lighted windows of the hotel. Lately I'd been breathless when I scuttled about, so

I had deliberately slowed my movements, and now I felt like a great barque gliding in the loose black-dyed teagown Mrs Bleeker had given me, for the striped dress was far too tight for me now. Although I heard and felt the water, I could not see the great sheet that covered the land, or the torrents that roared down from the hills. Were we all about to drown?

For a moment I wanted to scream, drop my tray and run. But I told myself yet again there was nowhere to run to and I was in the safest place I could be. The Royal Hotel, the best in Seymour town, stood on high ground; but so much ground seemed to have vanished.

I squared my shoulders, elbowed my way through the Royal back door, down the corridor and into the ballroom. A fug of hot cocoa, wet clothes, squelched carpet and steaming socks greeted me. Thirty-six refugee farm folk, mostly women and children, sat or lay slumped around the walls under the suite of pictures showing the principal rooms in Windsor Castle. Even the youngest were too dazed to show much wonder at the fairies and imps who were wrapping them in blankets and giving them mugs of cocoa. The local doctor, a fellow no more than twenty with spanking new boots, kneeled solicitously by each newcomer, feeling for scratches and broken bones, while Minnie handed him shiny objects from his black case.

Mr Bleeker was at the window peering through the curtains into the darkness, much as I had seen him peering through the curtains onstage at the Polytechnic Hall. From outside came a burst of screeching. He shivered and pulled the curtains across the window.

'What a night, eh, Mr B,' said Mr Guild the landlord, a bald fellow with an expansive apron. 'Didn't I tell you we'd get to use that boat?'

'D'you always have such spring rains?' said Mr Bleeker.

'Can't recall anything like it since '63. Our natives predicted it: big man flood.' With gloomy relish, Mr Guild cleared the mahogany table of empty cocoa mugs. As I set out my cargo of cabbage soup, now much diluted with rainwater, he delivered his bulletin. 'Mr Cameron the Presbyterian minister is missing. They say he and his lad were rowing away from the old hotel when their little cockleshell capsized. And we've lost Bill Regan. Mind you, it was his own doing. Drunk as Chloe. Must have fallen into his own fireplace. Drowned in two feet of water and the bottles bobbing around his head.'

I blinked water from my eyelashes. Heartburn lurched under my breastbone, and a sudden surge of rebellion, far stronger than the flicker I had felt in the wash-house at Adelaide. What was I doing in this Godforsaken place, run off my feet, at everyone's beck and call? Would anyone even notice if I gave in to my exhaustion and collapsed face down in the water? It was not right: no one should have to work so hard, especially one such as I. Perhaps I should just go off and find a rowboat and escape into the lake and the darkness and roaring, and never see the troupe again.

Then I remembered Belly, and why such an escape was impossible. And I thought that Franz and Rodnia, who had volunteered for rescue-boat duty and were somewhere out on the flooded plain, were probably in far greater danger than I was. I was ashamed of my anger and I wanted to pray for them, but I could not find the right prayer.

· · · · · · · ·

The rain had begun the morning before, after we had left Adelaide and crossed back into Victoria and had first arrived at Seymour. When we left the town, the rain, as if piqued, redoubled its efforts. We were aiming to cross a valley of seventy miles on our way to Sydney, which Mr Bleeker expected to reach in six days. Ned had already gone ahead, to spread news and playbills, and I found I could breathe much easier without any prospect of coming across his lounging figure or leering stare.

After two miles, one of the baggage coaches had become bogged, and we had all climbed out to lever boards under the wheels and dig it free, but it would not shift. Rodnia took a look and reported that the harness was damaged and the whippletree broken. Lavinia and Minnie observed with sorrow the wide chocolate rims around the hems of their skirts, and I thought of all that wasted washing in Adelaide. Mr Bleeker stood leaning on his spade, water bouncing from the brim of his hat. 'Every drop of rain,' he muttered to no one in particular, 'is one less gold coin for Mr Barnum.'

Some two hundred yards off, a covered wagon and four muscular Percherons stood on rising ground. A head poked through the canvas, watching us, and Mr Bleeker beckoned. Slowly the teamster crawled out and sauntered towards us, hands in pockets.

'You have some powerful animals. Will you help us pull out our coach?'

'For what?' The man seemed at his ease with rain. They haggled, and the man agreed on a sovereign. As he unhitched three of the horses, a bonnet popped out of the canvas on the wagon, followed by four tangle-haired little heads. There was talk, and suddenly the woman shouted: 'You fool, go tell 'em you want five pounds.

You've got 'em. If they won't give it, let them stick there till they drown.'

'Five pounds,' screamed the little heads.

Mr Bleeker gestured with his spade as if he would pound the heads like rivets back into the wagon. It took twenty minutes, four horses, a long chain and five pounds to release the coach, and the downpour never let up. The mud was now brown water rushing past our feet. From under a hat brim that sagged to his nose, Mr Bleeker ordered us to return to Seymour.

Mr Guild, showing no surprise at our return, waved his arm at the rowboat, sitting high and dry under canvas in the Royal Hotel garden.

'Give us a ride?' said Minnie.

'If this rain continues, little lady, you will see our Goulburn river become a mighty lake.' The landlord swelled with prophecy. 'And this boat will save many lives.'

• • • • • • • •

I stood alone in the middle of the ballroom among the dozing bodies, trying to dry my hair with a sodden towel. Charlie lay with his eyes closed, head propped up against the wall, a thin little boy lying asleep beside him, his head in the Man in Miniature's lap. Mr Bleeker and George, grasping a brandy bottle by the neck, had disappeared round the back of the hotel to erect a sandbag wall with Mr Guild: 'It's never reached the main building before, but can't be too careful can we, gents.' Of Minnie, there was no sign. Mrs Bleeker, for once with empty arms, sighed explosively, looked to the fire, and went to whisper with Lavinia, who was pegging out wet socks as if they were silk stockings. Then she turned to me: 'Quickly, we must find them.'

Find who? But Mrs Bleeker raised her lamp and the three of us were off, through the ground-floor rooms. Nothing but slime under our feet. Then we made our way up to the shadowy bedrooms, lamp swinging, flashes from the distant torches catching us in the stairwell. Oh, the pain of stairs, of climbing. Lavinia climbed with two feet on each step, like a child, and travelled with great speed. As we burst into each room, faces surfaced, squinting at the lamp, from piles of clothes and rolled-up rugs on the beds. From outside came a repeated bleat — myrrh, myrrh — of stupid terror.

In the highest attic room, we found Minnie Warren sitting on a chair, and the young doctor bending over her. He sprang back as we entered, and Minnie's fingers tugged together the gaping bodice of her dress. Mrs Bleeker set her lamp on the floor, gripped Minnie by one arm, pulled her up, thrust her behind her own skirts, and then advanced on the young doctor, striking him in the chest with a bony forefinger. How I longed to give her a hurrah.

'Get out. Now.'

'My dear madam —'

'Don't you madam me. Get out. If you dare breathe a word of this, my husband will cowhide you; and if you dare lay a finger on Miss Warren again, I'll personally throw you to the flood.'

The doctor's comely face twisted. He grabbed his black bag, dropping instruments, brushed past me, backed out of the room, and his boots helter-skeltered down the stairs. Mrs Bleeker slammed the door behind him and rested against the panelling.

Lavinia sat down on the seat Minnie had vacated, staring at the wall, and Minnie edged to her side, placed a hand on her shoulder. 'Vin. Dearest.' Her sister did not move, and Minnie sat down beside her. The seat, designed for one, was just large enough to take the two of them.

'Vin, do not blame Dr Arnott.' Minnie placed a hesitant arm around Lavinia's waist.

At the door, Mrs Bleeker bristled. 'That scoundrel ...'

'Hush, Mrs B.' Lavinia's voice was metallic, dead.

Mrs Bleeker whirled to face the door. 'Come, Mary Ann. We have work to do.'

'Please stay,' said Minnie. 'Both of you.'

Mrs Bleeker stood with her hands folded tight in front of her, and I copied her, immensely curious to discover how Minnie would explain herself. Had the doctor attacked her? But she had said he was not to blame.

'I asked Dr Arnott to come with me.' Minnie laid her head on Lavinia's shoulder. 'I told him I was troubled by palpitations, and we needed a private place for an examination, but we couldn't go to his consulting rooms because of the flood.'

Lavinia sat forward, dislodging her sister from her shoulder, and put her head in her hands.

'It's true, Vin, I swear it. My poor heart was beating so fast.'

'He took advantage,' said Mrs Bleeker. 'Oh, I have feared this for so long.'

'No,' said Minnie quietly. 'He was a gentleman.'

Lavinia raised her head, looked her sister in the eyes, then gave a little groan, and looked down. Outside, water gurgled from the Royal's eaves. A distant boom. The lamp sputtered, revived.

I thought suddenly of Matilda's papa, the chaise longue where he had invited me to lie so many times. He was a gentleman, but that had not saved me. Yet I could not imagine headstrong Minnie succumbing to any man.

'Vin, try to understand. I was frightened of the flood. I think Dr Arnott was frightened too. When we were in the ballroom, two old women behind us were whispering, they said the end of the world had come, they talked of portents from the realm of the spirits —'

'Portents from the realm of Mr Guild's bar,' said Mrs Bleeker.

'Minnie, how could you listen to such nonsense?' Lavinia flared with sudden anger. 'Why did you not tell the old dames to hush? Talk of spirits — where is your Warren spirit? Have you forgotten?'

'No, Vin.'

'William, Earl of Warren, married the daughter of William the Conqueror. We ventured to America on the *Mayflower* —'

'And General Joseph Warren laid down his life for his country at the battle of Bunker Hill. You see, Vin, we Warrens do not forget. We Warrens are not frightened.' Minnie exhaled her *Warrens* with great gusts.

'Don't mock the family name.'

'Then don't you tell me what I felt. I was frightened, and yet … It was a question of my heart.'

'Your *heart* was frightened? Then you are truly unwell.'

'Not at all, I was only agitated. But Vin, we are …' She took a deep breath, continued. 'You are happily married. You are' — she looked at me — 'about to be blessed. I am twenty-one years old and I have no one. Where in the world would I find a man my size?'

'You would not have the Commodore,' said Lavinia.

'No, and George would not have me, he would only have —'

'Miss Minnie,' said Mrs Bleeker sharply.

Minnie sighed. 'There's no spark between us.'

'Spark?' said Lavinia. 'What is that?'

'Sometimes it's just a moment, a flare.' Minnie's eyes glistened. 'Perhaps one day, it may be a steady glow. I can hope still.'

'Of course you can hope.' Lavinia took her hand, spoke softly. 'You are young yet.' She put a hand to Minnie's straying tendrils of hair. 'You must dress those pretty curls.' Mrs Bleeker handed me a hair brush from her pocket, gestured towards the sisters. I kneeled at Minnie's side and began to let down her hair. As the messy chignon loosened and the curls gathered around her face, Minnie raised one hand and wiped it across her nose like a child. But her voice, when she spoke, was unusually deep.

'You're right, as usual. I'm the little Queen of Beauty's younger sister, I'll always be younger. Even though we little people age so suddenly.'

'You must not say you have no one, Minnie. You have me. And Charlie, and dear Mrs B, and Mary Ann. We will all be here for you as long as you want us.'

'The Lord knows I'm grateful for it.' Minnie nodded. 'I've always looked up to you, Vin. Even when I was very young, I wanted to be like you, I didn't want to grow taller.'

'That's not true, you said you wanted to reach the cookie jar all by yourself.'

'I did not ... I remember your wonderful wedding, Vin, all New

York at your feet. Do you remember how many diamonds you were wearing?'

'Lord, I ...' Lavinia patted her hair.

'Two hundred and fifty-six. And I stood behind you at the altar and I prayed silently to God: *Let me have just one diamond.*'

'Minnie, you may have as many diamonds as you like, I will give you my spare bracelets and earrings ...'

'That's not what I mean. Oh, I don't know what to call it. A spark, for my heart.'

I wielded the brush, and sparks crackled from Minnie's curls. *For my heart* ... I thought again of the thing I had resolved never to think of, the reclining on the chaise longue, and a hand undoing the buttons on my bodice, slipping over my heart. *The hardest thing is to keep us weak women from the abyss.* My nipples hardened, a throb began somewhere beneath Belly's weight. But the hand on my breast was not the stubby hand of Matilda's papa. It was broad, with long sensitive fingers, thumb loose in the socket, a good spread, a good piano hand.

'You are too trusting, Minnie. We must keep you safe.' Lavinia took both her sister's hands, stared into her eyes. 'This heart of yours, this chasing after sparks, it is dangerous, it must never, ever happen again.' Minnie frowned, began to speak, but Lavinia interrupted her. 'I don't care about your Dr Arnott.' Mrs Bleeker gave a convulsive sniff. 'And I don't expect you to understand what I'm warning you about,' Lavinia went on. 'You must just promise me two things. One: take your medicine. Two: don't go looking for the spark.'

Lavinia glanced up at me, and I began to brush Minnie's hair with long, rhythmic passes. The younger sister's eyes slowly glazed over, like the eyes of a stroked cat. 'Vin,' she said drowsily. 'Do you remember before Barnum, those identical red cloaks and hoods Mother made?'

'The Little Red Riding Hoods.' Lavinia gave a faint laugh.

'I loved those cloaks,' said Minnie. 'Do you remember how we'd walk out together and people would call and we'd turn and they'd be so surprised?'

'Yes, indeed.'

'They expected to see little children, and they saw young ladies. Now I dream, Vin. I dream of the day to come, not so very far from now, when I walk down the street and some man calls out and I turn and I see —' She paused, took a deep breath. 'I see horror on his face.'

Lavinia sat in silence, holding her sister's hand. My brush rasped across Minnie's scalp. She began to sob. 'Rock me, sister.' Lavinia took her in her arms, rocked her gently back and forth, hummed *The Cottage by the Sea*. Five wicked pieces of metal, strewn on the floor where the doctor had abandoned them, gleamed in the lamplight. Brush poised, I looked over the sisters' bowed heads to Mrs Bleeker, still standing with her back to the door, arms folded, mouth a grim slash.

'Will you make me that promise, dear?' Lavinia murmured into Minnie's hair. She bit her lip, gave the faintest of nods.

For a moment, they seemed like children comforting each other. Then the sobbing Minnie gave a quick glance up at her sister when Lavinia's face was turned away, and Minnie's face reminded me of the way she had looked at me in the desert, made me think again of Mrs Bleeker's sewing machine: the whirring wheel, the needle dipping in and out. And I saw Minnie's hands, curled up in the folds of her skirt: her fingers were tightly crossed.

Yet the tears brimming in her eyes were real enough.

An aching petulant fury rose in me. Why did no one ever brush my hair?

• • • • • • • •

I had never been so weary. I snatched a couple of hours' sleep on the ballroom floor, sandwiched between a rolled-up rug and a snoring farmer's wife, but then Mrs Bleeker, herself pale and hollow-eyed, shook me awake as daylight began to seep into the room.

'Nooo,' I groaned, burying my head in my arms. But she kept shaking my shoulder.

Somehow I rose, and somehow my legs carried me to and fro as we helped Mrs Guild and two kitchen maids serve a breakfast of tea, bread and hard-boiled eggs.

I was beginning to hate the pasty faces of those farm people and their children as they grabbed their food and stuffed it into their mouths. Why was I waiting on them? Why would no one let me sleep? And most of all I hated the swaggering stride of Mr Guild around the room as the light grew and the roaring died down, his finger-wagging bulletins: 'Mr Vickers and Mr Greenwood are lost. I warned them not to go. Their buggy and pair fell over in the flush culvert on the Melbourne road. All that has been found are the hooves of the drowned horses, just above the surface … Only three buildings in town not under water. The bank, Maxfield's flour mill, and the Royal. The bank and the mill are at least as crowded as we are.' I waited in dread for him to say the rescue boat was lost, but he was silent on that score. Every time I was near a window, I peered out, but could not see any boats. I did not go out the back door again — the kitchen and bakery outhouses were full of water and had been abandoned — but Mr Bleeker and George were outside, attending to their sandbag wall. Charlie had commandeered a bedroom. The number of refugees in the ballroom had doubled, tripled, no one was counting: children whimpered and hiccuped, and some of the farmers' wives and older girls were folding up bedding as best they could with babies in the crook of an arm or toddlers clinging to skirts. They did not ask where their husbands and fathers were; they glanced out the windows at the virgin lake, calm and sparkling, and turned quickly back.

Mr Guild took a longer look out the window. From outside came a rattling and shouting. 'Glory be, the minister is safe,' he announced to the room. 'And his lad beside.' He hurried out the front. I was crossing the ballroom with a tray of mugs when Franz appeared at the door.

I turned towards him with a half-stifled cry of joy, came close and stopped. Had I fallen asleep on my feet, was I dreaming? His head and shoulders were sprinkled with white, and underneath he was smeared dark brown. He looked like an iced chocolate soldier, smelled of sweet almonds and foul drains. He held himself stiffly upright, his left hand held his side, blood trickled from his wrist, his hollow eyes were fixed on me as if I had rolled back the stone and called him forth.

It seemed to me then that time was frozen. No one was close to us, and everyone in the ballroom was so busy with breakfast and bedding, we could almost have been alone. He opened his mouth and I waited for a wild tale of fighting the deluge.

'You have not told me what you thought of my poem.' His voice was dry, cracked.

'I have been wanting to tell you … It is very fine. You are as gifted a poet as you are a musician.'

'Untutored scribble.' He shook his head. 'Any merit in it must have come from the inspiration of the subject.'

'The mermaid?'

'Exactly.'

'But the narrator of the poem is not a mermaid. She dreams of being one. *I would be a mermaid fair.*'

'Very perceptive of you, Madam Governess.' He smiled. 'Perhaps the writer of the poem dreams too. Would you like to know what he dreams?'

I could hardly believe we were talking so. I thought of Minnie, now asleep upstairs in the arms of her sister, and of the mermaid, who was sued and wooed and flattered by the bold mermen.

But the king of them all would carry me,
Woo me, and win me, and marry me,
In the branching jaspers under the sea;

'Yes,' I said. 'I would very much like to know what he dreams.'

There was just one mug on my tray that was still full of tea; the others were empty. I gestured to Franz to take it, and he reached out, a white smile flashing across his darkened face. It looked almost as if he were reaching to touch my breast.

At the same moment, Rodnia appeared before me like a miniature version of Franz's chocolate soldier: all brown sprinkled with white, the same sweet and sour smells. His eyes blazed at me from his piebald face, he clutched a dirty bundle to his heart. Had he just burst through the door, or had he been standing behind Franz and overheard us talking? He said nothing, but lifted his bundle and placed it on my tray, and the wrappings fell open to reveal a trembling black rabbit.

'Hail the heroes of the boat,' came Mr Guild's voice from behind the men in the doorway. 'Come, my lads and lasses, get 'em victualled.'

'I will get you tea directly,' I said to Rodnia, but a fat farmer's wife had moved in already, and Rodnia had his tea and a blanket around his shoulders, and the wife was drawing him to the fire with little clicks of her tongue. Another wife drew Franz in the same direction. The young doctor, who had been hunched over the fire, rose and made room and patted each man on the back, as if they could all share the glory.

'Here's the Reverend Cameron,' boomed Mr Guild. 'And Mr Carnie and the boy. Give the young 'un a glass of the Royal's ginger beer.'

'Give him whisky,' growled an old settler, to laughter and cheers.

'He is a wonder,' Mr Cameron said to the fellows around the fire, in his light, eager voice, waving his hand towards Franz. 'We were up the top of the cherry tree, me and the boy here, and I was preparing us both to meet our maker. Then there he was, in the tree too, all muddy and petalled, and the lad screaming. And he got us down into the boat. And that wasn't all he did, was it, Mr

Carnie?'

The man beside him grunted. 'Nearly put a hole in my boat.'

'But the rescuing, Mr Carnie, the rescuing!'

Mr Carnie looked gloomily at Franz and Rodnia. He sighed. 'I'll give him this much, he was keen as mustard. Every time we backed up my boat, he was out of it, up onto the roofs and chimney pots quick as winking. Mrs Vincent and her five grandchildren, they were sitting on the roof of their barn and they wouldn't come down for nobody. But he climbed up, got her down, took the children one by one in his arms, tossed them into the boat to their grandmother, and they laughed as if it were a game.'

I smiled towards Franz, but his face was buried in a towel. In front of me the rabbit crouched, its paws neatly together, as if my tray were a raft on the flood. Where did it come from? Should I give it back to Rodnia? He sat next to Franz by the fire, but they did not even glance at each other.

After a while Rodnia rose, the blanket still around him, holding his half-empty mug, and walked to the back door. Under the cherry petals and mud smears, his face held no expression at all. I followed him with my tray. He was sitting on the step and staring out at the roof of the kitchen, all that was left above water, while the rain fell on his knees and ran down into his boots. His silence and his back accused me of something I could not grasp. If he was sulking because Franz was the hero, it did him little credit, but I would try to be friendly.

'I'm sorry I did not have a cup of tea for you. Can I get you anything else?'

'That's all right.' He went on glaring at the rain. 'You made your choice.'

Why was he making me frown? 'I didn't choose anything. I offered the mug to the man who was nearest.' His neck hunched further into his blanket. 'At least move back from the rain, won't you? Where's the sense in getting half drenched?'

Still he made no effort to escape the deluge, but turned back and looked at me over his shoulder. 'He's been writing you poetry, then?'

'Are you referring to Mr Richardson? He has been showing me his literary work, he respects my judgement ... Please come inside, Rodnia. You can sit by the fire, and we will hear all about your adventures in the flood.'

'He can tell you well enough without me.'

'Why don't you like him?'

Rodnia shrugged. 'Who says I don't? He's a fine musician.'

'Yes, and a fine man. Did you know he has been wronged? I would do all in my power, small as it is, to help him.'

'We're all wronged, sooner or later.' He was frowning, fishing for something under the blanket. 'Your wish to help him shows you have a good heart. Just don't let it lead you —'

'My heart doesn't lead me,' I broke in, trying not to raise my voice. Why was he fidgeting? Why would he not look at me? 'It is my observation and judgement that leads to my esteem for Mr Richardson. Rodnia, you know very well what kind of man he is. You have just been out in the rescue boat with him.'

Rodnia twisted under his blanket, pulled out his clay pipe and tapped it on the step: a sodden plug of leaves fell out. He held it up, peered into the stem.

'Your Mr Richardson plays well,' he said, eyes on his pipe. 'He looks well. He speaks well. He rows well.'

'Well, well, well,' I echoed. It was too much: a day and a night of running backwards and forwards, dropping with weariness, in and out of cold, deep water, and rescuing Minnie from her amative fancies, while he squatted at his ease in a rowboat, observed a rescuing hero and then squeezed out his grudging praise. And how dare he sit there wrapped in self-righteousness, as if he were the wronged man? Suddenly I wanted to fetch another mug of tea and throw it in his face.

'Of all the stupid, petty, things to say ... I did not think you were capable of this ...' I was shouting above the pounding of the rain. 'Rodnia Nutt, you are such a ...' I opened and closed my fists, trying to grasp the right words. 'You are such a *little* man.' Before he could say anything, I turned and went back into the hotel. Only when I felt the empty tray dangling from one hand did I realise that the rabbit must have hopped off. I slumped against the wall, closed my eyes. It could fend for itself. I was too tired to care for any living creature but myself and Belly.

CHAPTER 13

'You should be playing,' I said to Franz.

'I fear I am not holy enough for Mr Cameron. And I would rather be here.'

I blushed, bunched up my skirts, wished they were not so muddy and my exposed ankles not so swollen. The rain had stopped; we were walking together around a new island. When our troupe had first come to Seymour, the Royal Hotel sat on a rise overlooking the town and the river. Now the hotel and its outbuildings sat on a small outcrop in the middle of a pearl-grey lake, a perfect picturesque scene were it not for the flies, the fringes of rubbish, and the stink of mud and excrement and rotting things. From the windows of the Royal came stumbling piano chords and a ragged chorus of *Abide with Me* as Mr Cameron rallied his flock. Despite the Sabbath, Mrs Bleeker had sent me out to look for anything worth salvaging, and Franz had volunteered to join me — in case, he said, there was a need for heavy lifting. Now I could not concentrate on my task at all.

I was refreshed from a long sleep, but I did not look as fresh as

Franz. He had washed, shaved, changed from his muddy clothes, his linen was white, his hair once again flowing in its careless waves. He extended his stick in an elegantly gloved hand and poked at smashed wine casks, sodden sacks, fence posts, bales of hay, logs cut for firewood, miraculously intact bottles of green glass. In front of us, a ewe grazed in a patch of grass at the lake's edge while not two yards away, a dead lamb floated. We had already counted twenty-six live sheep, two cows, seven goats and fifteen chickens picking their placid way through the mud. I turned from the poor lamb to look out over the lake, unbroken but for a few treetops and the chimneys of the flour mill. The sun peered through thin cloud, but all the light rose from the water.

'The flood is subsiding,' I said. 'We may be able to move on, after a few days.'

'After the deluge. Does it not strike you, we could be the only human beings saved? Adam and Eve, about to inherit a watery world.'

The ewe looked up from the grass and bleated at us, and I picked up one of the glass bottles and put it in my basket. What did that dancing smile mean? Why had he seemed so ardent when his face was black with mud, and now so bland when his face was clean and handsome again? Was he teasing me?

'I don't think we'd last long in such a world,' I said.

His smile fading, he scooped up the rest of the bottles, put them in my basket and slung it over his shoulder. 'You should not work so hard — you must think of the future.'

The floating lamb was swollen, with stick limbs, and the sheep, which might be its mother, had its contented head down in the grass. Seven months ago, I had a future. I might have one again, one day. He knew that.

As if reading my thoughts, he suddenly sighed. 'I have been thinking about the future, and the past. I have not been fair to you. I have not been completely honest. May I explain?'

We walked on, inspecting the flotsam fringe along the shoreline, and Franz talked. When he had told me he had been wronged, he should have clarified. He had been wrongfully accused of theft — not once, but twice. At the conservatory, just before he was due to graduate, a valuable trophy had disappeared, and suspicion had fallen on him because he was one of only two students with access to the room where it was stored. It was such a senseless, paltry thing, like a tale in some foolish girl's novelette, he said, raking his hair. The entire school was searched, the trophy was found in his locker, and he could only assume that his friend Martin, his admirer and rival, who also had access to the room, had tricked and betrayed him. Perhaps Martin could no longer bear it that Franz was indisputably the better musician. 'No one believed my protestations of innocence, and I was expelled.'

'What a treacherous friend.' Was this what it meant, this glow, to have your heart go out to someone?

'We never spoke again.'

'And the second time? You were wronged twice?'

'On the very day of my debut in Madame's concert. I had one teaching engagement that morning, a cheeky miss of eleven, and we were sitting side by side on the piano stool when the servants burst in and proceeded to search the entire room. Orders of the mistress, they said, who had lost her rings. So of course I insisted they search my holdall. To this day, I can see the bald patch shaped like a dollar on the back of the manservant's head as he bent to my bag and his hands stopped moving. Then he withdrew from my bag a small velvet sack I had never seen before, loosened the string and emptied on the carpet a number of gold and silver rings studded with rubies and diamonds.'

'But that is appalling.'

'The very air of the room became utterly still. Only my implacable metronome kept up its tut, tut, tut.' How superbly theatrical he was, waving his stick slowly back and forth, raising a cloud of flies from the refuse.

'Who would do such a thing?'

'Who knows? People are jealous of me, Mary Ann; it is my curse. Once again, I protested my innocence in vain, and my only reprieve was that no charges were pressed. I have hesitated to tell you these stories, and not only because they are painful to me. They seem so hard to believe.'

'Franz, you have borne your wrongs with great patience. I can only hope that one day you will have a chance to clear your name.' How honest he was. A lesser man would never have confessed to such disgrace, even if wrongfully borne. I longed to put a reassuring hand on his arm, but feared the touch would make me breathe too fast.

'Thank you, Mary Ann. You are a good friend.' A small catch in his voice wrenched me. He bent to a spar of timber, took off his gloves to get a better grip, and I sucked in my breath at the sight of blisters.

'Your poor hands. All that rowing, no wonder you would not

play the piano for Mr Cameron. Mrs Bleeker has some excellent salve, I will fetch it for you …'

'Please do not trouble yourself.' Franz straightened, glanced towards the hotel, where the hymn singers were now quiet, but Mr Cameron's reedy voice rose and fell, a discord to the twitter of sparrows. Franz dropped his rescued spar, hoisted the basket higher up his shoulder, took my arm and began to walk me round the island again. 'Have you given any more thought to your future, Mary Ann? I mean, after you arrive in America?'

After the child is born, you mean. After it is off my hands. I took a deep breath, as if about to plunge into the lake. 'That depends on many things, Franz. I have a question for you too, and you know very well what it is. You gave me a poem about a mermaid, and you asked me if I wanted to know what the author's dreams were, and I said yes.'

Again, I was appalled at my daring; I might as well have dragged him to the church door. But it was time to take a risk, and he had given me so many little signs. And Franz looked solemn, a little pale, he was clearing his throat. I waited.

'Mary Ann, I have been with the General's troupe for years. I have played fair to execrable pianos across America, through Europe, through Asia. I have endured blizzards in high mountain passes, grizzlies, marauding Indians. When our terrible war raged, I travelled back and forth across battle lines.'

He did not need to sell himself to me as a hero; and yet I warmed to his modest, melodious voice, the way he took on the lake's sparkle, and I could not resist adding: 'I have heard how you saved Mrs Stratton from the alligator.'

'Oh, that. It was in San Antonio, we were crossing a river, and I grabbed a log to use as a bridge. I let go very fast when it turned to bite me.' I put my hand to my mouth. 'Another time in Nashville, I saw a line of ghostly figures on horseback. Every man and every beast was covered from head to foot in white. Only the eyeholes were dark. They rode past us without a glance, and there was no sound except for the muffled thud of the horses' feet in the dust.' He paused, as he had done after playing *Liebestraum*, lifting his hands, letting the last chord die. 'I have never felt such oppression of silence and mystery.'

'Franz, you have had an adventurous life.'

He shrugged. 'These stories are not about myself. I witnessed these things because it was my task to be there. But the General and his lady ... I have seen them venture and survive, venture and survive. They are a courageous and cheerful pair. But in all that time they have never struck me as happy-ever-after people.'

'No,' I agreed, a little puzzled. But perhaps he would go on to mention other ways of being happy ever after.

'And yet,' he said, 'what you are telling me about your future — whatever you decide — is a happy-ever-after story.'

'I know no other.'

'I think you do.'

Amen, sang Mr Cameron's congregation.

Now, now, he would say the words; I would remember this moment when I was happy ever after. The island, the lake, his poor blistered hands. The stables, still high and dry, just beyond the hotel. The whining air, flies hovering over the floating lamb, for we had come full circle around the island and there was no sign of the ewe that might have been the creature's mother.

At that moment the stocky figure of Rodnia led two horses out

JANE SULLIVAN

of the stable and moved slowly round behind the building until he disappeared again. He did not once look in our direction.

'My dream is to make you happy,' Franz said, and my heart gave a great thump. 'And that is why I have something to give you.' He looked around as if to make sure no one was watching us. Then he put a hand inside his jacket, drew out a small box, presented it to me with a formal bow. I opened it with trembling fingers: nestled in the silk lining was a large hairpin attached to a crescent moon–shaped ornament, all in silver.

'Forgive me, but your lovely hair is sometimes a little wayward,' he said. 'I thought you might like this trinket to tame it.'

I drew it out, stared at the way it caught the light. Apart from my mother's locket and Mrs Bleeker's costume ring, no one had ever given me jewellery.

'It's beautiful. Franz, how can I ever thank you?'

'Take off your bonnet. May I?' He stood close, his breath on my neck, and I felt the pin slide into my knot of hair. 'Now you have the moon in your hair again, as I saw you in the night at Wellington,' he said softly.

I turned. His face was so close. I did what seemed to me most natural: I gave his cheek a kiss. It was so small, dry, chaste, and his response so fleeting, yet I felt it: he recoiled.

I stood still, afraid to breathe. Had I imagined it?

He stood back, cleared his throat, spoke louder. 'The moon is detachable, you could use it as a brooch, but I would not advise it. It should always be kept fastened; the brooch pin is much too sharp, you could cut yourself badly.'

'I will always wear it in my hair,' I whispered. We stood in

214

silence for a moment.

'Look in the box again,' he said. 'There is something else.'

What could it be, a matching ring? I fumbled beneath the silk lining and pulled out a small card. It was another of those *cartes de visite* that I had handed out to the besieging crowd outside the Polytechnic in Melbourne. But this one I had never seen before.

'It took me a while to find this; it was at the bottom of a box. It has not been used for some time.'

I gazed speechless at the image. A younger and slimmer General, with a hint of double chin and no beard, stood proudly beside Lavinia, who was seated on a chair in front of wooden panels and a luxuriantly draped curtain. In her velvet lap sat a baby. Lavinia's left hand disappeared into a magnificent christening gown, which spread onto the carpet, even further than her crinoline. All three gazed steadily into the camera.

'The Stratton baby,' said Franz. 'Born on December 5, 1863. Weighed three pounds at birth. An interesting thumbling, the papers called it.'

'I had no idea —'

'A medal was struck to commemorate its birth. At the age of one year, it weighed seven and three-quarter pounds, and was taken on an exhibition tour of Europe. Died in New York City when two-and-ahalf years old.'

'Poor Mrs Stratton,' I whispered.

'Oh, it was not so bad for her. The baby never existed, you see. It was all humbug to make Barnum more money.'

'What do you mean? This is a real baby, surely.' The child was enchanting. It held my eyes.

'Of course it is a real baby. How big?'

'I beg your pardon?'

'How big do you think it is?'

I stared. 'I cannot tell.'

'It is a very clever photograph, is it not?' Franz flicked at the photograph with the back of his forefinger. 'If we think of the General and his wife as a regular-sized couple, then that is an uncommonly large baby, for its head is nearly the same size as Mrs Stratton's. But the child does not appear huge, and the parents do not appear tiny. There is a perfect balance of illusion.'

'What are you trying to tell me?'

'Look again. Look at the photograph.' I could see nothing strange. Lavinia smiled her usual quizzical smile. 'Observe the size of the child's head. Unless it grew at lightning speed after its birth, how could Mrs Stratton ever have borne such a baby?'

I blushed. 'You mean … it was adopted?'

'Adopted. Borrowed. Bought. I don't know. I was not with them on that European tour and I never saw it.' I reached out, stroked the card where the christening gown spread. 'It is said they went to enormous expense for that gown,' Franz said. 'They got it back many times over in sales of that *carte de visite.*'

'One card, then.'

'And a tour of Europe. And there have been others. A Frenchie child on a visit to Paris. A daughter who went with them to visit the Prince and Princess of Wales.'

'A whole family?'

'One at a time. The public were wild for Tom Thumb babies. They always drew huge crowds, huge takings. They were not so hard to get. So many orphanages, foundling homes, baby farms. All that was wanted in addition was a wet nurse. For a short time.'

'What became of the child … of the children,' I whispered.

'I don't know. They disappeared. No one has ever mentioned them again. It was because they grew too big.'

Too big?

Briefly the island swirled, tilted, righted itself again, but something in me remained hanging at a crazy angle. *The golden egg. An individual of uncommon magnetism. They are mad for smaller and smaller men.* The words clicked — it was not so hard a puzzle. And yet I had never put it together before.

No wonder Ned had thought he could make a mint. But why did everyone expect me to bear a tiny child? Had Charlie's talk of strange magnetic influences spread about the troupe, and did everyone believe it?

'Now you see why there will be no happy ever after,' Franz said.

'I cannot believe it.'

'Don't believe me, then. Believe the photograph.'

I clenched my teeth and straightened my back. Babies coming and going like stage props. Lavinia would never stand for it. 'I will speak to Mrs Bleeker.'

Franz sighed. 'I am sure she means you no harm. But don't go to her for the truth. That is one thing she cannot give you.'

'But even if what you say is true, Franz, it is all different now. It is a proper adoption, not a borrowing or a buying. They will bring up the child as their own.'

'You did not sign any documents. Were any conditions mentioned?'

'No, of course not.' I stood with my left hand splayed over Belly, staring and staring at the beautiful baby in its frothing waterfall of a gown.

Franz watched me, slowly shook his head. 'I am truly sorry to be the one to say these things to you. My poor mermaid.'

My hand went to the unfamiliar shape of the crescent moon at the back of my head. What did he mean by his silver and his dark warning?

'Franz, you have done the right thing. I am in debt to you as always, for your beautiful gift, and for your candour and consideration.' I handed him the photograph. 'But I would prefer it if you did not speak to me of this again.'

For a moment, he looked as if some ruffian had struck him. Then he dropped his head. 'You do not believe me.'

'I believe that this time, things are different. Mr and Mrs Stratton will keep the child, and it will be in my charge for as long as I wish.'

'You are sure of that? They have said so?'

I could not remember such words. But surely they were there, underneath Mrs Bleeker's promises, Lavinia's tender stories of the nursery. 'I am sure.'

'And it is your wish?'

I closed my eyes. Why did this hot-and-cold man refuse to understand what my wishes were? A moment ago, I was walking towards the bright door of the New World, and he was waiting for me. Now the doorway was empty.

Angry shouts came from the windows of the Royal. 'Put that back, minikin.'

'Minikin yourself. Shan't.'

'By God, I'll make you ...' More shouts, a crash, a hasty piano chord.

'The General and the Commodore,' I said.

'Yes, we must go back,' said Franz tonelessly. He took my arm and we began to walk up the hill towards the hotel.

Something was growing in me that made my heart thump and my stomach heave and my body burn in moist waves so I could hardly put one foot in front of the other. Hurt pride? But I had so little pride left. Was it because Franz was abandoning me? But he was there, he held my arm, though with no closeness or warmth in his grip. Not a suitor's embrace — how foolish my hopes seemed now — and surely even a friend would hold my arm less stiffly, but he was by my side. And surely it was not too late: I could still stop him, pull him back to the edge of the island and the lake that shone like a great pearl but would disappear in a few days, and tell him once again that he was wrong; but even if he was right, it didn't matter. Whatever happened, I would fulfil my part of the bargain, I would get a handsome settlement. I had already tried to get rid of my burden; now I was in limbo for a little longer but once it was gone it would be gone forever and I would be free.

But the little men were still shouting, and Franz had a fixed smile, as if he had just told me something reassuring, and the thing blooming inside me was so fierce I could hardly breathe. What was it? Something Mrs Bleeker had said on the road from the orphanage back to Ballarat as she wiped her face with a pink cloth.

And then I knew that what lurched inside me was Belly's fear, and whatever happened, whoever might or might not abandon me, there was no way I could ever abandon Belly.

How impossible everything was.

CHAPTER 14

The flood receded, and we were off to Benalla in a flurry, and my heart felt as damp and crumpled and mildewed as all our costumes. My spirits fell still further as I saw Ned riding towards our convoy, shirt-tail hanging out, rolling in the saddle. From the coach window, I watched George run to him as he dismounted and reach up to embrace him, calling him his brave boyo, and Ned bend to pat him as if he were a puppy. Mr Bleeker climbed down from his coach, nodded curtly, demanded to know why Ned was not in Sydney distributing playbills, and Ned embarked on a long, slurred explanation. Shocking floods. Big river ahead. Bridge down. Put up in a miserable hole called Baddaginnie, and he'd already drunk them dry.

He was no longer clutching his animal hide. Had he sent it to the doctor, or bartered it for liquor? He had a lumpy canvas bag strapped across his back: perhaps it held more marvels for the collector.

George danced around, shouting of their adventures marooned on an island, but Mr Bleeker cut him short, asked Ned how they were to proceed. Ned took off his bowler, rubbed his brow and said they could wait for the river to calm itself down.

George jumped up and down. 'Won't do, won't do! Mr B wants to make money sharpish!' and Mr Bleeker frowned and said they should have been in Sydney a week ago.

'They do say there's an old crossing,' said Ned. 'A ford. But dangerous.'

'Take me to someone who knows the ford,' said Mr Bleeker. 'And straighten yourself up, man.'

· · · · · · · ·

At the riverbank, we all got out to inspect an evil river of rushing yellow, topped with patches of dirty foam. Not quite as wide as the Yarra Yarra or the Goulburn, and much more wooded round about, but fiercer. At the edges, the water was halfway up the tree trunks.

Belly fluttered and stirred. It felt exactly like my own fear: sickness, tremors, dry mouth, a constriction in my throat, a thumping heart. But I knew it came from Belly. Was there a point when the little creature developed its own feelings? This fear had not existed when I plunged into the Yarra Yarra, or was kidnapped by ruffians. Perhaps Belly had sensed danger creeping like a miasma from the photograph that Franz had shown me. I shifted miserably on the bank. I could not reason with Belly, who sensed peril round every corner, behind every curtain, under every tide. I could do nothing but hold fast and endure the fear as if it were my own.

A bloated calf bobbed by, and then, tilted at a crazy angle, a handsome mahogany writing desk. I looked round for Franz. I had resolved to stay as far from him as possible, yet still I burned to see him. He stood well back from the group, away from the water. The other men, including the guide and the two drivers we had hired in Baddaginnie, stood in a row along the river's edge.

'A hop, a skip and a jump,' said Ned, suddenly sober.

'Australia is one infernal river after another,' said Charlie. 'Nothing but Jordans and Rubicons.'

'The Styx is the infernal river,' said George. 'And anyway, you've forgotten the desert.'

'So you are now an expert on Antipodean geography, Commodore? As the sailor of the party, would you care to tell us how to cross this piffling little trickle?'

'Oh ho,' said George. 'Getting the wind up?'

'Charlie,' said Lavinia, on a warning note.

Mr Bleeker took a couple of swift strides so that he stood between the two little men. I could understand his caution. He had had to drag them apart in the middle of the church service at the Royal Hotel in Seymour. They had flown at each other after Charlie had placed a grain of gold, one of his Ballarat acquisitions, on the collection plate, and when it was passed to George, he had taken it back.

'We will cross, never fear,' said Mr Bleeker.

'Of course we will,' said Lavinia. 'I for one want to try the excitement of fording a dangerous river.' She stood close to the flood, clutching tightly to her sister's arm; since Seymour, the two had become inseparable.

The guide from Baddaginnie, a lean fellow with creases fanning from his eyes, dismounted from his horse and kneeled by the flood, peering downstream. 'She's very deep. Rains've swollen her to perdition. Another twelve hours' storm and a frigate wouldn't touch bottom.'

Mr Bleeker followed his gaze. 'Can we cross?'

'Dunno. Top markers are still above water. I'll give her a go. Wait here.'

He remounted, rode downstream and disappeared behind an overhanging rock, then re-emerged in the water, crossing at an angle, his horse going deeper at every step. Up to his waist in the stream, he turned his horse's head, guided it onto the submerged bar, and walked it on steadily to the other side. On dry land, he waved his hat to us as gaily as a man at a picnic.

'Are you afraid?' Mr Bleeker asked the ladies.

I wanted to say, *Belly is afraid*. It was something I had to hold in, like my urge to urinate.

'We Warrens are never afraid,' said Lavinia.

The guide came back without mishap, and the men harnessed two of the strongest horses to the first baggage carriage. Rodnia climbed to the coachman's seat, glared at the waters. 'Good luck, Roddie,' cried George. The horses went downstream and entered the water at the overhanging rock, and Rodnia sat like a small bear on a sinking island. About two-thirds of the way across, the carriage came to a sudden halt. Rodnia scrambled onto the roof to investigate. 'We are fast against a rock,' he shouted back to the bank.

Mr Bleeker looked at the guide. 'What kind of bar is it?'

'Hard sand, very narrow, full of boulders.' The guide pointed to the baggage carriage. 'He did not keep the line. Lucky for him he stuck. Few feet further, he'd be rolling in the drink.'

'Good God, man, it's like crossing on a tightrope.'

The guide shrugged. 'I told you ...'

'Yes, yes. Can you get him free?'

'Only God can help him now.'

Rodnia, still on the carriage roof, had found a long branch and was pushing with all his strength at something under the water. The horses stood still, the water almost to their necks, as if the river might not notice them if they did not give themselves away. Mr Bleeker strode back and forth, shouting: 'Courage, Rodnia! Push! Push harder! Not too hard!'

Everyone shouted and shrieked; George jumped up and down. The loudest voice, to my amazement, came from my own mouth. Every muscle in me was clenched tight, only Belly was shivering and shaking, but I would not pay any heed. 'Be brave! Be brave!' I yelled, to Belly as much as to Rodnia. He turned briefly, waved his long branch towards me, a stocky knight saluting his lady at a tournament with his lance, and I felt a fierce rush of pride — until I remembered how I had shouted at him at Seymour. He was not waving his branch at me after all.

Rodnia climbed back to the coachman's seat, shook the reins, shouted at the horses. They strained, and suddenly the baggage carriage lumbered forward, edged with agonising slowness towards the further bank, rose out of the water, the horses' flanks streaming. As he pulled the team up, Rodnia stood on his seat, turned and gave us a bow.

How we cheered. George danced a squelchy jig, Mrs Bleeker threw her arms around me — I was still yelling, without words

— and squeezed me to her bony corset. 'It's Roddie's finest hour,' shouted George.

Over Mrs Bleeker's shoulder, I saw Franz under a tree, his head bowed, biting his gloved thumb.

The second baggage carriage crossed safely with one of the hired drivers; Mr Bleeker would not let our guide take it — he wanted to hear his advice from the bank. Before the two passenger coaches followed, Mr Bleeker arranged the seating, with equal numbers in each coach: two performers in one, two in the other. Surely all were thinking what it would mean if one coach containing three, or even four, little people were swept away. Charlie protested that he must be with his wife, but Mr Bleeker insisted they be separated for the crossing. Still, he would not climb aboard until he had seen Lavinia's coach cross. So Lavinia and Minnie, still clinging to each other, made their way to the front coach, and Mrs Bleeker and I joined them. At the last moment, Franz volunteered to be our escort.

The carriage lurched forward along the riverbank, keeping close inshore. Under the overhanging rock was a growth of scrub, and at the roots of the plants, almost underwater, a small white cross stood in mud. The guide tapped on the window. 'Head so as to pass one yard above where the baggage coach stopped, and no further,' he shouted to the driver. 'Make it quick and short.' The incline was steep and, almost at once, water flooded into the carriage from wheel level. I pulled my feet onto the seat, drew my knees up to my chin, and Mrs Bleeker and Franz did the same; Lavinia and Minnie stood upright on the seats; and all of us watched the scummy bath fill.

'Courage, everyone,' said Lavinia. Minnie whimpered. Franz sat opposite me, his gloved hands tight around his raised knees. His face was very pale under his pulled-down hat, his eyes were fixed on mine, but I sat rigid, lips pressed together, and I would not return his look.

The carriage tottered, righted itself, and Lavinia risked a look back through the window. 'My husband is urging us on. He is running up and down the riverbank and waving his hat in the air.' The water level in the coach was dropping, and out the window I saw a white cross in the dirt. Were we back where we started? No, a different bush, no overhanging stone. Minnie's whimper turned to a shriek of joy. As we climbed out, Rodnia tried to take my arm, but Franz was helping Lavinia and somehow elbowed him out of the way.

We stood looking back over the river, to where the remaining travellers — Mr Bleeker, Ned, Charlie, George and their hired driver — were entering the river in the last coach. Halfway across, at a point
not far from where Rodnia's carriage had stalled, the coach stopped.

'Oh my Lord,' cried Lavinia. 'They are stuck.'

'No, the driver has pulled up,' said Mrs Bleeker. Faint above the roaring of the river came the shout of the guide from the other bank. 'Don't stop. Don't stop, or you are lost.'

'His mettle is gone,' said Minnie. Lavinia put her hands to her mouth.

A sparse-haired head on a long neck emerged from the right window of the coach and shouted something to the driver, who sat frozen on his perch.

'They must drive on,' said Mrs Bleeker. 'It is the deepest part of the bar. If they stay, the flood will overwhelm them.'

The guide on the far side was screaming, but the wind snatched his words away. One of the horses whinnied back. Then the scream came again. 'Urge them. Urge them on.'

I looked at my fellow watchers, who had all leaped and shouted for Rodnia, but were now silent as the coach shook in the flood's jaws. Lavinia, her face drained of blood, clutched Mrs Bleeker's arm, pointed. Something had burst out the left window of the coach; a puppet hung from the sill by its boots, arms flailing, head dangling inches above the foam.

'Charlie?' said Lavinia.

Charlie's body twitched, tried a jackknife, hung down again.

'Charlie!' Lavinia rushed to the edge of the river, began to wade in. Mrs Bleeker and Franz grabbed her shoulders, hauled her back.

Charlie's body had gone as limp as a rabbit hung in kitchen rafters. Hands grasped his ankles, thin hands with white-lined wrists, but still he slipped a few inches down towards the flood.

Lavinia made a choking noise, struggled against her saviours.

Belly was still and I was numb. A dull certainty filled me: *he will fall, I will plunge in again to rescue him, his electricity will draw me, it is fated, we will drown.*

Then a pair of arms reached out the coach window, and knobbly hands, much larger than the hands at his ankles, grasped Charlie round the waist, slipped off, grasped again, pulled. Back went Charlie into the coach, a jack-in-the-box in reverse. The vehicle shuddered, the driver jerked into life: his whip cracked and cracked. The carriage rose and sank: the water reached up to the horses' necks.

'They will all drown,' cried Minnie. But the carriage was rising again, and slowly the horses hauled their dripping cargo up the bank. The coach lurched to one side, one door opened and out tumbled a mass of arms and legs, as if the bodies in their soggy coats had fused together.

As the bodies separated, a stringy figure with hands clamped tight over his ears climbed slowly from the coach. Mrs Bleeker ran to her husband, shook his arm, shouted into his face. He gave her a blank red-eyed stare. Lavinia also ran to her husband, but when she saw his face, purple with thunder, she stopped dead.

Charlie looked around until he saw George getting slowly to his feet. He began to dance on the spot, his fists raised, shouting. 'Swine. Villain. Confess.'

'Confess to what?' said George, brushing mud off his hat.

'You know what. You pushed me out the window.'

'Utter rot. You got into a funk, General. You pushed yourself out.'

'So. First you try to upstage me, then to murder me, and now you accuse me of cowardice. Poisonous worm. Jumped-up farmer's turd.'

George looked up from his hat, his jolly face pouting. 'You've had your time. It's my turn now, you fat old has-been.'

'Can't wait to get rid of me, can you? It was you pushed me off the bridge at Melbourne, wasn't it?'

'Bunkum. I don't *need* to get rid of you. Who do they shout for? Who do they love?'

Charlie drew himself up, inflated his chest, bellowed: 'I am the littlest.'

'Little right enough,' snorted George. 'A sight too little' — he stared at a point just below Charlie's waist — 'in some departments.'

'What are you insinuating, sir?'

'Lots of huff and puff. But no delivery. No results.' George crouched like a man playing tennis, expecting a return shot. Charlie, breathing furiously, glanced at his dejected and puzzled-looking wife. His gaze slid on and came to rest on me, and his eyebrows suddenly lifted as he strode to my side, took my elbow and steered me until I stood facing George like a great shield.

'No delivery, eh? No results? Here is all the evidence you need! It is you who are the has-been. Here is the future. Here am I, about to father the greatest little man in the world!'

Suddenly I felt as if everyone could see beneath my shawl, my dress, my underthings, right through to the dark bobbing ball in my womb.

'Please, General, don't,' I muttered.

'Don't you worry,' he whispered back, tightening his grip on my elbow. 'I know what I'm doing.' He put his little hand on my navel and shouted again: 'Behold the Coming Man!'

Belly shrank, convulsed.

I looked round for escape or support, but everyone seemed frozen. Even Mr Bleeker stood unmoving, eyes shut, holding his head in both hands.

'And now,' shouted Charlie, letting go my elbow, 'you will pay for your loathsome innuendos. Put up, swine!' He rushed past me and jabbed his fist at George's nose. George dodged just in time, slowly raised his own fists. They circled each other. Even above the rush of the river, I could hear the suck and blow of their breath.

229

Charlie led with his right, and suddenly there was another person between them.

'No!'

Rodnia stood sideways, one hand out towards Charlie, the other towards his brother, and even though he was the biggest of the three, he seemed to push mountains apart.

'Stay out of this, Roddie,' muttered George, but Rodnia shook his head, red-faced, furious-browed, his glare fixed on me, as if it were all my fault. I stepped back just as Mr Bleeker's eyes flew open.

'Stop this, all of you,' he shouted, hands still over his ears. 'Stop this disgraceful show. Is this all you can do when we've been plucked from the jaws of death?' The combatants stood staring at the ground. 'General, Commodore. Meet me in private the first chance we get when we reach Sydney. In the meantime, shake hands like gentlemen. No more nonsense.'

The little men glared at each other. Mr Bleeker stood between them, placed a dripping hand on each shoulder, and Charlie looked up in wonder. 'Mr B, you're shivering.'

'Come. Shake hands.'

Charlie stood still, gathering dignity. 'I will do it for you, Mr B. You have led us through the flood and plucked me from danger and the ladies are safe and dry.' He held out his hand. George grunted, folded his arms. Mr Bleeker drew his spine up and his brows down, the river roared behind them and slowly George extended his own hand. The handshake was brief, each looked over the other's shoulder. Lavinia let go of her sister and moved to Charlie's side, clung to his arm as Minnie had clung to hers.

230

Mr Bleeker turned to me and I stared at his lowered brows. But then he put a hand over his eyes and turned away. Clearly he had nothing to say to a woman who was the evidence, the future.

The circle of spectators broke up. Rodnia and the hired men busied themselves with the horses and carriages; Franz watched them; Ned stared at Charlie and George, now with their backs to each other; Lavinia and Minnie were whispering together; and Mrs Bleeker was reaching up to pull an overcoat around her husband's stooped shoulders. I was invisible, and I was glad of it.

Why had Rodnia glared at me so intently as he stood between the warring little men? Belly shivered. For once, Belly was moving faster than my brain.

I was so weary of all of them. Especially Belly.

• • • • • • • •

But then I was relieved. I lay in a warm meadow, and Belly was close by, wrapped safely in the black stripes of my silk dress that no longer fitted me, floating on a pond like a child's ball. The long grass overhead parted, and I looked up expecting to see Franz, but it was Mrs Bleeker. 'Leave her be,' came her voice. 'She is not sick. She just needs a holiday.'

I had never had a holiday. I stretched and sighed in the soft green grass. Then the grass melted, and I was lying on a lumpy bed, blankets heaped over me. My head hurt, my legs prickled and a dull pain throbbed in my groin. Under the blankets I put my fingers down to Belly, taut and hard, as if I had turned half-egg, and I yearned to go back to the meadow with Belly bobbing on the pond.

A smell of beef tea announced Mrs Bleeker with a tray. She spooned the broth into my mouth. 'You have had a nice holiday. You slept all day in the carriage and you slept still when we reached Sydney — my husband carried you to bed. Try some bread and butter. No, I don't need you yet. Nor do Mrs Stratton or Miss Minnie. They have both been to see you, have asked after you constantly. Take some more beef tea, it is strengthening. The General has asked after you. So have Mr Richardson and Mr Nutt.'

'The Commodore?'

'No, his brother.' She pulled a pink cloth from her sleeve and wiped up the beef tea where a little had spilled. I nodded slowly, sat up in bed looking at the cloth.

'There is something I have been trying to remember.'

'Hush, don't tax yourself.'

'No, I have it now, but I am not sure I understand it. That day we were walking back to Ballarat and you told me about the adoption plan, I remember your umbrella and those beautiful gloves you gave me, and how happy I was.'

Mrs Bleeker smiled. 'Quite silly with happiness, you were.'

I frowned. 'There was something else you said. *Of course, there is a condition. The child must be suitable.*'

Mrs Bleeker put a spoon into the beef tea and began to stir it vigorously. 'You must be sure to drink the dregs too.'

'What exactly did you mean by that, Mrs B?'

Mrs Bleeker took out the spoon, sniffed it. 'Well,' she said slowly, 'it is a matter of what the General meant.'

'Should I ask him then?'

'That will not be necessary. And may I remind you that you

agreed that all questions concerning the adoption should be directed to me. All he meant was that the infant should be healthy and perfectly formed. That is why you have had a holiday. He was most particular that you should not be disturbed.'

'And that is all he meant? Nothing else?'

'Isn't that all a child should be?'

'And the adoption is for life?'

'Naturally.'

'I cannot tell you how much easier in my mind I am now.' I breathed a deep sigh. When Charlie had pulled me forward on the riverbank and shouted about the evidence and the future and the Coming Man, I had almost thought him cruel, but perhaps that was just Belly's fear. 'It is wonderful to know I have so generous a benefactor. Do you know, I —' I broke off suddenly, gasped, then laughed at Mrs Bleeker's face. 'Here, feel.'

I took the spoon from her, placed her hand over the spot, and we waited. The kick came again, a lusty one, quite different from the usual ripples and trembles: Belly had grown fighting fit.

Mrs Bleeker rubbed her sleeve across her eyes and blew her nose. 'Lord, Sydney is such a town for brick dust,' she said.

CHAPTER 15

Mrs Bleeker was in a tizz. So much to do in such a hurry. George and Minnie were to go to the Lord Mayor's fancy-dress ball to meet Prince Alfred, the Duke of Edinburgh, Queen Victoria's second son, who was also visiting Sydney. At first the plan had been for Charlie and Lavinia to go, and Mrs Bleeker had had a grand plan for thousands of silver sequins on the Queen of Beauty's oyster-grey ensemble. But then Lavinia succumbed to a vile cold, and the doctor prescribed plenty of bed rest to protect her voice, so Mr Bleeker's thoughts turned to the second couple. Charlie objected that the poltroon Commodore would disgrace them all. But then Lavinia had a word in private, and I saw her husband emerge from her boudoir to tell Mr Bleeker airily that he had had enough of fancy-dress balls and royal asses — his wife had reminded him of where his true interests lay. 'The Coming Man, Mr B. The time is near,' he said in a stage whisper, putting a conspiratorial finger on his nose. I waited for him to turn to me, to bestow his smile on Belly. But instead he looked back through the open door towards the day bed where Lavinia sat, her hands folded protectively over the bunched blankets so that it looked as if the Queen of Beauty were the one who was expecting.

Then Mrs Bleeker touched my arm. 'No time to lose, we must have costumes. The Commodore can go as Dandy Pat, his velveteen will need a good brushing. Minnie must go as Little Red Riding Hood. Her red satin dress will do, but you must cut and sew the hem to the length of a little girl's skirts. Red thread and tiny stitches, mind, this is for royalty. And she must have a splendid cape and hood in red velvet, with a red satin lining. Here is money, buy the best velvet you can find — crimson, not scarlet.'

Smiling at the thought that at last Minnie would be permitted short skirts, and that I would be spared the sewing-on of thousands of sequins, I made haste to obey. And when Minnie came to me later and instructed me to lower her neckline, again I complied. Lavinia would never see it under her cloak, and what harm could it do?

. . . .

The morning after the fancy-dress ball, I woke late. The hotel was quiet, no one was around to scold me for oversleeping, so I crept to the breakfast room to see if anything was left. George was lifting the lid on a dish of kidneys. He winced and screwed up his haggard face in the steam, dropped the lid with a clang, winced again. His curls were plastered to his skull, as if he had dipped his head in a bowl of water to wake himself up. I knew better than to offer him a cheery greeting. He must have only just come back from the Lord Mayor's ball, and either he had not enjoyed himself, or he had enjoyed himself too much.

Although the ball was over, the thousands of tiny stitches I had made were still running through my head and I had no more appetite than George, who was watching me with a bleary gaze.

'Buck up,' he muttered. 'You're lucky. You're doing a great thing for her.' He shuffled past me, out of the room, for once without the roses in his cheeks. Ned met him in the corridor, put his arm round George's drooping shoulders and offered him something from a silver flask, and then they wandered off together.

On impulse I followed: down the stairs, out the back door, across the courtyard and along an alley to a murky little pond, a stream dammed with rocks where I'd seen horses brought to drink and washerwomen slapping their clothes on the stones, but all was quiet and deserted at mid-morning; it seemed a dank place for a confab. I was pretty sure the gents had not noticed me, and even if they had, they paid me no heed. I stood behind a copse of straggly eucalypts and watched as Ned stood on the muddy bank and looked about. George sat slumped on a dry stone and began a slow grumbling monologue, punctuated by Ned's occasional cries. The wind blew too much of their exchange away from me — all I could catch were a few words.

'The wolf,' George was saying, 'and the robin fucking redbreast.'

It was easier to hear Ned. He was either outraged and excited, or pretending to be so. 'Surely not!' 'What happened then?' And once, with a great guffaw: 'Hah, the royal sceptre at work!'

But George wouldn't be cheered, mumbled on and on. At last he raised his voice: 'Don't you dare say a word, Ned.'

Ned uncorked his flask. 'You know me, soul of discretion. Come, drink up. This'll warm your cockles. Just wait a sec while

I take a piss.' He slipped out of my vision, and I watched George take a long draught.

Suddenly, before I could move, Ned appeared around one of the trees. He smiled, but his eyes remained lazy-lidded. He had the silver top from the flask in his hand and he lounged against the trunk, raising his silver glass in a toast. I folded my arms and stared at him, and he winked.

'Eavesdropping again?'

'You're not in the billiard room now.'

He attempted a hurt-puppy look.

'You hung the General out of the carriage by his heels, didn't you?' It came out before I could stop myself, but I felt a savage pleasure in the saying.

Ned laughed. 'Sweet Jesus, ma'am, how can you say that? All was confusion in that coach; we were so rocked about. I was thrown onto the Commodore, and the Commodore rammed his foot in Mr B's ear, and the water so cold. We thought our hour had come. We were like a sackful of cats.'

'Yes. All was confusion. So nobody in the carriage would have seen what you did. But I saw, I was close, I recognised those wrists — I thought at the time you were trying to pull him in. But now ...'

Ned tugged his cuffs down, almost to his knuckles. 'Now why would I hang the General out the window?' he asked, as if it were some armchair mystery.

'Because you are a troublemaker.'

'I never bandy words with a lady, especially when she's in pod. But you're mistaken.' Ned swigged at his glass, wiped his mouth with a grey handkerchief.

'I am not a lady and you know it. But I see what I see.'

Ned narrowed his lizard eyes to slits, then opened them wide. 'You speak like a lady. You've got breeding. Your pa and your dear departed were both men of God. I'm just a poor boy from Brooklyn who's hoicked himself up and got himself educated. Mr Barnum is my God, ma'am. I mean no blasphemy. I study his words and his art.' He put one hand inside his jacket, pulled out a little book. 'Here's my Bible: *The Art of Money Getting* by P.T. Barnum. You should read it, ma'am. I'm hoping for a sequel: *The Art of Practical Joking*. Mr Barnum's very partial to practical jokes. Good healthy harmless fun.'

'Hey, Ned!' George was calling from his stony throne. I thought for a moment he could hear us, but the wind had shifted and was now blowing our words away from him. 'Where are you, boyo? Can't get your piss out?'

'Coming!' shouted Ned over his shoulder. 'Just a mo!' He came close to me, peered into my face; his breath was brandy-sweet. 'Are you planning to tell Mr B? We can do a deal, you know. Just to save you the pain of making false accusations.'

I stared back. 'I am not interested in deals, Mr Davis, only in heading off disaster.'

Ned grinned. 'Sure, sure. What can I say, ma'am? You see what you see.' His protruding canine gave him a vampire countenance. I had expected protest, anger, even snarling and clawing, anything but these cheerful shrugs.

'Is that all? You have nothing more to say?'

He held out his hands. 'What can I say? I'm just a poor boy from Brooklyn.'

'Ned!' called George.

'Excuse me, I have company.'

'You blackguard. You offered to broker a deal to buy my child. And when that didn't work, it was you who had me kidnapped in Ballarat, wasn't it?'

'I have no idea what you're talking about.'

'You are in Dr Musgrave's pay, aren't you? It wasn't just a tiger skin you tried to sell him, was it?'

Of course I could not be sure of what I was saying, but it was time for a challenge. I willed myself to stand straight, look him in the eye. I waited for him to shout and strike me, to give me proof of his guilt. But he just stood staring back.

Then, very slowly, he smiled, showed me his teeth. 'You should take more care with your accusations, ma'am. Think where they're coming from.' He turned, then looked back over his shoulder at me, a coquettish gesture. 'Good healthy harmless fun.'

He strolled back towards the pond, to a cheer from George. I waited for Ned to pull him to his feet, for them both to walk away, but instead he sat down beside him on the stone and they passed the flask back and forth in companionable silence. Finally Ned upended the flask while George lit a cigar. 'All gone ... Tell you what, Commodore. Do the Yarra Yarra.'

'That old thing? You've seen it a thousand times.'

What a difference a shift of wind makes. Now I could hear every word.

'And I never tire of it. Gets better every time. It's a work of genius.'

'I can't do it here, somebody might come.'

'You mean, you don't dare.'

'Fuck you, Ned.' George gave a weary cackle, blew smoke in Ned's face.

'Come on.' Ned took his arm, helped him up. 'It'll make you feel better. And this is the perfect place. Upsadaisy. There you go. Good boy … Yes! Yes!'

I rose on tiptoe, peered through the leaves. George stood on the top of the rocky dam, about three feet above the black pond, his face screwed into agony or ecstasy, doing some frantic business to the front of his trousers with his hands, while Ned whooped and clapped. Was the little man in pain? No, he was … It was too shameful, even in mime, but I could not look away.

'What are you thinking of, General?' said Ned, suddenly all indignation.

'What am I thinking of? Of the water, Ned, the mighty torrent.' George had Charlie's pompous, ponderous tone. 'That's what gets me vim and vigour going. The bath at Madam Boniface's.'

'Come, baby, time for your bath,' cooed Ned.

'Yes, yes …' He was getting breathless, his moving hand never stopped. 'I'm floating on my back, rosy Cupid. The mother-naked molls close in on me. They make waves with their cupped hands, they massage my limbs with sandalwood soap. The darkie embraces me, I suck at her luscious cinnamon breast.'

'Oooh, greedy boy,' cried Ned.

'Now I'm in the Japanese bath house. Veils of steam are parting. The glistening geishas pat foam on each other's nipples, they fondle each other's hairless crotches. They see mighty me, at the barrier where Mr Bleeker has lifted me up. They laugh and beckon …'

'*Amellican, Amellican,*' simpered Ned, beckoning. 'Please to jump.'

'They open their arms to me. My manhood is massaged to perfection. The water, the roaring water, rushes beneath me. I am electric. My mighty army of spermatozoa is primed to burst forth and seek its prey.' George spread his arms wide, swayed, jumped into the pond. The water only came up to his knees, but he staggered up the bank and fell onto the mud, rolled and thrashed and screamed. 'Mercy me, I'm drowning! Save me, good woman!'

As Ned bent to pick him up, George grabbed his shoulders and pulled him down, threw his legs around his hips and thrust his pelvis up towards Ned's groin.

'Oh, sir!' cried Ned in falsetto. 'Do not take advantage of me! I am nought but a poor widow!'

'Ohh, ahh, don't you be coy with me, you frisky filly,' gasped George, thrusting away. 'Yes, yes, open your mantrap! You're a busy little beaver, aren't you? You like a ride, don't you? Buck and rear for me! Napoleon ain't retreating this time!'

Ned giggled and shrieked and returned George's thrusts with extra vigour. They rolled over and over, coating themselves with mud, until Ned emerged again on top.

'That's right!' yelled George. 'Go at it, beaver!'

'Ooh, ooh, ooh!' wailed Ned. 'Fuck me harder with your magnificent … miniature … sugar stick!'

George gave a final buck, screamed, 'I am the Coming Man!' and lay kicking his feet in the air, while Ned stood and adjusted his invisible skirts. Then George sprang up, sauntered to the stone where he'd been sitting, picked up his abandoned cigar in his black fingers and blew a perfect smoke ring.

Their laughter followed me as I crept away. Ned had wanted me to know my place. Everyone in the troupe had known my place all along. Charlie's trollop. How odd that I had not known it myself, with my education and my breeding and my men of God, my fine needlework and piano playing and stories woven around me like a shabby shawl.

You really should be more careful with your accusations. Think where they're coming from.

I went to the privy, the only place I could be alone, and wept hot tears. Belly was quiet, as if asleep; it was all my misery. After a while, though, a spirit came to me and began to scold me, and when my throat tightened and tears welled up again, I struggled to stop them falling. *Your reputation does not matter*, said the spirit. *Of course Franz does not want you, how could he, but you have given up that ridiculous hope anyway. Your name might be brought low and your own future murky, but you are still the future for others.*

Then Belly woke and kicked me. Kicks aplenty, but no shivers and tremors. No longer afraid, Belly was hard and ready to fight for a future.

I dried my eyes. Somehow I would devise a way to get Ned to confess to setting those ruffians on me.

SIDESHOW

Commodore George Washington Morrison Nutt

Commodore Nutt and Minnie Warren

ACT TWO

Funk, what, me? Never. I am pluck personified, always on the attack: Commodore Nutt priming the cannons on his flotilla, Captain Jinks with his sabre aloft, Dandy Pat brandishing his shillelagh. Now my weapon must be my trusty pistol, and I cannot fail, for I have an arsenal of rage in me. Look how I point Widowmaker at my head in the mirror, look at my fiendish scowl. Aim, fire, kickback. I am a holy terror.

But by God and my beloved's black tresses, how I wish it had never come to this.

• • • • • • • •

My rage began to stir at the Lord Mayor's ball, where I'd gone in my best Dandy Pat green velveteen, a tot of brandy in me for courage, hopes as high and sprightly as the extra emu feather in my hat, and not a smidgen of grumpiness. Burly lackeys held the crowd back as I lovingly took Minnie the minx in her red cloak and hood by the arm and escorted her into the Exhibition Building. The picture of the radiant Lilliputian couple, we were. Nobody would guess what we really thought of each other. And all went well as we stood back to back, smiling, nodding, shaking hands: I said howdy-do to nine Hamlets, five Othellos, Coriolanus, a Turk, a cricketer, a jockey (a foot taller than me), two cavaliers, seven demons in tights, fourteen pirates, twelve peasants and so many mysteriously costumed gents I lost count.

And then the music stopped and silence fell, and all eyes turned as in he came, the plainest-dressed man in the place, a tall fellow in the dark habit and cowl of a monk, His Royal Highness Prince Alfred, Duke of Edinburgh, Earl of Kent, Earl of Ulster ... There it was, my chance to shine, to be By Royal Appointment, Comicalities for the Commonwealth, and you can be sure I doffed my cap and played the sneezy idiot with the feathers up my nose, but he was looking over my shoulder saying, 'Who is this enchantress with her basket of delights?' So I turned round. She'd let down her hood and pushed back her cloak behind her shoulders, so for the first time I saw what she wore beneath. A red dress, knee-length, like a little girl's smock. But little girls don't wear satin, nipped in at the waist and cut scandalously low. She pushed past me, eyes fixed on the Duke, curtseyed with a rustle, and I swear every Hamlet, Othello, Coriolanus, Turk, cricketer, jockey, cavalier, demon, pirate, peasant and monk in the room had his eyes down her décolletage.

Upstaged, by God.

Not a word passed between them. Gravely the Duke took her hand, lifted her up, led her to the centre of the ballroom. His equerry motioned for the band to start up. As they played a waltz, the Duke and the minx circled each other slowly in a swirl of red and brown, the ladybird and the thrush, or was it indeed Red

Riding Hood and the wolf? And what was I? A snail under a leaf.

The crowd applauded, then began to join the dance, but always keeping a space around the star couple. I wanted to jump up and down: *Look at me, Your Highness, forget about that scrap of bewitchery, look at me for some real artistry, I'll cast you a spell or two, look at meee!* But my audience was over.

Of course I still had my entertaining to do, and now the ladies were queuing up for me. Duty called. I danced with a simpering miss or two or three and a huge Queen of the Night who kept coming back for more — I could not escape her. A dozen or so champagne glasses later, when the room was beginning a slow, stately whirl, I searched for a glimpse of Minnie and the Duke but could not see them anywhere. I walked, then ran, through the ballroom and up and down the side aisles, tripping over sprawling revellers. Finally I reached a door guarded by the royal flunkey.

He tried to stop me, but I was too quick: under his arm, through the door, up a narrow set of stairs to another door. This one led into a dark booth like a private box at the theatre; it had an open front that overlooked the ballroom, but it was recessed so that no one could look up from the floor and see inside. Gold curtains were half pulled across.

A hooded figure sat with his back to me. Ahead of and facing him, very close, Minnie sat high on the parapet, her back to the stage. Her stripe-stockinged legs dangled. She reached out, slowly pushed back the figure's hood. With a grave concentration she put her hands to the chest. She was searching for fastenings, I realised. The robe slipped back, staying on the shoulders but exposing the chest. Minnie stared, motionless. Then she reached out again and ran her hands over the man in the chair, from neck to waist, lingering over some places, as if she were massaging the royal skin, tugging gently at whorls of hair. I imagined Lavinia's fingers on my own chest, and I gave an involuntary groan. Minnie looked up at me, swiftly pulling down her skirts, and he turned.

'Ah, Commodore. Good to see you, do come in.'

Smooth customer. Unbelievably smooth. He lounged in his chair with his ankles crossed.

'We are getting to know each other, Commodore. Miss Warren is very curious about my military awards.' He swept a hand across his glittering frontage, and I saw that he was not naked. Under his robe was dark wool, epaulettes, brass buttons, a red sash and a chestful of medals.

Minnie looked hard at me, then forward again. She touched one of the medals.

'Knight of the Order of St Andrew the First,' said the Duke. 'A medal from Russia. Commonly called the White Eagle. I am also a Black Eagle ...' He took her hand and placed it on another medal. 'And a Red Eagle.' He moved her hand again. 'And a Golden Lion ... and ... an Elephant.'

Minnie giggled. I thought I would stop breathing. But somehow I spluttered out my apologies, was as deferential as I could be, no funny business — my heart was way beyond humour — said we must be going. He requested a moment or two alone to bid farewell to his fair companion. I sweated, I boiled, but he was royalty. So I left them and stood with the silent equerry outside the door, knocking back more champagne, while the moments stretched and stretched and I could hear nothing but a singing in my ears.

At last she emerged, wrapped in her cloak. We walked arm in arm down to the rapidly emptying ballroom and on towards the exit. No one came near us. I think they were all too tired or too soused.

'Trollop,' I hissed.

'Don't be ridiculous,' she said calmly, eyes lowered. 'And don't say anything to my sister. You will be silent for me because I have been silent for you.' She gave me a sidelong glance to see if I had understood.

Once she had caught me with my secret *carte de visite* of my angel, set up amid candles behind a tiny folding screen. I'd been on my knees, kissing the image as forlornly as the withered peasant women we had seen in France had kissed the priest's ring. She'd withdrawn at once and had never said a word, so sometimes I thought that perhaps she hadn't seen anything after all.

But that minx knew exactly where my heart was, all trussed up in its golden chains. One word from Minnie, and I would see what I never want to see in my angel's eyes: pity for me.

• • • • • • • •

I woke very late the day after, still sprawled on the bedcovers fully dressed, with a bodhran thrumming in my head. I peeled off my sodden velveteens, stood on a chair at the dresser and poured jugfuls of icy water over my head until the drumming had faded a little, put on my soberest morning suit and stumbled downstairs in search of breakfast. No one was about but Mrs Bleeker's little assistant, the sweet-faced young woman bearing Charlie's child. Even though I've always believed Ned's story about her, it's hard to reconcile her innocent looks with all that rumpy-pumpy. But Ned saw what he saw and, after Minnie's behaviour, who could trust any woman but my angel? And then Ned, God bless him, turned up with a flask of his best medicine, just when my stomach was telling me breakfast was out, and after cautioning him to say nothing to Lavinia, bit by bit I poured out my heart to the good fellow. Well, no, not all of it, but certainly all my disgruntlement at the ball, and the smooth Duke, and the way all the people looked at him and that sluttish minx, and not at me. And on top of it all I'd lost my Dandy Pat cap. That confession did me a bit of good, for quite apart from my indisposition there was some feeling building in me as steam builds in a kettle, and I could feel my lid wobbling with it, but I didn't know what it was, or if I dared let it out.

We went to the pond for a bit, and joshed a little, and I did one of my private performances to let off some steam, but still it seethed and my lid wobbled and wobbled. Then Ned gave me some more medicine and took me up to his low-ceilinged attic room where even I could scarcely stand upright, and we sat down on his bed, and he put his arm around my shoulders and asked me straight, man to man, what was troubling me.

'I'm angry,' I said, and by God, there it was: that was what the steamy feeling was.

'Well, I'm not surprised,' said he, 'for sure as I'm a Brooklyn boy there's a devil of a lot for you to be angry about.' I thought he meant the ball, but then he began to talk — when he gets going, Ned sure can talk — and it was all about Charlie. He said he had thought to keep mum, had not wanted to upset me, but could see I was upset anyway and it was better to have it all out in the open.

'Have what out?' I said, and on Ned went. How Charlie was saying I'd been trying to murder him. First on the bridge over the Yarra Yarra, when I crept up behind him and pushed him into the flood. Then crossing the Goulburn, when I'd hung him out the carriage window by the heels and tried to drop him. And how it was only a matter of time before I'd have another go at him.

'So every time we pass a river I get the urge to push him in, is that it?' I burst out. 'I know we've had our fights, but this ... this ... By God, I will grind him to powder and scatter him to the winds.'

Ned ran a finger round his neck, under his collar.

'And yet I cannot. Ned, I am no ruffian ... Well, I'll go to the police and get him arrested for slander.'

Ned shook his head. 'Can't do that. Would ruin the show. And the publicity might ruin you.'

'But this is crazy ... Why does he think I would want him dead?'

'He says you want to be the greatest little man in the world and because you cannot eclipse him on stage, you will eclipse him in life. Then you will marry his widow.'

My mouth hung open, and I must have produced a new comical face without even trying. 'I am flabbergasted,' I said. 'Outraged.'

'Of course you are,' said Ned soothingly.

I did not tell him that Charlie's last and most shocking lie was the one that filled me with wild, evil hope. I strove to push it from me. 'Why would I want to marry his widow?'

Ned looked sorrowfully at me.

'What does he say? Answer me, man.'

'Can't. I'm your pal, ain't I?'

'All the more reason. Come on.' I stood on the bed, shook

250

him by the shoulders. He curled up under my assault, began to whimper. 'Out with it!'

'All right, all right, just let go of me.' I sat back, and he straightened his weskit, slicked back his cap of hair. 'He says you are her slave. But if you were the last man on earth she would never have you. He says they laugh about you together. He says you are a green cockroach, and she says one day someone will stamp on you. Squish. And then they laugh.'

My eyebrows went up, my frown came down, my eyes glared, my nose wrinkled, my upper lip rose, my mouth opened, my teeth clenched, but I could not find the right face for the steam that was rising in me, a boiling black cloud. All I could think of was Widowmaker, my faithful pistol, lying under my pillow.

'I'm sorry, Commodore. Truly I am.'

I groaned, hunched down, put my head in my hands, tried to think. Dimly I heard Ned talking, about how there might be a way to stop it all.

'As gentlemen used to do, if you take my meaning. But of course, it's not to be contemplated in our new age.'

'Hang on. What are you on about?'

'You must know, Commodore. When a gent's honour is impugned, when he must have satisfaction ...'

Slowly, I sat up.

'We could do it,' said Ned, as if to himself. 'I could make the connections, scout out the land, get the, ah, equipment. We'd need seconds. We could keep it a secret, a gents' affair.' Then he shook his head. 'What am I thinking? That kind of bravery, nobody has it now.'

I took his arm. 'Ned, Ned. I have it. Doesn't all come out of a brandy bottle, you know. I will face anything, for ... for ...' I wanted to say *for my angel*, but finished, '... for my reputation. Surely it is only what the blackguard expects.'

'You're certain, Commodore? It's a mighty big step to take.'

'Well, I will take a number of small steps. And then —' I mimed it, raising my arm, aim, fire, kickback.

It wasn't much of a joke, and he didn't smile.

'Leave it to me,' he said.

Now I am alone, and I sit with my hand mirror and Widowmaker, a strange calm fills me. I hold it close, for I know it will not last. There will be nausea, sweats, a feeling like a fist in my stomach, and my hands will be all a-jitter, and these are not ailments that Ned's flask can cure. But when the time comes, my hands will be steady. The funk always vanishes when I step onto the stage.

It's just such a big stage this time, and all around is blackness.

CHAPTER 16

Two days after the ball, and one day after I had eavesdropped on Ned and George's Yarra Yarra show, Lavinia came to me at breakfast time, sneezing and sobbing. From the window of her room, she had just seen Minnie, dressed in her Red Riding Hood cloak, board a grand black carriage drawn by two black horses with white plumes. Now they were on their way to the house of the gentleman who, according to the hotel clerk, owned the carriage.

'I must get Minnie back,' Lavinia cried. 'And I can't find Mrs B, so you will have to do. Get the clerk to fetch us a cab, Mary Ann, and tell the cabbie to make haste.'

I wondered what the hurry was, but Lavinia was too agitated to explain, and she grew more and more so as we had an interminable wait for our cab.

Even when we were on our way, it was impossible to make any speed in the Sydney traffic. Again and again our cab lurched forward a few feet, then shuddered to a halt. I peered through the window, hands over my nose against the whiffs of animal dung, and could see nothing but carriages and horse flanks. Overhead, our cabbie damned and blasted each time we stopped, and Lavinia and I, sitting side by side on the cracked leather, jerked forward and back, Lavinia convulsing in sneezes.

'Must you really be out and about, Mrs Stratton?' I asked.

'Someone must collect my sister, and as usual it falls to me.' Lavinia fanned her face with her gloves and wiped her streaming eyes.

'Would you like some of my medicine?' I opened my reticule and handed Mrs Bleeker's bottle of elixir to her. She took the cork out, sniffed dubiously.

'It smells just like Minnie's medicine. I wonder if it works on colds? It does not seem to work on Minnie anymore.' She took a long unladylike swig, grimaced, wiped her mouth. 'It tastes so horrid it must be good for one. Does it do you good, Mary Ann? It certainly makes you grow.' She raised her eyebrows in the direction of Belly.

Perhaps it was the medicine, but as we lumbered on in our slow progress, Lavinia seemed to grow calmer. Another jerk of the cab, and this time she fell sideways onto me. She laughed, apologised, and then continued to lean against me.

'May I …?' She reclined across Belly, ear against my navel, and patted the great curve with her hand. I felt a sudden rush of tenderness, as if it were Lavinia who was my child. 'I can hear a heartbeat,' Lavinia said dreamily. 'Goodness, he must be strong. Does he wake you at night?'

'All the time.'

'It must be very close now. How long?'

I had tried so hard to keep up my calculations, but the days had passed in such a whirl. 'A week, I think.'

'I will get Mr B to find the best doctor in Sydney.' Lavinia closed her eyes, and I held my breath.

I was not the General's moll. Those rascals by the dammed pond had it all wrong. So what was I then? A mother, a Madonna carrying the General's child. Or so Lavinia believed, and that was all that mattered, was it not?

'What a brave one you are, Mary Ann,' Lavinia murmured. I gave an inward shrug: that was what people said to those who were giving birth or dying, because they could not help it. But I would ask a brave question.

'Mrs Stratton …'

'Hmmm?'

'How big do you think the child will be?'

I had not forgotten my instructions to reserve all questions concerning the adoption for Mrs Bleeker. Would Lavinia be angry? But she merely blinked.

'Who knows? My dear, I don't care two hoots if he is a pygmy or a giant. Just as long as he is bonny and healthy.' She delivered a few more pats, as if she could measure the inside of the womb.

'Were the others bonny?'

'Others? What do you mean?'

'I have been given to understand that you have had other infants in your care.' I spoke slowly, weighing each word. 'I have seen a photograph.'

'Oh, that old thing,' said Lavinia carelessly. 'I thought we had got rid of those *cartes de visite*. We used to borrow babies for shows and presentations and photographs, and pretend they were ours. It was Mr Barnum's idea. We did not mistreat them; they always went back to their loving mamas, I can assure you. That has nothing to do with this little one,' and she resumed her patting.

I allowed myself to breathe again. It all sounded so simple and harmless. Why had I not dared to ask Lavinia about it before? Why had I worked myself up into such a frenzy of worry?

'You know,' Lavinia said, 'on the eve of my wedding, my mother warned me that I must not have children. Giving birth would kill me, she said.'

'But I thought … you and the General …'

'That we were barren?' She made a sad little noise, between a laugh and a huff. 'I don't know, because we have never … I had a talk with my husband before our wedding day, and we came to an arrangement. He is an admirable man, has always respected my wishes. As for his wishes …' She gave me a quick upward glance, then continued to lie sleepily across my lap, lashes drooping over her violet eyes. 'Forgive my indelicacy, but you are — were — a married woman, so I can speak to you of things that I could never discuss with my sister. He taught me how to give him oral satisfaction. It is not hard, and he never seems to tire of it.'

I stopped my gasp just in time. Charlie was indeed admirable: I could not imagine how such a virile soul would ever be content with kissing.

'Before you joined us, I had been wondering,' said Lavinia. 'We are always taught to listen to our mothers. But was I right to listen to my mother?' She patted my stomach again. 'At least now there is no need for me to wonder anymore.' She sighed, sat up, straightened her coiffure, sniffed and sneezed. 'Indeed, now I worry that Minnie does not listen to her sister. I keep thinking of that dreadful doctor in Seymour. I fear she is chasing the spark again. We must catch her before it is too late.'

I thought of Minnie being caught, a red butterfly in a net. Was that what happened, when you chased sparks?

The cab turned onto the shush of a gravel drive and pulled up. I opened the cab door, blinking in the brightness of a day of high cloud, and saw a handsome frontage of pillars and sandstone, hidden from the road behind high walls. I beckoned to the cabbie, paid the fare and helped Lavinia down. He drove away as we climbed a wide flight of steps to the front door. It was a steep ascent for Lavinia, and she could not reach the doorbell. As I stretched over her shoulder, the door swung open, and a thin fussy-looking fellow in black peered down at us.

'I am Mrs Charles Stratton and I have come to fetch my sister.'

Lavinia stood straight-backed, chin high. If the young man was surprised, he gave no sign, but bade us come in. The hall stretched for acre after acre; our footsteps echoed. If all was so vast to me, how must it seem to Lavinia? I fought the urge to take my employer's hand.

We were shown into a handsome parlour. Lavinia declared the brocaded chairs would fold up and swallow her but, with my help, she climbed onto one nonetheless. In the tones of a cathedral bell, a mantelpiece clock tolled twelve. How long it had taken us to cover a few miles, and now we must wait again.

'Where has that young man gone?' said Lavinia. 'I would like some refreshment.'

I looked in vain for a bell pull. 'I will go and find someone'.

'Must you leave me here alone?' Lavinia's voice was low and trembled a little.

'I won't be long.' I propped up the cushions behind her back, gave her a clean handkerchief from her reticule and stepped into the hall. No one was about. I might as well have been in a mausoleum. Marble urns topped pedestals that could uphold the Parthenon. Ancestral ogres in ruffs and farthingales glared from the walls. I began to walk briskly one way, then turned and walked the other. Where did one go for a cup of tea?

Very faintly, a voice wafted towards me. Thin, high, sweet.

When other lips and other hearts
Their tales of love shall tell ...

At first I thought it Lavinia's voice, but the timbre was wrong, and it came from much further away, higher up.

In such a moment I but ask
That you'll remember me.

I followed the sound up a flight of stairs to a door, knocked. The voice stopped. An unexpected sound: a swirl of water. All at once I was overwhelmed with the sense that on the other side of the door lay Seymour, the glistening lake, the roaring torrents from the hills, the animal bleats of terror. There was only one way to tackle such a flood. I opened the door wide.

SIDESHOW

Miss Minnie Warren

Mrs Sylvester Bleeker and Minnie Warren

ACT TWO

So there I was, standing on a strange four-poster bed, undressing all by myself, pulling down my striped stockings, loosening my stays. Two days after the ball, when everything changed. Two days that had lasted forever, but now I was going to have what I wanted more than anything else in the world, and yet I could not stop my fingers fumbling and my heart thumping and my whole body shaking. And it was not because of any chill in the air, or the darkness and ancient perfumes of the embroidered bedcurtains that surrounded me and kept me hidden, or because I was frightened of discovery. It wasn't even because he was on the other side of those curtains. It was because of what Madame Clofullia told me, all those years ago, that seemed so funny at the time.

She was the bearded lady at Mr Barnum's museum, and it was she who finally answered my incessant questions about the Act of Love. I had gotten nowhere with Lavinia, even after her wedding. She just said something vague about kissing and such. I rushed out of her boudoir and took my questions elsewhere. Mrs Bleeker said an act of love was always rewarded in heaven. Not an act, the act,

I made plain; and Mrs Bleeker's cheeks turned plum and she said I would find out in good time when I was married.

I had to wait another two years until Madame Clofullia deemed me old enough to know. First, she made me swear I would never reveal who had told me. Then she explained.

'The Act of Love is for the creation of children and for the glory of the Creator. First, the lady must record the dates of her monthly emissions. Then she must arrange for the act to take place midway between her menses. Not a day or two before, or after. That is no good for children.'

I asked what exactly the lady should do next.

'She informs her husband of the date. Then he visits her at night ... What did your sister tell you?'

'Kissing.'

Madame Clofullia chuckled. 'So it begins. Then the member of the husband — you know of the member?'

I thought of the pee-pee tap on my little brothers and the bull's raised pizzle. I nodded.

'The member rises like a flower and the lady must climb up and sit herself upon it, envelop it and ride it.'

I tried very hard not to burst out laughing. I wondered if I would need a stepladder. I thought of Monsieur Clofullia — a thin twiggy gentleman who had a much sparser beard than his wife and wore a monocle in his left eye to make him look fierce — and I gazed dubiously at Madame's spreading crinoline.

'But does not the member get squashed?'

'Not at all. It is quite firm for the purpose.'

'And the act — is it very wonderful?'

For the first time, Madame looked down and blushed behind her whiskers. 'It is for children. Monsieur is most particular. To have children will be very wonderful. Birth is the miracle of marriage.'

I thought of Madame Clofullia cradling a baby with fuzz on its chin. But I could not see Madame riding Monsieur. And I could not see myself doing such a thing with anyone, ever. If the Commodore would not have me — and, to be plain, I would not have him either, for what woman with self-respect will take a man whose heart is already given away? — then I would devote myself to my singing and performance and live as a nun.

But I did not have the feelings of a nun, and as I grew older, and my figure and complexion improved, I began to realise that even though marriage might be impossible, and I was no Queen of Beauty, no Robber Bride who can walk down the aisle with two hearts dangling around her neck with her diamonds, there might yet be men who would want to love me. And they were not the size of the Commodore, or a Russian dwarf, or a miniature Hottentot, but regular full-sized fellows who shouted from the theatre floor or kissed my hand and murmured compliments when we lined up to present ourselves to the public. I learned to flutter my fan and my eyelids, but I also learned that the usual rules for a young lady did not apply to me. We were touring then, from city to city, and later from country to country, and I didn't have time to wait for a gentleman to declare himself. I had to come forward, to make discreet but firm declarations of my own, with my eyes and my fan and my voice.

So that is what I did, and what gates I unlocked, most particularly within myself. The gentlemen responded with great warmth and boldness. I know Mrs Bleeker would think they were evil men who had a horrid fascination with freakish forms of nature, but it was not so: they were my selected Kings of Beauty, responding to the frank attentions of an amative young woman. It is wonderful what you can do with the play of eyes, the brief caress of a hand, standing right next to your sister, and she does not see it. Under my dress I would squeeze and rub my thighs together and imagine the handsome stranger touching me. Once I did arrange a secret rendezvous, with a boy in San Antonio who had mesmerising eyes, but I would allow no more than kissing, and anyway he was frightened of me up close.

· · · · · · · ·

Then there was the young doctor in Seymour, with the face of a fierce angel, his passion, his healing hands on my bosom, and I was almost ready for the Act of Love, I swear, but then the storm came crashing in on us and the poor fellow fled like a rabbit. I was sorry that my little adventure had so pained Lavinia, but she didn't understand that everything I did was in homage to the Act of Love, to the moment when I would experience it for myself.

The moment I set eyes on him, I knew he would be the one. He was not a boy or a scared rabbit. He was a ruler of men and his broad chest was covered in glory. But I knew I would have to guide him, little by little. It is odd how grown men are frightened of little women. They think we are like fine rose-strewn teacups that will shatter under their rough hands, and then maybe the shards will hurt them.

He summoned me to this place, but he said he was my loyal subject, and mine to command. He arranged for us to be alone, and I asked to see the scar on his left side, where the bullet from the Fenian assassin's pistol entered his body. Then I asked him to take off all his clothes. It was a test. If he did it, but did not ask me to do the same, then I would know. I remembered the date of my last menses. My apologies to Madame Clofullia, but this would not be for children.

He waited very quietly for me outside the bedcurtains. He must have been shivering too. If I told him to go, he would go. We agreed on that. But I didn't make any sound at all.

We could not see each other. The bedcurtains were drawn against him. But I caught a glimpse. He was like a bronze of Poseidon.

The member rises like a flower, I told myself, and I will sit on it and envelop it. Dear God, what am I doing?

This is what you do when you have followed your sister all your life, and then a wall springs up between you, and you can no longer follow her.

George called me a trollop, and that word stung like a slap, but what would he know, to him all women are either goddesses or gutter creatures. There is no word for what I am. An adventurer is brave, but an adventuress sounds hard, calculating, even criminal. And it is true that if I want to be true to myself and yet not shock and hurt my dear sister, I shall have to scheme and deceive. If anyone, anyone at all in our little band, has even the smallest idea of my adventuring, they must be silenced, and I will do whatever I can to make sure of that, and all will be well.

I don't deceive myself that all will be well with me. I will grow old with no man, no babies. All I want is a few memories of beauty that I can hold in my heart.

And then I was ready to draw open the curtains and appear on my little stage, and I who had faced grizzly bears with impunity, I wanted to hide under the bed or tremble in my sister's arms. Courage, I told myself.

CHAPTER 17

By the time I made my way back to the room where I had left Lavinia, the fire was blazing again, a trolley stood before the hearth laden with tea, sandwiches, pastries, a brown bottle, a soda siphon and crystal glasses, and a tall handsome man with sailor's whiskers was sitting on a sofa and talking to Lavinia as if they were dear old friends. All that warmth and comfort, and yet suddenly I was watching it from far away, as if I were buried in a transparent mountain of ice.

I watched the redness creep from Lavinia's nose across her cheeks as she sipped her tea. I tried to catch her eye. Lavinia saw me and smiled.

'There you are. Your Royal Highness, may I present our assistant wardrobe mistress and indispensable helpmeet, Mary Ann Carroll.'

Lord, the Queen's son himself. I curtseyed deeply. The Duke beamed at me over the rim of his seltzer glass. 'Indispensable, eh? Young woman, your charming employer was just about to give me indispensable advice. I have confessed to a phobia. You know what scares me? Chaps in black with tight white collars. Hundreds of 'em.

They sweat like cheeses. They declare themselves loyal subjects. Their loyalty goes on and on … Mrs Stratton, I am so bored with public life and so worried I will lose patience. What should I do?'

Lavinia lowered her eyelashes. 'Pardon me, as a mere American citizen, I would never presume …'

'Presume away,' said the Duke. He stretched out his long legs. His boots were the softest leather I had ever seen.

'Very well,' said Lavinia. She sounded reluctant, yet I knew at once that all hope of speaking to her in private had gone, and the ice tightened its grip on me. Where were the tremors, the sneezing attacks, the anxiety? A new Lavinia spoke to the Duke in the voice of calm authority. 'You should be warm and gracious and sunny, but not too familiar. You should make everyone you talk to feel very special.'

'Oh, yes,' said the Duke eagerly. 'You are right. You put it so well.'

'You must be patient with pompous fools and rude fellows. Some people assume I must be very stupid because my head is small. And therefore my brain must be underdeveloped.'

'That is prejudice of the worst sort. You have a rare intelligence.'

'Your Royal Highness, please save your compliments. I have not finished yet.'

I topped up Lavinia's teacup. Would I ever get a word in? But even if I could, what would I say about what I had just seen?

'When a speech is very long and very dull,' Lavinia continued, 'you must open up a corner of your mind and picture something you love to do. That will make you appear attentive.'

'Lord, yes. Why did I not think of that?'

'We shall practise. I am a dignitary with a scroll. I am declaring my loyalty … Blah blah blah … Is there a picture in your mind?'

A pause. Then the Duke nodded. 'I am on the quarterdeck of the *Galatea*. A crisp morning. Stiff breeze from the south-west ...'

'Good ... Blah blah ... And again?'

'Hunting kangaroo. Blighters hopping everywhere .... Got one.'

'Yes, Your Highness looks most sanguine ... Blah blah ... and now?'

He smiled. 'A mere American citizen.'

'Are you playing a parlour game?' said Minnie. She stood in the doorway in her best morning gown, buttoned up to the lace at her chin, curls neatly pinned and fluffed, her red cloak and basket over her arm. 'I'm glad to see you're better,' she said to Lavinia. 'I suppose you have come to fetch me back.'

'There is no hurry,' said Lavinia. Then her hand flew to her mouth, in amazement at what she had uttered.

The Duke said he understood. The life of an artiste was so demanding. It grieved him to part with such a fascinating pair of sisters when they had only just met, and he had so much to learn, but ... The equerry ushered us all out. The Duke saw the sisters into the black carriage, arranged a mohair rug over their laps, kissed their hands, declared himself their loyal subject. I climbed in and sat opposite, unnoticed, as the Duke pressed a bottle of elixir into Lavinia's hand — 'For your cold, it works wonders' — and stood waving as the carriage swept away.

The ice mountain that had held me prisoner was gone. I wanted to scream. But I was silenced as surely as if my lips had been sewn together.

• • • • • • • •

The carriage was much better sprung than the rickety cab that had taken us to the Duke's Sydney quarters, and the journey back to our hotel was smooth and quiet. The sisters sat bolstered like figurines in ivory cushions. The only movement came from Lavinia, smoothing her gloves down her fingers, over and over again, until Minnie put out her own gloveless hand towards her.

'He summoned me.' Minnie's chin had a defiant tilt. 'He said he would like one of my red slippers. So I gave him one. The other is here.' She lifted the cover of her basket and gasped. 'I swear I didn't know this was here. I will send it back.'

Lavinia leaned over, slowly pulling out a string of rubies. She inspected each gem with a practised eye.

'I would not send it back if I were you. It might cause offence.'

'Whatever has come over you, Vin?' Minnie stared at her. 'Of course I shall send it back. I am not … You know I have never wanted jewels.'

'A diamond.'

Minnie frowned.

'That is what you said at Seymour,' said Lavinia. '*Let me have one diamond.*'

'Oh yes.' Minnie smiled, stroked the shoe in her basket. Lavinia shifted in her seat. The ruby necklace slid off her lap and I retrieved it, put it back in the basket, as Lavinia bent towards Minnie's neck. 'You are using a new scent.'

'Do you like it?'

'It reminds me of rosebuds.'

I leaned back, thoughts rushing to and fro, seeking escape. I closed my eyes.

After a while, Lavinia spoke. 'Mary Ann?'

I feigned a little snore.

'The poor soul, she works so hard,' said Minnie.

Another pause. Then Lavinia's voice, low and urgent. 'Minnie. We must speak plainly.'

'Yes, dear.'

'You have broken your promise to me. You have gone looking for the spark.'

'No, it came looking for me. And it found me.' Her voice was wondering, childlike. 'Don't think I am in love.'

'Lord save us, were you alone with him? What did he do?'

'Nothing you need worry about, dear. He said he was my loyal subject, and I must command him. So I did.'

'Minnie, how could you?'

'We are not as other women,' said Minnie with a new firmness. 'The rules are not the same for us. So I will be discreet, but I will follow the spark.'

'Do you not see? You cannot do this. You will be collected.'

'Collected?'

'You are rare. A prize. No matter how discreet your plans, no matter how honourable the … other party, in his heart of hearts you will be pinned like a butterfly …' Lavinia's voice rose, wavered. She broke off into sneezes.

Minnie answered in the deeper tones of a reassuring older sister. 'Something may be pinned. Some keepsake. But not me.'

A long pause. I opened my eyes a tiny slit. Minnie had grabbed her sister's hand, held it to her heart. Lavinia looked away, her clean handkerchief covering most of her face.

'Say something, Vin,' said Minnie. 'Or I will know only that you despise me.'

'Of course I don't despise you. It is only that I despise stolen kisses. And I do not want you to be hurt.'

'But it hardly hurts at all. That is the wonderful thing.'

I had to marvel at Minnie, at what a strange package she was. Everything she had said to her sister was totally sincere.

Minnie threw her arms around her sister. 'Vin, are you crying? What's the matter?'

'It is only my cold …' Lavinia lowered her handkerchief. 'Oh, see, Mary Ann is with us again. Did you have a nice nap?'

Minnie inched forward, patted my knee as I shrank from the touch. 'Mary Ann knows my secret.'

'Indeed?' said Lavinia, with a brave attempt at archness. 'And what might that be?'

'Ladies may collect too,' said Minnie.

'If you please, Mrs Stratton, I don't know anything.'

'I mean my beauty secret, of course.' Minnie's smile had grown a little steely. 'My new scent.'

'The attar of rosebuds? Then you should have a little bottle made up for her, Minnie. It is light, fresh, most becoming.'

Minnie looked at the bottle of elixir the Duke had given her sister, lying on the ivory cushions. 'Vin. You must remember to take your medicine.' She began to sing, motioning for Lavinia to join in, but her sister sat silent.

When hollow hearts shall wear a mask,
'Twill break your own to see:
In such a moment I but ask
That you'll remember me.

I sat very still. It was not just my lips that were sealed. My whole body was bound in a spiderweb. The strands stretched tight over Belly, but they did not break.

• • • • • • • •

When I had opened that door upstairs in the Duke's Sydney quarters, while Lavinia sat fretting in the parlour, the scent of a vast garden of roses had poured out to fill my head. I felt gusts of warm humid air and saw points of light dancing on a high ceiling. Slowly I moved into the room, as if I were swimming. The lights on the ceiling were reflected from a child's white bathtub in the centre of the floor. In the tub Minnie reclined, pink soapy water up to her chin, her curls fanned out over the rim. Her face was turned towards the ceiling and her eyes shone with delight or tears.

'Miss Warren?'

Minnie turned her head, blinked through the steam. 'Is my sister here?' I nodded. Minnie's face went blank, then contorted in panic. 'She is waiting downstairs? Is she coming up?'

'I don't think so.'

'Does she know where we are?'

'No.'

Minnie sighed, lowered her lids. Then she raised one glistening arm from the perfumed water, inspected it with studied languor.

From sheer habit, I looked for a towel. On the floor I saw a cambric shirt; a gentleman's trousers and morning coat, of very fine fabric and cut; a gentleman's undergarments; and a gentleman's boots, the softest leather I had ever seen. They were strewn carelessly, but they seemed to lead in a trail towards a huge four-poster bed, hung with embroidered curtains. On the floor at the foot of the bed were a little gown, petticoats, a camisole, drawers, stockings. I followed the trail, picking up Minnie's things, and pushed open the bedcurtains. The bedclothes were stripped back to rumpled sheets. On the pillow was a yellow silk cravat.

The rose smell was cloying. A sound of a small waterfall.

'Leave those things.' Minnie's voice from behind me had a sharp edge. I turned. Minnie was standing in the tub, pink and mother naked. She bent down to retrieve a white towel from the floor, beneath her discarded Red Riding Hood cloak. 'Since you're here, you may help me dry. But I'll dress myself today.' She wrapped herself in the towel, stepped out of the tub. I kneeled down and rubbed her briskly through its folds, fighting a temptation to rub much harder than I should. 'Pin up my hair.' The curls slipped and slid out of the pins. 'Mary Ann, let us be clear. You have not been in this room. You did not see me.'

'I …' How could I be party to such brazen deception?

'You know nothing of this room and I know nothing of where this' — she gently nudged Belly — 'comes from.'

'But —'

'It's quite simple. You keep my secret, I keep yours.'

'Miss Warren, you are mistaken. I have no secret.'

Minnie looked at me through wild impatient locks. 'For heaven's sake, what else would you call it? Fraud, perhaps? You come down to Melbourne alone, from somewhere in the depths of the bush. You have been a governess with a family. You had to leave suddenly for no clear reason. My brother-in-law finds you wandering in the middle of the night on the banks of a wild river. Suddenly the governess is a widow. And suddenly my brother-in-law is a father-to-be.'

The story was so trite, so obvious. The cheapest of tricks. Raw shame rose in me, tingled in my cheeks. 'Miss Warren, please listen —'

'Nobody asks questions. They don't need to. You are an answer to a prayer. My brother-in-law has a mad theory about electric conception. My sister knows it's mad, yet she believes it. For a while, anyway.'

A faint hope flared in me. 'She wants the child.'

'Of course she does. And she'll get it. As for you, if you say anything about me, you will be cast out. But if you keep quiet, I'll see to it that you go with the happy family to America.'

'America?' Suddenly the country seemed as impossible as the wonderland down the rabbit hole in Matilda's book.

'That's what you want, isn't it? When this tour is over, that's where we will all go.' She yanked back a strand of hair, looked me in the eye. 'Including Franz Richardson.'

I stopped rubbing. I felt as if I were the naked one. Was there anything that this cunning creature had not seen, did not know?

'I'll get you to America,' she said. 'That's all I can do for you, and it's plenty, believe me. Contrary to what you might hear, none of us little people were born small. So you have time on your side.

Lavinia listens to me, and she believes her husband. People believe what they want to believe. But only for so long.'

'So … she will not keep me? Or the child?'

Minnie shrugged. 'Not once it starts getting big. Not unless you were governess to a child whose father is the size of the General.' She sat down on the edge of the tub, dried between her toes. 'Never mind. You'll be in America.'

I imagined pushing her back into the tub, holding her under the water, feeling her grasp and claw like her brother-in-law in the Yarra Yarra.

'You'd better go down now. We mustn't keep my sister waiting. Remember what I said. We'll be good friends and keep each other's secrets, won't we?'

I nodded. I could find no words, no actions. The roses were suffocating me. I turned, fled the room.

CHAPTER 18

It had started to rain, and I lumbered out to the hotel courtyard to unpeg washing from the line and sort it out under the porch. Damp things in one basket, dry things in the other. Into the dry basket went Minnie's petticoats and drawers. I had gone at them furiously with my scrubbing brush, trying to drive out the scent of roses. Now I folded and smoothed them with care. I had to stay calm, had to remember that Minnie was not my enemy. She was only trying to survive, to escape from the need to be tractable. And she was right: I did want to go to America. Or rather, I wanted to go where Franz was going. Perhaps he might still take some notice of me, in a brotherly way. And I wanted the baby.

I paused in mid-fold, holding a sheet out before me, arms wide as angels' wings. What a strange trick my mind had just played on me. Of course I did not want it, not to keep. I wanted a good home for it; that was quite different. And I would not abandon it: I would first make sure it had the best possible home. The wind blew the still-damp sheet against Belly. Could the creature in my womb feel the moving air, the damp? I wanted it. Bonny, healthy. Not for myself, of course not. For Lavinia and Charlie. Lavinia did not mind if it turned out giant or pygmy, she had said so. But Minnie had said otherwise. Charlie was expecting the littlest man in the world, everyone knew that. *It must be suitable.* I turned sideways onto the porch's dark windowpane, trying to see my reflection under the sheet, how large my white sail swelled. Whatever was in there, pressing on my stomach and bladder, giving me heartburn, it was not a Lilliputian. And when would it be born? A week to go, I had told Lavinia. Seven days. One hundred and sixty-eight hours. But that was only a guess; I might have more time or less, much less.

I closed my eyes, imagined Belly exploding out of me in a rush of blood and slime, Mrs Bleeker tut-tutting, ordering me to mop up the mess and throw it down the privy. It was too much to bear. I dropped the sheet and clasped my hands tight. Lord, let me die in childbirth. Not too much pain, please, Lord, and then oblivion.

My damned throat, tightening. I would not cry. Someone, the Lord or otherwise, must help me.

'Mary Ann? What's the matter? Is the bab paining you? Are you sick?'

Rodnia Nutt, carrying a saddle over his shoulder, had come out of the archway to the stables and was staring at me from across the courtyard. In the rain his curly hair straggled down his forehead. I had a stupid urge to take each strand, wind it round my fingers and restore it to its corkscrew shape.

'Nothing is the matter, thank you, Rodnia.' I did not know how I could make my voice so calm, or stretch my face into such a smile. I only hoped he had forgotten my stupid dog-tired outburst at Seymour. He came closer and stood watching me, very solemn.

'Something's wrong. The way you look …' He took his clay pipe from his mouth.

Please, Lord, let him think these are raindrops on my face.

'You remind me of someone I knew once,' he went on. 'Emmeline. She was about to be wed. She said she was happy. Her fiancé rode the trapeze with her.'

'I don't see what some acrobats have to do with me,' I said coldly, but he went on, his voice rough and urgent.

'The fiancé. His name was Mr Ludovic. He used to click his tongue and call to her like she was his pony. And she'd just stop whatever she was doing, and go to him.'

'Rodnia, I'm sure you have your errands, and I have mine …'

'At least let me carry a basket for you.' He put down his saddle, reached for the basket, and I nudged it away with my foot.

'Emmeline died,' he said. 'At her wedding. She fell from the trapeze and she died.'

'Then I am sorry.' I picked up and folded the sheet, piled one basket of washing into the other.

'She fell with her arms out. Like she was diving into an embrace.'

I put the baskets on my hip and walked swiftly away from Rodnia, back into the hotel.

But still he called out after me: 'He was dazzling, that Mr Ludovic.'

How he spat out that name. It was almost as if he were angry with me. I was sorry that his story was still upsetting to him, but I had somewhere else to go. There had been another offer of help, and this one I could no longer reject.

• • • • • • •

Franz was writing in his windowless cubby hole of a room, hunched over a candle, cigarette dangling from his mouth, covering page after page with urgent scrawl. He looked up at me as I stood in the doorway, his gaze so fierce that I thought I had not been forgiven after all for my rejection of his help. But he pulled the pages hastily together, put them face down on the bed behind him, stubbed out his cigarette and came to the door.

'I am sorry,' he said with a smile. 'You startled me.' I stared at him across the top of my baskets and his brow wrinkled. 'Have you been crying?'

I turned my face away as his hand approached, and he drew it back.

'You were right,' I whispered.

'About the child?'

'Yes.'

Franz gave a long sigh. 'Put down that basket. Come, sit by me.' He stuffed his papers into his battered leather satchel and fastened the clasp, sat down and patted the counterpane. I perched on the edge of the bed, as far away from him as I could. 'Dry your eyes. Use that handkerchief in the basket, it is mine. That's better. Now, tell me everything.'

Where to begin? The horrible pantomime by the dammed pond? Minnie's ruthless bargain? My own pathetic yearning to escape to the New World with this man? I shook my head. 'I can say only that now I know. They will not want the child.' He was watching me steadily. 'Franz, help me. I don't know what to think. I don't know where to go.'

He made no move towards me. I put my hand to my head,

fingered the silver hairpin he had given me, thought with shame of the unwelcome kiss I had bestowed on his cheek. I told myself to be glad that he was always such a gentleman.

'You will stay with the troupe, of course. Will your confinement be soon?'

'A week to go.'

'Tell me, Mary Ann, do you want to keep the child?' His voice was shockingly brusque, urgent.

'I have never wanted anything else.'

Even as I said the words, I knew they were not true. But it was as if they became true when I said them. My mind had not been playing tricks on me. A savage hunger rose from my womb, tore at my heart. I wanted the baby. I thought again of Father's words: *The Lord giveth, the Lord taketh away.*

Not this time, Lord.

'Then don't say anything to anyone. Carry on with your work as usual. Have faith in me. I will devise a plan.'

He rose, tall and commanding, his hair burnished a deep russet in the candlelight, tucked his satchel under his arm and placed his hand on my shoulder, a priest's comfort. I placed my own hand on his, clung and squeezed, biting the inside of my cheeks to stop the tears coming again. Gently he patted my hand, loosened its grip and restored it to my lap as if it were a doll he had mended for me.

'You know my regard for you, dear mermaid. Be patient, have faith. You are always in my thoughts, and I will do everything in my power for you and your little one.'

Then I was alone with the candle flame, sitting on a man's bed.

• • • • • • •

Mrs Bleeker collared me at breakfast the next day. 'Ten reels white thread, ten black, five silver, three lilac, two yellow, four red. Buttonholing thread. More pins and needles and a really sharp pair of scissors. Here is a basket, here is a list, here is money. Find a haberdashery.'

'I cannot go,' I said.

'What is the matter? It is not your time, is it?'

'Not yet.'

'You are dressed, you are upright, you are eating oatmeal. You are well enough to go. Be off with you, quick.'

The Sydney market boasted pyramids of apples, piles of linen, tables covered with bottles, but nothing for the needlewoman: the stall I had visited to buy red velvet and thread for Minnie's costume was no longer there. Should I ask someone about a haberdashery? The faces around me seemed intent only on shouting their wares and, if I strayed too close, the stallholders thrust pieces of fruit or fabric under my nose.

My body was leaden, my skin itched like a too-tight corset, my feet had grown flat and wide — I could scarcely squeeze them into my boots. Only my head was light.

'Mama. Mama.' A little child. Sailing past, a lady in blue, forget-me-nots embroidered on her shawl, well-wrapped babe in arms, two small children clinging to her skirts, a slightly older boy in a sailor suit trailing behind, licking a toffee apple with a caramel tongue. 'Mama, I want …'

I turned slowly, around and around. The market was full of children. Mites with their mamas and nursemaids, ragamuffins with stealthy fingers. Three played hopscotch over squares scratched in the dirt. One with a grimy patch over one eye stood by a wall rattling a bowl, a smaller child squatting at his feet, gazing at me through matted hair.

I closed my eyes. I was back in the doll's house in Middleborough, Massachusetts. I went to the cradle, pushed back the apple-green blanket and picked up ... His name was Thomas. His crown shone through fine reddish-blond hair, his skin glowed, folded around his wrists and ankles as if someone had tied them with thread. He smelled of newness, and his closed eyes were little translucent fishes. What had changed? One moment I'd had Belly, swelling Mrs Bleeker's handme-down teagown. Now I had Thomas.

Had my memory failed me? Was the baby already born? But when I opened my eyes again, still I swelled. Why had I never thought of what lay inside, not even when he flexed his little legs?

Thomas tottered, clinging to my hand. He wrote on a slate with chalk. He went fishing in a creek. He rode a pony. I clapped my hands over my ears at the cacophony of voices, treble and cracking and deep, Thomases of all ages. *Mama, Mama.* I splayed my fingers under my shawl. *Here I am, Thomas. I will care for you.* And Thomas kicked, a reassurance and a warning. I thought of him in Lavinia's arms, his christening gown frothing to the floor. Then another photograph, of Charlie and his lady before the draped velvet curtain and wooden panelling, in exactly the same pose, but Lavinia's hands folded in her lap. No Thomas.

People believe what they want to believe, Minnie had said, but only for so long. The babies disappear, Franz had said. Not: The babies are returned to their mothers. They just disappear. He also said: Have faith in me. Wait. But Thomas was stirring and there were six days to go. Six days, one hundred and forty-four hours. No time at all.

I clutched the canvas awning of the nearest stall.

'What is it, dearie? Not feeling well are ya? Near your time?' The stallkeeper watched me from behind the canvas. 'Like a drink of water?' A wink. 'Something stronger?'

Behind her, a tut-tutting. 'In her condition. Shouldn't be out.'

I let go of the canvas and made my way across the square to a row of hansom cabs. The crowds parted to let my spinnaker through. I climbed into the nearest cab and spoke urgently to the driver. 'Take me to an orphanage.'

* * * * * * * *

The bland-fronted house, unmarked by any sign, stood in a terrace behind iron railings. A woman buttoned up to her chin in black opened the door and flicked her eyes over the doorstep where I stood.

'No infants.'

'Is this not the orphanage?'

'Orphan school. We don't take children under three.'

'But don't people bring you babies?'

The woman sighed, rolled her eyes. 'All the time. They dump them on the back doorstep, thrust them into our arms. You might at least have come to the tradesman's entrance. I suppose you're trying to get in early?' She folded thin arms, and I felt as if I had pushed in front of a long line of mothers carrying howling infants.

'I don't know where to go,' I said humbly.

'Should have thought of that before, shouldn't you? Try the

home for destitute women.'

'Do they allow children there?'

A sharp intake of breath. 'Of course not. Do you not understand English? It's a home for *women*.'

My gaze strayed behind the woman to the dark hallway, and I imagined Thomas toddling into that tunnel. I leaned against the pillar by the door, trying to ease the pain in my back and my feet.

'I can get you a glass of water, if you like,' said the woman, as if making an enormous concession. 'Then you must be off.' As I whispered my thanks, she turned and vanished into the tunnel. An insistent bell clanged in the dark maw, and boots clattered on stairs. There was a single cry, a sharp *Shush*, a whiff of something tarry and soapy. I slumped on the step, fanned my face, wriggled my toes in my tight boots.

'Get up, you can't sit there. What will people think?' Slowly I rose and received the glass, taking little sips. The water was pale yellow, like the woman's skin, and had a disagreeable smell. The glass was cracked. The woman peered into my face like a curious crow. 'Seen better times, haven't you?' Impossible to tell if this was sympathy or condemnation.

'The babies that are left here,' I said. 'What happens to them?'

'They are boarded out with respectable families.'

'Could you find a family for me? Could I visit my baby now and then?' My breath quickened. I would see Thomas, might even be allowed to hold him for a moment.

'Certainly not. Mothers who relinquish their infants are not permitted further contact. And an infant is only boarded out if one parent is found by a magistrate to be incapable of maintaining it.

You look strong enough. You can work.'

'What sort of work can I do and look after a baby at the same time?'

The woman shrugged, held out her hand for the glass. I lingered over the last drops. 'I don't understand the way things are done in Sydney,' I said.

'From the bush, are you? Well, you need to learn only one thing: beggars can't be choosers.' The woman snatched the glass. 'You run along now. Try the asylum for destitute children at Randwick. Only don't say I sent you.'

* * * * * * * *

The cabbie insisted on his fare in advance, and the coins in my purse were running out, but I was relieved to find myself in the cab away from the yellow-faced woman. I took off my bonnet and my shabby shawl, pinched my cheeks, pinned up the straggly fringe of hair that had worked its way loose at the back of my neck, rubbed spit on the curls in front of my ears, brushed off my bonnet, tied it on again and plumped up the bow. I polished my boots on the inside hem of my teagown, dusted off my skirts and smoothed out the creases. Then I opened my basket and took out Minnie's robe, which I had brought to match the thread I meant to buy, tucked the hood inside the collar and tied it around my shoulders. It fell almost to my elbows, a smart red velvet cape.

After a long ride, we left the streets behind and rode past paddocks. Finally, the cab climbed a grassy hill and pulled up at high wrought-iron gates flanked by six pillars. At the peak of the hill rose a great porticoed palace, glowing honey in the sun. This time, there was a sign: *Asylum for Destitute Children, estabd 1856. Suffer the little children to come to me.*

Remembering my last call, I walked round the palace, but could not find a tradesman's entrance. The sandstone walls were clean and new, still dented with the marks of pickaxes. Beyond, I glimpsed outbuildings, rows of raspberry canes, orchard trees covered with netting. Through a half-open window, tall and stately, came a regular hammering, treble voices and laughter that made me think of little princes and princesses at play.

Back at the front door, I drew myself up in the manner of Mrs Bleeker at her most august and rang the bell.

'Good morning, ma'am,' I said briskly the moment the door opened. 'I was wondering if —'

'Praise be. Come in, come in.' The woman was stout, yet whisked at astonishing speed into the depths of the building. I glimpsed a gleam of tiles, a staircase sweeping to great heights, a vase of dahlias, a mirror, myself with a startling splash of red across the breast, and then a parlour, three lofty windows full of sky and trees. 'Now,' said the woman, folding her pink hands across her waist, still a little fluttery from her passage. She had a dove's deep breast and a voice inclined to coo. 'What would you like to see first, Mrs … ah …'

'Mrs Carroll.' I was amazed to be asked my name.

'Mrs Carroll, I am Mrs Sweetman. Mr May is away at present and has left me in charge. Welcome to our model colony. We accommodate two hundred young people here in clean commodious rooms. They learn the value of honesty and industry and doing their duty. So many activities, and not enough staff, to

tell the truth, which was why I answered the door in person …
but we manage. The boys are at shoemaking and carpentry, the
girls are at their needlework. Baking and milking are finished but
they are still busy in the laundry. Later there will be singing and
marching and prayers … So where shall we start?'

'Wherever you wish.'

'We might take a turn in the garden; it is such a delightful
morning, is it not? Some boys are weeding the cabbage patch.'

More whisking through corridors and out a door I had failed
to find when walking round the house. We crossed a quadrangle
under two Norfolk Island pines — planted by the Duke of
Edinburgh, said Mrs Sweetman — and out another door towards
a cleared patch of earth, where rows of white-shirted backs bent
over the ground. Three boys aged about eight came down the
path from the cleared patch towards us, carrying spades and hoes
over their shoulders like toy guns, pushing a wheelbarrow full of
tangled greenery. They stood aside and touched their caps, bid us
good morning. 'Good morning, boys,' said Mrs Sweetman.

Another woman in brown, wearing an apron, gauntlets and a
calico bonnet and carrying a muddy trowel, came up the path. I
watched the boys trundle their cargo towards the house, imagined
Thomas with one hand on the wheelbarrow, shouldering his hoe
with a nonchalant air.

Mrs Sweetman nudged me. 'Such bright and open faces.
Doesn't it do your heart good to see the little souls? No more
listless downcast looks, no more hardening influences.'

'Indeed not.'

'Mrs Evans, can you show Mrs Carroll around the garden? I

must go and attend to one or two things ... and fetch the donation book. I expect Mrs Landon would like to know all the details.' Mrs Sweetman hurried back to the palace.

'Who is Mrs Landon?' I asked, half to myself.

The woman called Mrs Evans stared at me as she pulled off her gauntlets, then she chuckled. 'Mrs Landon is a rich old biddy who loves squeezing out driblets of money to worthy causes, and Sweets thinks Mrs Landon is your employer.'

'There is some mistake —'

'Of course there is,' said Mrs Evans comfortably, scraping a little dirt from her nails. 'Mrs Landon said she would send someone round today to inspect.' Her hands were burned brown, the skin flaking in places. 'Ma Vinegar send you here?'

'I beg your pardon?'

'Sour old girl at the orphan school. She really shouldn't do that.'

'Mrs Evans, please believe me, I am not here under false pretences. I just don't know where else to go. I need a home for my child.'

'Of course you do. And a home for yourself.'

'It is more than I dare hope for, but if there was some way I could stay here; it is such a paradise for poor children, and Mrs Sweetman did say they were short of staff. I am a governess, I can teach, I have good references ...' My words tumbled out in a terror — I was convinced that if I paused for a second, Mrs Evans would say: *No infants*.

'We don't need teachers. The children only learn Bible stories, marching, and how to do their work.'

'Then I will sew, cook, clean, anything — I don't need wages, just a roof over my head, a bite to eat. Please, Mrs Evans, I beg you.'

The woman stood back, folded her arms. 'What are you, a widow or a runaway?'

'A widow.'

The boys who had gone up to the house came in sight again with an empty wheelbarrow. They detoured around the path where we stood, again touching their caps. 'Make sure you clean out the furrows,' Mrs Evans called after them. She turned back to me, laid a hand on my arm, held the muddy trowel close to my chin. 'You're not of dissolute or abandoned character, are you?'

'Certainly not.' I shook off her hand.

'Pity. That's what you have to be to get a child in here: convicted before a magistrate and all. Then there's a maintenance fee to be paid. And another thing — we don't take babies.'

I clenched my teeth. To stand in a garden beside a golden palace, to be prodded with a trowel and to know I must leave, as surely as if the angel with the flaming sword stood prodding me back towards the smoke of Sydney.

'Where is the heart in this town?' I said. 'Is no woman ever allowed to live with her child?'

Mrs Evans shrugged. 'I don't make the rules.' We stood in silence and I heard the scrape of spades, a tuneless whistling. 'You'd better go before Sweets gets back. I'll make sure she doesn't set the police on you.'

'Yes. Thank you.' I wanted to scream but I kept my voice low and toneless. Mrs Evans peered over my shoulder up the path, took my arm, led me into the shade of a bushy pine tree so we were screened from the house windows.

'A word of advice: forgive my plain talk, but you know what you should do. Find yourself a man.'

'I beg your pardon?'

'Oh, I suppose you loved your dear departed well enough, but he's gone now, and he hasn't left you provided for. Sydney is full of bachelors, dear. All they want is someone to cook and clean, give them a word of kindness, keep them happy.' The callused fingers pressed through my sleeve. 'Tell me true, is there some man already sweet on you?'

Who is it loves me? Who loves not me? I dipped my head. Not me. Not the busy little beaver on the riverbank. But some tormenting vestige of hope thrilled along my arms and into my fingers, clad in Mrs Bleeker's smart gloves. 'I … I don't know.'

'Take him, do. Take him to the church as soon as you may. You know how, you're young yet, you still have your looks.' She stroked my scarlet shoulder, chuckled. 'This is not the only velvet on you, is it?'

I looked around wildly. A little distance ahead, the rows of white shirts bent over the furrows bobbed like dew-heavy flowers. Surely I could talk this woman round, and Mrs Sweetman too, for no one who walked within these golden walls or planted green things in the crumbling earth could have a heart of ice.

Mrs Evans followed my gaze and sighed. 'This place ain't paradise, however it looks.' A snort. 'Bright and open faces, my eye. Did you see how skinny those lads are? Scald head under their caps. Sometimes I'm glad I don't have any young ones of my own. Sickness breeds here, dear: they come in, we work them, they go out, usually feet first.' A gust of wind lifted the cape from my shoulders. 'We lost dozens last winter. Bronchitis, dysentery, measles, convulsions. Year before last, whooping cough. Who knows, cholera next ... What is it, dear?'

I followed her gaze, looked down. I had drawn my right hand into a claw and was rubbing at the palm of my left hand, scraping the leather of Mrs Bleeker's good glove. It was the way I had scrubbed and scrubbed my numb red hands with soap in the rectory.

I began to walk, almost run, back towards the quadrangle, the shady hall, the great panelled door, the iron gates.

'Remember,' Mrs Evans called out. 'Take your man while you may.'

· · · · · · · ·

'Where have you been?' demanded Mrs Bleeker in the hallway outside the troupe's rooms. I tried to stare back, but found I had to look down.

'I have been looking for a haberdashery, but I could not find one.'

'Never mind that, you can manage with what we have — but what took you so long? I have been worried sick. I remembered what happened to you in Ballarat, and then I thought, maybe your time —'

'It is not my time yet. But I am very sorry to have worried you. I wandered so far, and Sydney is so big ...' I spread my hands. How to say, if I had found even a hole to creep into where Thomas and I would be safe, I would never have returned? But I had not been able to think of anywhere else to go but back to the hotel. I had not had enough money for a cab, so I had put Minnie's cloak back into the basket and had hitched a ride from Randwick on a hay wain, beside a farmer who talked constantly of whelping and rutting. Even Mrs Bleeker's wrath was better than his fat paw straying towards my thigh. I did not dare slap him until I reached a street I recognised, and jumped down to his gasp and shout.

'Are you sure you are well?' Mrs Bleeker frowned, her grip on my wrist tightened. 'It should not take so long to look for a haberdashery.'

Before I could reply, a smooth melodious voice cut in from behind me. 'It is all right, Mrs B.' Thomas kicked, and all my body thudded. 'I asked Mary Ann to buy some sheet music for me, and no doubt she had to hunt around to find it. I am sorry if I put you out.'

'Well, really, Mr Richardson, you should clear any such errands with me first. Mary Ann has many tasks and I can seldom spare her.'

'Yes, I am sorry. I will not interrupt her further, but may I sit with her as she sews and enquire after her purchases?' Franz's smile had a boyish eagerness.

Mrs Bleeker sniffed. 'Take off your bonnet, Mary Ann, and get to work at once. The sewing basket is overflowing; our best costumes are reduced almost to rags. Mr Richardson may sit with you in the parlour as long as he does not distract you. And from now on, you are not to go out anywhere, or do anything, without my express instruction. I fear I was wrong to send you out before — your condition is clearly too advanced to risk any mishap. How long now?'

'Six days.'

'Lord. Well, I will be watching you.'

'Yes, Mrs B.' I sat in the parlour windowseat, where the light was best, began to let down the hem on Minnie's Red Riding Hood dress. The troupers were taking their daily turn around town, drumming up business in the walnut carriage; and the room was very quiet, for the windows were swagged with deep blue velvet curtains that stifled sound. Franz perched uncomfortably opposite me on an ottoman, bending forward with his hands on his knees as I sewed; he seemed far too tall for the furniture. He did not catch my eye but talked amiably of minuets and bagatelles and hummed snatches of melodies that faded into the curtains, while Mrs Bleeker bustled around the table with piles of garments, folding and refolding. When Franz began a lecture on the life of Beethoven, she finally took her bundles out the door.

'You did not have to lie for me,' I said at once.

'I don't think I was the only liar. Will you now answer the question you refused to answer before? Where have you been?'

'I was trying to escape from the fate which you painted so vividly for me.' I fixed my eyes on Minnie's satin. Why did Franz's calm coldness make my heart beat much faster than Mrs Bleeker's scolding?

'Ha.' Franz rose, began to pace the carpet. His stride was like Mr Bleeker's, but he held himself more proudly. 'I take it you did not find an escape. Anyone could have told you the prospects for a young homeless penniless female in a raw colonial town.'

'A female with child.'

'You think I had forgotten?' Franz gazed at me through his long forelock. Abruptly he turned to the fireplace, picked up the poker, raked the ashes. 'Why didn't you wait?' he flung over his shoulder. 'Why didn't you have faith? Didn't I tell you I would devise a plan, I would do everything in my power to help you?'

'You have been very kind to me, Franz. I never lost faith in you. I just … I felt I had to protect Tho … my child.' The thin words rang in my ears. They were no way to describe what had possessed me in the marketplace, that feeling that Thomas had taken my hand and was about to run with me off the edge of a cliff. I could not wait for anyone to devise a plan while we fell.

Franz stood with his back to me, then he walked to the door and peered up and down the corridor outside. He pushed the door until it was very nearly closed, slid the curtain across the window, then resumed his seat on the ottoman. 'My poor mermaid.' His voice was more gentle now, and he leaned towards me in the blueish light. 'Why did you run away from me, Mary Ann?'

I looked up, astonished. 'I was not running away from *you*, Franz. How can you say such a thing?'

'You are stubborn, dear mermaid. You will not trust me.'

'I do trust you, but I was at my wit's end. You have a plan?'

'I do.' His smile was like the sun on the honey walls of the palace at Randwick. Then he dropped his head into his hands, ran his fingers through his beautiful curled locks until they stood out like porcupine quills. 'But I fear to tell you it.'

'Tell me. Please.'

'I presume too much. I do not wish to take advantage of your position.'

'For God's sake, Franz.' I crushed the dress fabric in my hands.

'Yes. Yes.' He got to his feet again, stared into the looking glass above the mantelpiece, muttering so I strained to hear. 'Yes, I will, I must, and run the risk that I will lose what I treasure most — your esteem.'

'You value my esteem?'

'I value everything about you,' said Franz into the looking glass. 'From the moment I first saw you, you entered my highest regard. Surely you who see everything have seen that?'

'Franz …' The dress fell from my hands.

He turned swiftly, raised a finger. 'Let me say it: I don't have much at present, but I have great prospects — not as a piano player for travelling entertainers, not as a piano teacher, but as a pupil of the great Franz Liszt.' His voice trembled a little on the name.

'I don't understand,' I said. 'You are playing with me, Franz.'

'Never think that, never. I will soon be voyaging to Europe, where I intend to take up an apprenticeship with no less a tutor than Mr Liszt himself. I have a benefactor who will fund my journeyings and arrange the crucial introduction and recommendations.'

'I cannot believe it. Oh, not that Mr Liszt would refuse you — I have heard your wonderful playing. But that someone would arrange all this for you …'

Franz's smile burst out again. 'It is only just arranged, in utmost confidence, and I cannot yet tell you the details, but I have it on excellent authority.'

'Then I am very glad for you.' I tried to put warmth into my voice. First he accused me of running away; now he was going away himself.

'Naturally,' said Franz, 'my wife and child will travel with me.'

I picked up Minnie's dress and tried to rethread my needle, but the red strand trembled and blurred in front of my eyes.

'My dear mermaid, you cannot misunderstand me. Oh, I'm doing this so badly ... To be plain, my plan is to take you from here to somewhere where I hope you will do me the honour of becoming my wife.' The needle slipped, drove into my finger. I sat completely still, my eyes fixed on the scarlet bead that grew and fell onto the satin.

'You have hurt yourself.' He dropped to his knees beside my chair, took up my hand and kissed the red spot on my finger, and I began to laugh.

'You mock me,' he said.

'No, no, it's just that you are kneeling *now*.'

Franz laughed too. 'I told you. I am doing this badly.'

'You are doing this beautifully.'

He held my hand, splayed out my fingers and touched the webs between them. He reached an arm around my shoulders and kissed my cheek, and the blue light from the curtained window rippled around us. I turned to him, and for a moment our lips brushed; I tasted peppermint and tobacco and the salt of my own blood. *Take your man.* My finger throbbed, my heart thundered, fear and joy seemed like twins. Then a new doubt struck me. Something was strange. Was he holding his breath?

Franz drew back, gazed at my face, then at my stomach. I looked at his porcupine hair and felt a sudden gnawing need, whether to comb it back into shape or dishevel it still further, I was not sure, but before I could reach out, he stood up.

'You are sure, Mary Ann? I had thought ... perhaps you cared for that little groom.' He muttered the words through his teeth.

'Rodnia Nutt has been a friend to me. Nothing more.'

Franz's body stretched, straightened. 'That's a great relief, but I must still be sure that *you* are sure. It will mean betraying the troupe; we will both lose our employment, and we will have to steal away in secret.'

'An elopement, then?'

'I suppose we should call it that. I don't think there is any chance they will release us from service when they still hope for …' He looked again at the sleeping Thomas, hidden under the spread-out satin.

'No, they might let my baby go one day, as you warned me, but they would never let us go now. But I will steal away and go with you, Franz, to Europe, to anywhere. I trust you.'

'Maybe one day you will love me a little too?'

'That day is here.'

He smiled, his teeth blue-white, almost fierce in his joy. I willed him to sit down, to kiss me again. But he stayed on his feet, though his voice grew tender. 'My mermaid. I will arrange everything. You'll need to wait one or two days more. Six days, you told Mrs B. So there is still time? You are not by any chance mistaken?'

'It's all right, Franz.'

'Then I'll let you know when I have made arrangements.'

'Yes. You'd better go. I must finish my work, and I don't trust myself to be composed when Mrs Bleeker returns.'

'Nor I, nor I. Dear girl. Have faith.' He blew me a kiss and was gone. My heart still thundered as I threaded my needle, remembering Franz's mermaid poem.

But the king of them all would carry me,
Woo me, and win me, and marry me,
In the branching jaspers under the sea;
Would slowly trail himself sevenfold
Round the hall where I sate, and look in at the gate
With his large calm eyes for the love of me.

No, I had that wrong, that was not the merman king. The fabric glowed on my lap, but the small bloodstain, so close to the colour of the satin, had already disappeared. In and out went my needle, in and out.

SIDESHOW

Mr Charles Sherwood Stratton,
alias General Tom Thumb

General Tom Thumb

ACT TWO

My name is General Tom Thumb, and I won't die, I won't. Not before I have seen my boy.

Lord knows, I've thought of ageing often enough in the past few years. Can't avoid it, in that looking glass, in that ache in my right knee. Can't avoid it in the Commodore's face, that fresh rosy insult. But death? Who'd have thought my angel of death would come to me just now, wearing cheap pomade? And like any angel, even the darkest ones, he means well.

I had just left my lovely expectant Lavinia and was alone in the hotel garden, inspecting some undersized grapes on the vine that straggled over the pergola. Maybe I was musing happily about young, scarce-formed things; I don't know. And then there was Ned Davis, panting as if he'd just run a mile, gabbling a mile a minute, holding his bowler over his chest as if his heart would hop out into it. I sat him down on the step, got him to calm down, asked him what the matter was, and he told me what they were saying: that George deliberately tried to push me from the coach into the Goulburn river. Well, that was no more than I had said at the time, but I was very agitated then, and had thought better of it since. But had I been right after all? Could George really be so jealous of me?

Ned was still talking, about how George was plotting to write me out of the show, working against me both onstage and offstage, how he never lost a chance to lobby Mr B. Of course I just laughed, assured Ned that Mr B never listened to George. But my disquiet was growing, and more so when Ned told me that George had written those dreadful notices of the show himself, and had bribed the newspapers to run them. Why hadn't I thought of that?

'We will tell Mr B,' I said. 'Then the Commodore will be the one who is out of the show.'

But Ned said no, the Commodore was a desperate man. 'He wants to be you, sir. He wants your fame and your history and your glory. He wants your wife and your child.'

The moment he said it, I knew it was true. I felt cold to my marrow, and then a rush of electricity. The scheming ratkin. I told Ned I would go to the police at once and nail the villain for slander and attempted murder. But Ned put his hand on my arm, and his fingers had a strong grip. 'Please, General, hear me out. That's not all. There are things he says you won't want the police to know, or anyone else.'

What could be worse? Ned didn't want to speak then, but I urged him and urged him, and at last, stammering and staring at the ground, he told me. 'He says you are nothing and he is everything, and you can't bear it. You can't understand you're just a fat old man and people laugh at you in contempt. That your wife secretly laughs at you, that she is disgusted by you. That you are a little squirming pig with a little pink tail that will not rise to do its business.'

I sprang to my feet and clutched the pergola posts. Like Samson, I wanted to bring down the vines upon us.

'Take care, sir. The Commodore is angry.'

He was angry? How dare he?

Ned lifted his eyes to me. 'He has asked me to come to you with a challenge. For slandering his good name. For saying he pushed you into the river. I tried to stop him, I begged him —'

'What kind of challenge?'

Ned swallowed. 'Pistols.'

A breeze buffeted the pergola, and that's when I heard it: the beating of angel wings. All my rage froze; I was a stick of ice. I took a vine tendril in my hand and picked off a tiny grape, rolled it very gently between finger and thumb. Ned was on his feet, pacing back and forth, talking and talking, how he would tell the Commodore that of course I didn't accept his challenge, there was no shame in saying so in this enlightened age, and even if there were, it was better to be called names and thought a coward than to lie wounded on some beach at the end of the world.

I popped the grape into my mouth. It was very sour.

'Don't tell him that, Ned. Never fear, truth and right will prevail. I will show him who is the hero and who is the nobody.'

He was silent then, raised his hands in a helpless gesture.

'You have acted honourably,' I told him. 'I will not deal with the Commodore directly, but you can represent me.'

Ned clapped his bowler back on his head, gave a heavy sigh, said he'd be honoured to act as my second, and he knew just the man for the Commodore. 'Tomorrow, sir, at dawn? It's as well to do these things as soon as possible. I know of a secluded beach, just the ticket. And we'll keep it all a secret. Leave it with me.'

I watched Ned walk away, and I fancied for a moment that his shoulders were less bowed than when he had found me. I thought of George's pistol, Widowmaker. I had never seen him shoot it, but I knew he was rumoured to be a crack shot, or was that just his boasting? Whereas I was no marksman.

I had thought twice before I was going to die, and each time it was water that threatened me. The run and rush of water: that has always brought on my manly surges of electricity, has also been my undoing. But I could not remember how I had felt then. All that remained was a recurring dream, not by any means horrid, of dark velvet waves, and myself sitting on Mr Bleeker's shoulders to see the sirens.

I placed my hands on my belly. Somehow I knew that this was where George would aim. What would it feel like, to take a bullet in the guts? To have a ball of metal tear through the padding of flesh that had taken years to pack around my person, the comfortable result of all those roasts and desserts and decanterfuls of port? To keel over, to see my last vision on this earth? I hoped it would be light enough to see some sky, a cloud or two, maybe a wheeling bird. On a beach, Ned had said. I'd stood on so many beaches, waiting to embark, waving to crowds, but I had never wandered on a beach by myself, with bucket and spade, perhaps with a curly-haired dog, trailing aimless strands of seaweed.

I held out my hands before me. They wouldn't stop shaking. I thought of the fire in Mr Barnum's study, burning my side. The coil of black hair on Lavinia's forehead. And something I hadn't remembered for many years: the faded Italy-shaped stain on my mother's apron, in the days when she wore aprons, the days before she was the amusingly vulgar Mrs Stratton, the days when I wasn't the General, just little Charlie, who would bury his face in Italy and cry …

Stop it. I won't die, I won't. George will never have the gumption to shoot me. He just wants to scare me, he will shoot wide, and he will expect me to run away in terror. What will I do then? It is a godsend, this duel, for I will destroy him.

It is not the past I must think of, but the future. My beloved wife, my tiny little Tommy, the Coming Man, a miniature man in miniature. I want a moment for him, like the night I had at the Théâtre du Vaudeville in Paris, when the danseuses stood in line and lifted their skirts to form an archway with their legs, and I ran down their avenue of honour, laughing and jumping and grabbing like a boy let loose in an apple orchard. *Viens, mon petit poucet.* I will get him that triumph, the pure joy of those ripe apples, and I will be there to see it, and nobody will stop me, no sir.

CHAPTER 19

Thomas was lively, pushing and prodding, so I had no trouble waking before cock crow. Five days, one hundred and twenty hours. I had asked to lie alone because my sleep was so restless, and Mrs Bleeker had moved to a camp bed in the ladies' bedroom. Dressing in the dark, I bundled my nightgown and purse into the packed bag I pulled out from under the bed and slipped my hands inside to feel slippers, stockings, drawers, apron, spare shawl, petticoat, cake of soap, washcloth, hairpins, a tortoiseshell comb Lavinia had given me. Only these familiar textures could convince me that this was not a dream.

Franz had told me the previous night that it was time. In just a few moments he would come and knock, and then he would wait with a cab outside the servants' entrance, and shortly afterwards I would leave the troupe forever. I allowed myself to imagine the impossible farewells: Lavinia's peck on my cheek, Minnie's pats on my arm, Mrs Bleeker's rough hands drawing me to her bony bosom, and then an unbidden fancy: shaking hands with Rodnia, stiff and formal, in the stable. I could feel his leathery palm in mine, hear his gruff *Godspeed*, and all the time his frown, the pressure of his palm, his silent trembling, the reproach he would swallow. *So you're tractable after all, ma'am.*

It was too late for that. I had made my choice. Rodnia would forget me, if indeed he had ever cared for me at all: as long as I stayed within the troupe, I was nothing but a vassal, a vestal, a vessel … a container for a child. Now I thought of Franz playing on a grand stage, heard the crowd's roar, myself in the front row, slim-waisted and elegant in a white gown with Thomas beside me, his little feet sticking out over the chair; and afterwards, backstage in his dressing room, surrounded by flowers, how Franz would laugh and close the door and kiss me long and deep while outside the adulators knocked and knocked …

Yes, they were real, the knocks on my door. Six taps, as we had arranged. He was here. My body was all knocks and hammers, and Thomas kicked me for good measure as I ran to the door and opened it to throw myself into his arms. Then I froze, unable to move or think or feel, for the world had stopped breathing. Mrs Bleeker stood alone on the threshold, dressed but with her hair still in its night-time plait, her mouth in its grimmest slit, her umbrella in her fist.

Were we discovered? Was the elopement over before it had begun?

'Mary Ann, come quick. We have an emergency. The General and the Commodore are bent on shooting each other dead.'

· · · · · · · ·

The stretch of beach, overhung by sandstone cliffs, faced out of darkness towards a dim grey sky where surely no sun would ever rise. The waves were grey ruffles, hitting the shore with petulant slaps, and a mean wind plucked at my skirts. Although this bay was within walking distance of our Sydney hotel, there were no bathing machines, no fishing boats, no native fireplaces or middens; it was as if no humans had ever been here, or would ever come again. But now there were six of us spaced out along the strand: myself and Mrs Bleeker in the middle; one tiny man and one small man on our far left; and one tiny man and one tall man on our far right. We all stood motionless, as if waiting for the clock to strike and the machinery to whirr.

Then Mrs Bleeker turned this way and that, and I was astonished to see her biting the end of her plait. 'Come,' she said suddenly and began to walk towards the figures on our left; floundering in the fine sand, I followed.

I should never have opened the door, I thought. I should have hidden under the bed, or jumped out the window. By now I would be in the cab with Franz, on the way to my wedding. Instead he was waiting, waiting. How long would he wait before he gave up, judged me faithless yet again, left alone to pursue his dreams with Mr Liszt? Why did I go on jumping to Mrs Bleeker's tune? And yet I had known, with one look at her wide desperate eyes, that I had to go with her.

'A duel,' Mrs Bleeker had gasped to me as we had bunched up our skirts and had run — or as near to a run as I could manage — along the winding path to the beach. 'Rodnia Nutt secretly woke me and told me, just as they left. He thought maybe I could stop it. Why me, Mary Ann? I could not even wake my husband, he has been sleeping so badly lately, I gave him a sedating draught last night and not even the Devil could stir him before noon, but I still needed help, and you were nearest, and oh, these foolish men, what will they do.'

On the sand we reached Rodnia and George, buttoned up to his white face in a coat with many flaps.

'Mrs B, you too?' he murmured.

Rodnia stared at me, then turned back to his brother. 'For the last time, George.'

George shook his head. 'It's as Ned says: we're at the Rubicon. Matter of honour. A gent doesn't back off his word.'

'Honour be blowed, we're talking pistols,' said Rodnia.

'Mr Nutt, you must stop this madness,' said Mrs Bleeker to Rodnia.

He nodded. 'What am I going to say to Ma and Pa if …'

'You know as well as I do, I'm as safe as houses. I'm the crack shot. The General couldn't hit an elephant half a yard in front of him.' Rodnia and Mrs Bleeker both began to talk at once, but George waved a dismissive arm. 'I won't hit him.'

'You can't be sure,' said Rodnia.

George laid a hand on his arm. 'Roddie, you always took good care of me when I was Tiny George, but I'm not so tiny now. Let me be a man.' There was a deeper, graver edge to his voice. Rodnia stared hard into his eyes, as if looking for the cocky boy of old: then looked down, and there was now enough light in the sky for me to see that his face was a little pink.

'Do as you will, then, only take care.'

'Rodnia Nutt, how can you say such a thing? Will you let them get away with murder?' Mrs Bleeker swung her umbrella like a sword.

At the same time, we heard a shout, and I turned to see Ned walking towards us from the other end of the beach.

'What's going on? This is no place for females.'

'This is no place for any God-fearing person,' said Mrs Bleeker. 'How dare you, sir. You have put the gentlemen up to this deadly game. Just wait until I tell my husband.'

'Don't you worry about that. We're here, and your husband isn't. Besides, the gents don't need anyone to put them up to it. They're raring to go, and I'll be darned if I can talk them out of it. Devil knows, I've tried. Ain't that so, Commodore, you being the challenger and all?'

George was paler than ever, but he nodded.

'But what harm has the General ever done you?' I cried.

George was about to reply, but Ned cut in. 'We won't go into that. The dice is set. They will play. You'll just have to watch until it's over. If you've the stomach to watch.' He glared at my swelling teagown.

'Lay off her,' growled Rodnia. 'And if my brother gets hurt, so help me —'

'Remember what I said to you,' snapped Ned. 'If you try to step in …'

'Roddie, it's all right,' said George. He sounded very weary.

Mrs Bleeker rammed her umbrella into the sand, then pulled it out as if it had entered Ned's skull. 'Oh, you men, there is no sense in you. I will go and get the General to see reason.' She began to march down to the solitary little figure at the other end of the beach. Should I follow her, I wondered?

Then Ned said to Rodnia: 'Listen to your brother, wait here and keep an eye on our brave fighters while I collect the weapons,' and I knew that Ned was the one to watch. I set my face inland.

'Mary Ann,' Rodnia called out behind me, his voice hoarse, urgent, but I did not turn.

Franz, please don't go yet. Please wait for me.

Ned had headed off on a different path to the route Mrs Bleeker and I had taken to reach the beach. It wound around the overhanging sandstone cliffs and the scree at their base, then began to climb. I scrambled behind him, but soon was gasping for breath and had to stop, Thomas was so heavy. Ned kept climbing, but when he was near the top, at the steepest part, he turned and waited for me, smiling, holding out his hand. So he could be civil after all. I toiled up the path very slowly, pausing every now and then to get my breath, and finally reached for his hand with great relief. He gripped me so hard I cried out in pain.

'Want to come? Then shut your trap, missy, and keep it shut, or by God I'll hurl you and your brat down to the rocks.'

Now I was sure he had tried to kidnap me at Ballarat. His lazy mockery was gone; his eyes were slits, his breath rasping. This was the face of a man who would do anything to make a mint. And he had me in his grip.

I looked down and my head reeled: any fall from this height might smash my skull. He yanked my arm, one foot slipped, but I righted myself and climbed with him until we came out at the top, on a cliff edge that gave a view of the shore. The wind plucked at us with new spite.

Just behind the cliff edge was a grassy hollow where several logs of wood and a few camp chairs were arranged in rows, and on them sat some two dozen gentlemen, muffled in capes and greatcoats and deerstalker hats, facing out to sea and the beach view. Another man lounged on a shooting stick. They focused binoculars, chewed bread rolls, ham and sausage, and swigged at hip flasks. Some looked at me with mild curiosity: to them, I realised, I must seem like Ned's assistant. I wanted to cry out to them for help, but remembered Ned's threat and swallowed my pleas. My own fate might not matter so much, but Thomas did not deserve to have every limb broken before he was even born.

'What ho, Davis,' said the man on the shooting stick. 'Where's the action? Those little fellers look lost.'

Ned clamped his hat low on his brow with one hand and, with the other still holding me in a tight grip, he peered over the cliff edge. I followed his gaze and saw Rodnia in the middle of the beach, while George and Charlie stood at opposite ends, facing the sea. A taller figure in skirts stood with Charlie, apparently shouting and gesticulating, but we could not hear a word Mrs Bleeker said. Just as the wind blew away her words, so it seemed it would soon blow away these four puny creatures. Ned turned back to the shooting-stick man, a broad face framed in luxuriant whiskers. 'The action will commence very soon, sir,' he said, and the slight tremor in his voice surprised me. He cleared his throat, spoke louder. 'Gentlemen …' They continued to talk and laugh among themselves.

'You're downwind,' said the whiskery man. 'Get up on that tree, then they'll hear you, and smell you too.' He guffawed, winked at me.

Ned moved to the tree, pulling me close to his body, and began to shout. This time, he had their attention.

'Gentlemen, you're about to witness a unique event. A stupendous conflict between the two tiny Titans of our age. A genuine, no-holdsbarred duel with pistols, between the celebrated General Tom Thumb, on the beach to your right; and to your left, his equally celebrated rival, Commodore Nutt. Who will prove the greatest little man of them all?'

As Ned shouted, he straightened up and his chest swelled. His habitual nasal whine became a deep, thrilling tone, and the men listened in total silence. Ned was a natural showman, I thought, perhaps even more than Mr Bleeker. Something, maybe the same force that had scarred his wrists, had twisted and thwarted his gift and he would never forgive the world for it.

'What's their quarrel?' someone called out.

'What's not their quarrel? They are rivals from the cradle. They've always competed for attention. They can no longer bear to share a stage. See how they can't even share a beach?' The gentlemen peered through their binoculars and murmured. 'And what's more, gentlemen' — Ned tapped the side of his nose — 'Cupid's arrows've been at work. Churchy la fem, as the Frenchies say. They courted the same little lady, and the General won. The Commodore has never recovered from his broken heart. It makes him livid, roaring.'

'Seems awful quiet,' said a man with binoculars to his eyes. 'Which one did you say he was?'

'The convulsively choleric Cain-raising Commodore is on your left. The glowering grizzly grinding-his-teeth General is on your right. But it's not just rivalry and Cupid's arrows that sets these Lilliputians warring against each other. No. It is a pearl of immeasurable price!' He paused, then flung up his hand with my hand in it, so my shawl fell back from my shoulders and we both stood reaching wildly to the sky, keen children trying to attract their teacher's attention. 'Behold ... The Busy Little Beaver! See, gentlemen, the fruit she bears! Conceived on a dark and stormy night with a diminutive partner, but no one knows who! And now her time grows near! Will it be a child in miniature, the Coming Man, to grace the General's family tree? Or will it be a tiny Nutt on a half-shell, the Commodore's son and heir? All will be decided on this beach! Winner takes all, loser has a fall ... and never rises again!'

'No!' I cried. 'None of this is true!' But the gentlemen were laughing and leering at me and nudging each other in the ribs and making horrid gestures, and now Ned had let go of my hand and was patting me very gently on the belly with his long, nicotine-stained fingers.

When Charlie had patted me in front of the whole troupe at the ford, he had made me feel naked. Ned made me feel turned inside out, like a skinned rabbit.

I wanted to spring at him and tear his eyes out. But now the gentlemen surrounded me, peering and prodding, so that I had to cover myself with my shawl and push away their hands. Curiously it was Ned who came to my rescue.

'Back, gentlemen, please! Don't harm a little man's property or there will be the devil to pay!' Reluctantly they drew back. Ned raised his hand for silence and continued. 'Now you understand.

What you see on that beach is the calm before the storm. Soon they'll spring at each other like panthers. But first, gentlemen, I must crave your indulgence. You're hunting men, are you not?'

'We hunt, we fish and we shoot,' said the whiskered man.

'Then you know how to approach prey. Don't scare away the show, gents. They don't know you're here. You can see them but they can't see you or hear you in this hollow. Don't make too-loud noises. Don't stand too near the edge of the cliff. Think of them as your native bears.'

'We don't hunt native bears. Lazy little beggars.'

'Well, think of them as whatever you do hunt. I must leave you to present the mighty gladiators with their weapons. Any more bets?'

'Twenty on the Commodore,' said the whiskered man. 'I like his mettle.'

'Can't see any mettle meself,' said his companion. 'Twenty on the General.'

Ned walked up and down the rows as if at church collection and packed his already chinking pockets with more coins. 'I like your metal too, gents,' he said. They laughed and groaned and pretended to cuff him. He paused and had a few quiet words with the whiskered man, then suddenly turned and was off down the path, leaving me alone in the circle of hunters.

The whiskered man rose from his shooting stick and offered me his arm. 'Come, missus, you should not stand in your condition. Allow me to escort you to the best seat in the house. Make way, you rude fellows.' He shooed away the men on the log nearest the cliff edge and seated me at the centre — oh, the relief to sit — then sat down beside me and arranged my shawl over my lap. 'There. Nice and comfortable? Like some refreshment?' A whiff of brandy made my head swim as a flask was passed under my nose, to snorts of suppressed laughter from behind me.

I shook my head, breathed deeply, fought off my lingering exhaustion from the climb, tried to summon Lavinia's cool dignity. 'Sir, I call on your honour as a gentleman. You are all here on false pretences. This duel is a wicked charade, the little people have somehow been goaded into it, and everything Mr Davis has just told you is a lie. You must act now to call the whole thing off, before anyone is hurt.'

The whiskered man gazed at me in astonishment, then began a slow clap, and some of the men around him joined in. 'Bravo, missus, Ned has schooled you very well.'

'But I am not part of the show ...'

'Sssh, they are about to start.'

If Franz were here, I thought, he would knock all you fellows down like ninepins and push you over the cliff. The duel would be done with, and we would laugh as we left you floundering in the sand.

The whiskery man was nudging me and pointing. Ned had returned to the beach and was walking towards Charlie's end, carrying a long flat box. When he reached Charlie, he opened the lid, and the men murmured and craned their necks to see what was inside. Slowly Charlie lifted something out: there was a brief silvery gleam.

'Here, Mrs ... ah ... Beaver, take a look,' said the whiskered man, handing me a pair of binoculars. Charlie stood very still and stiff, holding a silver duelling pistol that seemed like Napoleon's cannon in his hand. Ned was talking to him. Mrs Bleeker stood a way off, arms folded, shoulders slumped. Then Ned broke away and walked down to the other end of the beach, carrying his box, ready for the second presentation.

'Fine weapons, by the look of them,' said the neighbour on my right, a folding telescope to his eye. 'Chequered butts. But far too big for those little fellows. Very hard to aim and fire. See, the General holds his as if it's going to go off in his face.'

'Ah, but the Commodore — he's your consummate marksman,' said the whiskered man. 'Watch how he handles his piece. Cocks it like a military man.' He took a bite of his sausage and grinned at me. 'I reckon you're going to crack a little Nutt.'

'Ten paces, d'you reckon?' said the man with the telescope.

'More like twenty, with the length of their legs. And three seconds to fire.'

As I watched, Charlie placed his pistol on the sand, thrust his hands deep into his pockets, then covered his face. He took off his coat, folded it carefully, put it down and retrieved his pistol. The two little men walked slowly towards each other, their seconds at their sides, nursemaids to toddlers who might keel over in the sand. Charlie was in shirtsleeves and a new red waistcoat that I had embroidered in gold thread. George had not removed his coat, but had undone the buttons; the dark wings flapped.

Far out to sea, a sun the colour of Charlie's old bodystocking pushed through smoky clouds, and orange-tinged gulls floated on the sulky waves. It was the Lilliputians' most spectacular theatre yet, but there was no performance: no capering, winking, confiding looks, bits of business, moments of triumph — just the slow movements of sleepwalkers.

They met, shook hands, stood back to back, pistols loaded, cocked and raised, monstrously large. A deep sigh and shudder ran through the spectators. Then they sat forward, utterly silent. A knot from my log seat dug into my thigh. I felt imprisoned by walls of tobacco, sweat and pomade. A tern alighted in front of me, on the edge of the cliff; the wind pushed its black headfeathers into a ruffled topknot. It stared out to sea, then took off again. I wished I could lift myself up like that, fly to Franz. But now the sun was up, perhaps he would not wait any longer. Something even heavier than Thomas filled my head and limbs.

'Come on, Commodore,' whispered the whiskery man.

'Go General,' said another out loud. He was angrily shushed.

Thomas kicked. Ned Davis says that one of those men is your father, I thought. It's all a show to him. What will happen to you if my elopement has truly failed, and if one of the little men dies? Somehow I can't see you growing up with the widowed Lavinia, and still less as George's son. Stay in there: you are better off floating and kicking than out on this clifftop with these creatures sniffing blood.

Now the little men began to walk away from each other, and the gentlemen counted their paces. One ... Two ... Three ... My neighbour was biting his nails. What's it to you, I thought, you have only money at stake. Ten ... Eleven ... Twelve ... I could still get up, wave my arms and scream, distract them, maybe even leap from the cliff edge. But I saw how still Rodnia and Mrs Bleeker stood. They knew it was too late: the game must be played out.

Eighteen ... Nineteen ... Twenty. Electricity crackled in my chest, down through my diaphragm and along my limbs to my fingers and toes. The duellists stopped, turned. My hair lifted on my skull.

Ned cried out, one word. Still we could not hear, but I guessed what he said. *Fire.*

Charlie dropped his pistol upon the ground, stood with his arms slightly out at his sides, as if wearing a too-tight jacket. George looked down. His duelling pistol was in his left hand. His right hand darted into the folds of his long coat, pulled out something, aimed, and on the clifftop we all saw the wrong weapon flash in the rising sun. Then, just as he had done on the riverbank at Baddaginnie, Rodnia sprang forward between the two little men.

In that quiet place, the shot shook the earth. All the birds were flung into the sky, screaming. Rodnia froze, clutched at his chest. But it was Charlie who fell on his back and lay still in the sand.

A ragged cheer burst from the men around me; they stood up and waved their hats. I jumped up, turned and ran past them, back along the path I had come in Ned's grip, heedless of the steep downward slopes and treacherous slipping stones, until I skidded onto the beach and attempted a slow dreamlike run in sand towards the little knot of figures around Charlie's body. Rodnia kneeled at Charlie's side; George stood like a statue of a shooting man. He looked up towards the row of cheering spectators on the clifftop. 'What's going on?'

'You've shot the General,' said Ned. Sweat and pomade were running down his neck into his collar. He took off his bowler and patted his drooping hair.

'It can't be,' said George. He looked at the pistol in his hand as if seeing it for the first time.

'The pistols I gave you were loaded with blanks,' said Ned. 'Nobody knew that but me. You weren't meant to use Widowmaker, damn your eyes.'

George put away his weapon, dropped the duelling pistol from the other hand and ran towards Charlie's motionless body and the kneeling Rodnia. 'Is he ... is he all right?'

'He couldn't have suffered,' said Rodnia, blinking rapidly and rubbing his nose with his hand.

'Get up that cliff,' said George, 'and see if there's a doctor among those fellows.' Rodnia's shoulders heaved. 'Roddie! Git!' His brother got to his feet and jogged towards the cliff.

George kneeled in his place, put his ear to the red velvet chest. 'I can't hear anything but his confounded pocket watch. Where's the wound?'

'You can't see for the vest,' said Ned.

George fumbled with the waistcoat buttons. 'Charlie, don't go ... I only meant to frighten you ... I aimed Widowmaker high ... I can't believe I'm such a bad shot ... Don't leave me, please, dear God, don't ...' His clumsy fingers gave up after two buttons. He placed his head on Charlie's stomach and sobbed.

Mrs Bleeker came forward and placed one hand on his shoulder. She gestured to me to help her, and together, very gently, we lifted George off the body. Then from somewhere inside her shawl, Mrs Bleeker produced a pair of scissors.

'No,' wailed George.

Ignoring him, she put the blades to the velvet and slit the waistcoat from bottom to top, peeled it back and ripped open the shirt. Charlie's nipples and belly appeared, three hairy hills, no blood.

'Where is the wound?' I said.

'Wait,' said Mrs Bleeker. As we watched, the chest rose.

'General?' said Ned, very faint.

'Charlie?' said George.

Charlie opened his eyes and stretched his mouth into a wide open grin. Between his clenched teeth sat a silver bullet. He sat up, spat the bullet into his hand. 'You owe me a new waistcoat,' he said to Mrs Bleeker.

I could go now. Nobody was dead, nobody would miss me. I could find Franz. There was still time. Five days.

But then, as George gaped at him, Charlie chuckled. 'Commodore George Washington Nutt, you must improvise faster than that. Don't you know anything? Aren't you even ready for your public?'

He gestured towards the cliff, where Rodnia and the gentlemen were coming in single file down the path. They gathered round, shaking hands, slapping backs, congratulating the little fellows on a capital show, and I was once again imprisoned in their circle of pomade and cigars. Charlie smiled and bowed, put his arm around George's shoulders, and I was astonished to see George lean into his embrace. Ned began to smile and talk fast. Rodnia stood to one side, a silent shadow. Mrs Bleeker, knowing better than to interrupt a show, also retreated a few paces, holding my arm in a tight grip. The gulls, orange in the climbing sun, were coming back. The whiskery gentleman threw them a sausage and they swooped, tearing.

'Jove, that was a fine show,' he said to the little men. 'And your fellow and Mrs Beaver here did a grand job of setting it up. I backed you, sir' — he turned to George — 'and I have made a mint.'

'No, no,' cried George. 'The General was also the victor. He's outsmarted us all. Including our fellow, who has no doubt made a mint too, eh, Ned?' Ned smiled and smiled, eyes darting this way and that.

'But we are betting men, sir,' said the whiskered man. 'How are we to tell who has won if there is no victor? I had all my money on you felling the General.'

The gentlemen frowned, glanced at each other, murmured.

'Felling the General? Bejesus, what an idea. As if I could harm a hair on the head of my beloved Charlie, the greatest little man on earth.'

'And as if I could harm my dear old pal George, who is like a brother to me. No, gentlemen, I fear we are shocking dissemblers, as all troupers are. Isn't that so, Ned?' Ned made a noise between a grunt and a wheeze, put his finger in his collar and circled his neck.

'Never fear, gents, you'll get your cash back with interest if you ain't satisfied,' cried George. 'You must apply to Ned here, the brains behind the show. No, don't protest, you modest fellow. It's all down to you. Why, even Charlie and I don't know the half of it.'

'No indeed. Nobody *knows*. He led us by the *nose*.'

'Say, Charlie, exactly how much d'you reckon he made?' George prodded Ned's jacket pocket, and Charlie prodded his other side.

'A big haul, George. Mighty big. Let's investigate.' The little men pulled at Ned's jacket.

'Ahhhahaha,' yelled Ned. 'Commodore. General. Please.'

'Gentlemen?' Charlie beckoned to the spectators. The laughing gentlemen yanked off Ned's jacket and turned out his pockets. Coins spilled onto the sand as George poked at Ned's trousers.

'Strike me lucky, Charlie, our Ned's a walking gold mine.'

'Let's have a look at his seams.'

Taking their cue, the gentlemen grabbed Ned, forced him down on the sand and pulled off his boots, trousers and shirt, shook the boots upside down and flapped his garments in the wind. More coins spun and bounced, and one gentleman began to collect them in a leather bag. Charlie and George capered around Ned, crouched in his ragged drawers, his hands folded around his chest.

'Hands up, Ned,' George growled. Widowmaker flashed in his hand.

'You wouldn't dare,' whimpered Ned.

'I would never dare shoot the greatest little man in the world. But I might shoot you.'

Slowly Ned raised his trembling arms.

'Oh ho, what have we here?' cried George.

I saw it, under Ned's right arm. A puckered pink circle. The third nipple, the Devil's mark.

'Ned, you dark horse,' said Charlie. 'You are one of us.'

I touched the webs of skin between my own fingers. Every one of us. And at once, I knew. I could see how and why he'd done it. Ned, the poor boy from Brooklyn, the secret freak. Fast talker, fast learner, brilliant troublemaker, but never rewarded with a high post in Mr Barnum's employ. Full of poison against his betters. Capable of spinning yarns that would convince both Charlie and George that one was out to destroy the other. Goading them into a duel, not to kill each other — that was too much trouble, perhaps — but to make them look foolish and fearful, and to make himself rich.

Was it in me, then, to feel sorry for Ned? But I could feel nothing but relief and a stab of savage elation at the comeuppance of the man who had plotted to kidnap me and my child.

As George lowered Widowmaker, Ned grabbed his trousers and ran along the beach towards the tumble of rocks at the far end.

At the same time, Rodnia burst out of his trance. 'Blackguard,' he yelled, and set off after Ned, stumbling in the sand. The gentlemen cheered and whistled. The little men bowed. Then Charlie put on George's coat and George put on Charlie's slashed waistcoat. They put their arms around each other's shoulders and passed Ned's abandoned flask back and forth between them, talking intimately in their biggest stage voices.

'I admired you from the moment I first saw you,' said George. 'I said to myself, Now I know a little man can be great.'

'That's big of you. You always looked up to me.' The gentlemen laughed as if they were the soul of wit.

'But, George, I say. If you always admired me so much, why did you try to shoot me?'

'Charlie, I would never shoot you. I used my own pistol and I shot so I wouldn't hit you. I wouldn't use Ned's pistols.'

George picked them up from where they had been abandoned on the sand, held them high, then shoved them under Charlie's nose. 'Handsome, eh? But the moment I held mine, I knew it was no good. The chequering on the butt isn't deep enough. No hair trigger. Wrong shape. Wrong weight. *Small* arms.'

'Bet you he got 'em from the theatre prop basket. But how did you know I would not shoot you?'

'Charlie, you don't have it in you, and that's the *size* of it.'

'George *Nutt*, you are *cracked*. You are the one who doesn't have it in you. I always knew you would never shoot me, that is why I planned my *little death*. I have a skinful of pluck.' He slapped his belly and crowed, and held up the bullet he had lodged between his teeth.

I guessed it was probably not the kind of bullet that would fit in either Widowmaker or Ned's pistols, but the sporting gentlemen cheered nonetheless.

'I have but one failing,' Charlie continued, 'and it is one I share with you. I believe in *tall* stories.' He winked at the delighted gentlemen.

'And no one tells a *taller* story,' said George, 'than our friend Ned.'

'Indeed. Ned has it in him. He is full of ...'

'Milk.'

'Enough for three bubs. What *tall* story about me did he feed you, George, to persuade you to challenge me?'

George's eyes grew round as marbles. 'Tell you later, my friend. There are ladies present.' The gentlemen whooped, and Mrs Bleeker raised her umbrella. George continued, 'And what *tall* story did he feed you, Charlie, that made you accept my challenge?'

Charlie blushed, for once without words, and I guessed it was something that would make the gentlemen whoop even more. He drew himself up. 'We shall be *short* with him, George. We shall cut him *down to size*.'

'I think he sighs already, out on the rocks, without his socks, with my brother giving him what for.'

'Say, gentlemen, what do you reckon? Ned has magnanimously refunded your cash. Do you still want to call in your bets?'

They laughed, shook their heads. 'Worth every penny,' said one.

Charlie held out his arm to George. 'Shall we proceed to our headquarters?'

All the way back to the hotel, as they walked arm in arm, the pistols in their box tucked under George's arm, the gentlemen pursued them. Mrs Bleeker and I brought up the rear, unnoticed, as the men clapped, cheered, hollered, whistled. The man who had collected the money kept pushing coins into their pockets, and others pushed in notes. Draining Ned's flask into their empty stomachs, Charlie and George sang *Yankee Doodle* in a rousing tenor, then switched to *Cottage by the Sea* in screeching falsetto. They were still singing as they reached the sleepy hotel, and their voices faded away through the doors.

And when life's long day is closing,
Oh, how pleasant it would be,
On some faithful breast reposing,
In the cottage by the sea.

Mrs Bleeker stopped in the courtyard as I was looking around wildly for Franz. There was no sign of him.

'Men,' she sighed, putting everything from sorrow to venom into one word.

· · · · · · · ·

There was no escape. All I longed to do was to run round the hotel, searching for Franz, just a glimpse of him to reassure me that he had not left alone in pursuit of Mr Liszt. But Mrs Bleeker sat me down, ordered me to put my feet up, brought me the still-overflowing basket of costumes needing repair, threw Charlie's ripped waistcoat on top and bustled around the parlour. 'All mayhem has broken loose and, in your condition, you are best out of it,' she said. 'Poor Mrs Stratton is in tears. My husband has summoned the combatants and is giving them what I am sure is his worst dressing-down yet. Rodnia Nutt has returned, all bruises and torn clothes, and there is no sign of that appalling Ned Davis. Good riddance, I say.'

I looked up from trying to thread my needle. My eyes were blurred and my hands shook so, I kept missing the eye. 'Is … is anyone else from the troupe missing?'

'Good heavens, isn't one enough? Haven't you threaded that needle yet? Use this one, the eye is bigger … Oh yes, here is something Franz Richardson has just asked me to give you.' Reaching over my shoulder, Mrs Bleeker dropped a small envelope in my lap. 'Tell him no, won't you?'

'I beg your pardon?'

She sniffed. 'I've had enough of that young man and his wants.'

I ripped open the envelope, dreading a farewell note, an avowal that he could wait no longer. I smoothed out an almost blank page, with one word on it.

Mrs Bleeker had her back turned, fiddling with her sewing machine. 'Lord knows, we are busy enough without the pianist seeking you out to run more errands for him.'

'It is all right, Mrs Bleeker, I will tell him no.' I folded the paper and put it in my bodice. *Tomorrow*, it sang to me.

CHAPTER 20

And then it was tomorrow, very early, even earlier than the time I had left for the beach, and I had left a folded note to Mrs Bleeker on her bed.

> *By the time you read this I will be married to Mr Richardson. I am sorry to deceive you for you have been nothing but kindness to me, but I had to decide what was best for my child. I have left my last month's wages by the treasury box and I have taken Mrs Stratton's gift of a comb as a keepsake — I hope she will not mind. Please tell the General and Mrs Stratton that I am sorry to leave their employ in such a manner and I shall always be grateful to them. I hope they will find another little one soon.*
>
> *Yours, with the greatest respect, gratitude and affection ...*

Franz was escorting me to the cab with his embrace about my shoulders. Four days, ninety-six hours. Just in time. He took the seat beside me, gave the signal to depart, asked how I was, and I replied that I was very well. My head was light; I had not slept. I wanted to laugh, to break into song, I wanted Franz to cover me with kisses. The poor brave soul kept an almost bashful distance, but I no longer feared his recoil, his held breath. The laughter and songs and kisses would come — there was time enough.

I smiled encouragement at Franz, who kept peering out the window at the dark streets of Sydney. Sometimes a guttering lamp caught his scissoring legs as they crossed and recrossed. He pulled out a cigarette case, then glanced at me and put it back in his pocket and gnawed his nails. All the waiting had unnerved him, I thought.

'I am so sorry I could not come yesterday, Franz. You must have been so worried. But Mrs Bleeker commandeered me.'

He sighed. 'I thought you had changed your mind ... But it doesn't matter, you are here now.'

'Yes, and my mind is made up.' I looked out the window into dark streets. 'Where are we going, Franz?'

'A church. It's all arranged. We must do it quickly, then no one can touch us. I'm afraid it will be a hole-and-corner affair.'

I laughed. 'Dear Franz, I didn't expect flowers and choirs and white satin.'

He smiled faintly, patted my hand.

When I tried to take his fingers, he drew back and peered out the window again. 'Are you worried we will be followed?' I asked.

'When I rose, I heard floorboards creaking.'

'But everyone was so exhausted after the duel affair, and we left so quietly. I'm sure no one suspected a thing. It's so strange. We are conspirators, we are deceiving generous people, and yet I don't feel guilty, I feel free ...' I talked on, of our voyage to Europe, of Franz's career, of how I would help him, of Thomas and his future.

'You must teach him to play the piano, Franz. Perhaps Mr Liszt will help. One day he may equal his father.'

Franz coughed. I entwined my arm in his, held his cold hand, felt the ragged edges of his nails, wondered if I had been presumptuous to call him Thomas's father. I had so much to learn and the lessons would be so exciting.

The cab pulled up outside a large, dark building.

'Is this the church?'

Franz got out to pay the driver. Through the window on his side, nothing but blackness. Out the other window, the upper edge of the sun at last, an orange sliver in charcoal clouds. As the weak rays touched my skirt, a wave of pain struck me below my navel.

Thomas, your handsome father is trembling, I thought, as Franz opened the cab door. The pain in my belly had receded as quickly as it had arrived. I picked up my bag — all I owned weighed so little — and allowed him to take it and escort me down stone steps to a basement door, where a man in an overcoat waited with a lamp, squinting at us through fogged spectacles. He had a round stubbled face and a glistening upper lip.

'My dear, this is ... ah ... the Reverend who will perform the ceremony.' The Reverend bobbed his head, muttered. I looked up high, saw the lamplight catch an arched and pointed window and a hanging sign with a device I could not make out. Then the Reverend opened the basement door and we came into a low-ceilinged room of stone arches. A few flickering candles did little to dispel the deep shadows. My spirits fell. It was like the crypt in London where Mother and Father were buried.

'Here, Franz?'

'The chapel is most convenient,' said a deep voice. 'The church above us is locked up this early in the day.' An elderly man approached through the arches. Something about his still-robust build, in contrast to the pale Reverend, reassured me at once.

'Here is our witness,' said Franz. 'Doctor …'

The doctor stood a little way off, smiled and took off his hat, ran his hand over his close-cropped white skull and shaven chin. I did not catch his name, and he remained in half-shadow, but he seemed vaguely familiar. I thought I had probably seen him in the audience at one of the little people's Sydney shows.

The orange sun sent an exploratory ray into the crypt through a grid in the wall, and a fiery hand gripped me and squeezed.

'Is anything wrong, dear?' said Franz. 'You are pale.'

'Perhaps the lady would prefer to adjourn the ceremony until after breakfast,' said the Reverend.

'That will not be necessary. Pray let us continue.'

The squeezing hand had vanished.

The chapel had no altar or lectern or pews, just a few chairs. The priest took off his overcoat, put down his lantern on a chair seat and stood at the top of a small flight of steps. Franz and I stood before him at the bottom of the steps and the witness, still in shadow, stood to one side. The Reverend cleared his throat and began the words of the marriage ceremony in a brisk mumble, blinking rapidly, fumbling the pages of his Bible and prayer book with his white fingers. How much better Father had performed this task, week after week, his sonorous voice reminding bride and groom of the sacred duties ahead. Perhaps this man was too ashamed of his part in a hasty secret wedding. But marriage was still sacred; he should remember that.

The crypt had a bittersweet smell of old wine, and another odour, damp and fungal, and I was glad I had kept on my bonnet and shawl as the cold of ages crept up from the stone flags beneath the thin soles of my boots. I stared over the priest's shoulder at a rosette lurking in an arch and breathed in an animal scent radiating off my poor husband-to-be. Thomas and I would have to take care of him. On my right, the witness stood serene, holding his hat in black-gloved hands. Had I first seen him standing this way, in the line waiting to shake hands with the Lilliputians? The orange sun pushed higher, shadows crept across the flags, the priest droned. Franz said 'I do' in a high, strangled voice I scarcely recognised. He pushed a ring onto my finger, the one that already bore the cheap ring Mrs Bleeker had given me. Franz's ring would scarcely pass the first joint, he frowned and breathed hard, wriggled the gold back and forth, and I thought of the way he had first felt the webbed skin between my fingers.

'*I do*.' My own voice was loud and clear.

The hand was squeezing me again, beneath my navel. Lord, I might have to dash for the privy. The pain gathered, peaked, and something warm and wet trickled down my leg. I opened my eyes wide. How could a mere pain hold me in such a vice? How could I still stand upright?

Four days, ninety-four hours. But Thomas would not wait. I turned, not to Franz, but to the man on my right.

'Doctor.'

'I now pronounce you ...' said the Reverend.

'Doctor. Help me.'

. . . .

A great vault, the colour of Thomas's eyes. I tried to sit up, but my body was jelly. The vault, framed by a church window, was sky. Or sea? Gulls karked. I was at the seaside. I would float in the waves and recover from whatever it was that ailed me.

It is one of God's blessings, Father had said, *that we do not remember pain*. I had been married in a crypt, or did I dream it? Dear Franz at my side. An orange finger of sun. The grip of a mighty hand. I had floated — or was I carried? — to a bed beneath a ceiling rose with a design of leaves and fleur de lys. It was still above me now. Poison had come shooting down from the rose, had transfixed me to the bed. Thomas, I had realised, was killing me. He squeezed like a little python. Something Mrs Bleeker had said about the infant Hercules, sitting up in his cradle and strangling two snakes in his baby fists. Was Thomas playing the snake or Hercules? Bravo, Thomas.

Faces had hovered, Franz's among them. Cold hands, clipped nails, a nuggety gold ring. A hospital smell, someone screaming — such language from a woman. A pain in my arm, a bee-sting beside the squeezing python. Was Thomas pinching me too? The rose above me whirled. Darkness.

Matilda was washing me, pulling a fresh nightgown over my head, brushing my hair, just the way she looked after her dolls. The sheets were cool, the towels crisp. My head lolled. From the window the sun spread its net.

Later, Franz sat at my side, holding my hand. I tried so very hard to stay awake for him, to give him a smile, because he looked so forlorn. Something had happened to the muscles in my face. At last I managed to say the words.

'Where is Thomas?'

CHAPTER 21

Now I come to a time when my memory was very confused. I did not know if I had had a child or not, but I believed I did. I did not know if I was hearing truth or lies. I did not know what was real and what was a dream.

There was a morning I sat up, looked out of the blue church window. I was alone, in bed, and I remembered.

'Thomas?' Franz had said to me earlier, as he sat by my bed. 'Who is Thomas?'

'My baby.'

'Oh … I am so sorry, Mary Ann. The child was stillborn.'

I had taken my hand from Franz's and had turned on my side, away from him. I would not believe it.

Later. My jelly limbs had firmed. I could get out of bed and use the chamber pot, though needles went through me as I squatted. I tried the door handle, but it would not open; the door was jammed. A large young woman with thick eyebrows and purpled hands lit the fire and washed me and brought me food and drinks on trays, and bitter-tasting medicine that I swallowed every night.

'Will you not bring me my baby?' I asked her. The nurse breathed heavily through her mouth, said not a word. When she had gone, I pulled the covers around my shoulders and sat on the windowseat, watching the cove through the bars. Water snaked in and out of the folds in the land, and ships crossed it to berth at the wharf below. On a headland nearby stood a strange Grecian temple, square and pillared, glowing white in the sun. I thought of another view, of apple trees, how I had sat in another strange nightgown, my needle dipping in and out of a tiny glove. No one but the nurse came to me. Sometimes I yearned for Franz's face; other times I yearned for another visitor, carrying a muff or a little pair of gloves.

'Am I mad?' I asked the nurse. 'Where is Mrs Bleeker?'

The woman frowned, bundled a pile of towels to her huge bosom and slid out the door.

I walked around the room, twenty circuits, then back the other way, knocking at the walls with my knuckles as I passed. I opened the wardrobe and the drawers and found my clothes, clean and neatly folded — there seemed no need to put them on. I put my hands to my stomach, slack and rubbery, like a puffball. At night, I fancied the ceiling rose sent down a black beam that dispatched me into dreamless sleep.

Franz would come to me, in time. Perhaps he thought it still too painful for us to see each other. But I was not sure where this pain was coming from, or who was feeling it.

And where was Thomas? Perhaps he was outside, somewhere in those snaking stretches of blue beyond the window. One time I had seen a small figure that looked familiar, walking close to the wall below me, and I had leaned out and looked again, but the path the figure had taken came to a stop and the wall dropped like a cliff, and the figure had gone. There was no way I could climb down, and in any case the bars would stop me. If only the door were not jammed, I would rush out and find them. Should I cry out? Who would hear?

I sat on the window seat, drew up my knees. I had found that gazing towards the serene Grecian temple on the green headland with its air of a painter's Arcadian paradise offered a little comfort to my agitated heart. I tried to find something firm in my woolly thoughts. The door was not jammed, it was locked; they had confined me for my own good. Perhaps I had gone mad with grief, but grief for what? Only my breasts felt anything — the nurse put cabbage leaves onto them, under my nightgown. They were hard as rocks, they burned, and sometimes they leaked white tears. I thought of the wet sheets hanging round Mother and Father. Perhaps I had been mad for a long time and had not known it. The Lord giveth, the Lord taketh away. The Lord might have waited a little, just long enough for me to hold my child. But Thomas would come back; he had wriggled and kicked so when he was inside me, he would never stay still.

I walked and walked. Thirty, forty circuits. When the nurse left me alone for the night, I poured my medicine out the window, and my dreams returned. Day after day, I put my ear to the door and heard footsteps, bangs, a bird's screech, faraway voices, rattling trays, a clock's distant chimes.

Once I heard an argument. Franz's voice was loud, furious: 'You gave me your word you would not harm her.' I could not hear a reply. Then Franz shouted again: 'Why did I believe anything you said? I have been under a spell, and I have woken up.'

Was I under a spell too? When would I wake up?

• • • • • • • •

It was always quiet between ten and twelve in the morning: that must be the time when everyone was out. I poked at the lock with a hairpin and, halfway in, the pin scraped on some obstruction I guessed was the key. I kneeled and stared under the door: the floorboards left a space large enough for me to slip in my fingers, but it was too dark to see anything.

The next morning, after the nurse had collected my breakfast tray, I took my shawl from the drawer, slid it under the door until half of it lay on the floor outside. Then I poked the end of Franz's beautiful crescent-moon hairpin into the keyhole, pushed the key backwards until it fell on the other side of the door, and pulled the shawl back, very slowly, holding the fabric taut. The key came with it. I unlocked the door from the inside, dressed quickly in my outdoor clothes and waited for the clock to strike ten.

As I turned the door handle, a fear shot through me that it would rot like an overripe peach in my hand, but it stayed firm, and I stole into the hallway, where silence and dimness enveloped me. I was in a short corridor leading to the top of a narrow flight of stairs, probably the servants' passage. Willing myself not to run, I descended, floor after floor, pausing every now and then to listen to the silence beyond my own ragged breath. My head seemed to work less well than my painful legs, and when Thomas or Franz edged into my mind, I drew down a blank sheet. I must leave the building without anyone seeing me; what I would do next, I had no idea, but for now there was only the need to be free of the house. Yet still there was the madness; that was why I was here. Was it not better to turn round, climb the stairs, get into bed and pull the covers over my head? But my aching legs kept carrying me down, the blank walls corkscrewed around me.

At last the stairs stopped, in another short corridor with a door at one end: I walked to it, turned the handle, but it was locked. When I walked the other way, the corridor rounded a corner and I flung a hand over my eyes, dazzled with red, purple and green lights, expecting to be seized and carried away, but all I could hear was a regular *tick, tick*. I took away my hand and looked around at a great oval saloon, unfurnished except for a handsome grandfather clock. A majestic flight of stairs, flanked by two black marble statues of Egyptian gods, spiralled upwards from the stone floor, to a distant blue dome that admitted light through a row of windows. The rainbow lights came through the hallway ahead of me, from a very high windowpane shaped like an open fan, too high to reach from the ground, which held a peacock's tail of stained glass. Beneath the peacock's tail were great double doors, and I ran to them, rattled the handles, pushed and pulled, but they would not budge. I stood to get my breath, licked my dry lips, listening, then turned to the room on the left of the double doors and found a bare echoing space, darkened by shutters locked over the inside of the great Gothic windows. The room off the other side of the hallway was dark for the same reason, but full of piled shapes I guessed were wooden boxes. Back in the saloon were more doors, all locked, and two doors under the stairs that were not even proper doors, just panelling: the staircase cut diagonally across them. I wanted to bang on the panels and shriek, but instead I sat on the lowest level of the spiral flight, loosened my bonnet and let it hang down my back. The black goddess on my left and the dog-headed god on my right gazed straight ahead as if I were beneath their notice. A lozenge of purple light fell on my left hand, and cool fingers brushed the back of my neck.

I almost screamed, then realised what I felt was air, a draught from upstairs. At once I was up, climbing, sniffing like a dog at the tiny breeze that came, with a stream of white light, from an open door on the first landing. Inside the room, I made straight for the sash window, raised a little to admit the air, and pushed it up as high as it would go. I looked out towards a pair of straggly eucalypts, a dusty shrubbery, a brick wall, tightly ranked slate roofs and chimney pots, and a row of iron bars, identical to the ones in my bedroom, across the width of the window. I pushed at the bars, tried to turn and squeeze a shoulder through, though I could see they were too close together for me to escape. What a fortress they had left me in. I stood, hands on the bars, as if my will could force them apart, and I could fly into the eucalypts.

A dull thump from the front of the house. Another, then another. They had returned early, they would catch me, punish me. But the thumps went on, as if someone were moving heavy objects, and they came from the window, not from the stairwell. Whoever was making the noise was outside the building, round the corner, out of my vision. If the window had been overlooking a street, I could call out; but there was not even a path. A taunting breeze, damp with salt and recent rain, riffled my hair and sent a drift of pale leaves against my skirts and onto the floor. When I looked down, I saw they were not leaves, but sheets of paper covered in writing. I made out a line:

As to my relation to the mermaid, it is entirely honourable ...

Somewhere behind the constant pain in my breasts, something squeezed my heart.

I bent to pick up the paper, which I saw now had not blown in through the window, but had floated down with other sheets from a desk in the centre of the room. In my haste to reach the window, I had not noticed my surroundings. The room reminded me of somewhere I had been before, but I could not think when or where. A padded leather chair sat behind the desk, a blue rug patterned with red octagons covered the floor. The remains of a fire glowed in the marble-fronted fireplace. Shelves of leather-bound volumes covered most of one wall, tall glass-fronted cabinets containing rows of slim drawers lined two more walls. The fourth wall, at the other end of the room, was hidden by a Japanese screen. It depicted three robed figures crouching. One unfurled a scroll, another drew a sword, and looming over them, goggling at them with its vacant eyes, was a giant skeleton.

On the maroon flocked wallpaper close to me was a framed drawing of a man's head in profile, with the skin of his face peeled back to reveal the folded muscles beneath; I shuddered at the naked eyeball. On the desktop, under a green-shaded lamp, was a blotter, a brass inkwell, a large crystal ashtray, a leatherbound ledger and two open folders. I opened the ledger, flicked the pages. There were long lists of mysterious names in tiny handwriting — *Nautilus pompilius, Dolabella callosa, Argonauta argo* — sometimes with prices attached, and more pages listing items — arsenate of soda, camphor, rubber tubes, bulbs. The last entry read: *16 Panes Glass, flat. Three Glass Domes. To the Temple. Lower Fort Street.* Something about these lists seemed familiar, but nothing made any sense. I turned to the papers on the floor, which had probably spilled from the folders, disturbed by the breeze. I picked up a few pages, leafed through them, gazing at the loops and curls of another hand, one I knew very well.

The mermaid is not at all like a common prostitute ...

Swiftly I put the papers face down on the desk, shut my eyes, put my head in my hands. The breeze from the window had died. I heard the distant ticking of the grandfather clock. Eyes still shut, my hands groped across the folders, pulling together the pages, holding them up. My eyes obeyed me, but my hands would not.

By the time the clock struck eleven, I was no longer thinking of escape. I sat behind the desk in the leather chair, reading sheet after sheet of paper, knowing that soon I must go back to the room upstairs and climb into the bed and try to rest my aching body, because here was the proof that I had indeed gone mad.

... Do you have more news of Mr Liszt and the Altenberg Eagles? I am most gratified to learn that the maestro replied to yr last letter with brief but favourable words — you must have been very flattering about my poor performance on yr magnificent pianoforte, the night you invited me to dine with you tête à tête at Athena Hall — would that my sadly unpractised skills could have matched your instrument. Tell Mr Liszt that I will endeavour to improve, da capo, da capo, despite the execrable quality of the Antipodean theatre pianos I am forced to play — I console myself with the thought that this is a purgatory that will end ...

There were dozens of letters, written on thin, flimsy paper with the marks of many foldings. Each was headed with the place and the month — Ballarat, March; Wellington, July; Seymour, September; Oatlands, May — but did not follow any sequence in the folder. Some were neatly written, others crumpled and smudged. These latter were scarcely legible, yet all the letters were in the same hand. All those I could read began *My Dear Doctor* and finished *Yr Grateful Servant, FR.*

With a sudden movement, I turned to the second folder on the desk. Again, a pile of letters, not quite so high, on finer quality notepaper, written to *My Dear FR* in a neat, cramped hand, the same hand that had filled the ledger. These were not signed: they must be copies of the originals, and the meticulous patience of this copying struck me as nightmarish. I flipped through the sheets.

I have had more news of the young Altenberg eagles. They perch on crags around Maestro Liszt's summer house. Under his tuition, they shed their downy feathers and grow pinions, evolve from promising musicians into angels of the piano. The Maestro endured years in an abyss of pain, haunted by the fear that he was squandering his God-given gifts in circus performances. Now he has found a new vocation — more humble, more noble — in teaching others.

I turned back to Franz's letters, staring at his bold loops and dashes, feeling a leaden reluctance to seek the word. At last I turned a page and it jumped out like a fin from water.

The mermaid is not at all like a common prostitute — she is young, well educated, well spoken, a little spirited but sweet-natured, passably intelligent, not at all grasping — not tall, not small — erect spine — abundant head of hair, chestnut brown — clear complexion — good hips — good teeth — small hands & feet — as to her constitution, seems lively, strong & hardworking, though given to occasional long spells of sleep — neither a drinker nor a partaker of narcotics — plays the piano quite prettily — handsome, if you desire such, tho I prefer a downy apricot to a cantaloupe ...

I gripped the side of the desk to steady myself, then turned to the second folder. Again, the word leaped at me.

What foolishness is this? It was as well your plan failed. In the first place, I already have two mermaids. One is a rare sirenoform infant. The other is as sorry as old leather and she stinks. Some rogue off Honshu stitched her together from a mummified monkey and a dried fishtail. I suspect Mr Barnum's Feejee mermaid came from the same source. I would not give you tuppence for that madam. As for a living female with webbed fingers, no tail ... commonplace. Not even Mr Barnum would bite.

Second, it is supreme folly to abduct an employee of General Tom Thumb's troupe and attempt to bring her to my door. I cannot be associated with such nefarious practices. My reputation is spotless, and shall remain so, no thanks to you. And I had taken you for an intelligent young man. You must pledge to refrain from any further wild deeds, lie low, watch, listen, keep me posted. Above all, heed my counsel.

I seized the first folder. A few pages on:

... to answer yr questions: the circumstances of the conception are as follows, viz: the General and his mermaid coupled under the bridge which spans the Yarra Yarra in Melbourne, on a stormy night in early Feb, whether in or out of the water I cannot be sure — there is one witness, the agent of the troupe — the General has put about some cock & bull story of a rescue from drowning & a miracle of his electric potency — no one believes him, except for his lady — I sometimes think she does not understand country matters — they say that dwarfs are not overly intelligent ... The

mermaid's history is unknown — she claims to be a widow & an
orphan & a governess — possibly she is a trollop hired in secret
by the General to bear his child — or possibly all was devised by
the wardrobe mistress, a cunning and formidable guardian …

I paused, passed a hand over my face. Surely these were not Franz's thoughts — an evil spirit had possessed his hand. I turned back to the second folder.

A mermaid that has bred with a little fellow such as your
General would be a treasure indeed. Not the fishy part, the little
part. I would hazard much for a living, healthy child of such
a union. It might be born small, ready for preservation in its
pristine state. Or it might be born full size, and would only show
its heritage as it grew. About four years old, I think, would be the
perfect age. Secure it for me and I will build it a glass Iranistan,
a beautiful grotto, I will preserve and plait and perhaps regraft
locks of its hair …

My fists clenched on the desk. On the blotter was the first sheet of paper that I had picked up from the floor. I smoothed out the crumpled page.

*her freedom is intermittent — the General's lady & her sister
adore her & cosset her like a puppy at one moment, & then expect
her to trot about serving them at the next — she is guarded — the
wardrobe mistress has a stern eye — but she is not a prisoner —
the General watches her as a man might watch a fine mare with
a racing foal on the way — as to my relation to the mermaid, it
is entirely honourable — I have taken care that we should not fall
under suspicion — I have been circumspect at all times — she is
sometimes complacent, sometimes confused & frightened for her
future — with all due modesty I should add that I have her eating
out of my hand ...*

The words blurred before my eyes. So the wedding had been
a sham, and everything had been planned to one evil end. Why
had I concluded that Ned was my betrayer? Because love was my
weakness, my downfall.

I thought of what must have happened as I lay in a swoon: the
doctor's clean white hands, pushing open my thighs, drawing out
his prize, and I reeled with faintness and nausea.

After a while I gripped the desk and looked about me at the
monster's den that masqueraded as a gentleman's study, and I
remembered another such study in Athena Hall where I had
feverishly written in a memorandum book and the kind doctor,
who in those days had a huge white ruff of hair and beard, had
shown me a much larger ledger with the same tiny handwriting.
A room full of treasures, some of them in drawers, some hidden
behind a burgundy velvet curtain. I stared towards the far end of

the room: the sun's midday rays fell on the Japanese screen drawn in front of the shelves. *It conceals my most precious specimens. I cover them to protect them from light, and also because, to the unscientific eye, some can appear … well, they are not for the eyes of the fair sex.*

I took a few deep breaths and arose, walked to the Japanese screen and folded it back. On the wall it had covered was a shelf at head height, holding seven glass jars, all slightly different sizes, all topped with glass domes in the style of an Arabian Nights palace. Each one was full of liquid, with a shape crammed in or floating inside, too cloudy to distinguish, except for the central three jars, the largest on the shelf. Inside the left jar was a little brownish creature in human form but for its face: it had a blank space where the eyes should be, yet below a stump that passed for a nose was a single eye on a patch of red skin, as if the eye were an inflamed wound. Inside the right jar was a similar creature: its face and closed eyes were perfect, but at its waist, instead of legs, it grew a stumpy tail. The largest creature nearly filled the space of the central jar. It was the colour of Lavinia's pink pearls. I leaned forward, my breath on the glass, and Thomas gazed back at me with a steady, milky look in his lidless eyes, his great round head bowed in thought, his arms and feet neatly folded to fit inside his glass coffin, his neck and wrists and ankles shackled with strings of black and white beads. As my gaze locked with his, he recognised his mother the gullible mermaid, who had betrayed him, and he opened his mouth in a high wail.

'No, Thomas. No.' I clamped my hands over my ears, dug fingers into my skull, but the wail went on, piercing me through and through. It was real, I realised. Not from a specimen in a jar, but from a real baby.

The grandfather clock began to strike. Twelve chimes. Far away, a door slammed, but I scarcely heard it. I was back in the house in my dream, with the blossom wallpaper and the tiny closed door, and Thomas's wail would not let me wake. My nipples tingled, my stomach cramped and a warm dampness spread across my bodice. My body knew him. But he was not there: I had to find him. I made my way from the room, the letters, the terrible jar, hand over hand on the velvety walls. The wail, the animal mew of an infant, came from higher up the stairwell. With an energy I did not know I had, I ran up two flights, along a landing, into a small, bare room with a tall unbarred window that looked out onto a dim lightwell. On the floorboards stood a child's cradle, crudely made. I crept closer and looked inside. It held only a small rug, but it was very gently rocking. I picked up the rug, inhaled warm, sweet milk.

So close. But where? I threw up the window sash. Below were bare walls, a three-storey descent to basement level, a lightwell with no doors. Gulls cried, carriages rattled in the distance, a tugboat horn blared. No one could escape from here. Somewhere else in the house, then. But as I turned back towards the door, heavy steps came, and then they were in the room with me, the faces that had hovered over me while I lay squeezed by the python and poisoned by the ceiling rose. So they were not apparitions of madness — unless I was still mad. I retreated to the window.

'Don't come any closer,' I told them.

'Mary Ann ...' Franz did sadness so well, I almost loved him again. When he took a step forward, I kneeled on the sill.

'If you come any closer I'll jump off.'

Horror filled their faces. Let them believe me mad, then.

'Come away from there,' said Franz. 'You are not well. You must go back to bed.'

'Bring me my baby.'

'Mrs Richardson,' said the doctor, 'I am afraid you are mistaken. You have no child.'

'He is here, somewhere.' There were no calm, sane words for my need.

'I am sorry to say your child passed away shortly after it was born.'

That lie again? 'No. Thomas is here.'

'Come, Mrs Richardson.' The doctor reached out his hand, his voice low and gentle. 'We mean you no harm. Step away from the window.'

I looked down into the lightwell: a man with a ladder stood there. Some servant, cutting off my one retreat.

I turned back to the men in the room: the priest from the crypt, smearing his hands on his apron. The doctor, shorn of his white ruff. Franz, all sweat and wretchedness.

'I have read your letters, I have seen the jars, and I know you all for what you are. Kidnappers. Deceivers. Murderers.' My words rang around the room, they would keep me strong, would stop me listening to their lies, would strike down the villains with their electricity. I shifted on the sill, glanced out the window and down. The servant, his face hidden under his hat, had propped his ladder on the wall and was climbing towards the window. He was short but muscular: he would be hard to fight. I turned my gaze back to the room; they were all dogs I could stare down. They were snarling into each other's faces.

'You should have followed my advice and thrown her into the harbour,' said the priest. 'It's not too late.'

'Don't listen to him, doctor. Remember, you promised me she would not be harmed —'

'But you said —'

'Gentlemen, gentlemen.' Dr Musgrave held up his hands. 'Let us be reasonable. Let us be civilised. What do we do with poor deranged women?'

'You humour them,' I said. 'You give them what they want.'

Dr Musgrave gave me a smile, shook his head. He was a cat releasing a mouse, then lazily stretching out its paw.

The servant's head appeared at the windowsill next to me; bearlike, heavy brows, a dark chin. I gasped with recognition. Broad shoulders followed, and a small, thickset body in a brown leather vest, a muscled forearm pointing a silver pistol into the room.

'Get back, the lot of you.' Rodnia swung a leg over the sill.

Why had I not known him at once? I wanted to cheer, dance, hug my stubby bushranger. I did not move.

'What is this?' said the priest in a thin voice. 'We have no money here, nothing of value.'

'Rodnia,' said Franz, 'you are making a mistake.'

'You know this man?' said Dr Musgrave.

'He is Nutt, the Commodore's brother. He drives the little coach.'

'I thought you got rid of that Bleeker fellow.'

'I did. But this man —'

'He followed you here?'

'Climb down,' whispered Rodnia to me, without taking his eyes off the men. 'Take care, don't be over-hasty. I'll keep these folks busy.' Then louder, to Franz: 'You blackguard, I ought to kill you for what you've done to her.'

'I can't go,' I whispered to Rodnia. 'Thomas — my baby — is here. I must find him.'

'I did nothing, I swear,' moaned Franz. 'It was her own wish. We are married.'

Rodnia went very pale. The doctor turned to him, raised a saintly hand. 'Poor Mrs Richardson is deranged from the shock of losing her baby. We caught her trying to steal another woman's child.'

'It's a lie,' I shouted, my fists clenching.

Rodnia rested against the window frame, folded one arm across his chest, kept his pistol aimed. 'The child is Bridget's, the servant, she has just taken it away to nurse it,' Dr Musgrave persisted. 'Mrs Richardson is not herself. She threatened to throw herself down the lightwell.'

'Then you must've frightened her,' said Rodnia. 'Who is this wizard, Richardson?'

'Rodnia,' said Franz, 'listen to me —'

'Be quiet,' growled Dr Musgrave. 'Mr Nutt, I am a doctor. I delivered Mrs Richardson's baby, which unfortunately did not survive, despite all my efforts. I implore you to put down your weapon and help us to help her, before she does herself any harm.'

Rodnia looked hard at me.

'You mustn't believe these lies,' I cried. But I sounded shrill, and Dr Musgrave sounded wise. My defiance had held me together, but now I was breaking into pieces. My mouth opened, but all that came out were whimpers, and my hands clutched at the air, tore my hair from its pins, reached out groping in front of me to hold emptiness. Dear God, was I raving? Rodnia watched me steadily, and something twitched under his stern brows. Not pity, not that. At last he addressed Dr Musgrave. 'She's never harmed anyone. But I'll do for anyone who harms her, so help me.'

'Harm is what we aim to prevent, Mr Nutt ...'

'Why should I believe you when you're in league with that blackguard of a pianist?'

Yes, yes, he saw things my way.

'We are not in league,' said Franz. Dr Musgrave turned to him, dark eyebrows raised. 'We are not in league,' Franz repeated. 'I've had enough of your promises and reassurances, doctor. I don't think you ever meant to send me to Mr Liszt. You have used me ill.'

'You wrote to me and you believed me because you are a dreamer,' Dr Musgrave said with a half-smile. 'For a while, our dreams have run together like horses in harness. They can continue to do so, I assure you.'

'I have lost a steady job because of you.' Franz shook his head. 'And the trust of my employers, my good name.'

I stared at him. There must still be some good buried in him. Perhaps I could unearth it.

'Franz.' My voice cracked, then steadied. When his sorrowful eyes met mine, I prepared to withstand the melting wave that always swelled inside me, but this time it did not come. 'I know you care nothing for me now. But if you ever cared for me, even a little, then I implore you to help me find my child and let us both go.'

'Don't trust the villain,' hissed Rodnia.

Franz stared at me for a moment, then dropped his eyes, ran his hands through his hair.

'I don't think your husband will be any help,' Dr Musgrave said in his soothing rumble. 'I regret to tell you that he never cared for you. Lovely as you are, Mrs Richardson, his tastes run elsewhere. You are — how shall I put it — too ripe for him.'

The mysterious words meant nothing to me. But Franz's face reddened, his eyes narrowed. The older man stood back and folded his arms, his head cocked on one side. 'I know why you were dismissed from your conservatory and your teaching jobs,' he said composedly.

I watched Franz shake his fist at the doctor and shout, 'How dare you?' but I was in a daze, my hands still groping for an invisible child.

Then Rodnia gave me the slightest of nudges with his elbow, jerked his head a little towards the window. 'When you get down,' he whispered, 'carry the ladder across and climb the opposite wall.'

'But I can't — I mustn't —'

'How d'you think you'll ever live to be a mother if you don't get out of here? Move. Now.'

My whole body was frozen. Why did Rodnia not understand, I could not leave while Thomas was in the house? But I had heard no more baby's wails since that moment when I had rushed from Dr Musgrave's study. Maybe they had smothered Thomas in his still-warm crib and had taken the body away, before I could find him.

No, no grief. Not yet.

Rodnia's finger was on the trigger of his fine silver pistol, and such a hurricane of rage swept through me that I yearned to snatch the weapon, shoot all three of my captors and run through every room until I found the body of my child. Then I remembered the little hands of Charlie and George, holding silver weapons aloft on the beach, and I knew where I had seen that gun before. The duellists' weapons had not been loaded. How long could Rodnia bluff them with a useless weapon?

If I did not leave now, this very moment, I would never survive to take my revenge. 'So, the dreamer wakes,' Dr Musgrave was saying to Franz. 'I note you do not complain that you have lost a wife and child.'

I stepped backwards over the sill onto the top rung of the ladder. The air sucked at me from a horrible depth. I clung to the ladder, my head all swirls.

From inside the room, Franz's snarl: 'Doctor, I should knock you down for that. You said you would not hurt her.'

'It's a little late to play the injured husband, particularly as your wife has read our letters.'

'And she is escaping!' came a panicky cry from the priest.

Surely they would stop me, or push my ladder away. But still, Rodnia's pistol kept them at bay.

'Let us all stay calm,' said Dr Musgrave. 'Mr Nutt, please listen to me ...'

Slowly my foot descended. One step. I could do it if I thought there was only one more step to take. One step. Above me Dr Musgrave droned on, but I could no longer make out the words. One step. Then I was at the bottom, moving the ladder to the opposite wall, as Rodnia had instructed. So leaden, scraping reluctantly across the stones. Would it tip and fall? I hauled with all my strength, got it into place and climbed once more. When I reached the roof, I paused to get my breath, looking down across the lightwell at the window where I had begun my climb, but from this height only a dark square showed, and nothing in my ears but distant squabbling gulls. I told myself to run across the roof, find a way down, get as far away as I could, but my feet would not move. As I stared at the blank window, a shot rang out. In a moment they would realise he had fired a blank and they would rush to overpower him.

Rodnia appeared at the window. He crouched on the sill, then leaped into the void. I screamed. A distant crash, the crunch of flesh on stone.

An updraft buffeted me, a rising wind of rage at the villains and rage at myself, and I fought to stay on my feet. It did not matter whether he had believed me about Thomas, he had believed in me enough to save my life and sacrifice his own, and what had I done? I willed myself to creep forward, to stare down into the lightwell. Now Franz's red head appeared at the window, he too was staring at ... nothing: the small stone square at the bottom of the lightwell was empty. I looked further over the wall's edge, at the ladder I had left below me, and there was the little groom, halfway up, a spider clinging to the rungs. What a miracle, where had he ... but of course, Mr Lillie's circus, the trapeze apparatus. He was still the secret star.

He climbed towards me. I held out my arms and helped him over the edge onto the roof. He breathed great gusts, shivered his flanks like one of his horses. Together we pulled up the ladder, Franz's twisted white face watching us from the other side of the lightwell.

He shouted at us: 'She threw your rabbit away!'

There were no words, only running. I followed Rodnia as he carried the ladder across the flat roof, dodging chimney stacks. How to explain how I could run and climb when my limbs had only just begun to work again, when my fear urged me to crouch and freeze? At the far edge of the roof, Rodnia lowered the ladder, and I peered down. A long way below stood a cab and a man who held the bottom of the ladder.

'Be brave, Missus Carroll,' said Rodnia. He helped me over the edge; my foot felt the first rung. One step, one step. Above me, a few rungs higher, his down-at-heel boots, his pistol thrust into his belt. When we had both climbed down, the man who held the ladder tipped his battered hat.

'Remember me, ma'am?'

'This is Mr Dennis Watts,' said Rodnia. 'The cabbie who brought you and Richardson here.' I stared at the man's shy smile. 'Never fear, he's my friend now,' Rodnia went on. 'Here's his cab. Hop in, quick.'

'No. You will take me back to the General and Mrs Stratton. I will not go and you can't make me.'

'I'm only going to take you to Dennis's place. I figured you'd had enough of being the goose with the golden egg.'

'Thomas was … is not an egg.'

'Oh, you poor goose. Well, come on. Let's get to safety and we'll talk about it.'

Was he lying? Was he really going to take me back to Charlie? But that was yet another thing I could not believe. So I climbed up, but refused his helping hand.

The cab went past a sign — *Cumberland Street* — and then another sign pointing backwards to Lower Fort Street, and then down a hill. It rattled past streets of cramped, mean houses: Gloucester Street, Miller's Buildings, Long's Lane. Rodnia patted my hand, then retreated to his corner of the seat. I wanted to weep, but the lump in my throat refused to soften, and a curious numbness was stealing over me, as if I were being wrapped in tight bandages.

'Feeling better?' said Rodnia. I nodded, though it was not true. It was more as if I had just run out of any feeling at all.

'Thomas —' I began, but Rodnia held up a finger.

'Hush. I reckon it does you no good to talk about it now. You must wait a bit.'

I sat back and held my straying hands tight in my lap, and Rodnia began to tell me how he had found me, and I knew I should be grateful, but it was like he was talking from a very long way off. He said something about how the cabbies at the market had directed them to a gentleman's residence — Isis House, at the top of the hill in Cumberland Street — and Mr Bleeker had insisted on going in alone, and Franz met him, told him a sorrowful story. But Rodnia had not believed I was safe and came back to try to discover a way to get me out.

'... And then that pale fellow with the spectacles crept up on me and tackled me,' he said. 'I was sure they'd push me out the window. So I jumped first.'

I tried to open my mouth to praise his courage, but the numbing bandages had spread to my face.

'Dennis and his missus'll look after us for a night or two. He's a good fellow: he took me in and stabled Zep for me. He got me the ladder and helped me build up a barrier to their door. And someone was fool enough to leave a key in the back door. Those blackguards won't get out for a while. When they do, they won't have a clue where to find us.' He kept his eyes on the road, his voice level. 'D'you still care for that Richardson?'

Care? What was care? I stared out my own window at more prosperous streets. Where to start unravelling the dark tangle of feelings, all tightly bound in their new dressings? Better not to pull any threads.

'Sorry,' said Rodnia. 'I won't ask you again.'

I turned, gazed at the centaur's snub nose and bristling chin. There was one small thing I could offer him.

'I did not throw your rabbit away at Seymour, Rodnia. It hopped off the tray, and I didn't find it again.'

'It went back to the boy. It was his pet, I'd got it down for him.'

'The Reverend Cameron's boy? You got his pet down from the cherry tree?' I fought to rouse myself from lethargy: once I had heard a different story. 'And you got Mr Cameron and the boy down too? And the woman, and her five children?' He nodded warily. 'Oh, I had thought ...' I groped through the numbness as the memory slid away and another came.

'Thomas played with me,' I said. 'I was in the room with the poisonous rose, and Thomas was outside dancing in the sky and the water.'

Rodnia closed his eyes and the lids trembled a little. Then the cab pulled to a halt, and he was out the door, shouting to Dennis.

Mrs Watts gave me a hot milk drink and said I should rest, I had had all manner of dreadful shocks, and not so long since my confinement, poor lamb, I must not take ill. I lay on my back in a small sagging bed, and my breasts were hard, painful mountains. The numbing bandages had spread, swathing my whole body, tying me down to the mattress.

Rodnia sat on a small, hard chair beside the bed with his hat in his lap as if visiting an elderly invalid. 'Can I get you anything?'

'I want Thomas,' I said, very softly. 'But he won't come anymore.' When I had been drugged, or mad, in another bed, he had come to me. Now there was nothing but glancing light through the half-closed curtains and the sound of hooves and shouts outside, and Rodnia's breathing.

'Mary Ann.' He took my hand. 'Consider. Your bab's gone to heaven.'

'He was in the house. I heard him cry. I saw his cradle rock. I smelled his blanket.' There, that was well done. No hysteria. My voice calm, my evidence clear. It seemed that I would not, could not believe that he had been murdered after all.

'But that wasn't your child. It belongs to the servant, Bridget. That doctor fellow said so.'

'And you believed him?'

'No reason to doubt it. There's a Bridget, isn't there?'

'Yes, but —'

'I don't believe that rot about you trying to steal her child, or anything else those liars said. But I think … you haven't been well, you're not quite yourself, you made a mistake.'

'Rodnia, he is in that awful house, I know it. We must go back and find him.'

'God's teeth, I've just got you out of there. Who knows what they were plotting to do to you. They might've thrown you out the window. And you want to go back?'

I nodded dumbly. I wanted to get off the bed and shake him, but the bandages held me tight, and it would burn my flesh to try to break free.

Rodnia bristled, clenched his fists tight, looked ready to battle a host of men. Then he sighed, shook his head. 'Mary Ann, listen to me,' he said, slow yet urgent. 'Mr Bleeker went to that awful house first, without me. Franz told him the bab had passed away at birth. He showed you to Mr B. You were sleeping peacefully. Mr B didn't meet the doctor or that other fellow. But he happened to see a servant girl nursing her baby downstairs.'

'But don't you see? That wasn't her baby, that was —'

'I talked to Mrs Watts. She used to work as a midwife. She says sometimes, when babs pass, the mothers can't believe it for ever so long. They talk to the mite as if it were still there.'

'It is not like that.' My hands flopped on the bed like empty gloves.

'Maybe not. But consider. Here's my plan. When you're up to the journey, we can go to the Blue Mountains. We should be safe there.'

The Blue Mountains. A fairytale place. Once there was a little boy blue who blew his horn … Thomas the mountain boy … Oh, why was I so drowsy? Had Mrs Watts put something in my drink?

Rodnia was talking on, something about how we could not return to the troupe, but he'd get work somewhere, he'd look after me, don't get me wrong, you're a married woman, whichever way you look at it, I just want to be a brother to you, like I was to Tiny George …

'Yes, Rodnia,' I murmured, like a good child. 'Can I sleep now?'

I went alone to the Blue Mountains: they were a deep azure, a frozen sea, and on the pinnacle of the highest mountain stood a palace of glass, its domes and minarets glittering in the sun.

SIDESHOW

Mr Rodnia Nutt

The marriage of General Tom Thumb to Lavinia Warren

ACT TWO

I walk round and round Dennis Watts's tiny parlour, round and round, hands locked together, fingers twisted into a knot, arms and shoulders pulling, pulling, as if my muscle can grow into wings to fly my way out of this bottomless hole and take her with me, but all I can think of is her on that bed upstairs. She lies as still as a statue, beyond fear, beyond misery, and yet she is falling further and further into limbo.

It is where they go sometimes, Mrs Watts has told me, when the baby passes. The good soul has given her a sleeping draught and hopes that when she wakes she will be back with us again, but no one can tell. Sometimes they stay in limbo. Sometimes the midwife gives a poor missus a doll to hold, and she clings tight and coos and tries to nurse it while she strokes its raggy hair. I don't want any doll for Mary Ann; I want her to know her bab is gone, for only then can she go on living. But what if that costs her too much? Isn't it better for her to stay in limbo land? I don't know, can't guess — I only know you don't float in limbo. You fall.

When I heard she'd eloped with Franz, I gave myself a talking-to. Get a grip on yourself, Rodnia, you've always tried to show her that she should strive for what she wants, even though you wonder if you made yourself plain, and you never quite knew what she wanted. And if this is what she wants, to keep her child and marry that man, however much you hate the fellow, then God's teeth, be happy for her.

But all I could see in my mind's eye was her toppling through a great empty void, her arms out as if to meet a lover.

So I was the first to urge Mr B to get on her trail, to seek out all the cab drivers at the market, find one who remembered picking up a gent and lady in the family way from the hotel very early in the day, and where he had taken them. And when Mr B told me how he'd found her at Isis House, and the story Franz had told about the stillborn child, I thought: So that's how she has fallen, and what a terrible hard place to land. But still my mind saw her splayed in the air and her fall was not broken, but went on and on. So I came to that huge fearsome tomb of a house on my own, and scouted around, and it came to me that I had one more place to climb up and do a rescue, as I'd done at Seymour, and though there was neither flood nor pouring rain, it was going to be quite the trickiest rescue I'd ever done.

Mrs Watts has a draught ready for me too and tells me I need to sleep, and Jesus knows I'm as done up and lathered as a nag that has galloped day and night, but still it comes to me I should keep watch, lest those blackguards find out where we are and come after us. And I want to be at her bedside when she wakes, though it might not be for hours yet.

What a ride I'm on, what a jade, up in triumph one minute

and down on the ground the next, back in the saddle, kick in the spurs, onwards. For there was triumph, I'll admit. Came too soon, perhaps. When I found the ladder, climbed to the window, how pale those villains at the sight of my pistol, how quick and brave Mary Ann in her escape. And how finally I'd done my trick again, so near the same as the one in the Big Top in Mr Lillie's circus, the leap to the ladder, the grip to stop myself sliding. Never thought I'd have the pluck for it again, but needs must ... And triumph too, I guess, though I'm not proud of it, that I'd been right about Franz Richardson all along. Not that I'd ever guessed he was in league with that wicked doctor. Always thought him the complete scoundrel, though, with his fancy airs and lady-baiting charm and, when he thought you weren't looking, his hard appraising stare.

Ah, Rodnia, you prize idiot, why didn't you speak out when you had the chance? Tip off Mr B, warn Mary Ann when you saw the way she looked at the fellow? Because I had no proof he'd done anything but play the piano like a pretty gentleman? Sure, but if I'm honest, there was more. It was because he was handsome and strong and athletic and graceful and tall as a tree, and all he needed to do was hang upside down with his red mop dangling and he'd be the spitting image of Mr Ludovic. Jealousy cripples the mind and withers the heart, I've always reckoned so, and I didn't want to go through all that crippling and withering again, no sir, all to no purpose or, even worse, to the purpose of destruction. I thought that if he won Mary Ann, and who knew if he would, maybe he'd turn out worthy of her. So for a long time I did nothing. But deep down I knew damn well nobody was worthy of her, least of all that red-crested rat.

It was when we were in Seymour, out at night in our rescue boat on the flood, that I truly saw him for what he was, and then I had my chance to take a leap, and I flubbed it.

I rowed in the prow, Franz rowed with his back to me in the middle of the boat, so at least I didn't have his noble mug before me, and a Seymour man by the name of Carnie sat in the stern with the tiller and a lantern under a tarp. We were all wringing wet, especially our feet. The world roared, the water ran hard, the rain seemed to fall only in the circle of Mr Carnie's lantern: beyond, all was black. Every now and then a sudden wrench of the tiller, to dodge an eddy or a drifting tree. We were following a distant screaming, whether man or beast we could not tell.

So far we'd rescued and taken to the hotel three families, a farmhand with an empty beer bottle in his mitt, a calf, a crate of hens. It was I who did all the rescuing. One biddy and her five grandchildren wouldn't come down from the roof of their barn. They sat in a row like jam jars snug on a pantry shelf, and that got me antsy. I yelled: 'Get in this damn boat or you'll be a-farming in hell.' Mr Carnie said there was no call for language in his boat, and Franz told me to pipe down, and I said I'd see them both in hell before I'd leave anyone to drown, and Franz said he wasn't taking lip from a jumped-up little horse wrangler, and I said that was rich, coming from a piano-wrangling streak of piss, and meanwhile the biddy climbed down into the boat. So then I shinned up to the roof and took the kids one by one in my arms and tossed them into the boat to their grandma and Mr Carnie, and the youngsters laughed as if it were a game. And all Franz did was what he did each time: hunch over his oars and scowl at me as if he hoped I'd miss, and a young one or two would splash into the black water.

The screaming was louder. Mr Carnie raised his lantern high and shouted. I stared over my shoulder at a huge cherry tree in blossom, and I almost wanted to laugh at such a festive sight in the blackness. In its high branches squatted a thin man and a scrawny boy clutching a bundle, and it was the boy who screamed, baring furious little teeth. 'Mercy,' said Mr Carnie. 'It's Reverend Cameron and his lad.' He steered our boat closer, and the white flowers rained on us. I stood in the prow with my coil of rope and threw one end up to the minister, who caught it and stared at it as if it were a snake. I shouted at him to lash it to the branch but I couldn't wait for his fumbled knots. I was up that rope like an organ grinder's monkey, and the boy stopped screaming, but his mouth stayed open. Slowly I coaxed Mr Cameron down the rope, and he fell the last foot like a bundle of wet umbrellas, muttering Bible talk. I slid down behind him with the boy under my arm. Franz reached out to separate us, then squealed, drew his hand back sharpish.

'The little bastard bit me.'

'No more than you deserve,' said I, and he took a swing at me. It wasn't a slap and it wasn't a punch neither, something in between, and it missed, and he nearly fell, and I hoped he'd go over into the water, but he didn't, although everything rocked to blazes and Mr Carnie shouted: 'No fighting in my boat'; and the boy screamed again and tried to climb back up to the tree, for he'd left his bundle behind. I stopped him, climbed back up myself, hoping Franz wouldn't seize the oars and row the boat away and leave me stranded. Back I came with the boy's treasure in my teeth, a bulging hessian bag the size of two fists, drawn tight at the neck. I offered it to the boy, but he shook his head. I ruffled his hair into wet peaks, pushed the bag inside my own shirt. It was warm and throbbed against my skin.

'For God's sake let us get back to the Royal before anyone punches a hole in my boat,' said Mr Carnie, glaring at Franz and me in turn while a pink glow rimmed the eastern sky, and Mr Cameron screwed his eyes shut and whispered his prayers.

The queer thing was I felt as frisky as a colt, for why would Franz shout at me and call me names and try to hit me? Only because he was jealous, realised he had a rival, someone with a lot more agility and pluck than he could summon as he crouched over his oars. If he took me serious, then maybe Mary Ann would too. I'm not sure how far I thought that out, but that mystery throbbing under my shirt pepped me up no end. And so when we came back into the Royal, I burned to go straight to her, to look up into her sad beautiful eyes, to declare myself hers. Didn't work out like that, of course. Such a fine suitor, dripping mud and showering sodden blossom over the ballroom, tongue locked in my mouth, no doubt stinking of the sewer, all I could do was reach into my shirt and draw out what felt like my own warm, beating heart and place it on the tray in her hands.

And when I next saw her, the boy's pet rabbit was gone, and she was angry with me, berating me for thinking so ill of her red-haired darling, prize poet, hero of the flood, who had rescued so many single-handed while I sat hunched over my oars. She had misconstrued, but how could I tell her the truth without laying bare my crippled mind, my withered heart?

The truth is, it is not enough to go out and rescue families from rooftops, or ministers and boys from cherry trees, or my beloved from a house of villainy. It is necessary, but it will never be enough. For she goes on falling, falling, as Miss Emmeline fell from the trapeze, and I cannot save her. The only one ever worthy of her love, her little bab, has been stolen from her — not by blackguards, but by God Himself. Can't fight that. Can't do anything but take Mrs Watts's sleeping draught and hope for blackness. For a while at least.

CHAPTER 22

When I woke, the bandages had gone and the flame of memory blasted me. I jackknifed in the bed, yanked my knees to my chest and down again, stuffed my hands in my mouth to muffle my cries. Still no tears, just pain so throttling it would not let me breathe. *Hold on. Hold on to something, anything.* And the name of the glass palace came to me: Iranistan, Mr Barnum's splendid pleasure dome in Connecticut. But it wasn't made of glass, was it? Another stab pierced me, not of pain, but hope. I sat up in bed, gasping. The room was dark and quiet, Rodnia's chair empty. *I will build it a glass Iranistan, a beautiful grotto.* Where had I heard that? No, not heard, *read.* The neat, cramped handwriting floated before my eyes, the pages fluttered to the floor in Dr Musgrave's study. *Iranistan.* That was where Thomas was — I felt it in my breasts, arms, hollow belly. Pray God he was alive.

But where was this Iranistan? I screwed my eyes tight, clenched my fists, willed my brain to race through all its corridors of memory.

· · · · · · · ·

Again, the same handwriting, in the same study, this time in a ledger. *16 Panes Glass, flat. Three Glass Domes. To the Temple. Lower Fort Street.* And into my head came the Arcadian picture I had seen from Dr Musgrave's window, the Grecian temple glowing on the headland. It was nothing like an Iranistan palace, and perhaps that was a flimsy hope, a mirage, but the temple was a solid stone building, and I could go to it. Must go to it.

I rose, peered through the curtains at a murky dawn. At least I could breathe now and must tell my hands not to tremble. My dress and underthings hung on a clothes horse next to a pile of linen. Quickly I took a towel from the pile and tied it around my leaking breasts, dressed, pinned up my hair, pulled on boots, shawl and bonnet. I might look a little frowsty but I must not look mad. Should I find Rodnia and wake him? But he did not believe in Thomas, he would only try to talk me out of going, or even change his mind and take me back to Charlie, and I could not risk it, could not waste a moment longer. Should I look for a police station? But if Rodnia did not believe me, what chance would a poor madwoman have with an officer of the law? I found a stub of pencil in a drawer, wrote *The Temple, Lower Fort Street* on a pillowslip, smoothed it out, left it on the bed, and crept out of the house.

I had assumed some huge magnet would draw me through the maze of Sydney to Lower Fort Street, but as I stumbled along a grey alleyway I had little idea where to go. North, I knew that much: the way back to Isis House, and Lower Fort Street was somewhere close by; it was one of the street signs I had glimpsed as Rodnia and I had fled in Dennis's cab. Fire in the belly burned me and drove me along. *Thomas, I am coming.* I walked faster and faster, almost running.

Then I began to slow down. I could not just fly to Thomas's arms — I must have a plan. If Thomas was at this temple, most probably Dr Musgrave would be there too. I had to outwit him, overcome him. No, impossible, he was too wise, too powerful. His words rumbled around me: *Let us be reasonable. Let us be civilised.* That was it, that was exactly how I would be: I'd tell him the truth, who Thomas's father was, how the baby would never be a tiny Coming Man, how he would be quite useless for the doctor's collection. Better to quietly hand him back, and Thomas and I would disappear into Sydney. He was a man of reason and science: how could he say no? Why had I never had the presence of mind to say it to him when I crouched on the windowsill? Again, my pace quickened.

As I moved further north and the morning wore on, the houses became smaller and crowded together. I pushed through drooping rows of washing, past foul gutters seething with dirty children. The air grew dark and thick, choked with coal fumes. The streets twisted and turned, became other streets, and on every corner was an inn: The Hen and Chickens, The Three Jolly Sailors, The Mermaid, The World Turned Upside Down. Where was Lower Fort Street? Was it close? Was I wandering around in circles? Would anyone help me? Men in flared trousers lurched across broken cobbles or slouched against walls blackened with slime; they called to me in slurred grunts and gurgles. A huddle of Celestials retreated from me in little shuffling steps, hands tucked into their sneaky sleeves. A fellow with tiger stripes tattooed over his face stuck out his tongue at me. A woman stood opening her shawl and baring a withered breast whenever a man passed by.

'If you please, ma'am,' I said when she had pulled her shawl closed again. 'Can you direct me to Lower Fort Street?'

She looked me up and down with her coal eyes. 'Second left, third right. Now clear off my patch afore I rake yer face.'

I hurried off, tried to follow the directions, fearing she had just said whatever came into her head. Soon I found another woman lying senseless in the gutter. Someone had thrown a bucket of filthy water over her matted hair, which streamed over her face. Next to her lay a naked baby. Not Thomas, I knew at once. Its limbs contracted and stretched, its mouth opened in a soundless scream. I came closer, bent down, stared at the woman's half-hidden eyes as if there were some message for me. A powerful reek of gin steamed off her. In a nearby house, someone scraped on a cracked fiddle, and the keening seemed to come out of the baby's mouth. When I straightened up, tears pricking my eyelids — why would I cry for another's child and not my own? — I saw the sign at last. *To Lower Fort Street*.

Suddenly I was out of the dark maze of lanes, in clean air, on a hill with a view of the harbour, a place for the gentry if ever there was one. And there was Dr Musgrave's Sydney mansion, unmistakeable with its dome and high walls. I felt so exposed to its arched windows, I wanted to turn and flee into the alleyways and hide myself. But I walked on, following the sign, down Lower Fort Street itself, right to the end of the road. Ahead and to the right there was a little park, and beyond it, the sea; and in between the park and the sea, the curious Grecian building, standing on its own headland, just as I had seen it from the window during my imprisonment. The Temple: it could be no other place, surely.

Slowly now, I walked down a stone path, between a row of young conifers, up the steps, round the side and on to the sea-facing frontage of white pillars and great double doors of heavy timber. At a distance, this elegant building had comforted me: close up, all I could see was cold and stony perfection. On either side of the doors crouched two sculpted figures, with the heads and breasts of women and the bodies and claws of lions. That's what I must be, I thought: a woman in instinct, with a lion's strength and courage.

I raised a trembling hand and knocked on the door. Silence. I knocked again, several times; I pushed the panels, I hammered furiously, with the same result. What was this place, so tightly sealed? Why were there no windows? And as the impassive sphinxes stared past me out to sea with their blind stone eyes, it came to me: this was no temple. This was a mausoleum.

I stood back, my eyes blurring. Either I had made a mistake and this was the wrong place, or Thomas was entombed. Surely this could not be the end. Should I give up, go back to Rodnia? Should I go hammer on the door of Dr Isis's home? Or should I run to the edge of the headland and hurl myself off into the ocean, just as I had once thought of leaping into the Yarra Yarra? As I began to turn, the double doors swung open onto a pool of mouldy darkness.

'Do come in, Mrs Richardson.'

I could scream, could run, and might have done both if I had stopped to think, but a need drew me that conquered all fear, all prudence. Without hesitation I stepped into the dark, into a hallway scarcely wide enough for one person. The doors slammed shut behind me, and for a moment I was in blackness. Then came the scrape and flare of a closed lantern opening, and Dr Musgrave's face floating behind it, and his mesmeric rumble.

'I apologise for not replying to your knock. I was not sure at first whether to let you in. But I must say, I admire you. Still the seeker after knowledge. I never thought you'd have the gumption to come after me. How on earth did you find me?' He thrust the lantern towards me.

'Dr Musgrave, the game is up.' I tried to sound bold, triumphant. 'The police have surrounded this place, they will break in at any moment now.'

He smiled. 'Oh, I don't think so. You might think my temple is blind. But I have my spy points. How do you think I knew it was you at the door? I can see a long way round about, from every angle, and all I have seen is sea, and birds, and trees, and yourself. Not that anyone would think of looking for me here. No one even knows it was I who built this edifice. Dr Musgrave lives in Isis House, everyone knows that. And this,' he waved his hand at the blackness, 'is not a place for the living.'

A shudder ran through me.

'No, Mrs Richardson, I don't believe the police are outside. I think you came here on your own, and no one else knows where you are.'

'They will follow me. They will find me and arrest you.'

He laughed. 'For what?'

This was all wrong. What had happened to my plan to be reasonable, civilised? As if he could read my thoughts, Dr Musgrave thrust his lantern towards my face again and I drew back, dazzled.

'You are suffering.' His voice was soft and full of wonder. 'I don't have medicine for that. But I can do one thing for you. I can let you see your child.'

'My child?' My heart gave a great lurch.

He did not reply, but held the lantern high, turned and walked further into the gloom, beckoning me to follow. I might still turn back, try the doors; he might not have locked or bolted them when they slammed shut. But I could do nothing but follow him, as if we were roped together.

My feet echoed on stone. My hand went out to steady myself, touched a sodden wall. It was even colder than the crypt where my sham wedding had taken place. The lantern flame bobbed ahead, casting monster shadows, until Dr Musgrave stopped at a door and opened it, stood back to admit me.

Warm, humid air and golden light. At first I thought I stood in a black dungeon illuminated by torches. The space opened out before me: it was huge, but I could make no sense of what was in it.

'Welcome to the Temple of Persephone,' said Dr Musgrave. 'Or the Temple of Isis, if you will. I like to mix my mythologies. I had it built as a mausoleum for myself when I should pass from this world. It is not finished yet, of course. Very bare, very unadorned. But now I have found another use for it, as you can see.'

On the wall were six glowing gas mantles, but there appeared to be many more of them reflected in a great wall of glass in front of me, and perhaps more gas lamps on the walls beyond the glass; it was hard to tell where the real flames stopped and the reflected flames began. As my eyes adjusted, I stared higher and higher. Not just a wall of glass, a whole cube, reinforced at the sides and corners by cast iron girders, filling almost the entire room from floor to ceiling, and from wall to wall. On the roof was a row of three great glass domes, the largest rising from the centre. Inside, the air was greenish. A dark rocky structure loomed from the floor to somewhere shadowy above my head, and shapes flitted like tiny bats around its towers.

'Iranistan,' I breathed.

'Well done,' boomed Dr Musgrave. 'I did not expect you to catch the allusion. I must say, you are surprising me more and more every minute.'

He held up his lamp and swept it slowly across the front of the glass. I almost turned away, but forced myself to look. The rocky shape behind the glass was like a ruined castle encrusted with moss and ferns. Perforated fanlike plants in yellow and rose sprouted from its walls, and in its centre, under the largest glass dome, soared a lofty tower with a platform at the top, but the light did not reach quite high enough to show it in detail. The ferns and fans moved in a queer, slow rhythm, and the miniature bats darting in and out of the ruins sparkled silver, gold, blue and red; they were not bats, they were … fish?

I saw it now, the way the plants moved, a circle of purple tentacles that bunched and swayed: the tank was a giant aquarium. Dr Musgrave smiled, suddenly lifted his arm high, and the lantern revealed the top of the platform: on it sat an open cockleshell, and in the shell a cradle, and in the cradle lay Thomas. He was wrapped in a white robe. He was perfect. He did not move. His eyes were closed forever.

From my mouth slipped a sound I did not recognise as a sound that any human being could make. I hurled myself against the glass. I spreadeagled myself on the surface, my breasts flattened as I willed my body to pass through the surface and into the water to join my son. Somewhere behind me Dr Musgrave talked and talked, at first calm and soothing, then more agitated, but I did not listen. Someone was howling, perhaps it was me. I threw myself again and again at the glass, hit it with my fists.

'Enough, Mrs Richardson. Calm yourself. Your child is merely sleeping.'

'But the water … he is drowned …'

'No, no, please, let me explain.' He took my arm and I wanted to fling him from me and smash his contraption, but all my strength had gone. I let him pull up a wooden stool for me and I hunched over, rocking to and fro, unable to look any longer at the beautiful glass tomb.

'The tank is not entirely filled with water,' said Dr Musgrave. 'There is an inner compartment at the centre, a cylinder from top to bottom, but you cannot see it because it is also made of glass. It is watertight, and inside there is air. That is where the tower and the cradle stand. The child sleeps soundly because I have given it a draught, but in an hour or two, it will wake.'

'I don't believe you,' I sobbed, hugging myself, tucking in my head and arms, rocking backwards and forwards on the stool.

'Then look for yourself.' He held up the lantern again, turned it this way and that. 'Can you see the gas lamps reflected? See that fish, how it cannot go forward, it stops, turns? Its head has bumped the glass of the inner cylinder.'

Slowly I stopped rocking, raised my head, and gradually the ghostly outline of the inner cylinder revealed itself. Inside were no fish, no floating ferns. Thomas was still alive. A vast euphoria flooded me. I prepared to jump up, reach out, seize my child and run into the street. Then I remembered the glass. My stomach lurched, I put my hands over my face as if grieving and watched Dr Musgrave between my fingers. He had put down the lantern and was standing back surveying his Iranistan like an artist before his easel.

'I did not mean to frighten you, Mrs Richardson. I have decided I owe you an apology.'

That was all he thought he owed me? Enough. I jumped to my feet, ran at him and hammered my fists into him as I had hammered the glass. But I could not even touch him: he raised his arms, grabbed my wrists and held them in the air, and as I struggled and shouted and tried to kick his shins, he gazed at me with such a look of pain and puzzlement, as if I were some ungrateful monkey he had shown nothing but kindness. His grip was very strong.

At last he let me go, and I spat at him. It was a gesture of defeat, and his look said so as he slowly took out a silk handkerchief and wiped his face. I retreated to my stool.

'As I was saying, I owe you an apology,' he said calmly. 'I hope you will forgive me. I should not have concealed from you that your child was still alive. You are an admirable mother: you have willingly put yourself into danger in the hope of saving the infant. And as you have now demonstrated, you are a fighting mother.'

Was I some new species to him, like a fighting fish? Oh, he would pay. I swallowed my bile, breathed deeply to calm myself, made my voice low and meek. 'I accept your apology. Please forgive me for my … outburst.'

He gave me a sharp look but then rubbed his chin, as if still surprised his beard had disappeared, and began to pace up and down the room. His fresh sweat, his breathing, the creak of his boots, the rasp when he ran his hand over his chin: he was worried. He had his treasure, but he did not know how to escape with it. He did not expect to be tracked down here, but he knew Rodnia might go to the police, and this cavern was just as much a dungeon for him as it was for me.

I would not take my eyes off him, not even to look at Thomas.

'Tell me how you made your Iranistan,' I said.

He stopped pacing, and a softness came over his features, as if I had asked him how he met his sweetheart.

'It has long been a dream of mine,' he said. 'I have spent many years in the study of the preservation of dead infants and small children. I think it began when I saw Willem Vrolik's Cyclops child in Amsterdam.'

Cyclops. One eye. The poor hideous creature in the jar in his study.

'A melancholy rose in me,' he went on, 'as I considered what might have been this child's fate, supposing science had the means to help him survive birth. Spurned by his mother, reduced to performing before the ignorant mob. Someone should care for him, I thought, even in death.'

Nausea rose in me. I struggled to keep it down, keep my face and body impassive.

'I began to search out other masters of the craft. I went to Leiden and inspected Doctor Ruysch's babies. Not the foetuses, not the little skeletons weeping or playing the violin. No, the faces. Such faces. Pink, framed in lace bonnets, lips slightly parted; you would swear they had just fallen asleep.' He smiled tenderly. 'Of course he had cut off their heads and faces, and he would insist on dangling an eye socket from one finger, like a precious earring. I fear vulgar sentiment was his downfall. I never cut up my own treasures. But I pay my tribute to his unborns — mine are all wreathed in his beads. No one knows why he did it, but I believe it was for the same reason that a woman adorns her wrists and her throat with diamonds.'

The floor was dropping away from me, but still I kept my look calm and attentive.

'When Franz told me of your child, the General's child, I conceived such a desire for it, I burned with such agony of longing. And I thought, this time I will build a palace, nothing else will suffice. I was already constructing my preserving jars with domed lids, but this would be on an altogether different scale. I engaged an architect in glass, instructed him to create to my designs a very special aquarium, a Crystal Palace for fishes — I think it was Franz's reference to you as a mermaid that made me think of a watery grotto. My architect was adept at all the fashionable touches, the Nullipores, the Retipores, the Gorgonias, the Medusas ...' He swept his hand towards the towers, the fish, the ferns, but I would not look: they seemed the home of fantastical and evil creatures. 'Of course this is just a prototype, it is not as refined as I had hoped, and the construction has its faults. The glass, I fear, is not quite thick enough. But I will have a sound and splendid one built by the time the child is ready for a sea change.'

'You mean a tomb.' I could no longer stay silent. Now was the time for my masterstroke. 'Dr Musgrave, all your preparations are in vain. This is not the General's child. I worked as a governess for the father, and he was an uncommonly tall man. Thomas will grow into a full-sized boy — he is no use to you.'

For a moment his face twisted into a sneer of revulsion. Then his features grew smooth and pink. 'Mrs Richardson, think of it this way. If I let you go now, with the child, what would happen to it?'

'To *him*. He is not a thing.'

'Yes, yes … Perhaps the General and his wife might reclaim it. They would exhibit it for a year or two to hundreds, thousands; it would be offered as a spectacle for ignorant gawkers. You would not be allowed anywhere near it, needless to say. Or perhaps you would attempt to escape with it into the streets of Sydney. This is a hard town for a single woman of no means. Chances are it would die of disease or starvation. Think now of the alternative.' He came close, bent down, looked at me with his mesmerising black eyes. 'The child will be treated like royalty, will lack for nothing. No vulgar crowd will be permitted near. Only I will worship.'

I fought rising panic. 'You don't believe me? You still think the General is the father?'

He sighed. 'Of course. But even if what you say is true, it makes no difference. I will just wait to find out. Months, years: I have plenty of time. And either way, the end, when it comes, will be swift and quite painless. A syringe. I will choose a moment when the child is … at its happiest and most unsuspecting. That is not such a bad fate, is it? What more could anyone want?'

'A mother.'

His lids fluttered, a slight frown, quickly ironed out.

'Where's your pity, sir?' My voice rose, trembled. 'Did you not have a mother of your own?'

He stood, turned his back, and I remembered something he had said long ago to Franz, when we had visited Athena Hall.

'She played the piano, didn't she? You called her your dear mother.' He did not answer and that made me bolder. 'Dr Musgrave, if you care anything for motherhood, will you grant me one request? I want to hold my child in my arms.'

My eyes raked his back, the close crop of his white hair above his neck, the dark tailored coat that strained over powerful shoulders. *Turn round, damn you.*

At last he turned towards me. 'Yes, yes, I should like to see …' I watched two pale candlelit faces, the second reflected in the glass. 'But not here, you will just try to escape and then I shall be obliged to …' His fingers hovered around his belt. Was a pistol holstered under his coat? 'Come with me.' He led me round to the back of the tank, lit by more gas lamps on the cavern walls, and pointed to a ladder that rose from the floor and rested against the iron girder at the top of the glass panel.

There seemed nothing for it but to climb; I picked up my skirts and edged up the rungs, remembering my escape from Isis House and wishing I could risk such an annihilating fall many times over if it meant I could escape with Thomas. Dr Musgrave followed, I felt his breath, but he was careful not to touch me. At the top of the ladder, he reached over my shoulder, pulled a small lever and with a loud whirr the great central dome of the roof tipped slowly outwards on a hinge, until there was a circular gap wide enough to admit an adult body.

I looked down over the edge, and a gentle hothouse breeze, warmer and moister than the air outside, caressed my face.

Directly below me was the inner cylinder, filling the space beneath the dome; and at the centre, about six feet below, Thomas's cradle. Since I had first glimpsed my child behind the glass, terror of the grief that might erupt and destroy me had stopped me looking at him. Now I stared and stared in the dancing light, at the whorl of strawberry blond hair on the crown, the closed fist, the feathery eyelashes on the porcelain cheeks, and I searched for any flutter, for any rise and fall of breath. No fear, no grief, only a yearning that overpowered everything. My iron breasts were suddenly damp with milk.

'The medicine makes sleep very sound, but it won't cause any harm,' said Dr Musgrave. 'Go on, go down.' He sounded eager. He indicated a rope ladder that hung off the iron girder and dangled down inside the cylinder, behind the pillar supporting the cradle.

I swung my legs over the side, climbed down as fast as I could — the ladder was only loosely fastened — and lifted Thomas out of the cradle. So little weight. His head lolled, he was warm, a pulse throbbed in his wrist and he slept very sweetly. His white robe was finely embroidered linen; Mrs Bleeker would approve of the stitching. Standing half on the ladder, half on a foothold in the pillar, I put Thomas over my shoulder, pushed the cradle aside, arranged my skirts and sat down on the cockleshell. I squeezed my eyes shut, hugged the little body to me, whispering over and over again, *Hush, I've got you now, sleep tight*, and other, nonsense words, surely more to soothe myself than my child.

Heedless for once of Dr Musgrave, I unfastened my dress, untied the towel from my breasts, pressed my left nipple into Thomas's mouth. Milk sprayed out, but Thomas slept on and would not suck. Damn the sleeping draught. What strange hands, miniatures of my own, tiny webs stretching between his fingers. White and rosy, skinny and plump. Wisps of hair standing up on his skull like a cockatoo crest. I had never smelled skin so clean and new, like honey flowers. His eyes behind his closed lids moving like tiny fishes.

Under my dress I was sweating. Was he too hot in his robe? I fumbled with the buttons, gradually releasing the awkwardly perfect body with its necklace, wristlets and anklets of black and white beads. Then I saw my mistake, gave a broken laugh, knuckles to my mouth. I had been so sure. I had known Burden, Belly, Thomas so intimately for nine months, and yet I had known nothing.

'I will have to call you …' I thought of the adventurous little girl in the book I had read to Matilda. 'Alice,' I whispered.

Were all mothers so happy? *Dear God*, I prayed, *let this moment last forever.*

'An affecting picture,' came the rumbling voice from overhead.

I peered up into darkness, trying to pick scorn in his tone, but finding none. Perhaps he truly was affected.

'Mrs Richardson, could you do me a favour? Could you please take off your bonnet and let down your hair?'

I was so surprised my hand went automatically to my bonnet strings and then to Franz's hairpin that held my knot of hair in place, and it tumbled down over my shoulders. I unfastened the crescent-moon brooch from the hairpin and stuck it carefully in my bodice; I would do whatever he wanted if it meant I could go on holding Alice. The sounds from outside the tank were muffled, but I guessed he was climbing down the ladder. Thank God, he was leaving. A pause. Then the lights in front of me dipped, swirled, brightened. I looked up from Alice's head. The doctor was holding up the lantern, speaking and gesticulating from outside the tank, his outline blurred by the water between us. The little jewelled fishes seemed to swim around a deep sea monster. I shook my head, mouthed, 'I can't hear you.'

He walked out of view. More scrapes and thumps, and then his soft purr from above. 'How like a mermaid you look. A mermother on your throne. Or a Madonna, perhaps.'

I sat with head bowed, holding my breath, imagining him softer and softer, kinder and kinder, to the point where he would let me take my child and leave.

After a long pause, he spoke again. 'You have had your wish. Time's up.'

Without relinquishing my grip on Alice, I turned to the rope ladder that I had noticed was so loosely fastened. My weight had tightened the knot during my descent, but by lifting the rope and pushing it around a little, I was as sure I could dislodge it at the top as I would be of unthreading a needle. But I could not see above my head, and at any moment I dreaded Dr Musgrave's shout as he discovered what I was attempting. Sweat poured down my face, I blinked it from my eyes, the child grew leaden in my arm, and still I pushed and pulled. At last the rope came away from the top of the cylinder and fell in loops and folds behind me.

'Stupid girl, why did you do that?' Now a tiger stood above me. But holding Alice gave me a new courage.

'I want to stay with my child.'

'But the pair of you could die down there. Is that what you want? I have only to put back this dome and move the lever to its tightest point. The air will give out, it will be slow and painful.'

I sat very still, willed my body not to shudder. 'You'll not do that, sir. Remember, I am a mother. Remember your own mother.'

A long pause. Was he moved? Was he doubtful? I twisted my head but still could not see his face in the darkness above me.

Then he spoke. 'At least pass me up the child.'

'So you can kill me now and kill her later?'

He would aim at me with a gun, or he would fetch a rope and climb down, or find some long sharp instrument to torment me. But not right away, please God. All I needed was more time, until Rodnia found the message on the pillow slip, realised where I was … But would he even realise? Dr Musgrave was so confident he could not be found, what if he were right? I clung to Alice. If the worst came to the worst and he closed the dome, I would breathe into her mouth until all air was gone.

'Remember,' I said again. 'Remember your mother.' Meaningless, perhaps, but what else could I say? Silence but for a faint lap of water and Alice's soft breath, as the fishes flitted around my throne.

'Desire is so huge, so ravenous, is it not?' Dr Musgrave's voice was surprisingly low and wistful. 'And yet the object of desire may be so small. I have been as one-eyed as any Cyclops. I have filled mansion after mansion with the rare and wonderful, yet all I ever wanted was one thing, and still I do not have it.'

Then go find it and let me keep my baby, I wanted to say. Instead, I hazarded a guess. 'Love?'

He gave a laugh that was more like a dry croak. 'I was such

a dreamer, and she saw right through me. A pathetic jellyfish of a boy. When I sat down at the piano to play she would push my fingers from the keys and make short work of my arpeggios. "Freddie dear," she would say, "you are in my light."'

'She was impatient with you?'

'She loved me so much, she wanted me to be as perfect as she was.'

What lost love was this?

After a long pause, he spoke again. 'I came home too late. At first I thought they had put some other woman on show by mistake. Her loosened hair, white as an albino's. But it was her, laid out in the drawing room in her finest morning gown. I sat with her through the night, my doctor's bag at my feet. There were jardinières of massed roses, to conceal …' A sigh. 'The candles gave her face a soft flush until I bent over her and cast her into shadow. Two marks from her pincenez dented her nose. I could swear she would open her eyes and tell me I was in her light.'

'I am sorry,' I whispered. But I felt no sorrow for him.

'I reached very slowly into the coffin and traced the central parting that divided her curious white hair,' he went on. 'I turned back the lace shawl that concealed her upper body, inch by inch. Her bloodless hands were folded over her breast. There was no rigor mortis: her arm bent easily and it felt quite natural to drape it over the edge of the coffin. I held her hand in both my own, to put a little warmth back into that chill palm.'

There was no mistaking the sorrow and passion in his voice. I wished I could see his face. But it was what he wanted, to gaze unseen at me and my child, my loosened hair.

'She must have loved you very much,' I said, with no idea if it were true. A brilliant spark of hope was kindling in me.

'Her poor jellyfish boy … When I reached down to my doctor's bag, I did so with great caution, so as not to wake her.'

A pause. A picture came to me of Minnie upstairs in the room at Seymour, and the wicked sharp instruments the young doctor had left on the floor as he fled, and suddenly I gasped.

'So that story about you and your hatbox was true after all.' The word rose, I could not stop it. 'You are nothing but a ghoul.'

'You have understood nothing,' he snapped. 'It was all I could take of her at that time. I had thought … but no one understands. Enough, it is time. You must come out of there, or hand me up the child.'

I shook my head, held Alice tight, waited for him to close the dome-shaped lid and fasten the lever. But the thumps were his steps down the ladder, and then an indistinct grating, as of a large and rusty tap. A deep metallic judder, and suddenly a shockingly loud sound of water gushing. Had he broken the glass of the tank? The sound was so close. I looked around, above, down. At the bottom of the cylinder, not far beneath my dangling feet, was glint and movement. I put Alice very carefully back in her crib, placed it in the centre of the cockleshell seat and slipped down to the base of the pillar. Instantly my feet were wet: water was pouring into the cylinder from the surrounding tank. I bent down and my hands groped around to discover the water was coming from the mouths of six pipes, spaced evenly around the circular base. If I twisted my body around the pillar there was just room for me to block two of the pipes with my hands and the opposite two pipes with my feet, but water continued to pour out of the remaining two.

The poor lovelorn jellyfish, the ghoul, how dare he?

As suddenly as it had begun, the gushing water stopped. I stood upright, panting, soaked skirt dragging, water swirling around my knees. 'You don't scare me,' I shouted. But it was the cry of a defiant little child.

'That's just a taste.' Heard from the bottom of the cylinder, his voice had a hollow, inhuman boom. 'Climb the pillar and hand me up the infant, there's a good girl, and I promise I won't harm you.'

'Never.'

'It makes no sense, you will both drown.'

'Better to drown than to give her back to you.'

He did not reply. Again the steps on the ladder, the groan of machinery, the gushing. I tore off my shawl and stuffed it into one pipe. Five closed, one left. I tried to rip the hem of my skirt, but when my hands left the pipes the flow came more fiercely, my wet skirt would not tear, and then the force of the flow pushed my shawl out again. Despite all my efforts, the water was rising steadily, past my knees, and soon almost up to my waist. I held my breath, put my head under to block the pipes with my hands, but soon had to come up for air. Then I tried standing with my feet in two of the pipes, but the flood pressed and pressed, lifted me off the bottom of the cylinder.

The roar of the Yarra Yarra, the filth, the icy clinging mud. This water was lukewarm, clear green, with a chemical smell. A clean drowning. Little fish bobbed beneath my chin. I looked up into steam and darkness, around into fog and vague haloes of light: the one solid thing was the pillar of stone. I climbed back to the top —

the pillar was rough-hewn, there were plenty of footholds — sat on the cockleshell and took my babe in my weary arms. How could any baby, however drugged, sleep through this deluge? The water was rising, rising: now I had to stand on the cockleshell and already it was lapping round my feet. Would the ghoul turn off the flood and give us one last chance? But it kept coming, up, up. I thought of how I had once borne General Tom Thumb out of the river. I kissed Alice's brow and lifted her high over my head, starfished and limp on my hands, and then I saw something, two things, dangling from the very top of the cylinder, and I knew then that those two forked things were not sea creatures but the ghoul's hands. He was waiting for the water to rise far enough to lift us, to place Alice in his arms, so he could whisk her away and push me under.

No. I pulled Alice down, pinched her sweet nose with one hand, closed her mouth with the other, took a deep breath and dived deep. Better to go this way together.

A thunder filled my ears, booming like the huge waves of Bass Strait, and I anchored my legs around the pillar, which was not so solid anymore; it shuddered and shook as if about to break loose from the bedrock. *Breathe out, open your lungs. The end will be quick.* Still some panicky fool in me kept my breath in, my mouth shut and my lungs bursting. The booming, the light growing, the water paling from dark green to light blue, muffled thunder. I looked down at Alice. Her eyes were wide open, she was gazing at the fish with utmost wonder, and a pearly trail of bubbles came from her mouth. And suddenly I had to get to the surface and get some air into her little lungs, Dr Musgrave or no. I released my breath in a storm of bubbles, let go of the pillar, kicked with my feet, rose to the surface, coughed and spluttered in cold wonderful air, held her high.

The arms reached down, almost touching Alice's head. I lowered her a little, still keeping both our heads above water, held her close with one arm. I trod water, waited and, as I expected, the arms came lower and lower. The ghoul could not wait for the water to lift us; his whole upper body was stretching out over the cylinder, wriggling forward like a serpent, coins falling from his pockets, clawing at the air above us, his upside-down face only a little above me now, contorted and swollen with his blood. The tips of my toes found the cockle throne at the top of the pillar; I was not yet quite out of my depth. It was time: I had one chance. I must be quick, accurate, use all my strength. I unfastened and drew the moon brooch with its extra-sharp pin from my bodice, crouched down momentarily under the surface, pushed hard with my feet, shot up out of the water and rammed the pinpoint as hard as I could into his left eye.

The hands jerked back, covered his face, he screamed, the water around me turned red. He was trying to pull back but he had leaned too far over, he toppled down headfirst into the cylinder, his boot caught my ear a glancing blow as he passed. A great churning and frothing rose as he wriggled and kicked, trying to shift his body from where it was stuck, wedged head-down under the surface, between the pillar and the curved wall of the cylinder. I felt the pillar rock perilously; it must have been shakily fastened onto the bedrock — the construction has its faults — it was never expected to undergo such a pummelling, and his struggles were loosening it further. I put my back against it, bent my knees with my feet up on the glass, and pushed with all my strength. With a great crack the pillar began to topple and slip sideways, and the doctor with it. Now we were all slipping, sideways and down, as the pillar fell: a great smash as it carved through the cylinder and more grinding and groaning and smashing to follow, but my head was under red water and I could only hold Alice tight and pray, deliver us, deliver us, as we were sucked and spun around in the maelstrom. And then there was quiet, and air, and I was lying face down in a pile of shattered glass, gasping like a fish, and high-pitched screams filled the cavernous space. Was it the ghoul? My own keening? I sat up and the screams grew louder.

Alice was lying on her back, puny face screwed up, fists that could crush serpents waving and wobbling in the lonely air, mouth a square of shock, red hunger and rage.

I stood, brushed glass granules and grit and rubbery sea creatures from my arms, ignored my trembling legs and the thin trickles of blood from my skin. I picked Alice up. She had small cuts on her knees and elbows and would surely bruise later, but otherwise she seemed unharmed. My enveloping body must have protected her from the glass. I carried her to my stool, still miraculously standing in the knee-deep water and debris, where I sat and held her upside down. I slapped her on the back to make her choke up any remaining water, and she screamed even louder. I put her to my breast with no idea how to make her suck, but somehow between us it happened, and she fell quiet. I could not stop shivering. My wet hair plastered my face and shoulders, my skin stung and oozed in dozens of places, my right ear throbbed. The whole front of the aquarium had collapsed in a pile of glass and rubble, everything stank of chemicals, little fish lay twitching all around me, and a larger body hunched in a corner, legs thrashing silently, red hands clamped to its face. But slowly a vast calm came over me, and Alice was all to me, and I did not flinch when, God only knows how much later, the door was hacked open and the room was suddenly full of men in dark blue uniforms.

When Alice paused from her feeding, Rodnia was in front of me. I rose, put her into his outstretched arms, then hugged his barrel chest and his leather–tobacco–hay scent to me with a furious greed. The top of his curly head was almost level with my collarbone. For a while, Alice endured being squeezed tight between man and woman with a shocked silence, and then she howled her protest. So I disentangled myself, sat back on the stool and began to feed her again.

'Will you fetch a blanket for the poor wet bab?' I said to Rodnia.

The policemen sifted over the rubble, prised boards off a window to let in light. One fellow kneeled by Dr Musgrave's now still body and felt his pulse. He talked in a low voice to a tall, gangly man leaning over him, and when I heard his American drawl, I knew Mr Bleeker had found us, and black spots swam before my eyes.

The man in charge, an inspector, introduced himself and made me a handsome little speech about my aid in capturing a dangerous felon long under police suspicion. Clearly there had been an accident. The felon was unconscious and had lost a lot of blood, and one shard of glass must have taken out his eye, but he would probably live despite his injuries, the inspector said. They already had his accomplices, including the red-haired man whom they had caught trying to burn incriminating letters. Then he turned to Mr Bleeker. 'What charges do you want to bring, sir? We will have plenty of our own, I reckon, especially once we have searched his house.'

Mr Bleeker stared at me in silence, and I began to tremble with more than cold. His eyes were red-rimmed. He slipped his hand inside his jacket and rubbed his chest with great circular motions.

'You said he had kidnapped General Tom Thumb's heir,' the inspector prompted him. 'This is the child, is it not?' He pointed to my bedraggled lap. Rodnia stood close to me: he had found a sack for Alice, and I was trying to tuck it round her to keep her from cold. He patted me on the shoulder, glared at Mr Bleeker. The manager stared at us, frowning as if he were trying to remember something, then dropped his eyes. I waited for him to confirm the inspector's question, to hold out his hands for Alice, to take her back to Charlie and Lavinia with the law's blessing, to leave me empty-armed, all my venturing for nothing. *The Lord giveth, the Lord taketh away.*

SIDESHOW

Mrs Charles Stratton,
née Miss Lavinia Warren,
aka Mrs Tom Thumb

Mr and Mrs Tom Thumb

ACT TWO

In the looking glass over my dressing table, I see a man and woman embrace. They are familiar, and yet strange. I think they will make a handsome couple.

But the Queen of Beauty is lost. Where has she gone? Not half an hour ago, I sat down at my dressing table and the woman in the mirror was a fright. Puffy, blotchy skin; lines scored across the forehead and down around the mouth; eyes red swollen slits; ragged black mane with the first hints of grey. Once I would have gasped, tutted, reached for my lotions and rouge sticks and powders. Now I slumped before the slack-jawed apparition, raised my hairbrush, lowered it again.

Steps behind me. Another stranger appeared in the mirror, put his hands on my shoulders. Charlie as I had never seen him: pale, almost gaunt, dark smudges under his eyes. Since Mr Bleeker had brought us the terrible news, we had embraced, and I had cried, and I thought Charlie might have cried a little on his own too, but I did not know, for we had scarce faced each other. At last, days later, we could meet each other's gaze, in the safety of the looking glass.

I leaned back into his embrace.

'My poor Vinnie.' His voice was hoarse.

'My poor Charles. And my poor Mary Ann.'

His hands stiffened. 'She ran away from us.'

'I will not blame her,' I said, and it was very nearly true. 'She is not the first young woman to have her head turned by love. I am only sorry for how she must feel now our … her …' Heavens, my faltering voice. 'Now the child is no more.'

Charlie sighed. 'I wish I could have seen to a fitting burial. I wish I could have kept something for you. A lock of hair, perhaps.'

For a moment I pictured a little crown with a whorl of colourless fuzz. How could I so miss a creature I had never seen, never heard described, scarce even imagined? I swallowed, forced the tears back, handed my hairbrush to Charlie. He ran it gently over my hair, my head, down my back.

'Harder.' I set my teeth. 'Do it as Mary Ann did, to bring out the shine … She will have other children, won't she? With her husband?'

'Of course.'

'I hope Franz will be good to her. I hope all her children will play the piano.'

My eyes strayed to the photograph I had placed in a corner of the mirror, the one of the pair of us with the last infant we had briefly adopted on our travels. It had never had a name. It was just Baby. I had never allowed myself to love it. Sometimes when it sat in my lap I felt I could not breathe, would turn to stone. It was a relief when Baby disappeared.

I took the picture out of the mirror frame, peered at it. My eyes were dim and viscous from too much weeping.

'You know we could not keep Baby.' Charlie spoke gently. 'He was already too big.'

I nodded, but I was lost in a memory. Not of Baby, but of an evening walk Charlie and I had taken, just us two, in the little sand-clogged township of Wellington, after crossing the desert. It was strange to be so alone. We passed pyramid dunes, coppery and blue in the shadows. The place had seemed deserted, but suddenly five barefoot children had popped up like rabbits from a burrow and followed us, silent and staring. It was impossible to tell boy from girl. They had ragged smocks and hair like taffy and were brown all over as if they wriggled all day in the sand.

The second-tallest child held an infant. It might have been a pretty mite under all the dirt and clag and mucus. When Charlie put his hand into his pocket, drew out coins and bonbons and threw them, the children dived like gulls, except for the child with the baby.

Even as he threw his treasures, Charlie was telling me that our son would know from the moment he was born that he was destined for great things. He was marked. It was all in *Dr Foote's Home Cyclopedia*.

'So it will be a boy?' I said.

'I know it will. Something in my waters. Would you prefer a girl?'

I assured him I would be happy to have a child of either sex, and I still could not believe how heaven had blessed us. At once he became very upset. *You must believe, Vinnie.* He said it over and over again, as if I had just said I did not believe in God. And of course

I wanted to believe, but I could not fathom what he meant me to believe in. So I found the courage to ask, with many apologies, what had always puzzled me: how could he be so sure that the child that Mary Ann bore would be as tiny as we were?

He stepped back, placed his right hand over his heart, his left hand over his right, and pressed inwards as if to keep his heart from bursting out of his chest. The sandy children leaned forward, mouths agape.

'My love, you must take no notice of those wicked rumours.'

I had no idea what he meant. I still have no idea. I told him so and added that whatever people might be saying, we must set matters right, but he shook his head, said it was of no consequence, I should forget it. 'The, ah, provenance does not signify. What matters is the medical science. Believe me, pet, our boy does not just grow in the womb. Under the constant influence of the man of destiny, he also shrinks.'

That did not sound very healthy to me, but my poor Charlie was so agitated I could do nothing but assure him I believed in our boy. Indeed, I took his hand and placed it just below my waist, as if an infant was growing in my intact womb, and I almost deluded myself I could feel a flutter of response.

'General Tom Thumb the Second,' I said. 'But we can call him Tommy, if you like.'

After we shared a kiss, the eldest child thrust a hand into a smock pocket, took out one of Charlie's coins, darted forward and placed it on the ground at our feet.

• • • • • • • •

Something in that memory was teasing my brain, which grief had made so sluggish. I pushed my hair back from my face.

'You were always so sure Mary Ann's child would be small,' I said. 'But suppose it was big? As big as Baby? You wouldn't have wanted to keep it, would you?'

'My dear, I was always sure he would be small.'

It was no answer and he knew it. I thought back further, to the night of his rescue from the Yarra Yarra. He had been unable to sleep and had gone for a walk by the river. Then he lost his footing on the bridge. He remembered nothing else. It was Ned who had witnessed the rescue. I had slept through it all, in my empty bed, and woke only when they brought in Charlie's cold wet body. Then I had wept and prayed.

Later, I had wondered how he could have fallen from a bridge that had such a high parapet. How some miraculous commingling of essences could produce a pregnancy. And how he knew such a thing had happened when he also claimed to remember nothing. I had never heard of so outlandish a conception in my life, and no woman of high intelligence ever believes all she is told. But what was important to Charlie was that he believed it. And if I believed in Charlie, I had decided, then I must also believe in his dream.

We were silent for a while and I felt the tug and hiss of the brush strokes. What had we lost? Perhaps it had never been more than a dream.

Slowly my wild mane was turning into a lustrous curtain. Slowly something was growing in me, a new gestation: I was not sure if it was fear or hope, but how fast it made my heart dance. I turned, looked straight into his face.

'Charlie. Is there not one sure way to have a child that will be as we are?'

'Well, I was sure, but medical men do not agree with one another.' He cleared his throat. 'Allow me to be a little indelicate, dear. As you know, I swear by Dr Foote, and he is quite clear on this. The chief factors that cause the child to resemble its parents are the hypnotic influence of the magnetism of the husband upon the uterus of the wife, and the magnetism from both parents on the foetus as it is formed. So it seems to me that the only sure way is to have two parents who are both as we are.'

I nodded. 'Well, then.'

He put down the brush, kneeled beside me. 'What's on your mind?'

'My mind has changed. I would like to try.'

His voice, when it came, was shrill. 'With me?'

Oh the dear man, I could not resist a tease. 'I was not aware of any other husband.'

He got to his feet, paced the room. 'This is … I can't tell you how I … I must know you are sure. I've always respected your wishes. And I've always understood your wish was … no such venture.'

I rose, placed a chair next to mine and asked him to sit down beside me. He sat heavily, tugging at his cuffs. I took his hands in mine.

'We have ventured much, you and I,' I said. 'Isn't that so?'

'What d'you mean, Vinnie?'

'We have entertained kings and queens and ruffians who throw us gold nuggets,' I went on. 'We have ventured into dangerous places around the globe. In Australia we have ventured across flooded rivers and parched deserts. So why have we never ventured into that natural consequence of loving unions?'

Charlie began to speak, but I raised my hand to hush him. 'I know, it was my wish, and I loved you for following it. I wasn't ready then. I listened to my mother, as a young woman should, and perhaps I listened to her too much. I'm ready now.'

He stared at me. 'I can hardly believe it. You don't know how I have longed ... But how come you're ready now?'

Suddenly I felt really small, insectlike. 'I'm not very brave, Charlie.'

'Nonsense.' He was warm in his vehemence. 'You're the bravest woman I know. Your bravery is an example to your sex.'

'Oh, it's quite otherwise. Mary Ann braved the flood to save you. She braved her growing belly and the pains she never spoke of. I wish I'd helped her more. Our dear Mrs Bleeker is bravery itself. And my sister ...'

'Minnie? Miss Foolhardy?'

'I think she has changed,' I said carefully.

'She still seems the naughty little sister to me.'

I was silent, unable to say how it was that for all her rebelliousness and shocking lack of decorum, I felt more hopeful for Minnie's future. She seemed to have reached some part of herself that would forever be lost to me. But I could not put this into words for Charlie, so I squeezed his hands. 'Anyway, I know now that I can bear more than I thought. I can bear childbirth.'

And I can bear conception too, I wanted to say, but felt the heat rise in my cheeks and could not go on. I tried another tack. 'I want us to be one, Charlie. I want us to be as close as husband and wife can be. I used to think we were that close. I gave you all the delight I could. But still I held myself back. Now …'

He reddened too when I said *delight*. His hands were warm and plump and motionless in mine. I thought of those countless times when Charlie had felt electric. It often happened when he heard or saw running water. It had last happened before Mary Ann disappeared, same as always.

Even in my mind, to myself, I cannot speak of what I did to him as he stood in his pose of Hercules challenging the Nemean lion. But he has taught me well, and it works as well as the knitting machine in Mr Barnum's museum, the one operated by a dog. As long as I stay awake. The strangest thing is he never seems to tire of it.

Now, I thought, when Charlie feels electric, other things will happen, things I can scarcely permit myself to imagine.

He was looking downwards, apparently deep in thought, his head on one side, and I stared at his left ear, the whorls, the hair curling around the lobe. It was soft and vulnerable, yet it was a little window to his body that would forever stay protected. Whereas I … I too had read Dr Foote. I knew what to do. I would eat food with very little calcareous matter, so the frame of the unborn child would not develop too rapidly. But not so little that the child would be rickety. I would think constantly of Charlie, so his magnetism would work upon the growing form.

And yet I could not be sure. Perhaps a huge infant would swell in my womb, pressing outwards, cracking my pelvis, murderously squeezing my lungs and heart. I shivered, and he looked up at me, his eyes full of bewilderment and trouble.

Everything you ever wanted is coming your way, I thought. Why can't you be happy? But of course: your Queen of Beauty must be happy too.

'Please, Charlie,' I whispered.

'Well ...'

I kissed his ear, a feather brush.

'If you're quite sure,' he said. 'We'll take it slowly. We can stop whenever you say. I won't hurt you.'

I put my arms round his neck.

'You can't hurt me. I'm ready.'

In the looking glass I see a man and woman embrace, and there is nothing in the frame to show how large or how small they are, only that they fit each other to perfection.

I think I will stop looking in the mirror now.

CHAPTER 23

So that is the answer to my beautiful Alice's inevitable question. That is where she came from. I am sorry it is not all good news: that her dadda is not her real father; that I thought I knew what I wanted, and I was wrong, and I did not find that out until it was almost too late.

Of course she is not old enough for me to tell her the whole story. Indeed, I cannot open my mouth and tell her anything yet, and probably there are things I can never tell her. I'm sure she will understand she was once Thomas, but how can she forgive me for the fact that she was once Belly and, before that, a burden I wished were gone? In my mind now I have to say goodbye to all those stages of her that were her and yet were not her, that I never even thought about, that Dr Foote's manual assures me really did exist, though I never saw them, though they sound like the transformations of a fairy tale.

I want to say goodbye to the tiny knot of matter, and then the little fish, and then the thing like a curled-up comma, and then a being like a water-child with sealed-shut eyes and ears and throat, floating, connected to me by a magic tube that snaked into my own flesh and blood. It is a way of saying goodbye to parts of myself too. Who is to say where I stopped and she began?

And I want to say goodbye to how she made me feel: all the aches and pains and bloating and heartburn and crawling skin and insistent bladder and lumbering heaviness and flat feet and fatigue, and the moments when all my insides rose in revolt and splashed over the ground or across my needlework.

It is good for me to remember my story, as honestly as I can, and then I can decide how much to tell her in reality.

Nobody but Mr B knows about her. He has kept our secret. He also kept Erasmus, the Australian cockatoo, when Dr Musgrave with his pirate eye-patch went to prison for a long time. Mr B writes from New York to tell us how Erasmus is doing. The bird can still say only 'Byebye', but Mr B tells us that is enough. Erasmus is his guardian angel, he says. It was Erasmus who screeched 'Bye-bye' at him when he left Isis House in Sydney, not knowing it was Dr Musgrave's house, after he had seen me sleeping and thought my child was dead. At first he did not realise what he had heard. Later, when his dyspepsia plagued him, the cry came back to him, and he knew black deeds were afoot and the child must be rescued and restored to the General. But when he saw me with Alice, all bedraggled from Iranistan, I reminded him of his wife when she was young, and still to be blessed.

So in the end, as the police inspector waited and waited for the answer to his question, 'This is the child, is it not?' Mr B took out his handkerchief and blew his nose and then said: 'No, I made a mistake. I'm sorry I wasted your time. I know this child. It's not the

General's.' And he held out a lanky arm towards us: 'It belongs to Mr and Mrs Nutt here.'

And so he rescued us. Actually it was Alice's dadda who rescued me, but he always says that, in the end, I rescued myself. I certainly rescued Alice.

I've just sponged her all over with her favourite sponge, and dried and dressed her, and she smells like honey flowers. She's galloping her wooden horses on the floor as I sit by a good fire, sip my tea and look at her.

So how did we come to England from the Antipodes? Mr Bleeker kindly paid for our passage from the show's handsome takings in Australia, and Alice's dadda and I were married on the ship, my first real marriage, for my wedding to Franz was nothing but a sham, and the so-called priest nothing but an undertaker's assistant. When we got here, my husband set himself up first as a groom, and then as a cabbie, and then as the owner of a delivery business, on Hampstead Hill. Now we often walk past a house with horse-chestnut trees leaning over the wall, and Alice demands to see the tall white flowers, so I lift her up and she tries to grab them above my head. One day I will tell her that was her grandparents' rectory, and whenever we walk by, I remember happy times before the cholera. Another family is there now.

One day we hope to pay Mr Bleeker back, and my husband hopes to write to his brother, and I hope to write to Mrs Bleeker, but not yet.

Charlie and Lavinia still believe my child was stillborn. Mr B says they were very sad for a while, but then an extraordinary change came over them, particularly Charlie. All his old vim and vigour returned and redoubled, and on his last night in Melbourne, when he shared a box with Mr B at the Theatre Royal, he jumped up on the stage as the Marching Amazons formed a guard of honour and he ran between the lady warriors' legs, his white opera scarf streaming. I don't know what happened to make him so perky, but I am glad to think that he and Lavinia are not suffering.

Our time in Dr Musgrave's Iranistan has marked us. I'm sure Alice doesn't remember it. And yet she screamed the first and only time I put her in a bath, she can't bear even a bowl of water to touch her skin; all I can do is sponge her. Iranistan is why she won't splash in puddles. Iranistan is why she won't let me walk near the pond on the heath, why the sight of its glitter makes her grow pale and whimper and pull back. I still have a white tracery of scars on my arms from all that glass. And then there are my nightmares, though I don't remember them when I wake, only the feeling, and my husband has to hold me until I stop trembling. We will just have to wait, Alice and I, and hope that in the end the dark current will cease flowing.

How her horses tap-tap across the floor, whinnying and snorting, but in a moment she will clamour to be in my lap. The grey cat watches her warily, in case she pulls its tail again. I have to keep separating those two.

Soon my husband will be home from work. He will stable Zep, give him a rub-down, feed him and Ludo and Emmy and the other horses. Alice will ride Emmy when she's older; Emmy is the more gentle of the little ponies. I can't wait for him to come through the door, sweep Alice up in his arms and kiss her on the nose, then embrace me, his springy curls at my shoulder, so different from

Franz's russet locks or the tightly shorn bristles on the head of Matilda's papa.

'How are you, dear goose? What've you been up to?' he'll ask me, sitting down to bounce Alice in his lap. 'God's teeth, bonny bab, you're so heavy. I won't be lifting you much longer. You'll tower over us.'

Long tall Alice. I wonder how she will like her brother, or is it a sister? That's one thing I have not told her dadda about yet, but of course I will.

When she is much older, I hope I can be brave enough to show her my heart.

I showed her dadda my heart before we even thought of leaving for England, when he first proposed marriage to me as I sat nursing Alice. At that moment I remembered the day in Green Ponds, Tasmania, when he had reached out to me, and I thought he would seize me, crush me to his leather vest in a wrestler's or a lover's embrace, and I shook with something I had not felt when Franz had put his manicured hands over mine at the piano.

After the proposal I shook again, but it was not fear I felt, and I longed to embrace him, but some scruple stopped me cold. Fate had thrown us together, but I did not want him to feel obliged to support me and my child, and was determined he should know the worst of me. If he then decided our ways should part, I would accept it, though something stabbed me deep at the thought of him walking away.

So first I asked if he was still in love with Emmeline, and he said he honoured her memory, but as for the rest, he thought it circus dazzlement. Then I said I had been dazzled too, and not just by

Franz, and I told him that Mr Carroll never existed, that I had made him up. He did not even pretend to be surprised. So then I told him about Matilda's papa and the house with the canary in the cage. When I finished telling him, his face was red and his fists clenching. Did he think me wicked? No, he said, he was angry at those who'd used me ill; there was no wickedness in me, only in the world, which feeds itself by making the virtuous feel wicked. But I was not so good neither, he said, for I wasn't tractable. And he smiled at me when he said it and clicked his tongue, and the thing inside me stabbed me again, but this time it was a good pain of longing, and I thought to myself that I never wanted to look up to a man again.

THE END

AFTERWORD

HISTORICAL BACKGROUND

This fictional story is inspired by a real event. General Tom Thumb and his troupe of little people visited Australia for nine months in 1870 as part of their world tour, and caused a tremendous stir wherever they went.

Mary Ann and Dr Musgrave are pure fiction, but I have used the names of real people in the troupe and have imagined their characters and doings. The route they followed around Australia is similar to the one in my story, and some of the events I describe did take place, though I have changed some details.

For example: to get to Adelaide the troupe had to cross a desert. In Seymour, Victoria, they were held up by floods. In Oatlands, Tasmania, they had to perform in a stable. They survived a perilous fording of a flooded river. At a fancy-dress ball in Sydney, Minnie Warren wore a Red Riding Hood costume, danced with the Duke of Edinburgh to the envy of all the ladies, and was said to have kissed him. 'I never kiss and tell,' Minnie told Mr Bleeker.

While the General and Commodore Nutt never fought a duel, they were rivals for the hand of Lavinia, and at one stage had a scuffle where the Commodore threw the General onto his back. I have imagined that their rivalry was rekindled by the Australian newspaper reviews of their shows. While these were generally favourable, some praised the Commodore as a natural comedian and denigrated the General, in either oblique or explicit references, as a portly, pompous has-been.

In some ways, the most important person in my story is a background character: Phineas Taylor Barnum, the quintessential American showman. The real Barnum was the discoverer and mentor of the little people, and the promoter who turned them into the equivalent of pop stars, so it is impossible to overestimate his influence on their lives. Barnum's life is well documented in two autobiographies, a collection of letters and a number of excellent biographies.

My main sources are an account of the world tour written by the troupe's manager, Sylvester Bleeker; an autobiography by Lavinia Stratton, 'Mrs Tom Thumb'; contemporary accounts and reviews of the tour in Australian newspapers; and, for background, books by and about P.T. Barnum.

The General and Lavinia never had a child, but it was widely believed that they had one, thanks to Barnum's spin doctoring. They were frequently photographed with a baby in Lavinia's lap. In 1863 a medal was struck to commemorate the birth of a child, who was said to have died two years later. The General and Lavinia also carried infants to visit royalty on their tours. The children were supplied by foundling homes and were given away when, as inevitably happened, they grew too big to be credible 'thumblings'.

The condition that characterised all four little people was probably what is today called pituitary dwarfism 1, or sexual ateleiotic dwarfism, caused by a deficiency in growth hormone. People with this rare genetic condition stop growing in early childhood and, though they may grow a little in later life, they remain at much below average height. Unlike in some other forms of dwarfism, the head, body and limbs remain in perfect proportion. They may be born to parents of normal height and may have average-sized siblings.

Some people with pituitary dwarfism are unable to have children; others have children who may or may not have the same condition. They are most likely to have normal-sized children. The genetics were not well understood in 1870, and it would have been reasonable then for a little person to expect to give birth to another little person. But there might also have been a fear of giving birth to a normal-sized baby.

Readers may be interested to know what happened to General Tom Thumb's troupe after the world tour. The little people continued to tour America, and the General and his wife built a fine miniature house in Lavinia's hometown of Middleborough, Massachusetts, where the General indulged his fondness for yachting and horseracing.

In 1881, the couple were travelling with Barnum's 'Greatest Show on Earth' when a disastrous fire ripped through their Milwaukee hotel. Mrs Bleeker died from her injuries in the fire, and the General was said to be so upset by the experience that he died from a stroke the following July. He was forty-three, and had been performing since he was four years old.

Lavinia's sister Minnie did eventually marry another little person, Major Edward Newell, in 1877. She became pregnant, and everyone expected a tiny baby. But she gave birth to a child weighing nearly six pounds. She died from exhaustion, and the baby died soon afterwards. Mother and child were buried together in the Middleborough family plot.

Although Lavinia was said to be devastated by all these deaths, she continued to tour on Barnum's advice. She appeared with two little brothers, Count Primo and Baron Ernesto Magri, and in 1885 married Count Magri. These three little people went on performing together for many years (it seems Lavinia's days of wealth were long gone) and, even after retirement, they set up a roadside stand for passing tourists in Middleborough, selling candy and soda pop. Countess Magri, as Lavinia became known, died in 1919.

Some reports say that Commodore Nutt never married. But according to The New York Times, he married a Miss Elston of Redwood City, California, sometime in the 1870s. She was a woman a little below average height. When Nutt died of Bright's disease in 1881, his wife sobbed over his coffin, calling him her dear little boy.

My Franz Richardson is a plagiarist: 'The Mermaid' is a poem by Alfred, Lord Tennyson.

FURTHER READING

Sketch of the life, personal appearance, character and manners of Charles S. Stratton, the Man in Miniature, known as General Tom Thumb (Van Norden & Amerman, printer, 1847)

The Autobiography of Mrs Tom Thumb, by Countess M. Lavinia Magri and Sylvester Bleeker (Archon Books, 1979 edition)

General Tom Thumb and His Lady, by Mertie E. Romaine (William S. Sullwold Publishing Inc., 1976)

General Tom Thumb's Three Years' Tour around the World, by Sylvester Bleeker (New York, S. Booth, printer, 1872)

The Life of P.T. Barnum, Written by Himself, by P.T. Barnum (University of Illinois Press, 2000 edition)

Struggles and Triumphs, or, the Recollections of P.T. Barnum, Written by Himself, by P.T. Barnum (Ward, Lock & Co., 1882)

Selected Letters of P.T. Barnum, edited and introduced by A.H. Saxon (Columbia University Press, 1983)

Barnum: America's Greatest Showman, by Philip B. Kunhardt, Jr, Philip B. Kunhardt III and Peter W. Kunhardt (Knopf, 1995)

Barnum: The Legend and the Man, by A.H. Saxon (Columbia University Press, 1989)

E Pluribus Barnum, by Bluford Adams (University of Minnesota Press, 1997) *Barnum*, by M.R. Werner (Harcourt, Brace, 1923)

Memories of Seymour, by John G. Jennings and Virginia Jennings (Seymour and District Historical Society Inc., 2003)

Reviews and accounts of the little people's tour: *The Age*, Melbourne; *The Argus*, Melbourne; *Melbourne Punch*; *The Sydney Morning Herald*; *The Courier*, Ballarat; *The Ovens and Murray Advertiser*; *The Register*, Adelaide; *The Mercury*, Hobart; *Daylesford Mercury and Express*; *Castlemaine Representative*; *Tarrangower Times*; *Avoca Mail*; *Dunolly and Bet Bet Shire Express*.

Dr Foote's Home Cyclopedia of Popular Medical, Social and Sexual Science, by E.B. Foote, M.D. (Murray Hill Pub Co., various editions from 1858)

ACKNOWLEDGEMENTS

Thanks to the many people who generously gave their time and critical skills to improving my manuscript. Some read extracts, some read a whole draft, and a few — hands up, my heroic writing group — read endless extracts and successive drafts.

My readers include Peter Bishop and Helen Barnes-Bulley from Varuna, the Writers' House; Gillian Barnett; Lyndel Caffrey; Jennie Drake; George Dunford; Anna Dusk; Alison Goodman; Jacinta Halloran; Matthew Hooper; Simmone Howell; Antoni Jach; Meredith Jelbart; Toni Jordan; Leah Kaminsky; Vivienne Kelly; Katherine Kizilos; Louise Manifold; Angelina Mirabito; Noni Morrissey; Rachel Power; Sally Rippin; Barbara Wels; and the late, great Louise Zaetta.

Thanks to my wonderful publisher and editor, Aviva Tuffield, and all the team at Scribe Publications.

Thanks to David and Christy Sullivan for their patience with author meltdowns, and to my book group friends for moral support.

And thanks to Joan Leslie for telling me inspiring stories about her days touring as Snow White with nine little people.